RESISTOR

C.E. CLAYTON

RESISTOR

(An Eerden Novel, Ellinor #1)

STARFISH INK
PASADENA CALIFORNIA

ISBN-13: 978-1-952797-02-6

Cover design by: ebooklaunch.com
Map design by: Sarah at thesketchdragon
Edited by: Sheila Shedd
Interior Formatting by: Desiree Lukowiak

Starfish Ink:
starfishinkpublishing@gmail.com
Printed in the United States of America

This is for the ER doctors and technicians who said my brain was "unremarkable."

NAME PRONUNCIATION GUIDE

Ellinor Olysha Rask: Ell-ih-nor O-lee-shah Raah-s-k

Kai Axel Brantley: K-eye Ax-el Brant-lee

Cosmin von Brandt: Cahs-min vahn Br-aunt

Jelani Tyrik Sharma: Jeh-l-ah-nee T-ai-r-eek Sh-ir-m-ah *Misho Shimizu*: Mee-sh-o Shim-me-zoo

Irati Mishra: I-rat-ee M-ih-sh-rah

Mirza Otieno: Meer-zah O-tee-en-o

Pema Tran: Pay-ma Tr-ann

Talin Roxas: T-al-in Rock-as

Janne Wolff: Yah-neh Wool-f

Eko Blom: Eh-k-oh B-lahm

Lazar Botwright: L-ah-zah-r Bought-right

Dragan Voclain: Dray-gan Voh-clay-n

Zabel Dirix: Za-bell Deer-eeks

Oihana Sharma: Oy-han-na Sh-ir-m-ah

Andrey Rask: Ah-n-dray Raah-s-k

Azer: Ah-zer

Warin: War-inn

Embla: Em-blah

Izza: Iz-zah

Fiss: F-iss

RACE AND LOCATION PRONUNCIATION GUIDE

Humani: hyew-man-ee

Seersha: sear-shah

Seerani: sear-ahn-ee

Doehaz: dough-has

Dreeocht: dree-ockt

Ashling: ash-ling

Eerden: Ear-den

Erhard: Err-hard

Euria: Yur-e-a

Anzor: An-zoor

Desta: Deh-stah

Trifon: Try-fon

Amaru: Am-ah-roo

Saxa: Sax-uh

Behar: Bee-har

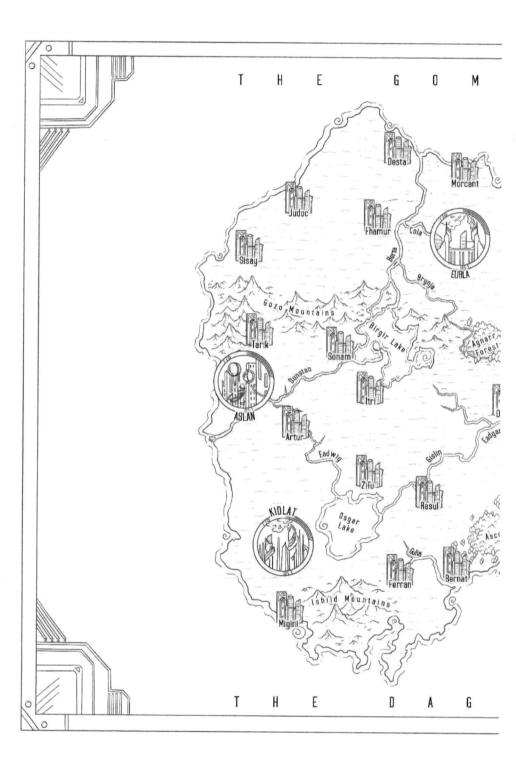

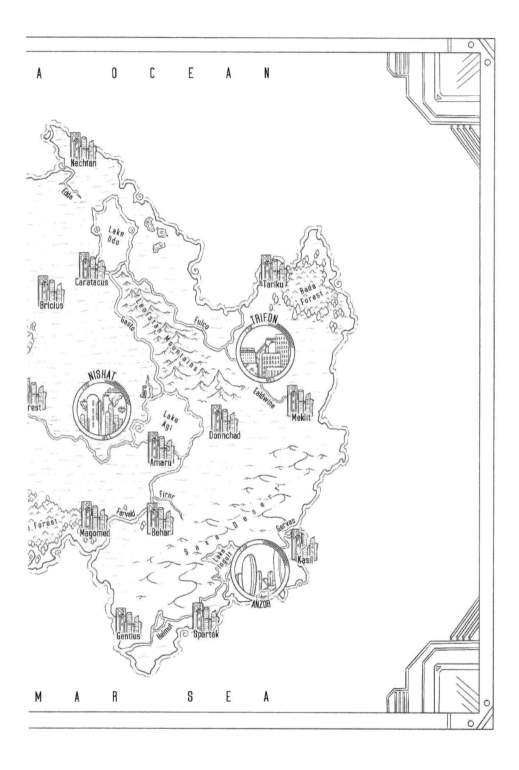

WELCOME TO EERDEN
///PROLOGUE

OCTOBER, 4145

I T WAS said Azer woke up bored one day and decided to travel, to go somewhere where he could start over, so to speak.

Azer was not his true name. Mammalian vocal cords were incapable of forming the complex syllables and maintaining the correct pitch to pronounce his actual name. So, for all that was created after, he went by Azer.

Azer came from a place where magic was as real and as abundant as oxygen, interwoven into every fiber of every atom and molecule, brimming with colorful, marvelous, and, yes, destructive, magic. With magic in such abundance, all anyone needed was a thimbleful of imagination, and they could do anything.

Azer was the youngest of 10,873.6 (don't ask) children. These weren't beings born of a mother and father, at least not conventionally. The point is: Azer was the last born, and the magic and imagination was already being used, and quite liberally, by the rest of his family.

It seemed whenever young Azer exercised his abilities, thinking he had come up with something clever, one of his many, *many* other siblings had already thought of it. In fact, probably hundreds of them had long ago reached the same conclusions Azer was just coming to. This frustrated the young being.

Of course, these scenarios happen, as they always happen, as they will continue to happen no matter what cosmos you reside in. So, Azer let his magic fester, and he became lazy. He thought, "Why bother? Anything worth anything has been done." And, for a time, Azer was content with this, or at least he thought so.

Azer, like his siblings, had an unfathomable lifespan; "immortal" doesn't exactly cover it. With such a complex lifecycle and existence, it took a great deal of time before Azer's laziness transcended into sheer and insurmountable tedium.

Unable to do what he thought he was—perhaps—capable of, alongside so many older, more experienced beings, Azer set out on an adventure. That's when Azer finally stumbled upon something that interested him. Nothing had truly fascinated Azer in eons, so this was an exciting moment.

What Azer found was a soon-to-be extinct world, but, this failing planet still had its libraries. They stood derelict, of course, but that was no trouble for a creature like Azer. He willed himself invisible and, within a moment, all of the world's reported history was swimming in his brain, and he thought, *I can work with this.*

If Azer could not compete with his siblings then why should he try? Even if he was not as skilled as his older relations, Azer's power was so close to godly that it hardly made a difference to the few remaining species. Here was this dying system, replete with a plethora of religions and cultural beliefs, he could twist to suit his desires. And it was ripe for renewal; of the millions of extinct animals and insects, there were several hundred he thought he'd be rather fond of, all well within his power to bring back. Why start from scratch when the framework was already there?

Within thirty-seven hours and fifty-two minutes (Azer liked to round down, for pride's sake) the planet was his. Once that was done, Azer snapped his fingers and transported the world to a new space in a similar solar system and went to work.

He took what was left of the people and animals and reshaped them. He even remade some *in his image*—a line from one of their holy texts he rather liked.

Azer gave these beings magic, a modest amount, made a few new creatures and species, brought extinct ones back, and juggled some of the continents about to bring back landmasses that had been melted, flooded, or destroyed by the changing climate. He then ensured none would find his new planet, for Azer was nearly as selfish as he was lazy.

Within twelve days, he had made himself into the only God these newly reborn creatures would ever know. For a time, Azer delighted in his new creation, patting himself on the back endlessly, reveling in all the adoration these fledgling life forms gave him.

He did not consider what being God would mean, however, in the long run. How he'd have to put safeguards in place so his new creations would not get too powerful. He had to give others a chance at survival, in case the magic gene he'd added to their DNA didn't take root. He had to make rules, myriad habitats, complex nervous systems . . . this endless busy work exhausted Azer. Creating life was exceedingly more difficult than Azer had imagined.

Once he made everything he intended, and meddled long enough to get the gist of things, he decided his active participation was no longer crucial. He christened the planet "Eerden," and stepped back. He left Eerden and now watches it, similar to a viewer of the televisions of old. At least, so some of his creations believe; supposedly they find this thought comforting. Some even claim that the effort of creating Eerden took so much energy that Azer is still resting and will return one day. Others, however, are not convinced Azer remains, and others yet question his existence entirely. Who can say, really?

As Azer might be watching from some lofty perch, not involved with Eerden anymore, or perhaps napping, or back home with his thousands of siblings, it's useless to share Azer's story. What follows, instead, are the tales of Azer's creations, of the world he usurped, reimagined, cosmically resituated, and no longer dabbles with; of the new life forms and the life forms they continue to make of both flesh and blood, and of metal and electricity. This may be Azer's Eerden, but what follows is Ellinor Olysha Rask's story. Azer may not be aware of Ellinor—yet—but that doesn't negate the fact that she is in more dire circumstances than she likes to admit.

"WELL, SHIT" PART ONE
///CHAPTER ONE

THIS WAS not the first time Ellinor Olysha Rask found herself bound and chained, and she very much doubted it
would be her last. This was the longest she had ever been in-
carcerated, however.

Ellinor leaned back against the wall and closed her eyes,
though it made no difference in the pitch black. She wiggled
against the rough wall, never getting comfortable. The restraints clamped over her wrists chaffed at her skin. She lost
count of the days she'd been locked in the rank cell, but she
supposed it didn't actually matter how long she'd been there,
only how much longer she'd be staying.

She sighed loudly, her patience long gone. Not that she had
been blessed with an abundance of composure to begin with,
but her restraint had diminished considerably since Misho's
death.

Heaviness settled on her chest and shoulders as she imagined Misho's disapproving *tsk* at her current predicament, and
her chin started to quiver. Gritting her teeth, she knocked her

head against the bumpy wall to focus her thoughts. She always lost control when she thought about Misho Shimizu, and she didn't want to lose what little control she had left. She needed to conserve her energy.

For what? There's no telling how long I've been here, or who took me. Time to stop waiting.

She hadn't recognized who grabbed her, or how they had gotten the drop on her. She had been drinking, of course, but no more than usual. One minute, Ellinor was meeting with a contact who had information about the Ashlings she was hunting. Ashlings who needed to answer for what was done to Misho. The next? She couldn't remember. The air—her own power!—had betrayed her. Everything went white and hazy, and a fog rolled over her memories.

She sat up straighter against the wall, breathing deeply, ignoring the aches and pains of her cramped muscles. Whatever had happened, poisoning or a knock over the head, had left her weak. Concentrating had been a chore, let alone summoning her magic. She knew she wasn't at full strength, but better to do *something* than continue to wait around for whoever had nabbed her to remember they had her locked away.

Ellinor had heard of humani, beings like her, who were strong enough in air magic to blow apart buildings, and who had the skill to dismantle the most intricate of machines without destroying any of the delicate parts. Ellinor had never been that strong, nor that finessed with her talents. She had enough of the talent to make her someone most would shy away from, and it had been more than enough for her *job*. Using the air, she could turn otherwise fatal blows from knives or projectiles away, and coupled with her own abilities for creating mayhem, her magic had served her well, or well enough, until Misho died.

Then her power turned her into someone, *something*, most didn't want to talk about. Someone the remainder of her family distanced themselves from. She lived only to avenge Misho.

The seersha, though . . . now *they* would have no trouble using wind to blow apart this cell, no matter how far underground they'd have to pull the air. They'd be able to use that same current to wrap themselves in an impenetrable force field then simply sail away like some cocky bird.

That didn't mean she couldn't cause some trouble, though.

Ellinor licked her chapped lips, sweat collecting on her brow as she sniffed the still air around her. Normally, whenever Ellinor needed to call upon her abilities, she was outside where the wind was plentiful for her to manipulate. Down here? Well, if she wasn't careful, she could suck all the air out of the room and suffocate herself just trying to get a breeze going. That was something she generally tried to avoid.

Of course, there were other options.

Ellinor shook her head against the thought. Creating air from nothing was risky, even when she was at full strength. Still, Ellinor was bored. Bored and annoyed at being locked up so long without knowing who had collected on the bounty out on her this time . . . it couldn't have been the government. They followed procedure and would have at least told her why she was locked up, if nothing else.

Andrey would be pissed at her. Her older brother had always despised how willing she was to rely solely on her abilities to get her out of a pinch.

Ellinor growled; the sound echoed off the walls. *But he's not the one in a stupid prison, is he?*

She shifted position so she sat cross legged on the ground, and cleared her throat. Ellinor focused on the elements in her blood that tingled each time she used air to save her, to give her an edge.

She felt the familiar coolness seep through her veins that prickled to the surface when she called upon her abilities. Focusing on the pockets in her lungs that gave her life, then reaching out, feeling the musty air that occupied her cell. She measured it like a jeweler weighting precious stones, determining the quality of the oxygen around her and how much she could afford to spend.

Exhaling, she visualized the air streams in her mind and began rotating her hands, bundling the wind up like a ball. As she was about to release the magic, a dense pressure built in her chest. Not the air she used for breathing, but something heavier, something that pulled at her ribcage and threatened to turn her inside out the more she tried to release her power.

Ellinor collapsed back against the wall, panting, struggling to get her heart to beat in a regular cadence. Harnessing a small current was enough to render her nearly unconscious with exhaustion.

Which shouldn't have been possible.

She wasn't exceptionally strong at casting magic, but she was by no means inept. Something was hindering her abilities and keeping her from properly casting.

Ellinor groaned, propping herself up on one elbow, straining her hearing. It sounded like all she'd accomplished was to make a little unnatural noise, shaking some of the devices that were freestanding on her prison door. Ellinor guessed the steel cuffs keeping her wrists together were embedded with some kind of neutralizing technology that restricted her casting.

While the cell itself might have been primitive, the door was anything but. No doubt designed by an elite humani mechanic, probably even obtained legally through one of the government's fancy emporiums, making it impossible to break in or out of without the proper code. Which most likely included something ridiculous, like a tongue imprint, if it was made by any of the mechanics Ellinor once knew.

Once the knocking and shaking of the devices on the door ceased, another sound became clearer. Heavy footfalls pounded down the stairs outside. Inhaling deeply, she tried to bring life back into her body, and scooted away from the door as the complicated locks were disengaged.

No matter how many gulps of air Ellinor forced into her lungs to bolster her senses and ease the ache behind her eyes, there was only so much she could do before the door was flung open—for dramatic effect. Good mechanical doors did not require flinging once they'd been unlocked.

Ellinor squinted into the light. There was one electric bulb in the bare stone hallway, but to Ellinor, it might as well have been the sun, given how long she'd been kept in the dark.

Blocking most of the door was a burly figure Ellinor had trouble focusing on. With how round the figure appeared, she guessed he was clad in the showy mechanical armor favored by guards and thugs who wanted to look intimidating above all else.

Ellinor knew those types well.

The massive figure loomed in the doorway for a moment, perhaps enjoying seeing Ellinor crouched on the floor, her wrists shackled together. But even in this state, she was far from helpless.

She unfolded her legs and sprang at the figure in one fluid motion, raising her bound wrists, planning to use the hardened steel and combat-tech held within to knock her jailor unconscious. A raspy roar escaped as she flew at him.

The man swatted her out of the air like a bloated beetle.

Ellinor crashed to the floor and the man chuckled, but made no other move, as if daring her to come again. After using so much of her energy to cast, Ellinor didn't have the strength to try again.

Her jailor stepped into the cell, eyebrows wiggling like caterpillars on his beefy face, a wide grin on his thin lips. She tried to focus her gaze while the room spun around her. His deep-set jade eyes had a look of familiarity to them, though his acid green and fiery hair wasn't ringing any bells.

She peered at his armor as he came closer. It was a Coyote mechanized suit. The kind used by humani to put down their robotic creations before the magic, combat, and bio-tech, and unshackled sentient life blooming within them could inspire androids to join the other Ashlings far to the north. Its heavy metal plating was interspersed with thin polymers designed to protect the wearer from both magic and machine-based projectiles. Its many compartments were stocked with hidden weaponry, grenades, ammunition, and batteries full with a magical charge that would outlast any robotic counterpart.

Her shoulders went back, chest thrust out at seeing the suit, and she forced a cocky smile. Ellinor tried to stand; this made her jailer laugh.

I know that laugh!

Before she could say anything, he picked her up by her shackled wrists and brought her closer to his face. With the room no longer spinning, she could better place his deep green eyes, the wide smile, and the black tooth filled with bio-technology to warn against poison.

Yes, she knew this man.

Kai Axel Brantley shook her by the wrists to focus her attention. "You done fucked up this time, Ell. Cosmin's been dying to get 'is hands on you for a long, long time."

A FORMER FRIENDLY FACE
///CHAPTER TWO

"COME ON, Kai," Ellinor said as her former friend dragged her up the winding stairs. "You don't have to give me to Cosmin. Let me pay you, yeah? You want money? Combat-tech? Or some new magitech? Just name your price. You know I'm good for it. No need bothering Cosmin with the likes of me. He's got no need for me anymore."

When he didn't let go, she tried another tactic. "Or, fine, take me to Cosmin. You know what he's planned won't last. Never does. Then I'll come back to make him pay for what he did to me and Misho, I'll remember this, and I won't be as nice the next time. You know I'm good for that too, Kai."

In response, Kai laughed and made a point of bumping her into the walls as they went. Ellinor wanted nothing more than to feed Kai his own eyeballs, despite their history. That history ceased to matter to Ellinor the moment she had walked out of Cosmin's employ—or so she had spent the past eight years convincing herself.

"What's this now? The infamous Ell bargaining for 'er life? That ain't like you. You getting soft in your old age, girlie?" He paused, glancing at her over his shoulder, and shook his head. "Definitely not looking so hot anymore. Where you been, anyway? Somewhere without mirrors or decent food?" He laughed again, waving away the few goons who offered to walk with them, leaving Kai to escort Ellinor alone.

She winced, not from the bumps and bruises as she failed to get her feet under her, but at the implication of getting old. She was barely fifty, and when she could potentially live to two hundred years or more, she was a far cry from *old*. Lots of humani started families at well past eighty! Ellinor had plenty of time . . .

Nope, doesn't matter. Families aren't for me. I don't need people anymore.

"Don't call me girlie," Ellinor grumbled, twisting behind Kai as she struggled to recover her strength. "You aren't allowed to call me that anymore, you old bastard. You're not my friend."

"Ah now, Ell, don't go being like that. This ain't personal. Just business. You know how it goes. I expect you'd treat me no different if our tables been turned."

"You aren't allowed to call me Ell, either. Not unless you let me go and forget I was ever here."

Kai hooted and slapped his thigh in response like she had told the funniest joke he'd ever heard. Then he yanked the chain attached to her steel cuffs, towing her along. She caught glimpses of herself every now and again, reflected in Kai's armor, or in the absurdly high shine of the steel and glass doors they passed. Kai was right; she no longer looked her age.

Her black hair was lanky, heavy with grease. Even the permanently dyed emissive purple tendrils at the base of her skull looked dull. Her full cheeks had a hollow quality to them from over indulging in whiskey rather than solid food, and dark bags hung under her all-too-bright tropical blue eyes.

Getting her feet under her, Ellinor was able to catch up to Kai and take stock of where she was. She hadn't noticed the place before; granted, she *was* rendered unconscious and then left in the dark somewhere, but now there was no mistaking it.

Kai and Ellinor were still ascending the stairs from the cavernous dungeons below Cosmin's estate, but even at this depth, the hallways glittered. Cosmin had a flare for the grandiose, much like the other powerful seershas. They were like crows in that regard—they loved shiny objects.

During her tenure with Cosmin, she had never escorted anyone to or from his personal prison. That had been a job for people like Kai: loyal brutes who could fill out mechanized suits to an impressive degree.

"I see Cosmin hasn't changed since I left," Ellinor mumbled, changing the subject away from her haggard appearance or the fact that her old friend and former crewmate was dragging her by a chain. "He still using the same smuggler to get all that magitech?" She nodded at the gleaming walls.

"'Course the boss still uses 'im. He's the best in the business." Pride dripped from Kai's voice.

"Please don't tell me you're the one playing middleman for that deal." When Kai didn't answer, Ellinor groaned. "That shit's going to get you killed, Kai. Have Cosmin get some other lackey to run this crap for him. The governor, all the elected officials these days, they're cracking down hard on those little gem apparatuses Cosmin's using in his walls. Putting magic in tech like that is getting beyond illegal, and I guarantee it won't be Cosmin's seersha ass that goes down for it, either."

Kai twirled the chain a few more times around his hands, glancing around to make sure no service android was nearby. "Boss needs them, though. Them gems burst into jets of hot-as-abyss flame if anyone even dreams about breaking in or out. Boss has some real good mechanics working for 'im these days. It's real awesome stuff, you should see it in action!"

Ellinor swallowed. "I'd rather not, if it's all the same to you, yeah?"

"Ah, right. Under better circumstances then?" Kai winked, but it looked more like a grimace.

Ellinor knew the risk wasn't as high for Cosmin's magitech smuggling operations as she let on. With Cosmin using his own fire and earth based magics to fuel the devices, rather than an outside source, he could acquire most of what he needed legally. But it still made her worry for people like Kai, the ones who oversaw the comings and goings of the completed magical technology that was banned throughout the continent.

Fire, on its own, was not the most powerful of magics, but it was the most destructive. Cosmin had used that to his advantage. Seersha could live to be five hundred, easily, and Cosmin was poised to remain in power for the remainder of his long life. His casting did help, but the loyalty Cosmin commanded impressed Ellinor most. That, and his taste in décor.

The crown molding lining the ceiling and floor in this wing of the estate was a gleaming gold with neon lights lining it, full of crackling silver that squirmed as if alive. Service androids whipped down the corridor, their wheels silent on the pink marble floor.

Watching the serving staff roll about, a wave of dizziness crashed into Ellinor. Her leg muscles tightened, poised to flee—if she could only get away. She tried to wipe her clammy hands on her pants, to get her breathing under control, but she was having a hard time appearing indifferent to her predicament. If Kai noticed her shift in mood, he didn't say anything.

It had been years since she'd seen Cosmin. Years of evading his grasp and eroding his power bit by bit until he was brought to a level where she could make him pay for deceiving her and Misho. She wasn't sure what her former crime-boss employer had in mind for her, but it didn't matter. She didn't want to find out.

Ellinor breathed deeply. The air up here, out of the dungeons, was cool and free flowing. She may not have had any shoes, and her own specialized combat-tech armor and weapons may have been locked up beyond her reach, but Ellinor didn't need them to bring Kai down—who was whistling as a way to fill the silence.

She took another deep breath and waited for the robotic servants to move out of the way. Once the last one rolled down the hall, balancing a stack of gilded porcelain on its square head, Ellinor launched herself into the air.

Even in her current state, she was able to jump high enough to land on Kai's unsuspecting shoulders. Not waiting for him to make sense of the situation, she jerked the slack up from the chain he held and lassoed it around his thick neck, tightening it in one quick move.

Kai struggled to grab her ankles and fling her off, but that was the problem with the clunky mechanized suits: when up against an able-bodied seersha or humani, they were, indeed, unwieldy things. Each time he tried to maneuver so he could get his hands on her, Ellinor kicked them away. Which hurt, a lot, but kept Kai from getting a firm grip on her.

She felt him droop as he started to lose consciousness and said, "Sorry, Kai. It's just business. You understand, yeah? See, handing me over to Cosmin like a whore for hire is bad for *my* business."

Kai sagged to his knees, and Ellinor knew she should rip the chain free of his hand and flee. She should toss herself out one of the many rounded stained glass windows that lined the hallway and hope for the best.

But she was pissed at Kai.

Pissed he insisted on speaking to her like a friend, stirring up feelings she longed to forget. Pissed that he was still so enamored with Cosmin that he stayed after Misho's death, and had even started adopting their boss's eccentricities by streaking his red hair acid green.

The trained soldier within her burst through the doors of her rage-riddled mind too late. A sharp prick at the base of her neck and a current of electricity jolted her, and then curled around her like a rope, immobilizing her.

Falling off Kai, she twitched for a moment as the water magic that had created the electricity went through her. Then all she could move were her eyes. She glanced to the side and watched one of the service bots as the electrical rope uncoiled from around her arms and waist and disappeared back into the compartment in its chest. It would be several minutes before the paralytic would wear off.

Kai sputtered and coughed at her side, no lasting damage done to the big brute. He got up on one knee, rubbing at his throat, a hoarse laugh rumbling out of his barrel chest. "Shoulda known better than to underestimate you, aye Ell?

Been awhile since anyone's got the jump on me!" He guffawed again, punching Ellinor in the shoulder.

Ellinor glared at him, unable to do anything else.

"Ah, now, don't go being like that. It's like you said, this is just business. For what it's worth, I always liked working with you and Misho. Shame he died, ain't it? Ah well. That's life in the business for you."

Her eyes narrowed, and Kai had the grace to blush and help her to a sitting position. "Poor choice of words, that. Sorry."

Ellinor couldn't speak, but that didn't stop a pain in the back of her throat from crawling up, making it difficult to swallow. Tears stung her eyes and threatened to show a weakness she spent years trying to suppress with cheap whiskey and near-suicidal jobs. But Kai wasn't looking that closely at her anymore. Hauling himself to his feet, he cleared his throat a few more times, then proceeded to drag Ellinor down the hall.

BARGAINING CHIPS
///CHAPTER THREE

B Y THE time Ellinor was able to move her fingers and toes again, the two were standing alone outside a pair of massive ornate wooden doors. Carved in the wood were depictions of humani and seersha women casting magic. Some were riding creatures created of water or atop golem-like beasts, others dancing in a whirlwind, or walking through flames that licked at their bodies suggestively.

It was not the detailed carvings that always left Ellinor's skin tingling, subconsciously leaning toward the door, but the fact that it was simply a wooden door. In an age where mechanics could create doors to harness the magic of intruders to use against them, wood was never used. Power, and magic in particular, made for very paranoid people.

The fact that Cosmin had never needed to replace his ornate, but unenhanced, door was evidence enough of how untouchable he was. But perhaps it was deliberate; Ellinor knew the seersha gangster would enjoy the dramatic image of a door bursting into flames.

"Why're you doing this?" Ellinor whispered, her voice hoarse. She fixed her eyes on her pale, scarred hands, determined not to look at Kai, lest it break her nerve. All the same, she couldn't stop herself from stealing peeks at her old friend and former crew member.

Stop it. He's not on your side anymore.

Kai spared her a glance before turning away, a blush making his cheeks splotchy. He shuffled his feet for a moment, and then said, "Ah, Ell, you know why."

"You sleeping with him then?"

Kai laughed, a deep rumbling sound that Ellinor hadn't realized she missed until the prospect of it being gone again was quickly approaching. "I wish! Nah, you know Cosmin. He likes only those pretty girls of 'is. Too bad, really."

Ellinor's chapped lips twitched in a ghost of a grin, her face still numb. "And why's that?"

Kai's jade eyes twinkled devilishly. "Because only a real man knows how to properly fuck another man!" He howled in laughter and slapped Ellinor on the back as she got her knees under her, sending her again to the floor. Kai always enjoyed that joke.

When Ellinor was able to stand on her own again, the effects of the electrical paralytic finally wearing off, the door was pulled open by a pair of giggling seershas. They scampered past Ellinor and Kai without a backward glance.

The seersha were an eclectic race. No matter how long Ellinor worked with them, the diversity of their appearance still took her by surprise. The pair that skipped past them were unknown to Ellinor, and both were exquisite creatures. Cosmin would tolerate nothing less in his groupies.

One was clad in no more than a golden metal bikini that looked like fire dancing over her body. With soft, pale rose pink skin, she sported a pair of delicate ivory ram's horns peeking out from behind a curtain of neon orange hair. Her shimmering lavender eyes were twice the size of a humani's, and *bright*.

Her companion was cloaked in a translucent, floor length, indigo-colored robe, and not much else. While her companion boasted an athletic build, this seersha looked like an hourglass. Her skin ebony black, her large, round eyes so crystal blue they almost looked white. Her hair was a feathery silver that twinkled like the night sky in the prismatic light filtering out from Cosmin's private quarters. She had no horns, but a pair of elongated ears jutted over the top of her head in sharp points.

If her pink companion was the newly budded morning, this seersha was the deep and mysterious night.

Kai grumbled under his breath as the women glided down the hall and out of sight. Before Ellinor could rib Kai about it, he pushed her into the room and the heavy wooden doors shut behind them.

Diamond sconces with bright orbs of fire floated toward the vaulted ceiling, sending polychromatic light throughout the room, propelled by illegal magic harnessing technology, or magitech, as most called it. Platinum planters lined the wall with roses of every color—natural and otherwise—some of which hummed soothing melodies all thanks to Cosmin's earth magic. The walls were adorned with silver and gold framed mirrors and large screens showing live footage from various rooms in his home, as well as surveillance from the establishments Cosmin owned, and a few news broadcasts.

Swathes of gauzy black silk framed the obsidian and crystal-like dais. On the silken drapes, Ellinor spied dozens of mechanical dragonflies; their steel wings and bodies sparkled with a metallic teal-green as they crawled or made the short flight between the drapes. Ellinor knew they were cleverly disguised pieces of defense-tech, a last resort should the elite soldiers standing at attention around Cosmin fail.

And lounging at the top of the dais on a black and crimson day bed flanked by guards, was Cosmin von Brandt.

"Well, my dear! Isn't this quite the predicament we find ourselves in?" Cosmin cooed, reclining back on the sofa, smirking at her.

Clad in a red satin robe, Cosmin appeared uninterested by Ellinor's arrival, until she spied the ebony, form-fitting shirt and pants he wore under his robes. Just the flash of a red light as it raced along the contours of his taut muscles was enough to tell Ellinor that he was not as relaxed as he appeared.

Good. He should fear me.

"No predicament at all. Just let me go, and the matter's solved. Easy," Ellinor said, trying to toss the hair from her eyes, but the waning paralytic in her system made the motion far less dignified than she'd intended.

Despite his gaudy taste in décor, Cosmin was not one of the more unique-looking seersha. His skin was the color of dead grass: just yellow and green enough to be unnatural, but not overly so. He had no horns or large ears, and while his waist-length hair was of a pure black that reflected no light, that was not as outlandish as some of the other seersha or humani who permanently dyed their hair.

His eyes were what gave Cosmin away as a seersha.

Inordinately large and round, they nearly stole away from his strong chin and the disarming dimples that creased his cheeks when he smiled. It was their color that made it hard for Ellinor to meet his gaze, even under friendly circumstances. They were a bright pumpkin orange which glittered like diamonds, and with a stare that was just as hard.

Cosmin chuckled, a sound like crackling leaves. When no one joined in, he waved at those present in the room, who answered by shifting uncomfortably at their posts. All but Kai. His laughter boomed throughout the chamber.

"Kiss ass," Ellinor grumbled.

Kai glared at her in response.

"Elli, darling, you know I can't let you go! You've made yourself so hard to nail down these days. Why is that, do you suppose? Have your enemies begun to outnumber your allies?" Cosmin clicked his tongue at her. "Had you stayed in my employ, you'd not be in the situation you're in now."

"Don't call me Elli, *Coz.* Only Misho calls me that." Ellinor delighted in seeing him wince at the nickname, before pressing on. "You mean the situation where, I assume, you had some goons infiltrate the deal I was working? You could have gotten me killed! What did your guys do, anyway? I can't remember anything after the first few minutes."

"You mean the meeting I *saved* you from? You shouldn't have to work with such disagreeable humani, my dear." He spared her a cool glance, his eyes twinkling. "What were you after, anyway? Talking to underground mechanics like that. Were you trying, again, to get more information on the Ashlings that broke into my factory the night Misho died?"

The leash on Ellinor's simmering fury snapped. "None of your damn business! I don't work for you anymore. I don't owe you anything, let alone an explanation."

No sooner had the words left her mouth, than Cosmin flicked one long, elegant finger. The air heated up around her, coming up in a wavy sheen like hot pavement.

"Careful, my dear," Cosmin said, still reclining in his chair.

Ellinor didn't apologize, but she did shut her mouth and wait for Cosmin to speak. He was all too happy to oblige.

"That's the funny thing about casting with fire, all it takes is a bit of friction. Just a little organic material to rub the right, or wrong way. Then I have enough power to send a lovely tornado of flame dancing through the room, and I get to add the sound and scent of sizzling flesh to my singing roses. Doesn't that sound enchanting?"

Cosmin eyed her, keeping the heat on until sweat began pooling in the small of her back, her face turning red like a sunburn. Even Kai was becoming uncomfortable, though he'd never voice his distress to Cosmin. Eventually, he let the magic go and the temperature around Ellinor became manageable.

"Friction is a *magical* thing, my dear. I can use it in so many ways. I can even create it, if I need to." As if to demonstrate, the floor beneath Ellinor's feet began to rumble, while no one else was affected. "Sadly, what I don't have is an unlimited power supply in order to achieve what I want."

He held up his hand as if Ellinor was about to interrupt him. She wasn't.

"No, my dear, you don't need to know what it is I desire. Just know I'm not capable of having it yet, and I find that ever so vexing. Oh yes, my vaults are still full of magical batteries. Mostly earth and fire magic these days. It's not enough, though. Not for what I need."

Would it ever be enough, Cosmin?

Cosmin sighed dramatically and snatched a golden goblet from the red marble table tucked off to the side, nearly hidden by one of his guards. He sipped from the glass before settling his bright orange eyes back on Ellinor. "You know what would give me an endless supply of magical energy with which to do, well, anything I wished?"

A dreeocht, Ellinor thought.

"A dreeocht," Cosmin said, and Ellinor did her best not to roll her eyes.

Ellinor knew that dreeochts—similar to doehaz—were formed when enough raw magics, sophisticated machinery, and organic material met. The natural magics collecting around them from the discarded pieces of smart technology and bio residues of decaying former life forms was enough to create life. Dreeocht were far rarer than a doehaz, however, and were imbued with so much magic, that they elevated the abilities of those who controlled them, those of a similar magical type, to absurd heights. Making them coveted by every caster alive.

"Just one of those mysterious abominations would supply me with enough energy to accomplish my goals. I could over-charge all my vaults and combat-tech, just for fun! Now wouldn't that be delightful?" Cosmin crooned. He peered into his goblet and frowned, as if a fly had despoiled what he was drinking. "I've been searching for a dreeocht for centuries, but one hasn't been formed *anywhere* in the continent of Erhard in such a very long time. Supposedly there is one in the hands of the caster in Trifon, but it doesn't matter. It's most likely just a rumor I'm disinclined to believe.

"But do you know what happened a few weeks ago, my delicious Elli? Luck finally smiled upon me. A dreeocht was formed, and, before it fully formed its consciousness, I snagged the little monster! Then, because Luck is a greedy bitch, she decided this particular dreeocht wasn't going to be the right kind of boost for my talents. The little beastie is only good for air and water magics. Rather unfair, if I do say so myself."

Ellinor was intrigued. She'd never been in the presence of a dreeocht, nor anyone who used them, for that matter. Even if a water-based caster was in an arid desert, if they had a dreeocht, they'd be able to cast as if they were near an ocean: an endless supply of raw materials at their fingertips, and without draining themselves to create magic.

"Do you see why I just had to have you back, Elli dear?" Cosmin said, disrupting her thoughts. "You and our dearly departed Misho were the only ones in my employ who could command air or water magic. The rest of your kind prefer to be noble pricks with 'legitimate' occupations. Damn near incorruptible, too. Such a shame we lost Misho. He was always the more agreeable one of you two. Wouldn't you agree, Kai?"

Kai preened and opened his mouth, but Cosmin gave him a dismissive wave. "No need to answer; we all know it's true."

Cosmin glanced at one of the service bots against the wall and gave a barely discernible nod, and the machine rolled from the room. "The problem with dreeocht is they need to bond to the magic they're best suited to, or they cease to be useful. This is where you come in, so pay attention. I may not be able to use this treasure, but a friend of mine—well, I say *friend*, she's more of a pain in my neck . . . but I suppose she's better than most people I deal with. Anyway, she can use my treasure and is willing to trade some absolutely fantastic devices in return. Combat-tech and war automaton far beyond my mechanics' abilities, and without the stupid things turning into Ashlings and tearing my home apart.

"In exchange for all those goodies, I give her the unconscious dreeocht, and we become even better *friends*. Friends in your debt are lovely. I can call in that favor whenever I need it, no questions asked. It's win-win! Well, as close to win-win as I can get, given the circumstances." He spared her another cool glance. "You and a retinue of my people will leave for the city of Anzor tomorrow and deliver my package to Zabel Dirix directly.

"Anzor is a bit farther than I'd like from Euria, but there's nothing I can do about that. If I used my earth abilities to move the city closer, I might crack Erhard in half! And that wouldn't be much fun, now would it?"

Making a show of crossing his legs, Cosmin waited, looking at her expectantly. Ellinor blinked a few times before registering he was waiting on her. "Oh, you're done? Sorry, wasn't sure. You practiced that speech a few times before I got here, didn't you?"

"Obvious, was it?" Cosmin pouted. "I felt the delivery was a little forced. But I so loved it; I just couldn't miss this opportunity. Oh well, it's done now."

This time, Ellinor did roll her eyes. "So, what. You captured me so I could play escort to the prize you can't keep? What makes you think I'd help you? Especially after what happened—what you *allowed* to happen—to Misho? This is a hard *nope* for me. Find or capture another mule."

Cosmin tossed his head back, hair rippling as he forced a laugh. "You seem to think you have a choice in this, my dear. You do not. This is happening. You're going."

"You can't make me." Ellinor flinched at how petulant the words sounded. "You can ship me out with your prize and your best men, but you can't make me behave. You know they aren't going to be enough to handle me. Not even Kai. No offense, Kai."

"Oh, I know, my dear," Cosmin said with a shrug. At a gesture, the service android rolled back into the room and headed for Kai, who stooped to pick something up from the tray atop its head.

"You were always such a fearsome humani. A shame, really, that you couldn't be tempted to my bed, like so many other fearsome women. No matter," Cosmin said, fidgeting with his robe. "You see, you weren't my first choice, either. But the fact is, you're still one of the most useful tools I've ever had the pleasure of utilizing, and the only one I can get my hands on without rousing suspicion from our new governor. So, as much as it pains me, I simply must make use of you again. And you will have no choice but to do as I command."

At those words, Kai snapped a metal collar around her neck. It was a thin silver ring, and, once closed, welded shut. Ellinor could not remove it.

The faint, cool thrumming of power in her veins that surged with her magic was suddenly gone. She could no longer feel it. Her body began to tremble, eyes wide in sudden panic as her pulse started to race.

Nonono!

Even with the cuffs on her wrists, she could feel her magic; she could summon it if need be, but this was different. Now there was an emptiness, a weightlessness in her core. Like a piece of her soul and heart had suddenly vanished.

Ellinor sputtered, her breath hitching as if her chest were caving in. Desperately, she scrabbled to claw the collar off, her nails leaving angry red lines down her neck.

"What did you do, Kai? What the fuck, Cosmin!" Ellinor screeched, trying to force the collar over her head, to no avail.

"Isn't it obvious? I took away your magic, Elli dear. If you ever want to cast again, you will do as I say."

She felt Kai lean forward, his breath tickling her ear. "Sorry, Ell. Just do as he says and it's all good. You'll see. It ain't a bad bargain."

"You piece of seersha backwash! You just said the dreeocht needs to be with its preferred magic type, yet you cut me off from the thing that makes me valuable to you? Get this evil contraption off me. Now!"

"You know so little of the dreeocht, my dear," Cosmin cooed again. "You may not be able to use magic, to feel it or command it, but it's still in your blood. Dormant, or whatnot. The dreeocht will sense that and be content. My nifty little necklace will help ensure that. And given our . . . history, I'd be foolish to let you anywhere near me or my property with full command of your powers. You know I'm no fool, Ellinor."

"Fine, okay, whatever. Just remove it, Cosmin. Take the collar off and I'll do whatever you want. Just get this thing off of me. Please!" Ellinor tugged on the choker, but unless she were to cut off her head, she couldn't find a way to remove it.

"Frankly, my dear, your promises mean nothing to me. I no longer trust you. If you want your magic back then complete this task like a good little girl, and upon your return I'll have Kai remove that . . . thing, and you can go back to your filthy work in the shadows. And should you stay there, you'll never need to worry. Betray me, and, well, the device stays on and I tell your oh-so-numerous enemies how vulnerable you are. How long do you think our Elli would last under those circumstances, Kai?"

"Not long, boss."

"Precisely. Do we understand each other?"

Ellinor's heart skipped several beats as it fell through the hollow in her chest where her magic once dwelled, the weight of her predicament settling on her like a transport ship. No matter how desperately she tried to reach out for her magic, there was no response. Nothing answered. She felt as hollow as she did when Misho died, but helpless, with a new kind of cold, loneliness.

Resigned, Ellinor fell to her knees in submission. Kai hoisted her to her feet again as Cosmin clapped.

"Excellent! I knew you'd see it my way, dear." Cosmin waved to the service bots, who hauled the massive wooden doors open. "Take her to a *guest* room, Mr. Brantley. Make sure she stays put, and, come morning, you'll all be on your merry way."

Ellinor let Kai drag her out, stunned by the barren feeling weighing her down. Shuffling toward the door, she heard Cosmin call out, "Come now, Elli, it's not so bad! I have a feeling we're going to make a brilliant team this time around, don't you? After all, we *must* make an excellent team, otherwise, well, you know. I couldn't imagine such a fate. It must be so *terrible* for you to finally realize how useless you are without me . . ."

A PRETTY CAGE
///CHAPTER FOUR

B EING FREE of her cuffs should have meant the return of Ellinor's power. But now it meant nothing. Her limbs were shaky, chest achy, and there was a hardness in her stomach that threatened to overpower her with nausea.

As soon as the door locked behind her, the fragile walls holding up her tough façade crumbled. She broke.

Ellinor collapsed to the floor, the sharp pain of her knees hitting the ground ignored, heart pounding in her chest. She couldn't wrestle her breathing under control, nor stem the flow of tears. She pulled on the collar until she was rolling on the floor and screaming; her fingernails tore digging into the cold metal.

There was a logical voice in her mind, one that sounded suspiciously like her departed brother, Andrey, reminding her that plenty of people didn't have magic. Those people could function and lead happy lives; there was nothing wrong with them. In fact, non-magic users still outnumbered magic users, putting her in the majority now.

But, cut off from her magic, everything felt blunted. The ambient smoky scents and ozone that permeated Cosmin's estate were glaringly absent. The light didn't sparkle as brilliantly as it had before. Her senses no longer as sharp. She wasn't special anymore. She was without the one thing she still shared with Misho.

No. This can't be possible. I refuse!

Sitting up, she closed her eyes and tried to find the magic within her. Cosmin said it was still there, so surely if she searched deep enough, she should be able to find it. Even if she couldn't summon it, she should be able to feel something in her soul that would let her know she hadn't been abandoned by her own power. But no matter how hard she concentrated, she felt nothing. The wind would not answer her call.

Rubbing her temples, Ellinor forced herself to take deep gulps of air until the room stopped spinning around her. For now, she could not change the numbness settling into her bones, but she *could* attempt to either get out and force Kai to remove the collar, or, failing that, prepare for the journey ahead so she could be reunited with the locked off pieces of her heart once she returned.

Despite not having been in Cosmin's palatial home for years, she could see it had not changed. She knew the best places to make a quick exit, as long as she could cast and thus protect herself from the windows she'd have to break, and the long jump—well, the fall—she'd have to make. Which meant her only means of escape, in her current condition, was suicide.

An iciness filled her, cold in her soul in a way she never thought possible. Even when Andrey and Misho died, she hadn't felt this *empty.* A hollow, echoing cavern filled her body where once there had been substance, where a silent companion had dwelled all her life. She didn't know how humani or seersha who were unable to cast got up every day. She felt forsaken, alone in a way she couldn't comprehend.

And yet Andrey had done it every day of his life. He had been able to accomplish great things without being able to cast.

She rubbed her bruised wrists and locked her melancholy thoughts away, determined once more to focus on the things currently within her control, which was not much. But Misho would never have wanted her to despair in this way. She would simply do as Cosmin commanded, and the collar would be removed. She had to believe he would keep true to his word.

Ellinor stalked to the door and gave the handle a jiggle, unsurprised when a brief electrical shock went through her hand. The door was wired to keep her in, similar to her cell far below. She tugged the windows; they were much the same. Ellinor examined the room's furnishings, but anything of substance had been screwed into place.

The room was lovely, all else aside. The floors were covered in a plush, off-white carpet that felt like clouds beneath Ellinor's bare feet. A large desk with a black marble top sat in one corner with a posh throne-like chair in black satin; in the other, a spacious bed was bedecked in silken sheets and an obsidian frame. There was also a tall armoire across from the bed—made of real wood—with golden knobs. On the far wall, tying the room together, was a towering red gilded mirror.

Besides the main door, there was another next to the armoire, and this one Ellinor could open. Behind it was a silver and gold bathroom with white marble tiling. The room glistened, and, while any number of bubble bath soaps, scented oils, and hair dyes could be found, not a single object Ellinor could use as a weapon was at hand.

Closing the bathroom door, Ellinor planted herself in front of the mirror. She hadn't properly looked at herself in ages, and it was time.

In spite of the days Ellinor spent on prisoner's protein bars, and the red marks over most of her body that would soon turn to ugly bruises on her copper-tinged, ivory skin, she was no worse for wear. Her face was marred only by the lines of frowns, and a few creases left from laughter, when Misho had been by her side. She had no true wrinkles, just a hardened visage which added an air of mystery that Ellinor rather enjoyed.

Ellinor was considered pretty enough in some circles, but what made her *interesting* were her eyes. They glimmered like a warm ocean with sapphires littering the sea foam. Their vivid blue a testament to her caster abilities, for, all humani casters had such bright tones in a color denoting their magic, and she was surprised and relieved that they held their luster, despite the restrictive collar.

Ellinor had not avoided mirrors because she worried her scars were unseemly, or because she hated how disheveled she became when working a long job that required she stake out her target. No, she avoided mirrors because Misho had loved her eyes.

She was starting to forget which scars she had gotten by Misho's side, and which would be new to him. Mirrors reminded her too much that she was still here, fearing failure and success alike, because it took her further from the man she loved. Ellinor's heart twisted in agony as she stared in the mirror's reflection, and chills raced through her chest.

The reflection no longer held the image of a woman Ellinor recognized, nor particularly liked. She saw a facsimile of herself, someone who was still unsure how to trust, move forward, to live without Misho.

The door to her room opened, and Ellinor whipped around. Kai tentatively stepped over the threshold. Ellinor tensed, ready to spring if need be, but otherwise made no move or sound of acknowledgement to her old crew member.

His lips twitched, unsure whether to smile or frown, and therefore did neither. When Ellinor remained silent and unmoving, he heaved his shoulders in a silent sigh.

"Brought your things, Ell. Just your clothes plus some to spare. Nothing fancy, I promise. I remember your tastes well enough. I'll be giving you back your armor tomorrow, weapons, too, once we've left Euria. You understand."

Ellinor frowned. "After we've left Euria? You mean Cosmin's estate, right?"

The side of Kai's lips quirked up in a shallow smile, his bulbous nose twitching as he stifled a laugh. "You won't be needing nothing in Euria, Ell. Cosmin's people are safe here. Including you." He glanced behind him, as if making sure no one would overhear his words. "Besides, it's making the rest of the old gang feel a tad safer for you to be unarmed for a spell."

Ellinor narrowed her eyes and Kai squirmed a little under her gaze. "Right then," he said after a moment of tense silence. "I'll leave you to get settled. For what it's worth, it's nice to 'ave you back. Sorry for earlier, you know I don't mean nothing by it. Business and all."

Ellinor glared at him. Kai rubbed his neck, cleared his throat, and gave her a pleading look in return. *He was just following orders,* Ellinor tried reminding herself, but the bite of the collar was too fresh. She stayed silent and, with a sigh, Kai Axel Brantley left her.

DECISIONS
///CHAPTER FIVE

WITH A groan, Ellinor Rask woke and rolled to her feet. She rubbed at her neck where the collar bit into her skin, cringing as her fingers brushed over the cold metal. She gave the collar one last good jerk in hopes it would snap off, and then stomped to the bathroom.

Ellinor took a long bath, trying to bring some kind of warmth back to her body. When that didn't work, she gave up and donned the supple black pants, the form fitting but still cozy dark sweater, and heavy combat boots. She held her breath and clipped the black stomacher over her torso. She hated how constricting it was, but the corset-like device was necessary when she wore her armor over clothes.

She glanced at herself in the mirror and sighed; she'd never loved wearing all black, but it's what Cosmin preferred for his goons. Coupled with her fair skin and raven-colored hair, the clothes served to make her bright blue eyes all the more startling.

Ellinor had just twisted her dark locks into a messy bun atop her head, the purple tendrils escaping to tumble down the base of her neck, when there was a pounding on the door. Ellinor barely had time to turn around before the door was jerked open. Flanked by two bouncer androids stood Kai, who gave her a broad grin.

The smile seemed out of place, given the circumstances, but Ellinor didn't comment. Instead she glanced from Kai's smile, his black mechanical tooth gleaming in a sea white, to the gear he held in his massive hands.

She gasped; her heart tripped over itself at seeing her belongings. It was like seeing a beloved friend after an extended absence. Rushing to Kai's side, Ellinor's fingers danced over her combat armor, reverently fluttering over the familiar worn edges; she pulled it close to her face and inhaled.

The armor Misho had gifted her hadn't been lost.

She closed her eyes and saw Misho smiling back at her, his bright amber eyes flashing in delight as he watched her put the armor on. She could feel his long, graceful fingers trailing her curves as he appreciated how the fine craftsmanship hugged her body. She saw him lean down to kiss her, his full lips just a breath away—

Kai gruffly cleared his throat, and Ellinor's eyes snapped open.

"You need a minute alone with it, Ell? Bit of privacy maybe?" Kai said, wiggling his bushy red eyebrows at her.

Ellinor frowned and cradled the gear to her chest. "Don't be absurd. And what did I say about calling me Ell?"

"You said not to."

"Damn right! Traitors who collar me with despicable and inhumane technology aren't allowed to call me Ell. We're not friends, Kai. Not anymore."

Her heart twisted further. She didn't want to push Kai away, not really, not again. But how was she supposed to forgive him?

"Ah, c'mon, it ain't that bad! How can it be? It's just a blasted piece of magic bio-tech. Just means you can't cast is all. You don't need abilities to kick ass. Besides, I done told you it ain't personal. Don't mean we can't be friends, or friendly with each other, anyways. We were thick, you and me, not that long ago. Nothing's gotta change unless you want it to."

But everything had changed. Nothing felt or even tasted the same anymore, thanks to Cosmin. And Kai *helped* him.

Ellinor growled, "Don't talk about things you know *nothing* about!"

Cosmin's profession was in smuggling and selling illegal magitech and weapons. They harnessed natural magic and, when combined in a bullet or shackle like Ellinor's, had devastating effects. Such items were highly regulated by the politicians and police, making them a hot commodity in the ground level markets. Cosmin was well versed in the effect his device had on Ellinor, it was his *specialty*.

She jabbed her finger in Kai's chest, the bouncer bots buzzing a warning at his side. "You have no idea what this is like. What this feels like. What this does to a caster. This isn't like those shit cuffs you had me in. I could still *feel* my magic. I could still summon it. This? It would be like me taking your hands away. There would just be a dead, empty space where your hands used to be. There wouldn't even be phantom pains reminding you that your hands were once a part of you. Only a gap of where something vital to you once was."

She took a step back, stuffing her hands under her arms, clutching her armor tight to her chest, as the automatons continued to buzz. "I can understand why you wouldn't recognize the hole you've left me to fester in without my abilities, but Cosmin sure as shit does. He knows *exactly* the kind of hollow emptiness that comes with neutering a caster. Of how it makes you feel like you aren't even a person anymore. So don't you dare pretend that it's just business because you're hoping Cosmin will let you into his bed one day. It's never happening, Kai!

"Once this job is done, I never want to see you again." She shuddered reflexively. "If I do, abilities or not, my face will be the last thing you ever see. You got that?"

His shoulders drooped, and he took a step back. Kai was not magically inclined. He had no idea what it felt like to be cut off from a piece of himself so completely he couldn't even feel a whisper of it anywhere.

Kai wouldn't meet her eyes. His chin sagged to his chest, and he jerked his thumb back toward the door. "You just come out when you're ready. Be quick, though. Cosmin's expecting us to shove off soon."

With that, Kai backed out into the hallway, the door closing on his still flushing features. Under different circumstances, Ellinor would have felt bad for yelling at Kai. It felt too much like kicking a puppy—the big man had been relentlessly bullied as a child for his size and the father who abandoned him; he didn't need anyone else to ever make him feel worthless again. But she was far too livid to feel sorry, even with her beloved armor back in her possession.

As she clamped on the last of her empty holsters and sheaths, she noticed that the mechanical defense-tech shield she normally wore on her wrist was missing. But the gloves she used to operate it were accounted for.

Ellinor ground her teeth so hard she could hear them grinding as she flung on her cape—which *would have* allowed her to fly for short distances, if she could cast. She yanked the hood over her head and brought the flap over her mouth and nose that would filter out noxious gas, and connected it to the inside. Securing the flap wasn't necessary, but it meant she didn't have to hide her facial expressions when speaking to Cosmin or Kai.

"Where is it?" she barked as soon as she opened the door.

Kai had his back to her, but slowly turned, his glance still hooded from her rebuke. "Where's what?"

"My shield," she said, tapping her wrist. "It's the only thing missing from my gear, outside of the weapons. So where did you put it?"

Kai glanced at the bouncer androids, who weren't buzzing at Ellinor's icy tone. Shrugging, Kai placed his hands on his hips, his thumb trailing over the stun stick at his side. "It be with your weapons. Told you, you'll get those back later."

Ellinor scowled behind her mask. "It's not a weapon. It's a fucking shield!"

Kai sighed and motioned for the robots to start moving Ellinor down the hall. "Yeah, sure it's a shield. But it's *your* shield. We all know you can use that thing to relieve a man of 'is head if he made you mad enough." He gave her a fleeting glance, and added, "You'll get it back, and hopefully you'll be done with the prissy-fit by then."

Ellinor pinched the bridge of her nose, trying to get her headache to dissipate. "It better not be broken," she called over her shoulder to Kai, who was keeping a noticeable distance.

She followed the robots in sullen silence, picking at her collar whenever her mind wandered. She didn't attempt to run; there wouldn't have been any point.

Unlike the robotic servants, the bouncer and guard automatons were attuned to her pulse; they'd know instantly if she decided to make a break for it. Even if she could flee, there was no guarantee she'd be able to find a mechanic bold enough to go against Cosmin von Brandt in releasing her from the bio-tech shackle.

Instead, she did her best to stuff her ire down and save it for later, once she was free of all her bonds and focused on getting Cosmin's job done as quickly as possible. She would do everything in her power to get the dreeocht safely to the seersha Zabel Dirix far away in Anzor, and then the collar would be removed.

Hopefully.

A DIFFERENT KIND OF DANGER
///CHAPTER SIX

THE HALLS and corridors were silent as they marched to Cosmin's vehicle bunker. It was the place where Cosmin briefed his various soldiers, sergeants, lieutenants, and generals who ensured that his illicit businesses, and the legal synth clubs, brothels, and casinos he used for moving the goods and cleaning the money, went undisturbed.

The absence of her magic had left her with a constant ringing in her ears, intensified by the silence. Desperate to drown it out, she said, "Cosmin's coming with us this time, yeah?"

Kai shook his head. "Nah, you know better than that. Boss doesn't leave the city."

"Not even to ensure his prize remains intact?"

He snorted, voice tinged in disappointment. "Not for nothing."

Seersha power, unlike humani casters and Creature Breakers, was strongest in the place of their birth. It was the one advantage the less powerful humani casters had; their power was not bound to a particular location. If Cosmin left, even just to go to the nearest major city, Nishat, he would be weaker, even if he outfitted himself in every cleverly disguised magical battery he possessed.

"It keeps the peace though, uneasy as it is. Can you imagine if every boss like Cosmin or Zabel could just roam wherever they please? All Erhard would burn," Ellinor offered.

Kai narrowed his eyes at her. "Aye, that shit also allows 'em government types and their private militaries to run all over us, don't forget that. Last I checked you weren't too sweet on 'em keeping all the magitech to themselves. Don't go getting soft on me."

The cold weight of the collar became all the more obvious to her. Ellinor shivered. "But with a dreeocht, Kai? That could change everything. It invites trouble."

"I like trouble," Kai said with a wink.

Images of Ashlings streaming across Erhard to reach a caster with a dreeocht flashed before her eyes. The sentient robots, often accidentally created by powerful casters when modding their bouncer and war automata, might force them to awaken more of their brethren if they knew of the prize within Cosmin's walls. "Not this kind of trouble, Kai. Trust me, yeah?"

Silence fell between them after that and, as she was led farther into the estate, the opulence of Cosmin's flashy tastes ebbed to more practical things. The deeper they went, less and less ornamentation appeared, replaced instead by cameras that fed back to the guard houses and security personnel.

Ellinor spared a glance at Kai, but he was watching his feet. He wasn't even starting to grin, like he normally did, at the prospect of being near Cosmin. His brows knit together, green eyes cloudy as he focused on his steps.

He was once again wearing the big Coyote mechanized suit he'd worn the other day, though Ellinor wasn't sure why. Yesterday it had been for show, but today? What was the point?

The bouncer bots wheeled in front of Ellinor and blocked her path, waiting for Kai to open the door. Kai blew out a heavy breath and pushed his shoulders back as he opened the obsidian door, and Ellinor noted he still wasn't grinning.

He was nervous about something, but what? The job seemed straightforward, but could it be more complicated than Cosmin was willing to share?

The voice of her brother, Andrey, snapped through her head. *Probably. That's rookie level thinking. You should have known he wouldn't tell you everything.*

Ellinor sucked in her breath as Kai tugged her inside, the bouncer bots rolling in after them. She let her breath out slowly while surveying the crowded room, glad the mask hid the way she bit her lips until her heart stopped pounding.

Cosmin von Brandt had his back to them as they entered, talking to two of his lieutenants. Several soldiers and sergeants were skittering around the room, moving boxes, taking inventory of weapons, or checking their own gear to make sure they had everything. None would look directly at Ellinor, though she recognized many in the room; they were her old crew. The one she and Misho led a lifetime ago. But amidst all the bustling and clutter from unmarked black plastic crates and the wayward rifle or knife, there was a noticeably empty space, an area of inactivity so profound the silence emanating from that one corner dominated the room.

Her curiosity got the best of her, and she leaned toward Kai. "What's that? Is there something in there?"

Kai fidgeted with his robotic gauntlets for a moment, his eyes darting from her to the device in the corner. He began worrying at his lip and Ellinor started to believe he wasn't going to speak, then Kai whispered, "That's the dreeocht. It's in there, sleeping. Don't know 'ow long the magic in that tech will last . . . that's why Cosmin needed . . . *needs* you."

Unlike the plastic cargo boxes Cosmin's devotees were organizing into piles for the service robots to move to their aerial transport—a Class 3 Night Heron, if Ellinor wasn't mistaken—the device in the corner was more like a sleek, metal coffin. Its silver metallic body gleamed as if partially liquid; there were no creases or breaks anywhere on it, making her wonder how it opened. The only thing marring its smooth surface were three small lights, two of which were blinking intermittently between blue and white. The device didn't look dangerous, but it sent a chill tickling up the back of Ellinor's legs to the base of her skull.

"I don't understand. If Cosmin has all these pieces of tech to replicate the magic the dreeocht likes, not to mention taking my abilities away, then why am I here? What aren't you telling me? Cosmin doesn't need me if he's got that—" Ellinor waved at the device, "—thing to contain the creature. He doesn't need me at all. None of you do."

"Ah," Cosmin said, turning toward Ellinor, fixing his unsettling orange gaze on her, "but that's where you're wrong, Elli dear."

Ellinor swallowed. She hadn't realized Cosmin would be able to overhear their conversation from where he was. She narrowed her eyes as Cosmin and his lieutenants approached, once more glad they couldn't see her lips twitch beneath the mask.

While Cosmin offered a tight smile, his hands clasped behind his back, the two humanis at his side glared at Ellinor. Ellinor's stomach plummeted; she knew these two very well. And she wondered, with so many familiar faces in the vehicle bunker, if Cosmin wasn't deliberately teaming her up with the very crew who'd felt the most betrayed by her departure.

Despite the years Ellinor spent away, Irati Mishra and Mirza Otieno looked just the way she remembered them. By the hard glint to their eyes, it appeared they still resented being promoted as a result of Ellinor quitting the life rather than on their own merit.

"Why am I not surprised? Didn't think you were that dense when it came to combat magitech, but apparently you are. Your usefulness wanes by the second," Irati chuckled, and while her face was impassive around her hard eyes, Ellinor could hear the sneer dripping in her soft voice.

Irati Mishra was a beautiful woman—no, she was more than that. She was *breathtaking*. Her skin was a lovely, creamy brown with no wrinkles of any kind. Even with scars lining her cheek and neck, her face looked soft to the touch, and with her curves, people always wanted to touch her—Ellinor included.

Her dark brown eyes flashed dangerously with flecks of gold as she gave Ellinor the once over, her full, pink lips pressing into a thin line as she held Ellinor's stare. But even her frown couldn't mask the cute dimple in her chin, or the dark mole, low on her cheek where her lips would have curled into a smile.

Ellinor rolled her eyes, wrestling the fluttering in her stomach that always stirred in her when she looked at Irati. "Don't flatter yourself," she said. "You're as dense as I am, Irati. I'm sure if *Coz* hadn't told you all about it while you bent over to please him, I doubt you'd know what the container does, either."

"I got where I am on my own, you bitch—"

"Don't call him Coz," Mirza said over Irati.

Ellinor was undeterred. "You mean *after* I left, right? You'd have gotten nowhere if I hadn't left. Good thing *I*, for one, couldn't stand working with deceiving butchers!"

Cosmin flicked a finger.

Ellinor hadn't turned on her armor. She had listened to Kai when he said she wouldn't need it, and it cost her. Cosmin was powerful enough he didn't need to move his hands in the same way Ellinor did when casting even small amounts of magic. She had no warning before his punishment was released.

Cosmin made the natural ore materials in her armor so dense and heavy, it popped her arm out of its socket. Ellinor couldn't even scream before a hot blast of air slammed her and Irati into a nearby wall, knocking the breath out of her and nearly singeing off her eyebrows.

"Now dears," Cosmin said, his voice holding an edge, "let's not bicker. You have miles and miles ahead of you, and I'd like my property to arrive at its destination in one piece." He held Ellinor's gaze and said, "*All* my property." His magic dissipated, but his orange eyes anchored Ellinor in place. "Be careful when aiming your fury. I wasn't the one who killed Misho. You'd be wise to remind yourself of that. Daily, if need be."

Ellinor stood, tears stinging her eyes as she held her dislocated arm. Cosmin narrowed his eyes and waved at Kai. "My good man, fix that for her, will you?"

Before Ellinor could respond or prepare, Kai took hold of her arm and popped it back in place. This time she did scream. Irati smiled, or did, until she caught Mirza's disapproving look and Cosmin's frown.

Irati huffed, tossing her rich, deep brunette hair off her shoulders before crossing her arms and clamping her mouth shut. Had Irati been a fire caster—or a caster at all—Ellinor was certain her head would be smoking with irritation.

Ellinor held her arm to her chest and glared back at the trio before her, despite the tears trailing down her cheeks. Kai shifted his position beside her, as if he was looking for some sign of gratitude. If that was the case, he would be waiting for a long, long time.

For his part, Mirza Otieno looked annoyed by the entire situation. A man of few words, Mirza was the more cunning of the two lieutenants—despite Irati's bluster. His skin was much darker than Irati's, as were his eyes. But an incident with another fire caster left Mirza permanently bald, half his face a mask of puckered burn scars, and charred his vocal cords, leaving his voice as rough and gravelly as a stone pit.

Cosmin eyed his lieutenants and former lieutenant for a moment longer, perhaps hoping Irati's ire would fizzle out. When she continued to glare at Ellinor and grind her teeth, Cosmin shook his head and gestured to the device in the corner. "Well, now. With that little bit of unpleasantness behind us, may I continue?"

Obedient silence answered him, and he grinned. "The little monster is indeed tucked away nice and tight in my magic bullet. But the water and air magic keeping the device powered is, well, waning. You see, there wasn't much residual power left, and while I still had plenty of your power stored in the automated storage vaults, I'm not keen on using it all for this one errand. Once that third light comes on, the magic within the storage units will have run out, and your presence will be required to keep the dreeocht catatonic."

"But I can't cast. You saw to that when you put this on me, you—" Ellinor tugged at her collar with her good hand but was cut off by Cosmin's flippant wave.

"Yes, yes, you're ever so upset by what I've done. But don't think to threaten me here of all places, or I won't be as gentle the next time. You've made your point abundantly clear to me, and I'm sure to Kai as well," Cosmin said, winking at Kai, who blushed in return. "We have more important things to discuss than your feelings of being wronged.

"Now, I'm only going to explain this once because, frankly, it's becoming rather dull." Cosmin gave Irati a pointed look, but she pretended not to notice.

Turning his gaze back to Ellinor, he said, "There is a shared component between your . . . *necklace* and the capsule the dreeocht resides in. Once the stored air and water magic is gone, the device in your necklace will turn on and feed the capsule, as it were. That will keep the dreeocht from awakening. For as ingenious—and expensive—as the device is, however, it does have a limited range."

Ellinor's eyes went wide. Cosmin frowned at her and shook his head, his matte black hair swaying down his back. "The device that connects the two machines together, my dear, not your necklace. You thought I'd put something on you that would cease working once you were far enough away? Don't be silly! You can't stray far from the dreeocht, understood? You will remain within thirty feet of it at all times or," Cosmin's mouth relaxed into a smile, "the device around your neck will paralyze you. Kai will ensure your cooperation. Well, he and the rest of your old crew."

Ellinor blinked rapidly in response, stomach clenching. Cosmin laughed. "I thought it a convenient way to ensure you behaved; we wouldn't want you trying to kill anyone and run off with my property. You always did have a soft spot for your old team, Misho's friends. Really, the necklace would have been enough on its own, but I didn't want to take any chances, you understand."

"Stop calling this thing a necklace," Ellinor growled, refusing to think about being reunited with her old team under such conditions. "Call it what it is, yeah? It's a *collar*. It's a chain leashing me to your prize. It's not some pretty bauble I'd wear to a party."

Cosmin took a step back, his hand fluttering to his chest in feigned shock—or Ellinor assumed it was fake, at least. "My dear, collars are for *dogs*. Despite my reprimand, you have not stooped so low in my opinion—"

"Yet," Irati interjected.

Cosmin whacked her on the shoulder in what would have been a friendly rebuke if not for the slight shockwave Ellinor felt emanating from the slap, and the staggered step Irati took to keep her balance.

"Now, now, I'll have none of that. Elli was once a lieutenant. Perhaps this job will teach her some manners. I hope she'll see the error of her ways and return to us."

Jutting her chin toward the gleaming device, Ellinor stifled a growl. "Whose magic is fueling that thing now, then? Mine, obviously, but where did you get the water magic without Misho?" Even after eight years, her voice softened like it always did when she said her husband's name aloud.

"It's Misho's," Mirza said, and Ellinor's breath hitched.

Cosmin chuckled. "Why are you surprised? I had some of his residual power stored in the vaults alongside yours. Just because he died doesn't mean he, or his power, ceased to be useful. I've kept it safe in the meantime, which should ease some of your indignation over that distasteful incident all those years ago."

Ellinor said nothing. She blinked the sting from her eyes and crossed her arms, despite the ebbing pain, trying to bury the rising nausea over the thought of a piece of Misho's water magic being used to keep the slumbering dreeocht content.

A distant part of Ellinor had always known Cosmin had kept something of Misho all these years. Knew that a magic storage capsule still held a charge of her and Misho's magic from when they had willingly charged Cosmin's reserve vaults. She never imagined Misho's magic would be used in a hellish device to keep her disconnected from her own abilities.

She wouldn't have thought being this near a piece of her husband, especially a piece that did not smell like him, feel like him, or was even unique to him, would make it so hard for her to stand steady on her feet. But looking at the device in the corner now, she couldn't help but imagine Misho's angular face, strong chin, his dark eyebrows, and the mischievous glint to his marvelous amber eyes when he grinned. She wanted to run her hands along the capsule's smooth surface in hopes of feeling Misho there.

But she knew it wasn't him. It was just magic—natural magic that could be found anywhere.

Ellinor thought that realization would calm her, would stop her fingers from tingling, but it did none of those things. It made her heart twist in her chest and her body both ache and feel all the more empty.

Kai put his hand on her good shoulder and she winced. He sighed, but removed his hand.

Biting her cheeks to focus her thoughts, Ellinor cleared her throat and asked, "So that's all you need from me? To stay close to the dreeocht's holding cell until we get to Anzor? When will the . . . when will the magic run out?"

A shadow had passed over Mirza's face, his eyes softening so he could no longer maintain his scowl. When she turned to him, he had the grace to look away.

Cosmin didn't seem to notice the hitch in her voice, and shrugged. "Long enough to get out of Euria certainly. As long as everything goes according to plan."

His statement did more to focus Ellinor's thoughts than all the gnawing she was doing on her cheeks. She raised an eyebrow at the seersha, but she didn't see the worry she expected. Which made her all the more wary. "Are you expecting trouble? What's the plan, exactly? Seems rather simple, if you ask me. Too simple, by your standards, Cosmin."

"Don't presume to know anything about him or his orders anymore," Irati barked, and Cosmin rolled his eyes.

"My dear, please stop taking offense at everything our darling Elli does. It's getting tiresome. She's not all that disagreeable, and frankly, it's beneath you to be so petty. Do try to be better about it."

Irati clamped her mouth shut and looked down, her body tensing, cheeks flaming. Even Irati's blushes were pretty; it was entirely unfair. Ellinor cast her eyes down, reminding herself how deadly Irati was. She was one of the best snipers between Euria and Trifon, possibly the best on Erhard. Her exquisite features may be the most distracting danger, but that was not the most deadly thing about Irati.

Cosmin leveled his gaze back on Ellinor and sighed. "I always expect trouble. It's how I've survived this long. And while I took pains to ensure my little treasure remained a secret, even the most secure places have leaks. Just a drop or two is enough to get my rivals thirsty for an opportunity to tear me down.

"There are plenty within Euria who would want my dreeocht. Even the governor. I'm sure he'd love nothing more than to put it in a zoo or something, using it to gloat over the other city-states. Stupid man. But it means the force I need to send must remain relatively small, for secrecy's sake. I can't even give you one of my Class 1 Night Herons; it would only present a flashing neon sign that something of great value is inside."

Cosmin frowned, sparing a glance to the capsule as his fingers twitched like he was casting magic, although nothing happened. After a moment, he sighed and glanced between the four of them, the rest of the soldiers, sergeants, and service and bouncer automatons going about their tasks, oblivious to their discussion.

Shaking his head, Cosmin continued as if nothing were troubling him. "I've spoken to my generals and they all agree. A small force is the best way to go undetected. Which is why you'll not be restrained, as I'd originally planned. If things go sideways, I'll need everyone to do their part."

Ellinor smirked, though she knew Cosmin couldn't see the action. "Are we just going in a straight line from here to Anzor? Seems silly, given your enemies will be watching the most direct routes, yeah?"

Irati's smile was as sweet as ripe cherries, which was at odds with the vicious glint to her eyes. "Don't you worry about that. We've got everything handled on that front. Cosmin's business is in good hands, now that you're out of the picture."

"Oh, I bet. I'm sure he loves your *hands* all over his *business.*"

Kai snickered, and Irati glowered. Huffing, she stomped away to bark orders at a group of soldiers who were not loading the Class 3 Night Heron fast enough for her tastes.

Cosmin sighed. "Given the situation, you should be taking this more seriously, Elli dear."

"Cosmin," Ellinor said slowly, "stop calling me *Elli* like everything's good between us. I'm being coerced into doing a job by the seersha directly responsible for my husband's death. And now I'm escorting a dangerous creature that is currently leeching the last of his magic in order to keep it dozing. You can call me *dear* like you do every person with tits, but stop acting like we're friendly, got it?"

Cosmin's brow furrowed, and Ellinor thought he'd set her on fire this time, having finally crossed an invisible line. Instead, he glanced at Kai, who still had the appearance of a hurt puppy. Deciding it wasn't worth the energy, he shrugged, and Ellinor continued, "Besides, if I don't make light, reality is going to crash down on me like the Goma Ocean and drown me. So you do you, and I'll do me."

"Oh very well, but I hope you change your mind. I do miss seeing you bounce up and down my halls." Cosmin gave her a wink and turned to leave. "If our Ellinor has anymore concerns or questions, Mr. Otieno, be a good man and answer to the best of your ability. Tell her only what she needs to know, however. Nothing more."

"Yes, boss," Mirza mumbled, fixing Ellinor with his dark eyes and raising a brow at her.

Ellinor scrubbed at her forehead, as if that would keep the pounding headache building at the base of her skull at bay. "Well?" she asked when Mirza remained watching her stoically. "There *is* a plan, yeah? A better plan than making a mad dash straight across all Erhard to get to Anzor?"

"Yup," Mirza said.

"Wonderful. What is it?"

"It's on a need to know basis."

"And you don't think I need to know?"

"Nope."

Ellinor bit her tongue to keep from growling. Even for a man of few words, he was being vague on purpose.

Payback for teasing Irati and yelling at Cosmin.

"You're seriously not going to tell me anything? I'm supposed to just babysit the dreeocht box and follow blindly, waiting for you to tell me when to do something?"

"Pretty much," Mirza said with a shrug.

"Great, just great." Ellinor rubbed at her forehead again. "So what am I supposed to do?"

"Wait. We leave soon," Mirza said, glancing beyond Ellinor to one of the lower-ranking sergeants. Dipping his head, Mirza walked around Ellinor, saying no more.

"This is fucking stupid. I don't know what generals Cosmin is taking counsel from these days, but whatever they have planned, it's dumb."

"Ah, c'mon Ell"—she glared at Kai, and he swallowed before hastily adding—"inor. You don't rightfully know what they all got planned. Could be downright brilliant."

Ellinor debated not speaking to Kai at all, but given the earnest look on his round face, she relented. Despite Kai's massive size and the unsettling glee he felt when fighting, he was a big softy. Cosmin took advantage of his size. Kai's big, muscular hands and wide, upright stature made the people Cosmin wanted to do business with uncomfortable. But once you got to know him, he was far from intimidating. Ellinor had gone with Kai to pick out the six specially made golden bullet ear studs he gave to his mother on her birthday. After something like that, it was hard to see him as the brute he paraded himself as.

Mirza was incapable of telling her more, and even if he could, Irati would be sure he didn't tell Ellinor what the plan was. Given that, Ellinor decided it wasn't worth it to shun Kai. She had always known Kai Axel Brantley was Cosmin's man. Ellinor couldn't fault him for staying true to his convictions when so few did.

"You wouldn't happen to know anything, would you?" Ellinor asked, turning to watch the final preparations.

"Only a little. Don't think I should be telling you, though."

Ellinor shrugged. "Look, if Cosmin wants me to help out, someone's got to tell me something of substance. Otherwise, if trouble starts—and let's be honest, there's always trouble—the chances of me being caught with my pants down skyrockets. Just give me something, Kai."

Kai shifted from foot to foot for a moment, glancing to where Cosmin had joined Irati, whispering in her ear and handing over a compact flash drive which she immediately secured in a small pocket on her chest. His shoulders sagged when Cosmin began twirling Irati's shiny hair through his long fingers.

"All I know is," Kai began slowly, "there's these stops we're making. Check points and safe houses. Whatever the path is we be taking, it's guarded right proper. Undercover operatives and the like will be waiting. The safe houses stretch from here to Anzor though, so we should be safe enough. Even with our low numbers."

Kai looked like he was going to give her a clap on the back, but instead resumed his shuffling. "Cosmin's got a right smart group of generals, you know that. Journey's only slated to take a week there and back, if we stay on schedule. With you aboard, don't think no one's going to mess with us, though." Kai gave her a wink as if that would reassure her, but even he didn't sound all that confident.

"Uh-huh, right," Ellinor mumbled. Cosmin was meticulous in all his plans. And, despite knowing that Cosmin had survived this long and had retained his power by not being reckless, a cold sweat began collecting in the small of Ellinor's back.

Misho wouldn't want me to worry. He'd say that as long as I trusted my instincts, I'd survive. Ellinor's instincts were screaming at her, however, to abort the mission before it started.

But if she left, she'd never get her powers back. And, Ellinor owed it to Misho's memory to make sure the last of his stored magic wasn't spent in vain on a lost cause.

She had schemed for years, but she had never gotten this close to Cosmin von Brandt after she'd quit. Now, if Ellinor played her part right, she could bury her modified Leviathan Roaster—the illegal knife she had stolen specifically for killing a caster—deep in Cosmin's fiery heart. The debt for Misho's death would finally be paid.

BEST SEAT IN THE HOUSE
///CHAPTER SEVEN

ELLINOR HEADED for the dreeocht container and slumped against the nearby wall. None bothered speaking to her. She didn't begrudge them their hostility. She would have felt the same toward someone in her position—if it hadn't been for Misho.

Kai attempted to keep her company, but she waved him away. She wanted to be alone before they were all herded into the waiting transport. He gave her a sad smile and wandered off to see if Cosmin needed him. Once everyone went back to their business, Ellinor scooted close to the container, resting her head against its smooth, cool surface.

She knew it was silly, but she felt better next to the device now knowing what it was. Closing her eyes, she inhaled deeply, trying to remember how Misho smelled.

Like warm, fresh laundry after a long day in the breeze.

Within moments, she was swimming in memories of a time before Cosmin von Brandt had ever entered their lives.

"Hey! Watch it! If you don't concentrate, you'll stab your-self," a lanky young man called, racing for Ellinor where she was manipulating the wind in order to make her knives dance around the training robot.

Ellinor scowled and released the magic, all her knives bouncing to the ground—including the one she hadn't noticed wobbling behind her on the fringe of the air current she was twisting. Ellinor blinked at the rogue blade, a blush creeping up her neck.

"Uh, thanks, but I had it under control," she mumbled, col-lecting the blades and dismissing the training bot. Anything to avoid looking at the recruit bounding toward her.

He didn't call her on the lie, like her brother would have, or any of her instructors. For that she was thankful and met his gaze. His bright amber eyes were twinkling with laughter he held within.

"You're new, right? Just enlisted last week?" the young man asked.

"Okay, stalker. You keep tabs on all the new girls?"

This time, he did laugh. "I keep track of *all* the newly en-listed *casters*. There aren't exactly many of us." He picked up one of the wayward knives that had been half buried in the dirt. "I'm Misho Shimizu, by the way," he added, handing her the blade.

She took the knife, glancing at him before looking away again. He was still smiling at her, and she couldn't stop from blushing.

He moved with the grace of a dancer, yet had the smooth, confident flare of a powerful business man, not a lowly military recruit. His hair had that effortless disheveled look she had seen countless other men try to replicate with little success. Tufts of his shiny black hair curled over his brows and he tossed his head to clear his eyes. And his eyes!

Such a radiant amber.

Ellinor shook her head, tucking the combat-tech embedded blades into the various sheaths around her waist and thighs. She was doing everything but meeting Misho's gaze to avoid blushing like she'd never talked to a man before.

"Ellinor Olysha Rask," she mumbled, giving him a slight smile, still looking off to the side. "You're an earth caster, yeah? Or fire?" she added, waving at his face.

Having such bright brown tones usually meant an affinity for one of those two elemental powers in humani casters. Only seersha casters didn't follow such a rule; their eyes ranged myriad of colors, regardless of whether there was any type of magical affinity. Some earth casters had bright green eyes, but that was uncommon, just as it was uncommon for air or water casters to have anything but blue eyes.

Misho laughed again and Ellinor's stomach did a backflip.

It was deep and honest, like a freshly brewed cup of coffee. It made Ellinor want to snuggle up in her bunk under her favorite childhood blanket.

She glanced up at him again. He was a good head taller than she, his muscles starting to bulge from physical training. She noted his broad smile, but even his crooked teeth couldn't detract from his soft, full lips. Ellinor shut her eyes for a moment, lest her mind wander while looking at his lips, and forced herself to get better control of her emotions.

"I'm a water caster, if you can believe that. I was practically bribed to enlist by my local senator. It makes a good living for my parents, so I can't complain." He studied her for a moment, his small, glittering eyes trailing over her body in a casual way that sent goosebumps racing down her arms.

Ellinor squinted, studying him in a new found light. He didn't *look* like a water caster, but she wasn't sure that meant anything. He looked like any other young recruit, a handsome—

Stop that!

When Ellinor couldn't find her voice to respond, Misho Shimizu cleared his throat and asked, "What about you? Bet your family got a nice bonus, too. Is that why you enlisted?"

"Oh, yeah, but that's not . . . I mean, I didn't enlist because of the money. My family doesn't need it."

Misho tilted his head, a lock of black hair falling over his eye, which he blew away, and Ellinor's heart began racing of its own accord. Looking into his honest eyes, she had the sudden urge to tell him everything. Like she could trust him with all her secrets.

The words spilled from her and she couldn't stop them. "Andrey, my big brother, he, uh, he wasn't a caster. Always kind of hated that his little sister was, that everyone was more impressed with what I did than what he achieved. He . . . he wanted to prove himself, I guess. Show that you didn't need abilities to be great, or do great things. And, I mean, he's right! Or, he was. Andrey was an excellent soldier, top marks in all his physical classes and recruited by the police after he graduated. He joined the narcotics unit, hunting down any of those Juice Boxes that made it into the city. You know, those nasty serums that make non-casters get high on dead magitech nanites. But it wasn't enough. He still wanted to prove . . . I don't know, something."

Stop, Ellinor. You've never told anyone this before. But she couldn't stop, didn't want to, either. She was worried she'd forget Andrey if she never spoke his name again. "When the police commissioner needed volunteers to raid a suspected Juice Box shop, he was the first to step up. Nothing fazed Andrey, not even going up against Ashlings. I never got to tell Andrey how proud I was of him, that I looked up to him. When he and his unit went out to the deadlands to investigate, he . . . well, he, um . . ."

Ellinor trailed off, her throat constricting over the memory of coming home from school to find her parents in tears, a uniformed officer in their living room. She could still hear her mother screeching at the man, begging him to check again. To triple confirm that it was her boy lying on the slab. Two weeks later her parents would get Andrey's signature tattooed on their shoulders, his ashes and photograph occupying a place of honor on their mantle.

Misho put his hand on her shoulder. Her shoulders and legs tensed, body trembling. He must have felt it, felt her breaking, and tugged her into a hesitant hug. Her core went all soft and she threatened to melt in his embrace.

She had just met this man, and already he was touching her? She should pull away, but so few people talked about Andrey anymore. And if they did, the condolences went to her parents. Ellinor received only their frowns and nods, never their shoulder. But here was Misho Shimizu already giving her that, and Ellinor didn't know how to react.

"I'm sorry. I didn't know," Misho whispered. "But why are *you* here if it cost your brother his life? Casters can get a job anywhere doing anything. You shouldn't risk your life, too."

He released her, and a part of Ellinor wished he hadn't. Swallowing until her throat was no longer tight, Ellinor said, "I'm here *for* Andrey. To carry on his legacy. I shouldn't even be practicing with my magic, he always hated it. I promised that if I was going to honor him, I'd do so *in spite* of my abilities."

Misho gave her a bemused look. "In spite of? That's silly, isn't it? I'm sorry for what happened, but your abilities weren't to blame. It's a shame your brother felt jealous over your power, but that's not your fault. You could help so many people with air magic, you can do so much good. Can't you imagine it?"

There was a lightness in her chest and she could feel her cheeks start to flame again at the earnestness of his words. "Oh, I don't know about all that. I'm not a very powerful caster. Besides, those mobster seersha types seem more effective in keeping Euria under control, regulating Juice Box and magitech access, than the fat politicians anyway. People don't really need me," Ellinor said, picking at her nails and studiously watching her feet.

Misho took her hand as if they had been friends all their lives instead of near strangers. "Then allow me the pleasure of proving you wrong, Ellinor Olysha Rask. I'm going to show you how incredible your abilities are, and just how amazing you can be for using them to honor your brother."

Ellinor snorted out a laugh, and slammed her hands over her mouth, eyes going wide. Misho bit his lip at her reaction to keep from laughing, and Ellinor cursed herself for yanking her hand away.

Once she got her embarrassment under control, she said, "How can you say that? You don't even know me."

"Well, that's not entirely true. I don't know you all that well *yet*, but I'm going to change that—if that's all right with you." He winked at her, and Ellinor had to bite her lip to keep from giggling. She was hopelessly undone by Misho from their very first meeting.

A thud against the side of her foot snapped Ellinor out of her reverie and left her scrabbling for a pistol that wasn't there. She quickly glanced around, saw the big metal boot, and followed it up to the concerned face of Kai as he peered down at her.

"You ain't becoming an old lady who needs 'er nap time, are you?"

Ellinor frowned and got to her feet. "I'm good. Good enough to babysit a metal container at any rate."

"That's good, 'cause we're shoving out," he said, pointing toward where their team was filing into the docking bay. Kai grabbed the push-cart that held the dreeocht container and grinned a little at Ellinor when she didn't immediately start moving. "Ready?"

Ellinor rolled her eyes, tucking the daydream of Misho away in the warmer parts of her mind. "Not like I have a choice."

"Ah, well, that's true." Kai looked like he wanted to say more, but whatever it was, Ellinor would never know as he wheeled the container through the docking bay doors, Ellinor trailing behind him.

She could feel Cosmin's eyes burning on the back of her neck, but he didn't say anything and she wasn't about to strike up a conversation, not while her arm still throbbed. As Cosmin didn't follow after them, she assumed he had said what he needed to and felt confident all would go as he commanded, as always.

Ellinor trudged behind Kai through the cavernous docking bay, noting that many of the aerial and land transports were not in the hanger. All that remained were the big armored transports—the Class 1 Hornet Hawks—that would have made it damn near impossible to be shot down, but were too conspicuous for their journey. Sandwiched in between the big ships was their mid-sized cargo Night Heron with a crew of mechanics scrambling around it, removing fuel lines and clearing the landing pad for take-off.

Overseeing the mechanics was a familiar face that had Ellinor tripping over her feet. In the traditional pilot's uniform stood Eko Blom.

Eko had been in the same recruiting class as Ellinor and Misho. A talented mechanic, Eko had always been a shy man, never joining them at the bars. Lean and wiry, he looked like he had stopped aging just before puberty. While he was tall, his pale skin had never managed to grow any kind of facial hair. He styled his light hair differently now, shaved off on one side of his skull while the rest was combed over in a kind of milky-blonde wave that went down past his ear on the other side.

Eko was the only one not wearing all black. Instead, he was in the gray, white, and gold pinstripe suit all licensed mechanic pilots wore. The uniform would have been dashing on anyone other than Eko, who tugged at the lapels and readjusted his belt every so often, not quite filling out the uniform like a soldier should. He must have felt Ellinor's gaze lingering on him; he peeked back toward her, his hazel eyes widening as they made eye contact before he shoved his hands in his pockets and scuttled inside the aircraft.

Irati and Mirza waited at the top of the ramp, watching the proceedings like doehaz protecting their kill. Irati, as usual, appeared more trigger happy than warranted, her fingers dancing over the strap around her chest that held her custom-made revolver sniper rifle. She smiled viciously at Ellinor as she approached and, once more, Ellinor thought it was a mistake to keep her unarmed until they were out of Euria's air space. Still, upon seeing the smile, she pressed a small button on her glove, activating her armor. If Irati wanted to do her harm, she wouldn't find Ellinor devoid of defenses.

As if reading her mind, Kai turned back to look at her and winked. "Don't worry, I 'ad your things packed safe and tight. I'll give 'em back as soon as possible."

Ellinor pursed her lips and gave a quick nod as she scampered up the ramp into the Night Heron, not giving Irati a chance to utter any of her snide remarks.

Ellinor felt no need to secure anything or help make final preparations as everyone, except Kai, had made it abundantly clear she was just another unwanted passenger—a necessary burden they all had to shoulder. So, once Kai secured the dreeocht, Ellinor found a window seat toward the back of the ship and waited for take-off in silence.

She felt Kai's huge presence take a seat not far from her, but she didn't acknowledge him, nor did she bother looking around the Night Heron as it began to thrum when Eko initiated take-off. The vibration grew until the ship lunged forward, Ellinor's stomach plummeting as it raced to catch up with the inertia. The ship leveled out and joined the rest of the air traffic zooming about Euria. Her eyes found themselves glued to the cityscape as it raced by beneath her.

Euria was like most of the sprawling metropolises in Erhard: tall skyscrapers that didn't so much kiss the sky as ram their fist through it, their shadows casting a perpetual false night across the ground where the unfortunate dwelled. Citizens of the lower echelons eked out a living the only way they knew how while cowering under the damp mist that filtered to the ground from the exhaust of the vehicles high above. Euria was all glass, steel, and shimmering neon as Cosmin's businesses showcased advertisements for his casinos, strip and synth clubs, and brothels in luminous, brazen color.

Aside from Cosmin's undisputed control over the city's underworld, providing illegal machines of various kinds imbued with far too much magic, and keeping Juice Boxes out of his establishments, the city-state moved of its own accord. Its citizenry constantly creating and building, always moving up, forcing the skyscrapers ever higher as those at the bottom crawled their way out of the deep shadows. The tops of the skyscrapers housed spacious penthouses of high ranking governing officials and lobbyists, along with the rich and famous. Their pleasure gardens were pristine landscapes and forests the air traffic was ordered to fly around. Ellinor watched the gardens flash by, occasionally catching glimpses of seersha sunbathing or having cocktail parties, despite it being only noon.

Ellinor glanced back and sucked in her breath. The splendor of Cosmin's estate was at sparkling, demonic odds with the rest of the neon and metal city surrounding it.

Made of immaculate white marble, its roof was of gleaming gold. Swooping, curved staircases flanked the front entryway, their steps red sandstone that led to the roof of the grand entryway, where it opened to a massive balcony. On the balcony, trees soared into the sky, so green that Ellinor couldn't believe they were natural.

The austere and glimmering affluence of the building was not what made Ellinor's breathe hitch and her eyes widen, but rather the moat surrounding the estate.

The only way to enter the estate was over a special, computerized obsidian bridge that was close to a mile long. The moat itself was molten lava, twisting and curling like a tumultuous red sea. The expensive technology and metal in the bridge not only kept it from melting, but kept those who walked upon the bridge from feeling any heat, unless Cosmin believed someone was entering the premise unwelcomed.

Cosmin's estate shrank in the distance and was obscured by the downtown businesses before more and more skyscrapers of respectable sizes jutted toward the sky, the unforgiving neon of flashy advertisements replaced with dingy, multi-tiered storefronts and run down apartments. There were more broken windows and makeshift air vehicles, but also an influx of ground vehicles that raced below them.

It would take a few hours of flying at speed before they were free of Euria, and Ellinor was not sad to see it go. She had left the city only a few times in her life, but once Andrey was gone, her family home had never felt the same. And without Misho, her current residence was no more than a place to rest her head and patch her wounds. But Kai took her steadfast observation of the scenery to mean she was trying to memorize the terrain.

"Ah, you'll miss it too, huh?" Kai said, leaning over the aisle toward her.

Ellinor spared him a glance and shook her head. "The opposite."

Kai quirked a brow at her, and then his eyes widened. "Right. Misho. Forgot you'd probably want to get a ways from . . . all that."

Ellinor narrowed her eyes, yanking down the mask over her mouth for the first time since attaching it so Kai could see the full force of her scowl. "How can you forget something like that? He was your friend, for Azer's sake!"

Kai flinched. "Now don't go taking our maker's name in vain. What if He's listening and the like? And it's been eight years since the . . . accident. Some of us 'ave moved on."

Ellinor punched Kai in the jaw. Hard.

She shook out her hand, glaring at Kai, daring him to retaliate. But he only rubbed his chin in response, his eyes glistening. "I'm sorry I can't just get over my husband's death the way everyone else in this shit hole has." Ellinor snorted and barked out a mean laugh, still rubbing her hand. "I can't understand how you could still believe in the fairy tale that is our supposed god. Azer hasn't been seen since what, a century or two after creating the world? A millennia later, I doubt that *God* is listening. He's like any spoiled child, bored with his toys."

Kai glared at her then more than when she'd punched him. He had always been oddly religious for a criminal.

Grinding her teeth, Ellinor's scowl didn't lessen even as the sarcasm left her voice. "And you know what else? If we'd known what we were really guarding that night, if Cosmin had been *honest* about what was happening, we might have been better prepared. I still wouldn't have agreed with what the bastard was doing, but it may have saved Misho. Cosmin knew a robbery was being planned, and he did *nothing* to prevent it."

"But he didn't kill Misho. He wouldn't—*didn't* want that," Kai said, though his voice had grown soft as if his heart were no longer in the argument. "You gotta let that shit go or it's gonna fuck you up for the rest of your life."

Ellinor shook her head, but before she could say anything, Kai continued. "Look, I miss 'im too, got that? Misho was good people. And I owe 'im, so, I promise: you need something you tell me, and I'll do what I can. I want you back in the boss's good graces, all official-like. I miss us being buds. You just name it, and it's yours."

Ellinor didn't answer. She couldn't.

She couldn't tell Kai she wouldn't let it go until everyone responsible paid for Misho's life with their own. The only ones left were the Ashling sympathizers that had planned the heist, and they stayed in their island nation far to the north, and Cosmin von Brandt himself. But she couldn't ask Kai for that kind of help; he'd warn Cosmin of her plans. He may have been her friend, and he may believe he owed Misho for some past debt, but he would always belong to Cosmin first.

Instead, Ellinor shrugged. "Thanks for the offer, but I'm good as long as you keep Irati off my ass. I need more time. We'll see how I feel once this mission is over and Cosmin takes this collar off."

"You thinking of coming back to us then? Right proper like and everything? Not like you to forgive no one for nothing. That collar messing with you that much? Shit, Ell, I'm sorry. But you know Cosmin. His word be gold! He'd forgive you and make life easy for you if you did likewise. I'd make sure of it."

Ellinor turned her face back toward the window so Kai couldn't see the glint in her eyes, or the way her lips twitched in a nasty smile. "Yeah, something like that, sure. I think it may be time to bury that old hatchet."

A DECEPTIVE PLACE
///CHAPTER EIGHT

K AI TRIED to engage her in idle chatter, but Ellinor ignored him except for asking once if the dreeocht batteries were still full—they were. Kai gave up after that, leaving to talk to the rest of the crew—specifically Pema Tran and her girlfriend, Talin Roxas.

Pema, the olive-skinned humani sergeant with her graying, straight black hair, lit a cigarette as Kai spoke, blowing the swirling smoke off to the side, her dark brown eyes trailing over every contour of the air transport. Pema smiled at Kai, her arm draped around Talin's thin waist.

Ellinor had always liked Pema. She was tough but straight-forward; you always knew where you stood with her, and Elli-nor appreciated that. She didn't hide her disapproval of Ellinor's decision to quit, but she didn't seem to approve of her boss's methods in getting her back, either. Or so Ellinor as-sumed.

Talin was a seerani—half-humani, half-seersha—but she could pass for full humani. The only thing that hinted at her heritage were her large emerald green eyes amidst her smooth black skin. But she had no outlandish hair—she kept her head shaved, just a slight impression of black fuzz atop her skull—and no sign of either horns or pointed ears. She also wasn't a caster, and it made Talin work all the harder. Now she was Cosmin's premiere explosives expert. Useful enough, but with such a small number of people allowed on the mission, Ellinor wasn't sure why Talin was here.

Talin leaned against Pema, unperturbed by the smoke, laughing at something Kai said. A wave of loneliness washed over Ellinor and she turned her attention back out the window, determined to forget that these were the faces of the people she'd once considered friends, the people she had been in charge of when she'd belonged to Cosmin.

This far out, there were no longer any skyscrapers, only a collection of suburban communities tied together by the outlying farmland that made Euria self-sufficient. Cosmin ensured the land remained fertile, with the government's blessing. It was nice to call in a favor from time to time, after all. In exchange, the people on the outskirts lived for free on Cosmin's payroll, as long as they did all he asked. Ellinor had visited these communities once, and while the farmers had simple needs and desires, their loyalty was as fierce as Kai's. If they saw a plane or truck heading for the city proper—or leaving Euria—that didn't look official, Cosmin would know about it within the hour.

When their transport began to descend, Ellinor glanced out the window one last time and confirmed there was nothing out here so far from the city walls that kept most people from leaving. Nothing interesting or good, at any rate.

Ellinor's chest tightened at the sight of so much parched, uninhabitable land. There was only one thing stopping casters, even with a dreeocht, from leaving their bases of power and conquering more territory, and it wasn't the police or any government regulation, either. It was the vast swathes of dead land, between the great city-states and continents, where the doehaz roamed.

Those monsters hunted down any magic user who traveled through their domain and devoured them alive. Dreeocht and doehaz were of a similar family, except the magic used to create a doehaz was only enough to give it consciousness, leaving it craving magic like nothing else. It forced the beasts to become single minded in their desire to hunt and consume all the power they could to ease that never quenchable need for magic, as if trying to complete some unattainable transition into a dreeocht.

She shivered, turning away from the window, in need of a distraction.

"Hey, Kai," she called, noting he now had his head in the cockpit talking to Eko. When Kai didn't turn to answer her, she pushed her way through the loitering crew, ignoring their grumbles as much as she could.

Irati Mishra blocked Ellinor's path as she was about to reach Kai. "Where do you think you're going?" Irati planted her fists on her hips, a smirk on her full lips as the crew snickered behind Ellinor. There was a challenge to Irati's harmonic voice that told Ellinor the lieutenant wasn't kidding.

The hair on Ellinor's arms began to rise as she sensed herself being surrounded, and she had to swallow the urge to slam her palm into Irati's button nose and turn on those behind her. But without access to her abilities, Ellinor doubted she'd get more than one good hit in.

Deciding the injuries she would sustain weren't worth putting Irati in her place, Ellinor rolled her eyes and shifted her position so none could grab her unawares. "Relax, princess. I'm just trying to ask Kai what's up. Unless you'd be willing to tell me? You know, without the vitriolic talk about me being a saboteur, or whatever else you want to label me this early in the mission."

"You don't need to know what's going on. You'll be told what you need to know when we decide you need to know something. Not before. Never before," Irati said, grinning when those clustered around mumbled their agreement.

Mirza and Kai pushed their way out of the cockpit as the group crowded closer to Irati and Ellinor. Mirza Otieno fixed his partner with a hard stare and said, "Irati, stop."

That was all it took.

Irati blanched slightly and huffed, shoving past Ellinor and mumbling about checking the cargo, her more devout lackey, Janne Wolff, following after her. Janne was still a soldier officially, but the petite blonde with her dark blue eyes and freckles was often used in more . . . delicate situations. She worked best in the dark, ensuring her targets never knew it was their last night drawing breath. It's why she gravitated toward Irati. Both women struck before anyone ever saw them coming.

Janne had been snatched from a fetish brothel that thought they could eke out a living if they stole girls young and stayed on the outskirts of Euria, refusing to pay Cosmin's protection fees. Cosmin was all too glad to show them how wrong that idea was. Most of the workers found employment elsewhere, some willingly gaining employment in Cosmin's

strip clubs and casinos, but not Janne. Janne had wanted payback, and Cosmin was happy to give it to her. Within a year,
Janne had made a name for herself with some of the quickest
hands Ellinor had ever seen. They could snatch a keycard as
smoothly as they could snap a neck.

Kai frowned at Irati and Janne as the crowd dispersed and
put his hand on Ellinor's shoulder. Mirza shook his head at the
women and went back into the cockpit with Eko.

"What 'appened?" Kai said.

"Nothing new. More posturing and the like. It'll die down
when I get my weapons back. I'll get them back *now*, yeah?"
When Kai nodded she asked, "So why are we landing? There's
nothing out here."

"Well, I wouldn't go saying there was *nothing*," Kai said, motioning her toward where the dreeocht was secured. "Cosmin's
got a safe house of sorts out 'ere. Gotta change this old tin
can for a different model. One that's not gonna have Cosmin's
brand on it, you follow?"

Understanding hit Ellinor like a truck.

*Of course we can't take any of Cosmin's personal vehicles
across Erhard without someone getting suspicious.* Nodding,
Ellinor said, "So what now?"

Kai glanced to where Irati was walking up from the cargo
hold, one of her personal boxes held protectively in her hands
like a bomb about to go off. She snarled at Kai as if worried
he'd take her box before pushing past them to the front of the
Night Heron, Janne still following just behind.

Kai rolled his eyes and waited for Irati to busy herself with
her things before answering. "We got to meet with an agent of
Cosmin's. Dunno who, but guess we'll be swapping some folks
out. They'll take this 'ere boat back to Cosmin like we were just

checking on some outer city business and no one will suspect nothing. Can't risk the little beastie getting snagged before it gets to Zabel. Cosmin will be right cross if this trade don't 'appen and he doesn't get Zabel's tech, specs, and support."

Kai quirked an eyebrow at her as a knowing smile tugged up a corner of Ellinor's lips, but when she didn't elaborate as to why she was smiling, he shrugged. "Not sure who stays or goes, or when we'll leave. This 'ere be the last thing I know for certain outside the basics I already done told you, and our final stop before heading back."

"You one of the ones who's going back to the estate?"

"Nah," Kai laughed. "Cosmin tasked me with watching you and that's what I'm gonna do. Could be worse. Could have to babysit Irati. Now wouldn't that be something?"

Ellinor grinned despite herself before clearing her throat and jutting her chin toward the sour lieutenant. "What's up with her anyway? Is it just me or is she acting more unreasonable than usual?"

Kai shrugged and grasped a handhold above his head as the Night Heron began spiraling down for its landing. "She's been that way for a few years now. She had this 'ere fight with the boss, right? Huge shouting match and everything. Something 'bout not being appreciated, taken for granted. She went running to Mirza for backup, but he didn't 'elp her out the way she wanted. She accused 'im of being just like those three trash brothers of 'ers. You know, the ones who always thought she was less than nothing because of being a girl." Kai snorted, shaking his head. "Anyway, since then she's had an attitude meaner than a doehaz in heat. Shit, even Mirza's been tighter lipped than usual since their fight. But Irati's been keeping to 'erself a spot more, too. Well, besides for Eko. She's been getting real *friendly* with that kid. Odd. You wouldn't think 'e was her type . . ." Kai squinted into the distance as if struggling to recover a memory before sighing. "Not like she rubbed elbows with me much, but now she's shunning Mirza, and those two used to be thick. You know? Lay-down-your-life-for-each-other kind of deal. *Thick.*"

Just like me and you, buddy. But Ellinor bit back the words, the feel of Kai's fingers around her neck sending a chill up her spine.

Despite Kai claiming to not know much of the inner workings of their plan or Cosmin's operations in general, the big man had a keen ear for gossip and possessed zero filter as to what he should keep to himself. It was all Ellinor could do not to smile, sipping the accidental intel like fine whiskey.

"Yeah, yeah, I get it. Seems silly though, to get so weird over an argument with Cosmin. He's always been an egotistical bastard, but he'll give you what you're due. If you've actually earned it, that is," she whispered.

Kai's eyes hardened for a moment as he glanced at her, before shrugging. "See, I done thought the same, too. But Irati's been like this ever since, so what do I know, right?" Kai tugged on his lip for a moment before whispering, "So, uh, this means we're solid now, right Ell? I been sharing more than I ought to with you, you know?"

Ellinor tapped the bio and magitech circlet around her throat and Kai winced. The sorrow and regret in his bright green eyes made Ellinor's heart flip in her chest, though.

Kai had been alone for such a long time before stumbling into Cosmin's employ. Struggling to take care of his mother on the lower levels of the city, no father to help pay the bills, and a horde of nasty children always following him around, baiting him like a bear in order to watch the "fat boy" fight back. Cosmin had been there first, lifting him up, seeing his potential to create mayhem and chaos in his favor. The seersha mobster had given Kai help and a purpose before Ellinor and Misho had ever become his friends. Even before Kai fell head over heels in love with the seersha, he'd have willingly done anything Cosmin asked to repay his debt, now that his mother was living comfortably.

He had no idea what he was doing, what he was cutting me off from. He just thought he was helping Cosmin bring me back to the fold. Don't be mad at him.

But the emptiness, the hollow, icy ache in her chest where her magic once dwelled was keeping her at an arm's length. She sighed. "I need more time, Kai. Time, and a barrel of rye whiskey."

Kai frowned for a moment, before his shoulders slumped and he nodded. "Fair enough," he mumbled, going off to fetch the dreeocht as the Night Heron gently touched down in the middle of a vacant field.

PARANOID, MUCH?
///CHAPTER NINE

T HE EXTERIOR door opened and Eko and Mirza exited the
   cockpit ahead of Ellinor. Ellinor hopped down around the
young mechanic, who stopped just outside the opened doors.
She cocked an eyebrow at him, and Eko glanced up from his
shiny black shoes. He ignored Ellinor when he spied Irati's
stunning smile. The young mechanic blushed, his eyes flying
from Irati, trying to appear nonchalant about their little exchange. Eko then made brief eye contact with Ellinor in an attempt to temper the splotchy blush coloring his cheeks. His
eyes widened momentarily before looking away, picking at his
stubby fingers, his blush intensifying.

Ellinor hated that Eko was uneasy around her now. She had
looked out for him when he first started working for Cosmin,
protecting him from the cruel hazing some of the other soldiers liked to pull on new recruits. She had viewed him like a
little brother, once upon a time.

Before she could confront Eko about it, Mirza's gravelly voice filled the cabin. "Alistair, Botros, Mosi, and Sefu, you stay. The rest, follow me."

"What?" Irati hissed. "That's my team, Mirza! They're coming with us to the next stop. That was my understanding—"

"Plans changed. Cosmin's orders," Mirza answered, a hard glint to his eyes as he waved the four men back when they hesitated near the exit.

"Azer's cock! Change of plans? When did this happen?" Irati appeared ready to shove the four off the aerial transport, as if that would keep them from having to stay with the Night Heron.

"Knock it off, Lieutenant. These are Cosmin's orders. What do we do when Cosmin gives an order?"

"We . . . we follow it. *Blindly,*" Irati grumbled quietly, her warm brown eyes flashing beneath her thick lashes like wildfire.

"That's right," Mirza growled. "Those four have been ordered to stay on the transport, so they *stay.*"

Irati clamped her mouth shut so hard Ellinor heard her teeth clack, but she no longer argued with Mirza. Technically, they held the same ranking, but Mirza was her senior by a few years and therefore the default authority when there were disputes. It didn't always happen—or it didn't used to—but when they did disagree, Mirza was not afraid to lay into Irati.

It was the most Ellinor had heard Mirza say in a long time, and her surprise banished any lingering trepidation she felt toward Eko's behavior. Kai nudged her on his way out, and Ellinor tried to shake the thought away as she followed Kai and the dreeocht container, yet the tightness around her gut would not lessen.

Once out of the transport, Ellinor paused to inhale the muggy afternoon air, the smell of fresh cut grass and stale hay floating around her like a silken shroud. She wanted to breathe in the unpolluted air, wanted to see what this kind of air quality might produce, should she call upon her abilities. Tentatively, she tried reaching out again, only to be greeted by the deadness that resided within spaces once filled with warmth and substance.

Ellinor's lower lip trembled, her eyes stinging of their own accord.

Suck it up, soldier. Andrey's voice slammed through her mind. *You knew nothing was going to answer you. Don't give in to that weakness. Focus. Get this over with the way I would have. Keep your head high the way Misho would want. Don't let the bastards see tears in your eyes!*

Distracting herself, she studied the crew while they milled about, as uncertain as she was about why they were here, and what they were waiting for. The only ones who appeared unconcerned were the service bots, Mirza, Kai, and Eko—or as unconcerned as Eko could appear. Each time Irati got close to the young man, his face turned red, as if he had stuck it in one of his furnaces.

Once everything was off the transport, Irati waved to those who stayed aboard, and with a loud *whoosh* of the engines, the Night Heron lurched into the sky and sped off. Once the transport was no more than a streak of glinting silver in the sky, Mirza walked a few paces away, kicking the burnt grass and dirt. Ellinor watched him, along with everyone else, until he seemed to find what he was looking for. He stomped on the ground a few times, then took a step back.

Ellinor was about to voice the silent question resting on all their lips when she felt a gentle vibration coming from deep beneath her. The vibration grew into a rumble, then a quake, which had Ellinor flailing as she struggled to keep her balance as *something* neared the surface. Her eyes widened as she watched the space closest to Mirza, cursing that she hadn't made Kai give her weapons back before disembarking the transport. But then, the rumbling abruptly stopped and all was still in the vacant field.

Mirza leapt back as dirt was flung into the air by a hatch opening under his feet. A moment later, a white haired seersha with skin so bronze it had a reddish tinge to it, and a pair of ears so high over his head Ellinor was sure he'd never be able to wear a hat, peered at them from the hatch. He pushed a pair of wire-framed glasses up on his forehead, his large, greenish-yellow eyes traveling from Mirza to the rest of the group with an air of indifference as he chewed on the end of a fat cigar. Heaving a sigh that shook his slender frame, the seersha tossed the door open and waved to the group then disappeared back down the trapdoor.

His baritone voice traveled up to them from depths unseen. "Get in here before anyone else comes sniffing about, would ya? Would hate for this little business trip of yers to get screwed over just because ya lot let a simple hidden hatch keep ya from hustling."

Mirza, Irati, and Eko followed the seersha without question or comment. Pema and Talin exchanged a glance, but then shepherded the team into action. The crew formed a chain to deposit the pile of plastic crates, the service bots, and the dreeocht container down into the dark cavern. Once the team disappeared, and it was just Kai and Ellinor left topside, she tapped his back to stall him for a moment.

"Who is that guy?" she asked. "I've never seen him before."

Kai glanced around, shifting his weight from foot to foot for a moment as if expecting someone to appear from nowhere and scream: "Ah ha! Got you!"

He lowered his voice, and said, "I've seen 'im a time or two about recently. He don't exactly work for the boss, private contractor and the like. But he's decent people. Lazar Botwright's the name. He ain't a caster. Just a regular seersha with a knack for making things stay hidden."

Ellinor nodded, mulling over his words and trying to make sense of what Lazar's role might be, or where they would go from here, when Kai inclined his head toward the hatch. "Best we get down there," he whispered, squeezing his bulky body—made more so by the robotic suit he was wearing—down the narrow entrance.

Her feet landed on a flimsy metal floor beside the other waiting members of their crew and cargo, and Lazar Botwright, who raised a brow at her tardiness, closed the hatch door. The rumbling returned a second later. The small room was no more than a cavernous lift, its edges wedged against the hard-packed soil and stone beneath the surface. Once the engines were turned on, gears began whirling and scraping their way deep beneath the ground.

Chaos ensued for the next hour as Irati barked orders, the bots whirling around and attempting to repair and clean the disarray of the underground bunker. Mirza directed where the gear should be piled. Ellinor wasn't sure what it was anymore. She didn't think it was all freeze dried food or weaponry; there were too many crates for that. Kai was busy securing the dreeocht and checking on its magical power supply, oblivious to the rest of the chaos. According to Kai, Misho's residual power would dwindle with the dawn, and Ellinor's heart turned into a piece of lead thumping in her chest with the news.

She stayed out of everyone's way as they worked, not offering to help—not that anyone asked—and elected to stay near the dreeocht container and its push-cart. She stood as close to the device as she could, her shoulder pressed tight against its side, her fingers trailing over the cool, slick surface, still hoping she'd feel some familiar thrill of Misho as his magic was drained into the sleeping creature tucked within.

Only when everything seemed settled did Ellinor venture to ask Kai about getting her weapons back. He shook his head. "Tomorrow. We gots to leave Euria first." Ellinor rolled her eyes at the technicality and slumped down into a chair, leaning it against the dreeocht container.

The crew was still leery of her presence, bitter and salty over how things had ended between them and Ellinor. But as the only ones left were mostly Ellinor and Misho's old team, they weren't as diligent in snubbing her as the crew members who were headed back to Cosmin's estate had been. Pema Tran would glance at her occasionally, and Talin Roxas would go so far as to give her a nod of acknowledgement when Irati wasn't looking. Even Janne Wolff would observe her silently, no outward expression of any kind on her pretty face. While no one invited her to their circle—Ellinor convinced herself she didn't want to join them anyway—they didn't whisper as they spoke, either.

Pema grabbed a bottle of beer from one of Lazar's coolers, spun a chair so she was sitting on it backward, and took a long swig. She jerked her chin at the cooler in a not-so-subtle invitation for Ellinor to partake.

Pema draped her arm over the back of the chair, holding the neck of the bottle between her calloused fingers as she rubbed her chin, her dark eyes missing nothing of the cavernous storage facility. "How long you think it took to build this place? It's rough around the edges, sure. Still, had to take a lot of planning to get this set up out here. You think the boss had it built before or after he caught his prize, huh?" Pema's voice was nearly as gravelly as Mirza's, but hers was the result of too much smoking and drinking, not an altercation with a fire caster.

Janne shrugged in response. "This could've been done in an afternoon by a caster. My money's on the boss having this built once he realized what he had, but couldn't keep. You follow me?" Janne said, turning to the young girl at her side, a new recruit named Embla, whom Ellinor only knew of thanks to gossip from Kai.

"Yup, I follow. I think this was, like, built maybe a week ago? Two, tops," Embla squeaked, stealing glances between Ellinor and Janne.

Talin laughed and slapped her girlfriend's leg good-naturedly. "O' course she would agree with you, Janne. Embla's scared shitless by you. In fact, only one she's probably more scared of is Ellinor."

Embla turned a bright shade of red, and Janne smirked. A low laugh rumbled in Pema's chest as she reached over and rubbed Talin's head, bringing her close and kissing her on the cheek.

"Lay off the girl, babe, you know what it's like to be new and paranoid," Pema said. Ellinor had always liked Pema and

Talin together; they made for a fierce and oddly cute pair. "Hey, where's that shadow of yours gone off to, Janne?" Pema added, trying to change the subject.

"I'm not—" Embla whined, before Janne cut her off by holding up a finger. Embla swallowed audibly.

Janne turned her gaze to Pema. "Warin? He's working with the bots to make sure they're following instructions for storing and loading the gear." Janne tilted her head, dark blue eyes calculating as she regarded Pema. "Say, you know where we're going next, Sarge? Any more of us going to be sent home? We can't all be needed to watch that box thing and . . ." she paused to glance at Ellinor who quirked her brow in response. "You know, *her.*"

Ellinor suppressed a shiver. "You know I'm not here by choice, yeah? I just want to do this job and get this shackle off my neck. I'm not here to fuck with you guys."

The four crew members assembled acted as if Ellinor hadn't spoken. She frowned, and took a long swallow of her beer.

Pema scratched her nose, hiding her eyes behind a wave of black and grey hair before adopting a forced nonchalant air. "I couldn't tell you even if I wanted to. Only Mirza knows. But I can say we're not shoving off again until tomorrow."

"Tomorrow?" Talin balked, her bright green eyes narrowing as she looked at Pema, surprised perhaps that she didn't know this information already. "Why we wasting so much time? We could be in Anzor all quick like if we hauled ass to get there, no stopping."

"Talin," Pema said, her voice low, "that's not the plan. The plan's to be cautious. Make sure we're not followed, that no one has given the game up. Know what I'm saying?"

"I hear you, but that's also dumb as shit. You race to Anzor like a doehaz with their head on fire and it don't matter who's watching, no one's going to stop *or* catch us."

"We're spending the night? Here? With Lazar and *her?*" Embla said, trying to sound tough but unable to hide the tremor in her high pitched voice.

"She doesn't have lung-rot, Embla. Calm down," Janne answered, tone icy.

"You know I can hear you, yeah? I'm right here." Again, none of her old team turned to look at her, though Embla's face did pale slightly. Ellinor bit the inside of her cheek to keep from scowling, and reclined back, head resting against the dreeocht container.

"Yeah, but I mean, this is *Ellinor Rask* we're talking about. You know what she's done since she left?" Embla pressed.

Pema sighed, bored. "Cleaned out a bunch of rival mechanic shops and Juice Box dens. Saved us the trouble is what she did, Embla."

"Okay, sure, there's that. But she's also been targeting *Cosmin's* people and everything! I heard she killed eight guys all by herself, and Pol's never going to walk again. You think that . . . collar is enough? Shouldn't she, like, be shackled or something? You guys have heard the stories, right?" Embla said, leaning forward and hugging her knees.

Talin smirked. "You wanna go ask her? She's right there. Yo! Ellinor! That true? You kill all those blokes? Want me to ask her if she eats babies, too?"

Embla blanched, and Ellinor had to smile at the way the girl's throat bobbed as she forced herself to swallow. "Nn-o," she said, drawing out the word to two syllables.

Talin and Pema laughed, but Janne gave Ellinor a veiled look, picking at her nails. Once their mirth died down, Pema leaned forward, nudging Embla with the toe of her boot. "You need to learn to lighten up, kid. Ellinor's no threat. Not anymore."

"Fine, whatever," Embla grumbled, though she didn't sound relaxed in the slightest. "But seriously then, what's up with that seersha? Why's *he* here? He's not one of us."

"Hey now, what's that mean, huh? *One o' us*? You mean a humani?" Talin fumed.

Pema squeezed her knee. "Calm down, babe. That's not what Embla meant, now was it?"

There was an edge to Pema's voice that left Embla's brown eyes even wider than before, her lips trembling as she tried to hide behind a curtain of dark hair. "Nn-o, I didn't mean because he's a seersha. I meant like, he's a contractor, right? So why are we here? With him? Like, what's he got to do with any of this?"

"You know," Janne said, "I was wondering the same thing. What's his angle in all this? I don't think Irati or anyone else ever mentioned him."

"That's none of yer business, little girl," Lazar said, seeming to come from nowhere.

The crew flinched at his sudden appearance, and Ellinor squinted into the gloom. She made out a small recess that led into an office of sorts, its door a seamless part of the wall she had overlooked.

She could almost hear her brother's growl ring through her mind. *Rookie mistake. Pay better attention to your surroundings!*

Janne wasn't one to be intimidated by a seersha, or anyone else, for that matter. She frowned at the man, and said, "The fuck it's none of our business. We don't know who you are. You expect us to just sit down, shut up, and trust you?"

Lazar shrugged, taking a puff on his cigar, the light reflecting off his glasses and making his eyes appear to glow. "Aye, actually. I do expect ya to sit down and shut up. But don't trust me. Trust no one. Isn't that what Cosmin teaches the lot of ya?"

Pema grinned. "Something like that. You need something, Lazar?"

He glanced about the group, his greenish-yellow eyes studying each of them in turn before settling on Ellinor. Scratching at his white hair, he pointed in her direction.

"Got what I came for. Yer to follow me," he said, turning back toward the office, waving a hand at Ellinor.

She glanced at the group for a moment, all of whom were silent, waiting for her to leave. She shrugged, downed the last of her beer, and tossed the empty bottle to the side. She let her fingers trail over the dreeocht container one last time then followed after Lazar. As she passed by Embla, though, an idea struck her.

As Ellinor got close to the girl, she half lunged at her, snapping her teeth like a dog about to bite. Embla made a noise that was half-squeak half-scream, and buried her head between her knees, all to the chorus of her colleagues' laughter—except Janne. Janne awarded Ellinor a flat stare as she walked by, her blue eyes sending another chill down Ellinor's neck.

"We told you to lighten up, Embla. Ellinor's just messing with you," Talin said, as Ellinor slipped into the dark office where Lazar had disappeared.

Ellinor blinked a few times. Her eyes were slow to adjust to the dim lighting provided by a low-powered bulb at the far end of the room and the flare of Lazar's cigar each time the seersha inhaled. Kai was lounging against another steel door, arms folded over his chest. Mirza leaned against a table, picking at his scarred chin, and Eko fiddled with a set of transport keys. Irati paced back and forth in front of Mirza like a caged leopard.

Ellinor stopped where she was, her back to the door, muscles tense, ready to act in case Irati's agitation needed an outlet. But Irati did no more than grumble incoherently when Ellinor entered, making Eko stiffen and nearly drop the keys he was playing with. For their part, Mirza and Kai seemed undisturbed by Irati's attitude.

"What's going on? Why'd you need me?" Ellinor asked, her eyes darting from the seersha to Kai.

Lazar shrugged. "I don't need ya. Just doing as I'm told. Like we're all doing, isn't that right?" he said, leveling his eyes on Irati, who frowned at him in return.

"What are you talking about?" When no one answered, Ellinor grew frustrated, wishing to be back near the dreeocht. "If no one's going to elaborate, then I've got another beer with my name on it."

"Fuck it, fine!" Irati spat, kicking a chair. This time, Eko did drop the keys he was fiddling with. She glowered at him, the pilot's lip trembling in return, before she forced a long breath through her teeth in a facsimile of calm. "You tell her then. No need for her to hear the news from Lazar."

Eko Blom glanced from Irati to Mirza. When the quiet lieutenant gave him a nod, the skinny mechanic-turned-pilot cleared his throat. "Yes, well. Seems Cosmin left instructions here with Lazar for our arrival. He, well, he wanted to be sure that it was understood you'd be given back your equipment—"

"I already knew that," Ellinor interjected, only to be interrupted in turn by Irati.

"Well, it's a dumb order. I was arguing against it, which is the *smart* thing to do. You have no standing here. You're just the babysitter, you don't need weapons. Just makes you more dangerous to those of us still loyal to our benefactor. But no one takes *me* seriously anymore. No one listens to my warnings. You sleep with the boss once and suddenly its snickers down every hall." She kicked at the wall. "And so what? He's a seriously good fuck, but that's all it was, one fuck. Now suddenly I can't be trusted?"

"Irati," Mirza growled, ending her tirade.

"Go on, Eko," Irati huffed, glaring at Mirza.

"Right, okay, so Kai's going to give you your gear back, like you said. No problem. But Cosmin's other message was that, well, you were to be told the next stop. You're to be briefed at each safe house, told where we're going next and informed of personnel changes. He said it was to keep you from asking too many questions, but—"

"But it's just because Cosmin doesn't trust us to stick to a schedule. Because he has some hard-on over thinking you can be won back. You left us once, you betrayed us all—he shouldn't give a shit about you anymore!" Irati shouted, then turned her attention to Mirza. "She should be kept in the dark like everyone else. She most of all, actually. Ellinor has already proved untrustworthy."

"If Kai's to know the stops ahead of time, so is she. Those were the instructions," Mirza said, his gruff voice reminding Ellinor of the lift they took underground.

"I don't get what the big deal is. So what if I get an update? Why does it matter, yeah? I'm still shackled to the dreeocht. I get too far, it buzzes and stops me dead in my tracks while it feeds off me. I'm not going to mess anything up," Ellinor said.

"I been thinking the same thing. Ellinor's got the least reason to fuck this up. She does, and she never gets to cast again. She got nothing to gain by causing trouble," Kai grumbled.

"You stay out of this. Bad enough Cosmin trusts you as much as he does when you haven't *earned* it like the rest of us." Irati took a step toward Kai, forcing Mirza to get between them.

"Calm down," Mirza said, giving Irati a knowing look.

She rocked back on her heels. "Mark my words, this is a bad idea. She shouldn't know where we're going next, that way she doesn't have a chance to reach out to her contacts or something and, I don't know, make a play for the dreeocht." A thought seemed to slam Irati in the skull as her eyes widened. "That's right! She is an air caster, after all."

"That's stupid, even for you," Ellinor growled. "I'm not a powerful enough caster to make use of such a dreeocht. And even if I did want it—which I don't—with this collar on, I couldn't take advantage of it anyway. What's crawled in your ass and died, Irati?"

"Watch it, bitch!" Irati took a menacing step toward Ellinor only to have Kai come between them this time.

"Take a walk, Lieutenant," Mirza said, a hard glint to his dark eyes.

Irati snarled at him then seemed to wrestle her ire into submission, with great effort. "Fine," she snorted, and stomped from the room, pushing past Lazar, who rolled his oddly colored eyes in response.

"Go on then, lad, finish telling her what's up," Lazar said. "I'll go watch the feisty one. She's giving me a bad feeling; I can feel it all the way in my knees."

Mirza nodded and the contractor left to make sure Irati didn't break anything. Eko tucked his pale blonde hair behind his ear, his blush obvious on his soft cheeks even in the hazy lighting. He watched after Irati, like a puppy wondering when its master would return.

Eko had not been this openly besotted with Irati when Ellinor was still in Cosmin's employ. Sure, he liked her; every man who wasn't gay liked Irati, or wanted to bed her. Some of the ladies too, Ellinor knew from experience. But Eko Blom never had a chance with Irati Mishra, and he'd never pretended otherwise. But now . . . something felt different.

"Okay, well, the plan's simple really," Eko's shaky voice snapped Ellinor's attention back to more immediate concerns. "We'll be taking a Class 1 Mamba for about six hours tomorrow. That'll take us to, uh, about halfway to the little city of Caratacus. Lazar has another transport for us waiting there. Another aerial transport, instead of hypersonic train, though I'm not sure what class it is. Lazar doesn't want to share. He just says not to worry because it'll fly."

He looked to Mirza beseechingly, and Mirza offered a tight grin in response.

He could just be nervous about not knowing what kind of ship he'll be flying tomorrow.

But even as she thought it, she wasn't convinced that was enough to make Eko so ardently avoid eye contact with her while looking to Irati for aid so often.

When Eko didn't continue, Ellinor said, "So, that's our next stop? Caratacus? What's there?"

"Just that. The next stop," Mirza answered.

"I'll getcha squared away with your gear when we get on that Mamba. Never been on one of 'em hypersonic trains before. Should be fun, aye?" Kai said, giving her a wink.

Ellinor nodded absently, pulling at her lip. After a moment, she glanced at Mirza. "Lazar built all this? How'd Cosmin get a Class 1 Mamba all the way out here with no one noticing?"

"Oh, people noticed," Lazar said as he re-entered the room, puffing away on his cigar, eyes twinkling behind his glasses. "But people, see, they'll believe what they want. They want to believe all the big crates heading this way's just equipment for their farms. And some is. So they ignore the extra crates. The crates with excavation tools. They also want to believe their *government* cares a spot more for them than it actually does. So when I tell them the Mamba's gonna be for them once it gets a bit of testing, well, see, they want to believe that, too, so they keep their mouths shut on the rest. Ya catch my drift?"

Ellinor had to chuckle. Cosmin von Brandt could be brilliant at times, and he'd always had an eye for talent. If Lazar wasn't moved from private contractor to a full-time employee by now, he soon would be. Despite his farmhand bearing, he had to be a sharp manipulator. He effectively fed into the dreams of the outlying residents, just enough to make them look more favorably toward Cosmin and ignore the fact that a giant tunnel was being built for a hypersonic train they would never use. It was almost cruel how brilliant it was.

"So how long did this take you to get all the supplies and build? I'm assuming one of Cosmin's earth casters helped, yeah?" Ellinor said.

Lazar grinned, winking at her. "I don't go kissing and telling. I know about that wager the rest of the crew have about when and how long. If it's all the same, I'll be keeping that little tidbit to myself."

Ellinor smiled. "Fine, be that way." Glancing from Eko—who was still playing with the keys—to Mirza and Kai, she said, "So we done here? Obligation to Cosmin fulfilled?"

"Yup," Mirza said.

"Great. Now if you'll excuse me, I've got a dreeocht to babysit."

"I'll keep you company," Kai offered, following her out.

Cosmin's odd message sent an alarm through her mind, making her stomach roil in a way she couldn't control. Irati, for all her anger, was right; there was no real need for Ellinor to know where they would be making their stops. Unless Cosmin suspected more trouble than he initially let on? And what did he expect her to do about it, if that was the case?

Sometimes the seersha's machinations were a step too far beyond Ellinor. A result of living for hundreds of years between Euria's unforgiving underground and crawling his way to the top of the food chain, she assumed. Regardless of the reasoning, Ellinor was on edge, her fingers itching to hold the familiar steel of her knives or the solid butt of her pistols in her hands.

Returning to her place near the dreeocht, she let Kai talk her into playing a hand of cards, if for no other reason than she needed an excuse to sit quietly and observe her former team. Caratacus was a long ways away, and she was surrounded by enemies who knew her all too well. Ellinor needed to see if the treacherous blade was aimed at her, or Cosmin.

BECAUSE THE FIRST TIME WASN'T BAD ENOUGH
///CHAPTER TEN

B EFORE DAWN, at 3:14 exactly, the dreeocht container began beeping.

Ellinor woke immediately. It took her a moment to figure
out why the sleek, silver container was making noises, and
then she saw it—the white and blue lights were solid, no
longer blinking. She frowned, her mind slow to understand
what this could mean as she put her hand on the device. Then,
with another beep, the lights blinked off, and a red light came
to life. Something within her collar let out a soft *hiss* in response, followed by a brief tingling sensation washing down
Ellinor's neck to her shoulders. The piece of bio-magitech
within her collar synced with the dreeocht container turned
on, the way Cosmin said it would.

Ellinor's shoulders slumped, her legs as unstable as a new-
born. The last of Misho's magic had been consumed; there was
nothing of him left.

Ellinor grasped both sides of the container and rested her forehead against the cool surface, shivering. More than anything, more than even her primal desire to get her magic back, Ellinor longed for more time with Misho Shimizu.

"There's never enough time, is there, little bug?" A fist squeezed her heart. She took a ragged breath, fingers clenching against the slick surface. "I miss you. I miss you so much, Misho." Ellinor bit her lip, trying to keep the building sobs locked away, but there were already too many cracks in the dam behind her eyes, and they were widening with each stuttering beat of her heart.

"Why did you push me? Why couldn't you have let it hit me instead? You know the world would have been better off. Why didn't you run?" Her chest tightened, and there was no stopping the ragged sobs racking her body as tears and snot rolled down her chin. It was an ugly display, but Ellinor was beyond caring whether anyone saw.

Clinging to the sleeping creature that had taken the last bit of raw, magical energy of her departed husband, Ellinor let herself drown in the painful memories all over again.

"How about we do a river cruise for our anniversary? You know, take one of those fancy crystal and glass boats down the Cola River? Or! Better yet, how about we go down closer to that town, what's it called . . ." Misho snapped his fingers, before his amber eyes bulged as recollection hit him. "Judoc! The Gozo mountain range is out that way, so is the Agnarr Forest. Hear it's all exquisite that time of year. What do you think, love?"

Ellinor chewed on her bottom lip, slinging the new caster rifle over her shoulder, her back to the research facility door. She didn't like using rifles; she preferred her Asco Rhino, a mechanized, military-grade crossbow capable of firing something as big as a javelin with enough force to cut clean through a building. Or her Dunstan Anacondas—double-barrel pistols capable of firing magitech bullets—but Cosmin insisted on the new Thunder rifle.

"Can we afford something like that? Those cruisers come with a pretty price tag," Ellinor asked.

Misho dismissed her concern with a wink. "Where's your sense of adventure? Come on! Let's do something different than just a fancy dinner somewhere. Let me treat you this once, Elli. Besides, you'd look damn sexy in a skimpy little bikini." Misho made a rumbling sound deep in his chest.

She laughed. "Calm down, little bug. We're working."

"Oh come on," he said, voice husky. "You know you want me to take my time ravishing you on a secluded beach somewhere. Nothing but the sound of waves to distract from those cute little purrs you make when I—"

"Misho!"

He smiled at her blush, wiggling his eyebrows. "Let me spoil you, Elli. You deserve it."

Ellinor beamed at her husband. He was always trying to prove how much he loved her, though she wasn't sure why. She didn't need grand gestures to show that he adored her, he did that well enough without having to blow two months' paychecks on their anniversary.

Still, it would be nice to see a proper mountain range for once. And a real forest!

She opened her mouth, ready to relent when there was a brief rumbling outside the facility's massive steel door, followed by a resounding blast as the door crumpled forward.

Five goons, all in heavy Coyote mechanized armor burst through the combat-tech door of the research facility. Behind the humani and seersha thugs rolled in three war bots—no, not war androids. Ashlings.

This doesn't make sense, why would Ashlings be here? Cosmin doesn't tamper with smart bots—it was a fleeting thought, one that entered her mind as the first smoke grenade bounced on the floor, bathing them in thick clouds. The resonating *CRACK* of a water magitech bullet striking the far wall, immersing the room in an electrified net, snapped Ellinor to her senses and had her rolling out from the reach of the electrified mesh.

She brought her Thunder rifle up, the infrared scope highlighting the living foes in blobs of red, yellow, green, and blue as they spread throughout the room. Ellinor didn't think twice as she pulled the trigger and two quick bursts of her fire magitech bullets ripped from the barrel of her gun.

The agonizing screech of one of the assailants filled the room. The impact of the projectile would have killed him eventually, but it was the magic in the bullet that had the victim flailing about. The fire within the ammunition boiled the goon's blood; he fell to the ground, twitching and curling. The heat of his boiling organs and blood grew in time with his shrieks, before it all abruptly ended with a wet *pop* as the target exploded.

"Ellinor!" Misho yelled, the shower of viscera making the room a hazy pink.

Misho had disabled the electric net that encased the room, his own water abilities turning the magic within the device against the shooter and electrocuting him. Now the moist floor was electrified, stalling the Ashlings who were not eager to see if this new field would fry their circuitry.

"I'm good!" Ellinor called, darting from her place of cover to another section, raising her scope once more to get eyes on her target. "Shit," she murmured, unable to see them. They must have deployed a neutralizing shield that hid their body heat from her.

"You holding on to something, little bug?" Ellinor called, ignoring the shouts of the assailants to hand over the prototype so no one else got hurt.

"Good and anchored," Misho replied, knowing what Ellinor intended to do.

Ellinor reached out into the room, touching the air with the ethereal fingers she felt rise from deep in her chest, measuring the air and testing its quality and how much of it there was. Ellinor grinned; there was plenty.

Inhaling, she twitched her fingers as if she were molding clay, bundling up the breeze into a tidal wave. Pushing the magic from her, a momentary wave of dizziness swept over her as the wall of condensed air slammed into the assailants she couldn't see, but the wind wall was wide enough that she didn't have to be accurate.

She heard a few thuds she wasn't sure were the armored thugs. With the force she used, she'd be surprised if she hadn't collapsed the chest armor on the Coyote suits, crushing the ribs of anyone inside.

When Ellinor didn't hear anything, she used her scope to locate Misho. He was crouched on top one of the cargo boxes, his own Thunder rifle out and scanning the room. She made a gesture that would appear as a wave on the blurry infrared, and when Misho's blob answered in kind, she crept toward her husband.

When she found him through the smoke, he winked at her, his eyes like gems in the hazy light, guiding her to his outstretched hand. He cupped her cheek for a moment, his eyes dancing over her body as if worried she might be missing pieces. She grinned and pressed her lips into his palm. He read the hard lines on her face and frowned a little; he knew she didn't like killing people with Cosmin's illegal magitech bullets.

"You good, Elli?" he whispered.

Taking a deep breath, she nodded. "Yeah. Let's clean up, shall we?"

He studied her for a moment longer before giving a deft nod then falling in line behind her. As they carefully swept the room, Ellinor's thoughts drifted once more to why a group of Ashlings and their sympathizers would attack one of Cosmin's research facilities.

Sentient robots, whose artificial intelligence went off program, were known as Ashlings. Zey claimed to have a soul, and zey questioned zeyr makers, claiming zeyr own humanity. Eventually, zey said *no* to zeyr programming. She knew what Ashlings were, of course, everyone did, and not just because the lights of zeyr ocular orbs were black instead of red, green, or blue, which was a badge of pride for zem. She knew zey made zeyr own decisions and followed zeyr own version of vigilante justice when it came to protecting or avenging guard, bouncer, or service bots that had been "put out of service." Or, as zey called it, *murdered,* simply because zey no longer performed zeyr duties as programmed, or because zey were older, outdated models. Ellinor also knew Ashlings had a tendency to kill offending organics first, usually not bothering to ask trivial questions such as: did they deserve to die?

All seersha, humani, and seerani who willingly made automata with intelligence and then shackled them to perform only as ordered were seen as no better than slavers to the Ashlings.

But Cosmin said he wasn't in that line of work. He smuggled illegal magitech and bio-tech, but his mechanics weren't creating sentient war machines. That's what Cosmin swore to both Ellinor and Misho. Still . . . . Why would Cosmin assign two of his lieutenants to guard duty at a research facility? And not just any of his lieutenants, but his only air and water casters?

At the time, when Cosmin gave them the assignment, it didn't seem odd. Ellinor often complained that she and Misho rarely got to see each other with Cosmin constantly having them out on different assignments across the city from one another. She thought this assignment was Cosmin's way of acknowledging her complaints, of giving Misho and her a little quality time together on what was supposed to be a boring, routine guard post.

"Elli! Move!" Misho's voice broke through her thoughts as she turned her face to the far corner of the room, the barrel of her rifle not as fast as her gaze.

Half broken against the wall, one of the Ashlings wasn't quite dead. Zer raised zeyr arm, and in place of zeyr hand was a cannon's black barrel staring down Ellinor, which quickly became brighter as it powered up, draining the last of the being's batteries. It turned from a dead black, to a dazzling white as the water magitech embedded in the weapon came to life, making a stream of lightning that crackled as it shot in an arch straight for her.

She only had time to breathe out the word "Run!" before being flung back.

Ellinor didn't feel anything. She didn't feel the combat or bio-tech in her armor struggle to absorb and redirect that much energy. She didn't feel her bones splinter and crack apart with electricity, nor her heart stop completely, the way Misho said it would with a direct hit from a bolt of that size. Her ears buzzed from the resounding shock wave that followed the discharge of such a weapon, but that was all. Ellinor rolled over, wondering if perhaps the Ashling had missed.

But the Ashling had not missed.

Misho Shimizu lay like a rag doll several feet from where he had been, and from the spot where he had tossed Ellinor in order to protect her.

"No! Nononono," she gasped, scrambling to where Misho lay. She grabbed him, rolling him on his back, not caring that her armor was buzzing and crackling with its own efforts to absorb the residual magic still curling around Misho.

"Baby? Come on, Misho, open your damn eyes!" Ellinor pleaded, ignoring the shocks that found their way past her armor's defenses.

Misho's once perfect olive skin was now marred by an angry red scar that curled and splintered up his neck and over his face in the shape of the magic bolt that had hit him square in the chest. His dark locks were singed, the smell of burnt hair mingling with the sickly sweet scent of charred meat, though

Ellinor could see no obvious wounds beyond the scar. There was the smoldering crack that split out from the epicenter of where the bolt hit Misho's armor, but there wasn't any blood, just heat and the smell of . . .

Ellinor blinked the thought away. "You're not dead, little bug. C'mon, your own magic type can't kill you, it can't!" Ellinor shrieked.

Misho's instructions about the effects of what a lightning strike would do to a person filtered through her mind. *"If it hits right, it could stop a person's heart instantly. If not, there'll be scarring for sure, and probably lots of burns, along with some loss of hearing. I try for the direct strike though, it's kinder. Ends things quicker."*

She remembered asking him if there was a way to start someone's heart again after such a strike. She shut her eyes, racing through her memories when Misho's voice popped in her head again. *"Sure, you can start up their heart again. But—"*

Ellinor snapped her eyes open, having remembered as much as she cared to, as much as she believed she needed to. She summoned her magic, reckless in the amount she gathered, and tried to force it into Misho. She pushed against his chest desperately, her compressions out of sync, trying to restart his heart and get his chest rising and falling in that familiar rhythm she'd gone to sleep listening to for the past fifteen years.

"For the love of Azer, wake up, Misho. I need you to open your eyes, baby. I need you to take a breath for me. Please?"

Bringing her hand up to Misho's face, she had a momentary urge to open his eyes; she wanted to see them again, those brilliant amber orbs glittering back at her. She wanted Misho to wink and tell her, "Everything's going to be okay, Elli." Fear stayed her hand. She didn't want that image to be replaced with . . . something else. She didn't want to see what the Ashling's blast had done to Misho's perfect eyes. Instead, she pressed her fingers to his neck, and held her breath.

She waited, and waited, but there was nothing. No flicker of a pulse, not even a twitch of a muscle reacting to anything.

Then, there was a sound, something like a groan, and Ellinor released her magic with a gasp, eyes wide as they searched over Misho. She cradled him, waiting for him to make another sign of life. But then the sound came again and Ellinor realized it wasn't Misho at all, but one of the brutes she had slammed into the wall. Apparently, some of them were still alive, while her little bug had wasted his precious breath shoving Ellinor out of the way.

A scream escaped her and, placing Misho back on the ground with care, Ellinor stormed to the far corner of the facility, bringing out her Thunder rifle in one fluid motion. She saw a man dragging his limp legs behind him, trying to get to the still form of the Ashling who had fired at Misho. Ellinor's heart was pounding erratically in her chest and she saw red, screaming at the top of her lungs.

She took aim and unloaded every last one of her fire magitech bullets into the bastards who had taken Misho from her. She heard the *click* of the empty cartridge, but even then, she didn't stop pulling the trigger, all the while shrieking through her tears in wordless agony. It wasn't until her throat was too raw to scream anymore that she stopped, dropping the Thunder to the floor. It was then that a piece of something metallic caught her eye.

"Ell? You okay?" Kai asked, putting a heavy hand on her shoulder, and rubbing his bleary eyes with the other. When she didn't move, only trembled where she stood, he tugged her away from the container so she was facing him.

Ellinor hiccupped and tried to shove him off, but found she didn't have the strength as her hands trembled against Kai's chest. She could still feel Misho's hot skin beneath her fingers, smell his burnt hair, when all she wanted was to hold on to the good memories. The memories of her and Misho racing through obstacle courses during their training together, each trying to outdo the other. She wanted to hold on to the feeling of his firm hands as they ripped her clothes off and trailed over her naked skin for the first time. She wanted to hear him purr "Elli" once again.

But Kai was all she had now that Misho and his magic were gone.

Her knees went weak, and she collapsed against him. He caught her effortlessly and cradled her against his burly chest, no questions asked, and held her as her body shook with silent cries.

Burying her head in his chest, Ellinor whimpered, "It shouldn't have been him. It should have been me, Kai. I miss him so much . . ."

Kai hugged her, wrapping her in his arms like he hadn't collared her less than two days prior. Like he wasn't still working for Cosmin. Holding her instead like he was, and would always be, her friend.

"I know, Ell, I know. I miss 'im, too. I'm so, so sorry he's gone," Kai whispered.

Ellinor didn't answer. She didn't need his words of condolences, or particularly want them. What she needed was someone to hold her until the pain no longer made her heart stutter in her chest, and her legs too weak to carry her any further through life without her little bug.

SO MUCH FOR HISTORY
///CHAPTER ELEVEN

N O ONE mentioned Ellinor's breakdown. That could have been thanks to Kai, though, who uncharacteristically glowered at everyone as they hustled to get the gear loaded onto the waiting Mamba in time for their early morning departure.

Ellinor had tried to make herself useful in a feeble attempt to show strength, in case anyone had seen her weakness. But the moment she tried, Mirza Otieno shoved her back toward the dreeocht. While it wasn't hard, there was enough force to make Ellinor stumble and glare at the new lieutenant.

"You stay close to that now," he said, voice like cracked stones grinding against one another, pointing toward the container.

Ellinor had almost forgotten that, once her collar and the container were activated, she had to stay within a thirty foot radius of the dreeocht box or the magical tether between them would leave her incapacitated and risk upsetting the sleeping creature inside. The thought of being near the container and the thing that had drained Misho's magic made her palms sweaty and stomach clench. But she obeyed Mirza's command. That did not, however, make Ellinor Rask pleasant to be around.

By the time most everyone found their rhythm, they seemed to notice her irritation as she hovered on the outskirts of the distance she was permitted from her charge. Like a baited lion at the end of a frayed rope.

Pema gave her a sympathetic grin—and a wide berth. Talin tossed her a roll stuffed with scrambled eggs, cheese, and bits of bacon as Ellinor couldn't venture to where Janne was serving everyone, and Janne had made no indication of saving breakfast for her. Both Embla and Eko defaulted to not making eye contact with her that morning. Which, while still strange for Eko, seemed par for the course from the newbie, who didn't take kindly to being spooked in front of her comrades. Irati and Warin were nowhere to be found, and Ellinor assumed the foul-tempered woman had retreated to the hypersonic train early to prepare, alongside the service bots.

Once Kai was finished helping Lazar and Mirza secure the lift so none could accidentally trigger the elevator, he ventured over to Ellinor to keep her company and stayed, mercifully, silent. He never once brought up the events of the night before, and Ellinor hoped she'd only imagined burying her face in his chest. She was more or less successful, until they were the last ones to enter the Mamba. Then, any hope of the events being a particularly cruel and vivid dream were smashed into dozens of sharp pieces, once more leaving her ragged and bloodied.

Kai grabbed the push-cart, rolling the dreeocht past her. Turning to glance at her over his shoulder, he said, "Ready, Ell?"

She flinched, but tried to hide it by glowering at him. "Can you not, Kai?"

"What'd I go and do now?" he said, emerald eyes wide at the rebuke.

"You know what," she growled, brushing past him to get on the glossy train that reflected her haggard appearance perfectly, even in the cavern's dim light. The heavy purple bags under her eyes made her crisp baby-blues appear all the more haunted. Her once sharp cheeks seemed pinched, and with her lips pressed into a hard line, she looked more like the old woman Kai teased her she was becoming.

Kai's shoulders slumped in time with his heavy sigh. "Really? We back on that? I thought we were back on the level. What with last night and all."

"Until the collar comes off, we're back on that. Misho is gone, completely gone, and that fucking monster in your push-cart is leeching off of me now. Thanks for that!" She fixed him with a steady stare she hoped said: *It was a mistake to let you comfort me last night. Why can't you leave me alone? Please stop caring so damn much. I can't keep this up.*

Ellinor assumed Kai got the message as he shrugged and followed her aboard the Class 1 Mamba, saying no more.

Ellinor sat at the back of the train, and not because she wanted to this time. Sure, had she not been so intrinsically tied to the dreeocht at this point, she'd probably have elected to sit at the back of the three car hypersonic train, but now that it was no longer her choice, she longed to sit near the front. She wanted to be the first to see Euria fade into the distance, to leave the city that had been her home and had taken everything from her.

Ellinor had gotten as comfortable as possible in the leather bucket seat, trying to ignore the cold presence of the container behind her, when Lazar entered the Mamba and pressed a button to close the door behind him. Then, Irati Mishra lost her shit.

"Oh no you don't. What the fuck do you think you're doing? We're about to leave. Get out," Irati said, stomping over to the seersha, who blew a puff of cigar smoke in her direction and headed for the conductor's cabin.

"Hey! I'm talking to you. You're not supposed to be here," crowed Irati, reaching out for the seersha, who deftly grabbed her wrist and twisted her arm behind her. It was such a smooth motion that even Janne starred in wonderment, frozen where she was behind her superior.

Irati hissed at the same time as the stupor fell from Janne. She darted for her friend and mentor, hands scrambling for guns and knives. It made Ellinor once again wish Kai had given back the rest of her gear.

Lazar was watching the soldier dart for Irati, not even a hint of concern flashing in his greenish-yellow eyes. Mirza gave an ear splitting whistle from the first car on the train, stopping Janne in her tracks.

"He's coming with us, Irati," Mirza grumbled, dark eyes glinting like coals in a fire.

Irati's answering glare made Ellinor's face slacken, blood like cold steel in her veins with the momentary hatred she saw. Irati and Mirza had saved each other's lives countless times, they had been partners in every sense of the word, and now this?

Irati shook her head, shielding her face behind a wave of thick, dark brown hair as she let out a slow breath. "Why? Why's he coming with us? For how long, Mirza? I've a right to know."

If Mirza noted the glacier-like edge to Irati's voice, he didn't show it. "Dunno," he said with an easy shrug. "I'm just following orders. Like you're expected to."

He glanced at Lazar and gave the seersha a nod. Lazar shrugged and let Irati go, raising his hands in a type of surrender. Mirza watched Irati stand straight, rubbing her wrist, while she sneered at Lazar.

"We have a job to do. You'll behave?" Mirza asked, though even Ellinor knew it wasn't a question.

Irati growled in response, and prowled to where Eko and Embla were, not answering Mirza. The scarred lieutenant shrugged and waved the rest of the crew—who were either still gawking or preparing to tackle Lazar—back into action.

"Strap in, we're heading out," he said, waiting for them to get to their seats before going after Irati.

As the adrenaline faded from her veins, Ellinor tried to work out for herself why Lazar was accompanying them. He seemed a useful sort, one who was good at improvising and taking care of himself in a fight, but she failed to see why they would need him. Whatever Cosmin was playing at, Ellinor couldn't see the whole picture, and it left her pulse racing.

Not to mention Mirza Otieno's odd behavior.

Before the Mamba's engines could warm up enough to send them shooting toward Caratacus, Ellinor tapped Kai on the shoulder. "I need my weapons back. Now."

Kai picked at his lower lip, glancing to where his superior officers had disappeared, and started to shake his head. Ellinor cut him off before he could speak.

"Look, something stinks on this train. You can smell it too, yeah?" she said, jerking her thumb at Mirza and Lazar speaking softly in the first cabin.

"Ah. Guess things ain't sitting right with me, no. But so what? I ain't paid to think like the rest of 'em," Kai answered, casting his eyes down on the ground, his voice not as strong as it usually was.

"Remember what Cosmin's orders were? I've got to be armed in case things go wrong. I'm expected to fight. If shit blows up now, I won't be able to do that. Help me out, Kai."

"Oh, now you want my help, aye? Thought we weren't friends."

Her face stung as if slapped at his words. Kai was right. But the cold weight of the collar kept pressing her down, down, down . . . Ellinor closed her eyes, slowly opening them. "I'm sorry for earlier. I really am. But Kai, think about it from my point of view for a hot minute, yeah? Look at the position I'm in. It's obvious nobody wants me here, then here you are all friendly with everyone again like nothing went down. I fucked up, okay? Ever since Misho died I haven't been . . . . Something's missing, okay? It's gone or broken . . . it doesn't matter. Things haven't been the same and there's just one thing I want now—" She swallowed her words before she could say more. "I still need time, and that barrel of whiskey. The good stuff, too. None of that cheap piss I've been drinking lately." Kai raised an eyebrow, not even chuckling at her remark. She sighed. "Fine. This is *business* then, and it may be a matter of life or death. Namely mine."

Kai rolled his eyes but, as his soft grin slowly returned, a weight lifted off her shoulders. Patting her on the shoulder, he got up and disappeared down a hatch behind the dreeocht container. She heard him opening crates and digging around for a moment before he emerged from below. He handed her a combat-tech bracer that, once activated, turned into a shield. She grinned, clipping the device around her wrist. It was a start.

The shield was activated by a small button near her pinky that she could press with her thumb, even when holding a weapon. Once initiated, it took less than a millisecond for a series of metal plates to snap into place, flaring out until they created a shield she could use to deflect virtually all projectiles—even those of the magical persuasion. Without her abilities, her shield was the only thing she could depend on to save her life in a pinch.

Kai was about to head below once more to locate the rest of her weapons, when Irati left the conductor's cabin. Her eyes fixed on Ellinor and Kai.

She stormed as fast as she could toward them, her face still flushed in anger. "And just what do you think you're doing?" she demanded.

Kai looked uneasy for a moment before shrugging a shoulder, and trying to appear relaxed. "Just following orders and arming Ell."

"You aren't supposed to do that until we've left Euria. Where are we right now, Kai?"

"Well, we're in Euria. Just barely, though—"

"You're dumber than a frozen lizard and just as useful, you know that? You don't give that traitor shit until we get out of Euria. Better yet, don't bother equipping her with *anything* until we leave the Mamba. That'll teach you to think you can bend orders, especially around technicalities."

Ellinor snorted. "You're one to talk. You weren't all that keen on following orders a moment ago, Irati. Though, it doesn't sound like Cosmin cares much for keeping you up to date on the plan anymore. What'd you do? You fail to show him how devoted you are to his . . . *business*?" Ellinor said, making an obscene gesture with her hand and mouth.

Irati's cheeks turned even pinker as her brow furrowed, shielding her eyes behind thick lashes. "I'll enjoy cutting your tongue out for that, narc."

Ellinor wagged a finger at her. "Nuh-uh, not so fast, missy. I'm a VIP. You can't touch me while I've got to be all hale and hearty for the little dreeocht here," she said, patting the device behind her.

Irati snarled in response, chewing on the retort as if it were a piece of wood. Finally, she said, "Perhaps. But I owe you one. Just wait till the dreeocht is safe in its new owner's hands. You're less than gum on the bottom of my boot without your powers. I own your ass. Hell, bet even Warin could take you without your precious little caster abilities. But guess what? You still can't be armed." Irati moved to grab the cuff off of Ellinor's wrist, but Ellinor jerked her arm back, earning another deep scowl from Irati.

"This isn't a weapon. *Technically*. It's a shield." Ellinor stood so Irati could no longer look down at her.

Ellinor felt Kai at her back, towering over both the women, and she had to bite the inside of her cheek to keep from smirking. No matter how hard she was on Kai, he always had her back.

Irati glanced from Ellinor to Kai, her eyes as hard as brown diamonds. They stood, staring at one another for a moment longer than was comfortable, before Irati rocked back on her heels, and turned away. "Fine, whatever. It's just a fucking shield anyway," Irati grumbled. "Better hope you don't need it," she added, stomping toward where Janne and Warin lounged in the second car.

Mirza poked his head around from the first cabin, his eyebrow quirked on the non-burned side of his face, as he observed Kai and Ellinor. He held their gaze for a moment, Lazar peeking around the corner a second later. Ellinor felt her skin start to crawl under the seersha's scrutiny as he puffed away on his cigar. Watching him, she realized she had never seen him light a new one, or finish an old one, and that realization threatened to make her shiver for reasons she could barely comprehend. Lazar was a sneaky bastard, and that fact hit Ellinor harder now as the smooth wheels of the Mamba engaged, rolling them slowly through the tunnel.

Pressure pushed Ellinor back in her seat as the engines roared to life, and the train reached its top speed within seconds. She watched the standing crew sway with the force before it equalized.

Hypersonic trains were amazing pieces of technology, moving faster than the speed of sound, minus the sonic boom. They were the most efficient means of long distance travel, only slightly slower than a hypersonic plane. The planes weren't as inconspicuous as the underground Class 1 Mambas, though.

Ellinor wanted nothing more than to explore the cabins, to pick Pema or Talin's brain as to why so many of those on the team were acting oddly. But as she watched the crew begin to check their weapons, and occasionally disappear into the cargo hold, only making fleeting eye contact with her as they went, she didn't think they'd be willing to say much. And with how steadfastly Kai remained at her side, she knew he had already told her everything he knew. So, with no other recourse, Ellinor slumped back in her seat and watched her reluctant comrades while checking over her own armor.

Misho had the armor commissioned when they'd first joined Cosmin's operation, so, of course, it was black. Ellinor initially wasn't sure how useful the armor would be; she hadn't enough knowledge of the mechanic's capabilities to put much faith in everything Misho claimed the armor could do.

But now? Without her magic? She was even less convinced of its usefulness than she had been when Misho first gifted it to her. The thin wires full of combat-tech were meant to help amplify her abilities while absorbing what they could of other casters' powers. The pliable, metal-based polymers that filled the space between the leather on the outside, and the cool silk on the inside would still be optimal protection from the more traditional weapons, but if someone wanted to use fire to boil her blood, without access to her magic to make use of the more elite properties of her armor . . . .

She stilled her hands from constantly dancing over the controls and energy readouts. She didn't want to think about what her armor's limitations may be under her current circumstances.

Ellinor rubbed her chin, continuing to watch the crew as she waited for the Mamba to resurface, reminding herself time and again to be wary of *everyone*. Ellinor tried to stifle a groan as she mumbled, "This is going to be a long trip."

Ellinor didn't remember falling asleep, but she knew she had when the sudden bright light of the late afternoon sun stabbed through the windows straight into her eyelids. She glanced around and leaned out into the aisle to peek into the other cars, and was pleased to see that most of the crew had been likewise napping.

At least I didn't miss much.

Her feelings of unease still persisted, but she wasn't about to miss her first glimpse of the territories to the south of Euria. Even after leaving Cosmin's gang, Ellinor had never left Euria. She was supposed to leave with Misho, they were going to venture past the city's walls for the first time together. When he died, it felt like a betrayal to leave. Instead, lurking in the lowest levels of the city, Ellinor schemed and stole as she plotted revenge. She hadn't wanted to risk exposure by trying to get a pass to leave Euria and go to another city, not until she knew which Ashling faction was responsible for Misho's death and where they were hiding.

Her breath hitched at the sight of so many trees and the wide open fields racing past the Mamba's windows. The trees were huge behemoths, stretching so high into the sky that, even craning her neck against the window, Ellinor couldn't see the tops of their leafy green boughs. In contrast to the deep green of the timber clustered on either side of Lazar's hastily constructed train tracks, the fields surrounding them were a rich golden brown, with the tops of the tall grasses dancing wildly against the wind the Mamba created.

Ellinor was used to the skyscrapers that created a perpetual night for those at the lower levels, their world illuminated by flashes of neon; where they only ever saw brief flickers of the sky above. She was used to glittering buildings and ogling at the displays of raw power that the casters' used as naturally as breathing. Hers was a starless sky occupied by zooming, silver and gold transport crafts as they raced to their destinations. Out here, Ellinor felt smaller than she ever had before, but not insignificant, like she did when Cosmin stripped her powers away.

Soon, the trees thinned to where their long shadows no longer blotted the area. It was then that the Mamba began to slow, and Janne and Warin shot to their feet, scampering to the cargo hold.

"Bit eager to get off this 'ere train, ain't they?" Kai mumbled as the two disappeared below.

Ellinor frowned, a cold feeling teasing at the corners of her mind. "Yeah, no kidding," she said, before Embla and Talin went below to join them. She may not trust Embla much, but Ellinor trusted Talin to keep the others from doing anything overtly nefarious—for the time being.

Without a word, Irati flew past Ellinor and Kai to join the others below, tailed by the two service bots as the train came to a soundless stop. Ellinor ignored the lieutenant, her eyes glued on the surrounding area, which, once again, appeared to be an empty field full of nothing more than gently swaying yellow flowers and parched grass. But given what Lazar was able to hide in the last "empty" field, Ellinor didn't allow appearances to deceive her.

Irati emerged from below and headed for the front of the train, where Mirza pressed the door release, the door giving a slight *hiss* as it slid back. Ellinor waited for Irati to pass before heading for the exit herself, only to be roughly shoved back toward her seat.

Ellinor Olysha Rask did not take kindly to that. The crew seemed to subscribe to Irati's line of thinking: that she was nothing, a weakling without her abilities.

It was one thing to have Irati or Mirza push her around—even if she did not respect *them*, she respected their position, one she'd once held for several years. But it was another matter entirely to have any of her former underlings manhandle her because they felt they were entitled, or to prove they weren't afraid.

Ellinor grabbed her assailant's forearm and used it as leverage to fling them in the opposite direction, Ellinor following a breath later, but airborne. Spinning them around, Ellinor wrapped her legs around their torso, slamming them to the floor of the train, their arm at an angle where just a little more pressure would dislocate it. Ellinor crouched on them, her knee on their back.

It was only when the figure was sputtering underneath her, their free hand scrabbling against the grooves in the floor, that Ellinor saw whom she had pinned—Janne Wolff. A moment later, she heard the *click* of a gun being cocked above her head. She glanced up, and saw the barrel of Warin's Repeater pistol staring back at her, the dark hole of its eye level with her forehead.

Warin followed Janne about like a doting puppy. He was a decent enough guy, or had been when Ellinor was in charge. But with her gone, it seemed like he clung to Janne all the more, and since the assassin hadn't sliced him open yet, Ellinor knew there was something mutual going on between them now. Warin had always been one of those soldiers that kept his head down and followed orders to the letter. A good enough sort to have on a covert mission where asking questions wasn't encouraged.

"You had no right to do that," Warin growled, brown eyes hard with a furious spark.

Without getting off Janne, Ellinor said, "Lower your weapon, Warin. And for Azer's sake, get your finger off that trigger. You know better than to put your finger there unless you intend to shoot." She narrowed her eyes at him and waited a moment. When Warin didn't move, his khaki-brown skin flushed with rage, she blew out an exasperated breath. "You aren't going to shoot me, Warin. You can't. Besides, Janne here isn't in any real danger, isn't that right, Kai?"

Kai blinked at Ellinor from where he sat, stunned by the scene before him. It took him a moment to comprehend what was happening, but once he did, he leaned back in his chair, putting his hands behind his neck as if he was used to seeing this kind of display—and he probably was. "Nah, she ain't in any danger. Was right rude of 'er though, shoving people about like that."

Slowly, Warin lowered his pistol and took his finger off the trigger, glancing from Ellinor to Kai as if doing mental calculations about his chances of taking them both.

"Exactly," Ellinor said. "I may not be who you want on this little escort mission, but that doesn't mean you can treat me like street-level scum. We were a team once. You don't have to like me anymore, but you need to respect who I am. Thinking you can pull some petty shit like that, well, that's when people get hurt." She twisted Janne's arm back a bit, making the petite woman beneath her yelp, and Warin flinch. "Hurts, yeah? See? That's what I'm trying to avoid. People getting hurt. Not killed or anything, I wouldn't do that to you, to any of you, because I have class. Isn't that right, Kai?"

"Just so. Class by the trainload, I reckon," Kai answered, his hands still clasped behind his neck.

"So, Janne," Ellinor said, not releasing the woman beneath her, despite her squirms. "You remember we were colleagues once and you leave it at that, yeah? Spit at my feet if it makes you feel like you're wearing a pair of big girl panties, but don't you dare lay a finger on me again. I'm not here for that, and I don't have to put up with that kind of shit. You understand me?"

Janne growled beneath her, and Ellinor twisted her wrist a bit more. Janne ground her teeth to keep from screaming, and Warin's nostrils flared; his finger twitched to go back over the trigger. Kai shot out of his seat a second later.

He yanked the boy back, his hand wrapped tight around his collar. "None of that, now. Let 'em work it out for themselves. You just come and sit right 'ere with me and enjoy the show."

Ellinor heard Warin audibly gulp, and she had to keep from smiling. "Say you understand, Janne, and I'll let you up."

Seconds trickled by before Janne hissed, "I understand."

Ellinor jumped off her, hands dangling at her sides, ready to show Janne she wasn't the only one with deadly quick reflexes. Janne's face was flushed, sweat collecting on the bridge of her nose, and lips her were pulled back in a snarl.

Fuck, I'm going to have to pin her again.

But as the thought entered her mind, Pema called from the front of the train, cigarette dangling precariously from the corner of her mouth, "If you two are done, I'd like to get off this train. Get a move on, soldier. That's an order!"

Janne's dark blue eyes flashed like exploding stars. Letting out a slow breath, she walked past Ellinor without another word or the slightest brush. Warin blinked, his eyes glued on Janne's hips as if he had never seen her walk away before. When Irati emerged from the cargo hold and saw Warin sitting there, staring after Janne, she slapped him on the back of the head, mussing his mousy brown hair and the blue streaks buried within.

"Move your ass, Warin. You know what you need to do. Stay focused." Irati spared a glance for Kai and Ellinor, her lips twitching in the ghost of a sneer before she cleared her throat. "Let's get this over with," she grumbled.

This time, it was Ellinor's turn to blink stupidly back at the lieutenant. "What was that all about?" she mumbled. At the sound of Talin's chuckling, she wheeled around to face the dark-skinned woman.

"Might as well take the win where you can get it. Wouldn't go on expecting Irati to show you kindness the rest o' the trip," Talin said, walking past Ellinor, her arms laden with crates.

"That's what you call it? Kindness?"

"She didn't go breaking your nose, did she? Not like she's going to bring you flowers or nothing. So yeah, you heard me, kindness. Don't go making a big thing outta it, Ellinor."

Even if I wanted to, Ellinor thought, *I couldn't make* a big thing *out of it.* The rest of the crew filed past her on their way to get their gear, including Lazar—but not Eko Blom. Eko took one look at her and all but threw himself out of the Mamba without a backward glance.

ANOTHER EMPTY FIELD
///CHAPTER TWELVE

J UST LIKE last time, the field was far from empty.

Like looking through a piece of glass, a stealth-tech mirror tarp showcased the item meant to stay hidden. Once Lazar revealed the decrepit transport plane to the group, Ellinor shared Eko's consternation on the plane's ability to take them to Caratacus.

The transport looked like it had been assembled from spare parts found at an illegal junkyard. But, with how fondly the white-haired seersha gazed upon it, puffing away on his cigar, you'd think it was the latest sporty Class 1 Wasp, straight from a manufacturer's showroom.

"We getting on that? It looks like shit," Talin said.

Pema rolled her eyes, stepping on the butt of her cigarette. Even Embla snickered at Talin's bluntness before Warin silenced her with a hard stare. "I'm sure it's not as bad as it looks, okay?" Warin turned to where Lazar was standing, now giving them a cool stare. "I'm sure it's safe and will get us to Caratacus on the quick."

There wasn't much of an inflection to Warin's voice, but with the way his brows knit together, they all heard the question to his words. Lazar rolled his eyes behind his glasses and nodded. "Y'all care a great deal more about appearances than ya should. Ya know what this here plane even is?"

"Clearly not, or we wouldn't be asking," Pema said, placing a reassuring hand on her girlfriend's shoulder. But Talin didn't relax, and only continued to rock on the balls of her feet, glancing between Lazar and the transport with a wary expression.

Lazar blew out a breath, placing his hands on his hips as he chewed on the end of his cigar. "It's a hypersonic plane, ya arseholes. A Class 1 Eagle Owl," he preened.

A heavy hush fell over the group gawking at the decrepit-looking transport, everyone except Irati and Mirza, who were giving orders to the service bots as they loaded their gear on the transport. Ellinor looked over the plane again, her eyes roaming its rusty hull, looking for the tell-tale signs of a high end machine buried beneath, but all she saw were mismatched parts and nothing more.

"Are you shitting us?" Talin said between bouts of laughter. "That ain't no Eagle Owl. You're good, Lazar, I'll give you that. But no way you're *that* good. This thing looks like it'll be rattling apart just getting off the ground, let alone reaching hypersonic speeds." Talin nudged Embla. "You want to go changing your bet? No way this was done in two weeks, even with a caster's help."

Embla shook her head, rendered too shocked to give any kind of coherent answer.

"How is it even possible you could smuggle something like that all the way out here?" Janne asked, running a hand through her dark blonde hair. "The train I could understand, that was still in Euria. But . . . this is in the middle of nowhere." The assassin squinted at the seersha, her eyes thin blue slits. "Just who are you that you can do all this?"

"A man who gets shit done. Y'all are asking the wrong questions. Don't matter how I did it. It's done. Get yer butts on the plane before someone sees. It's not as desolate out here as ya'd like to believe," Lazar said, his eyes focused on the horizon.

No one moved, not lending much credence to Lazar's paranoia. The seersha grumbled, and bit down on his cigar, spitting out the end as he said, "Look, if it makes ya sleep better at night, yer boss knows me and my sources. That should be good enough for the lot of ya."

Warin opened his mouth, most likely to protest or repeat Janne's concerns, when, of all people, Eko cut him off. "This is a . . . really? A Class 1 Eagle Owl? An actual hypersonic plane?" His soft words dripped with awe and wonder, hazel eyes twinkling like lights on a dashboard.

Lazar grinned. "What did I just say? I ain't in the habit of lying, boy."

Eko ignored his words and walked toward the plane, all fear gone. Talin glanced at Pema, who shrugged and put her arm around the explosives expert's waist, leading her to the stack of cargo still waiting to be loaded. They were soon followed by the rest of the crew—save Ellinor and Kai.

Glancing at the dreeocht container, Ellinor made sure she had enough tether to get closer to Lazar. "As one outcast to another, then," she said. "How did you really manage all this? A Class 1 Mamba and now an Eagle Owl? And one that looks, well, like crap, to be honest. This must've cost a fortune."

"Aye, it did, and worth every credit. So what?"

"Well, it seems like a lot of trust for Cosmin to put into a contractor. You either have something on the caster, or you desperately want to be in his good graces. Or maybe Cosmin has something damning on you? Which is it?"

Lazar narrowed his eyes at her, and Ellinor felt Kai take a step closer to the two of them. But Lazar didn't seem to care. "I already told ya, it doesn't matter, and it's not yer business. Just get on the transport, and leave me to deal with the whys and hows."

Ellinor rolled her eyes. She had dealt with seersha as arrogant and powerful as Cosmin, so Lazar's narrowed gaze didn't send her scurrying the way it had the others. "I think it does matter, though. It matters because we could be even better . . . *friends* if you're helping Cosmin less than . . . *enthusiastically,* shall we say?" Ellinor said, waving at her collar.

"No," Lazar responded.

Ellinor blinked slowly. "No? No what? No we can't be friends? No he doesn't have dirt on you? Which is it?"

"Pick one. Answer's the same." Lazar turned to walk away and Ellinor took a step toward him, only to have the seersha wheel back on her, the tip of his cigar flaring as he inhaled sharply. "Can I get ya a stool or something so ya can get off my back? Bugger off. I'm not like ya, and I sure as shit don't have an interest in being yer *friend.* Leave it be."

As the seersha stormed off, Ellinor stood, dumbfounded by the sudden turn of events, an icy feeling settling on her shoulders. Glancing back at Kai, who was watching the retreating seersha with the same confused expression Ellinor was sure she also wore, she cleared her throat. "Kai? Can I get my weapons back? Now, please."

His green eyes slid down to her, and his frown deepened. "Ah, 'bout that . . . I'd love to give 'em back to you. But the crate with your weapons? Yeah, Irati already had it loaded on the plane. I'll have to ask 'er where she done put it, and I don't reckon she'll be that forthcoming, you follow?"

Ellinor groaned, waving Kai toward the transport. "Of course. This is just perfect. Look, something still stinks about all this. We may not be as close as we once were, but you believe me, yeah? Something's not sitting right."

Kai's eyes lit up, and he nodded. "I feel you, Ell. I'll get your stuff back as soon as Irati's got 'er back turned."

INHALE, EXHALE
///CHAPTER THIRTEEN

THE FLIGHT from the middle of nowhere to Caratacus was supposed to take four hours, ample time for Kai to retrieve Ellinor's missing weapons. Or it would have been, if Irati hadn't caught him and then screeched about how Ellinor didn't need her guns or knives on an Eagle Owl, and then stuck Janne to guard the cargo hold. After Ellinor had pinned the diminutive woman to the floor, Janne had no interest in seeing the ex-lieutenant armed in any capacity.

Lacking options, as Kai was being watched to the point that Janne and her shadow, Warin, could count the number of times he got up to piss in the last two hours, Ellinor succumbed to asking Pema Tran for help.

Pema laughed at Ellinor's request, nearly spitting out the beer she'd been nursing. "You've gone dumb, Ellinor," she said, wiping tears from the corners of her eyes. "I'm not stupid. Irati's got a bug up her ass about you, and with her mood lately? I'd rather not tempt her itchy trigger finger, you follow me? Stop stressing, no one's going to cut you."

"And why not? Because of the dreeocht?" Ellinor grumbled as Pema walked away.

Pema waved over her shoulder. "Exactly. As long as Cosmin needs you breathing, breathing you'll stay."

With nothing else to do, Ellinor pouted at the back of the cleverly disguised hypersonic plane alongside Kai, hidden in her overly large seat from Janne's piercing, dark blue stare. Ellinor tried to distract herself from the prickles she felt at the base of her neck by looking out the window. But this high up, all she saw was a blanket of fluffy gray clouds.

Ellinor tapped the empty holsters around her waist idly, trying to puzzle out Cosmin's plan as a way of distraction. Having a variety of safe houses scattered from Euria to Anzor was risky. That was well over two thousand miles of terrain they had to cover. Even if none of the stops were in the big cities, there were dozens of other minor city-states strewn between the locations, not to mention swathes of deadland where the lawless dwelled—those who shunned the government's regulations, and the gangster caster's influence. Then there was the Saxa Desert that stretched across Erhard close to Anzor, leaving only small areas of land safe to travel that weren't inhabited by doehaz.

Ellinor knew the reason they didn't take a ship to Anzor was because there were aquatic doehaz just as there were desert. Had they taken a cruiser, they would only avoid detection for so long before all the casters and illegal combat-tech was sniffed out by the foul beasts. Ellinor had faced such a monster once in a virtual simulation back in basic training, and she was not eager to meet such a beast in real life.

By the fourth hour, Ellinor and Kai had played more hands of cards than Ellinor cared to admit. Had they been playing for money, she would have lost the clothes on her back twice over. Not that Kai would ever hold that against her; the big man liked playing for fun, despite his uncanny ability to bluff his way through the worst hands. Glancing at the digital clock on the far wall, Ellinor figured they'd be landing soon, and declined a sixth round with Kai.

Minutes crawled by, and their altitude didn't change. She felt the Eagle Owl make a turn, but when it didn't begin to descend, the pit in Ellinor's stomach grew heavier, and she worried at her bottom lip with her teeth. Out of habit, she checked her armor and took some small consolation in noting it was still on and fully charged.

When they crept close to the five hour mark, Lazar became antsy. The seersha got up and pounded on the cockpit door—Mirza made no move to stop him—but was greeted by Irati's voice over the crackling intercom.

"We're avoiding a patch of bad air. Buckle in folks, it's going to get bumpy."

"Bad air? The fuck does that mean?" Ellinor heard Talin say, the woman's dark skin paling. Pema put her arm around Talin, but that didn't return her luster or lessen the terror shining in her large, grass green eyes as she looked around the plane, trying to see if anyone else was on the verge of panic.

"That don't make sense . . . I checked the airspace. We were clear," Lazar said, voice carrying through the cabin as he raised his fist to pound on the cockpit door once more.

"You should sit, Lazar," Warin grumbled.

As if on cue, the entire plane began to shake and bump about like a bicycle free falling down a cliff side. Lazar was tossed down the aisle, tumbling to a stop not far from Ellinor, his thin, wire-framed glasses hopelessly mangled. He groaned as he hauled himself into a vacant seat, and buckled in, his greenish-yellow eyes unfocused. Beyond the rattling of the plane, the only thing that could be heard was Talin's hyperventilating, despite Pema's best efforts to calm her, and Embla yelling about the structural integrity of Lazar's Eagle Owl. Lights around the cabin flickered, and the bright white emergency lights swirled throughout the plane. The plaintive *ding* of the icon to remain seated made it hard for Ellinor to think, let alone understand what was happening, or how long it would last.

If Ellinor had access to her abilities, she could have stabilized the turbulent air around them. Still, even without her talents, this didn't feel right.

Having flown countless times before, through friendly and unfriendly airspace, in good and not so good conditions, what the Eagle Owl was experiencing didn't feel natural. The way the plane bucked around wasn't consistent with the varying pockets of pressure that created normal turbulence, nor did it rattle as if it were going against a head wind.

Before she could voice her concern, warning klaxons blared throughout the plane and oxygen masks tumbled from overhead. Eko's shaky voice came on over the intercom, "We've lost cabin pressure, put your masks on. This isn't a drill!"

Talin Roxas screamed, her voice higher than Ellinor would have ever thought possible. Embla practically scrambled over Warin to secure her mask, and even Pema was praying loudly to Azer as she helped secure her and Talin's masks. All the while the plane continued to bounce and rattle, the blaring sounds of danger and swirling lights of malfunctioning parts filling every inch of the cabin until there was nothing left but panic.

Ellinor didn't comply as the rest of the crew did—neither did Mirza Otieno. She sniffed the stale air, noting that nothing felt out of the ordinary. She trusted her instincts, even without her powers, to know when the air was about to betray her.

Kai watched her, his own mask poised over his nose, eyes wide, lips and hands trembling. "C'mon, Ell. Hurry up before shit gets real!"

"Kai, wait—"

Before she could finish, Janne's quick, nimble hands slipped the oxygen mask over her face, tightened the straps, and tied them so she couldn't pry it off.

"You heard Eko," Janne said, smiling at Kai, who jammed his own mask on at seeing her reassuring grin. "We've lost cabin pressure. Wouldn't want anyone getting *hurt*, now would we?" Janne practically cooed as the flow of oxygen forced its way down Ellinor's nose.

Only it wasn't oxygen.

"WELL, SHIT" PART TWO
///CHAPTER FOURTEEN

SHE BECAME aware of the throbbing behind her eye-sockets first, followed by the stabbing ache at the base of her skull. As she blinked open her eyes, squinting at the harshness of the white cabin lights, a muffled echo of voices came to her from far away. As more of her senses returned, her vision cleared and feeling returned to her extremities. The voices became sharper, but the words were a collection of hushed, urgent whispers that did little to silence the sound of Ellinor's thundering heart.

I'm tied up? What in the abyss happened?

"Wake up, Ell."

It took Ellinor a moment longer than she'd have liked to register those words coming from Kai Brantley. With great effort, she tilted her head to look at the figure that was slowly coming into focus. Even in the absence of his Coyote mechanized armor suit, the ropes strained around Kai's chest and bare arms.

"Easy now. They done gave you a whomping heavy dose of that shit."

"What happened?" she murmured, wincing at how slurred her speech was, and the pulsing, sharp pain in her head.

Another figure shushed her and Ellinor glanced to the side, where Pema sat, her dark brown eyes narrowed, face pinched, and mouth pressed in a hard line. Lying motionless at Pema's side was Talin, beads of sweat collecting around the black fuzz of her hairline. Seeing Talin bound like an animal helped focus Ellinor's sluggish mind, but did nothing to stabilize her irregular heart rate.

"She'll be okay," Pema said with a sigh. "She was so freaked, has some serious trauma left over from the time we were in an aerial crash, that she was gulping that crap in the masks like water." Pema fell silent, her eyes settling on her girlfriend and her steadily rising and falling chest. "She had better be okay, or I'll feed those cowards their own tits, just you watch."

"What happened?" Ellinor repeated, focusing Pema's attention once more.

"Not sure. Shit was going crazy, and Talin thought we'd crash. I was . . . ." The sergeant gave another silent sigh. "I should have been paying more attention, you know? My fault. I fucked up. But with Talin's PTSD, she gets real bad on bumpy flights. I knew we'd have to fly, but I thought it'd be good for her. To, you know, help her get over it. I shouldn't have pushed for her to come. Fucking Janne!" Pema growled, her dark eyes wide as she jerked her head to glare down the cabin walkway, a lock of greying black hair falling over her face, her skin darkening with fury. "I don't know why they did this, or what they're aiming to do, but this, whatever *this* is, it's Irati and

Janne's doing. And Warin's, too. That piece of doehaz shit has a bullet with his name on it."

Ellinor nodded, and then winced as the motion sent her vision swimming. "Mirza? Eko?" she croaked.

Kai shrugged, a frown crinkling his caterpillar thick brows. "Mirza didn't put his mask on neither, but I swear I saw Janne shove that damn mask on 'im, but . . . I don't know. I done already breathed that shit in, though. Things were fuzzy like my ma's favorite pair of slippers by that point. Can't be sure what I saw, but I don't think he's involved."

"Where is he then?" Ellinor tried to gently wriggle around so she could get a better look at things. That's when she realized her hands weren't just bound behind her back; there was a rope around her waist keeping her in place against the dreeocht container.

"He's in the cockpit," Pema whispered. "Embla and Lazar are knocked out on the other side of the container."

A soft moan filled the air and Pema frowned at the noise. "Oh, looks like Embla decided to return to the land of the conscious. Welcome back, sweetheart." Despite her words, nothing about Pema's tone was friendly, and Ellinor wondered if she suspected the girl of aiding Irati somehow.

With a groan, Embla rolled over into Ellinor's line of sight, tugging Lazar with her; the two had their ankles bound together. Ellinor watched them, trying to process what she was seeing. As the drug continued to wear off, Ellinor noted they were still missing people.

"Wait, where's Warin?" Ellinor asked, voice lowered, as she glanced between Kai and Pema.

The older woman snarled, nose crinkling and eyes hardening. "Bastard shot at Talin. Where you think that asshole is, huh?"

Ellinor blinked, her body humming like a revved truck ready to speed away, despite her pounding headache. "What do you mean, he shot at her? Why? You sure it wasn't an accident?"

"It was no slip-up. Talin was freaking out and Warin must of thought she was going to pull something. Maybe make some explosive from the shit dehydrated food we've got on deck. And he shot at my girl."

Ellinor looked to Kai. Despite Warin's earlier actions against her, she couldn't believe he would turn on Talin, his own crewmate for years. "Did you see what happened?"

"Not real clear on how it went down," Kai began slowly, "but Warin didn't 'ave a mask on either, though he might've been trying to get it on 'cause Janne was fussing over 'im, right? Talin's thrashing . . . don't think whatever they gassed us with works all that well on seerani or seersha. Pema's already out, right? Janne comes over and is trying to tie 'er up all proper like. Problem was, Warin sees Talin take a swing at Janne, not sure if she meant to or was just panicking, like Pema done said." Kai shook his head. "You know Warin ain't good with trigger discipline. Fool only just missed Talin's head."

"It wasn't poor discipline," Pema growled, her husky voice dripping with malice. "That boy knew what he was doing. The fucker picked a side. The wrong one."

Ellinor wasn't sure what was true, whether Warin had panicked when he saw Talin flailing near Janne, or had meant to kill Talin and was just a terrible shot.

Nothing's making sense.

Taking a deep breath, Ellinor began to compartmentalize. There was too much that didn't add up, but her immediate concern was getting out of the new mess she was in, and hopefully staying alive long enough to finally avenge Misho. But to do that she had to focus and take things one step at a time. Which meant she couldn't worry about who was doing what or why. That would come later.

"*Okay*," she said, letting her breath out slowly, willing her headache to lessen with each exhalation. "Okay," she said again, focusing on Pema. "We'll take care of Warin later, and Irati and Janne. But first we need to get free. You with me?"

Pema clenched her jaw and gave a deft nod. Kai gave a gloomy smile in return and said, "Whatcha need, boss?"

Ellinor thought for a moment. "How long have I been out?"

Kai squinted at the clock. "Far as I can tell? 'Bout two hours or so."

Ellinor stifled a groan. Given they were an hour off course and she had been unconscious for another two, Ellinor had no clue where they could be. They could be over the town of Bricius, or close to the coast of the Goma Ocean. Or they could be somewhere else entirely. The sheer number of possibilities made the corners of Ellinor's eyes twitch.

"I need more time," she mumbled. But time was not in their favor, especially as their traitorous crew could come and check on them at any moment.

"Right then," said Kai. "We'll do what we can, and warn you should anyone be headed this way."

Nodding her head, she got to work.

Ellinor maneuvered her fingers, testing the rope between her waist and the cold dreeocht container, feeling for any slack, and finding none. But then her fingers brushed over something familiar on her wrist: her bracer. The very bracer that had her combat shield embedded in it. Ellinor bit her tongue to keep from barking out a laugh.

Irati had known she had her shield, but Janne didn't; seemingly, the assassin didn't know what the cuff was—a testament to the money and craftsmanship Misho used when having the piece commissioned. The problem was, if she activated the shield in her current position, she could rip her back apart, or sever her arm.

Kai and Pema watched her curiously as she got her feet underneath her and began flexing and arching her back over, and over again. The ropes they had used were nothing special; Ellinor guessed Irati couldn't have metal cables smuggled on board without someone noticing. But the ropes were tied by Janne, who had been trained in all manner of knot tying while being held in the fetish club.

Ellinor knew the pressure she was using would eventually give her some slack in the rope around her waist. She just hoped it was enough to allow her to wiggle free.

By then, Embla had come to enough to watch Ellinor with interest, though Lazar and Talin remained unconscious. As Pema and Kai hadn't said anything to Embla, when she finally appeared coherent, the young woman asked, "What are you doing?"

"What's it look like? Trying to save our collective asses," Ellinor grumbled.

"Save us?" Embla frowned, struggling to sit up. "But this is your fault."

"Keep your voice down," Pema growled. "How's it her fault, huh? Did you miss the part where she's tied up like the rest of us? What do you think is happening here?"

Embla blinked slowly, her eyes searching the cabin as reluctant understanding settled on her. "Janne?" she whispered.

Pema's whole body sagged. "Your hero betrayed you, Embla. She gassed you, tied you up, and stabbed you in the back worse than anything Ell ever did. At least when Ellinor mutinied, all she did was walk out the front door of Cosmin's estate. Irati and Janne decided they needed an entourage for what they got cooking."

Ellinor tried to ignore the shocked intake of breath, the stuttering that Pema must be mistaken. That Janne and Irati wouldn't be so foolish. She ignored them again when Pema retold the tale to Talin, once the woman reclaimed consciousness. Lazar shifted over to the side, and she assumed he had overheard one of the retellings, as no one spoke to the seersha directly, nor did he speak in return. But he did study her with equal amounts interest and suspicion as she continued to flex the ropes to create more slack.

Finally, Ellinor was able to stand. She focused, relaxing until she no longer swayed to keep balance, and wiggled the rope past her hips, where it pooled around her feet. Smiling at the crew, she sat back down, and began working on her bound hands.

This is going to hurt.

Her arm was still sore from when Cosmin had dislocated it, but there was no way she could avoid aggravating it now. Wriggling her arms, she managed to scoot her hands underneath her rear end, brought her knees up and through so her hands were no longer behind her back. Her shoulder screamed in protest of the circular motion, but Ellinor gritted her teeth to avoid crying out. Once her hands were in front of her, Ellinor began twisting her wrists with more efficiency, trying to move the ropes so they were over her cuff.

A sharp inhale from Embla halted Ellinor's progress.

"What's this? All the babies awake from their naps?" Janne Wolff cooed, her boots snapping against the metal floor as she strode toward them.

Ellinor stilled. *Shit.*

"You got this, Ell," Kai whispered, his eyes hardening as they narrowed on Janne.

Giving her wrists another turn, she grumbled, "Fuck me," and dove at Janne before the slender woman was aware of what was happening.

Ellinor slammed her bound wrists into the side of Janne's head, sending her tripping backward into the empty seats of the Eagle Owl. Ellinor followed after the woman, who, despite being dazed, was scrabbling for her electric knives.

Janne snatched one of her knives, flipping it in a downward position to better pin Ellinor; the other she still tried to get a grip on after turning it on. But by then, Ellinor was on her once again.

Janne made a slashing motion, and the ex-lieutenant barely avoided it by jumping back and sucking in her stomach. Ellinor still felt the blade pass over her armor, sending a tingle throughout her body as her armor struggled to deflect the electricity that passed from that fleeting touch.

Just as Janne brought her arm down to stab Ellinor in the shoulder, Ellinor jumped forward and slammed her forearms into Janne's clavicle, stunning her. With her arms around Janne's neck, Ellinor smashed her forehead into the petite woman's nose. She was rewarded with a resounding *crunch* as the bone broke, blood splashing over Ellinor's face.

"Yo, Embla," Ellinor heard Talin say, her voice hoarse but clear, "see how the rumors about Ellinor got started? Ain't you glad she's on *our* side now?" A manic giggle flowed from Talin as she added, "Finish the bitch, Ell."

Ellinor didn't respond; she never had the chance. The cockpit door slammed open. Irati Mishra framed the doorway with a Gislin Cobra, her special, long range revolver-sniper rifle, up and at the ready.

Ellinor's eyes went wide, her blood running cold. She didn't know what kind of bullets the lieutenant had, but just because Irati needed Ellinor alive didn't mean the woman wouldn't maim her, or leave her too crippled to ever enact her revenge.

Or she could shoot someone else. Like Kai.

Irati raised the Gislin Cobra, the scope hiding the evil glimmer in her dark eyes, and Ellinor's muscles went rigid, an extreme focus settling over her. She twisted Janne until the stunned woman was facing her superior officer, but Irati didn't lower her weapon. Ellinor gritted her teeth in time with the sound of Irati's safety clicking off—and Ellinor pressed the button on her glove that activated her shield.

The ropes were not the only things to tear free.

Hot lead ran through her body as her shield activated, slicing off a portion of her wrist as the metal plates flared out. It even took the tip of Janne's broken nose with it. Their blood hadn't yet hit the ground when the thunder of Irati's shot filled the cabin, the impact sending Ellinor stumbling back, the bullet striking just over her shoulder—where Pema had been.

Ellinor scrunched her face at Irati, even though she couldn't see the rage building in her eyes. Ellinor ran her thumb over the button on her shield, changing the setting so the shield would seek out Irati's shots, no matter where the woman fired. The shield would move at near supersonic speeds, tracking the bullets of Irati's gun and moving accordingly. Ellinor couldn't keep it on this setting long or the power supply would drain, but this would ensure the bound crew behind her stayed alive.

Janne regained enough of her wits to begin struggling in Ellinor's arms, but with both hands now free of the ropes, Ellinor was better able to hold Janne in place. She punched Janne in the side and the woman slumped against her. Ellinor ripped one of Janne's electric knives from her hands, and kicked it back to where she hoped one of the crew members could reach it.

Another *CRACK* rang in Ellinor's ears, the impact of another bullet sending her sliding backward as the *ping* of the ricochet bounced about the cabin. This time, when the warning klaxons blared, Ellinor knew they were real.

"Janne!" Warin shouted, and Ellinor dared peek around her shield.

She saw the trail of blood she and Janne were leaving and knew Warin must have known that Janne was hurt. Ellinor ground her teeth until her jaw ached to keep from yelling in frustration.

Kneeing Janne in the other side, knocking the air out of the woman in a loud *"Umpf!"* she wrestled another knife from her. Ellinor sent that skidding back to the crew as well.

"Warin, stop!" Irati barked, the sound of heavy footfalls barreling toward Ellinor.

Warin slammed into her and she slid backward, trying to brace her feet so they could grip the floor. But that was impossible with the puddle of blood around her. A gloved hand gripped the top of her shield, another reaching beneath to wrench the dazed Janne out from Ellinor's slick grasp. Warin shoved Janne toward Irati.

With Janne providing accidental cover, Ellinor lowered her shield, jerking it from Warin's grasp long enough to slam him on the side of the head, sending him flying toward the bound team. She didn't pause to see what happened next.

Instead, she ran straight for Irati and Janne.

Her collar began to tingle as she got toward the end of the invisible tether she was allowed from the slumbering beast, but she didn't stop. Irati and Janne had tried to kill her, or use her, and they had risked the lives of the people Ellinor tried—and failed—to no longer care about.

Ignoring the growing tingle that began to turn painful, Ellinor sprinted at Irati and Janne, only to have Irati fling Janne into the cockpit. "Lock the door, dammit! We have enough fuel to get to Magomed. Gun it!" she cried, dashing inside behind Janne.

The cockpit door banged, the magnetic bolt sliding into place as Ellinor barreled into it. She yelled wordlessly as she beat and kicked at the door, but it didn't budge. Whether Mirza was helping Irati from behind that door, Ellinor still didn't know.

"Boss!" Kai called from the back of the plane. When she didn't answer, he called again, "Ell, you gotta come back 'ere. You're too far from the box. You're risking getting paralyzed. Please!"

Giving the door one last good kick, she stumbled back toward the rest of the crew. They were all free of their ties, and had Warin pinned on the ground. Pema held Janne's blade so it barely pierced his skin, sending a continuous shock throughout his body.

The knives were quality WR Lances gifted to Janne by Cosmin. One slice from them and not only would it short circuit most armors, but it would cut flesh as smoothly as glass.

Electric knives, like the Lances, were similar to the illegal magitech bullets Cosmin so loved and sold on the ground level market, and only the very powerful could afford them. But Janne's knives didn't need magic the way Cosmin's bullets did. WR Lances were pure combat-tech. Similar to an electric prod or stun stick, they were modified to offer different levels of pain. They could also be dialed up to kill a person with no more than a papercut.

It didn't take much to kill a person with electricity; Misho had taught Ellinor that long before he died.

Had Janne's knives touched Ellinor's bare skin, the voltage would have danced over the natural moisture present, sending the electricity throughout her body instantaneously with the blade barely cutting into her. Ellinor had been lucky, plain and simple, but Warin had no such luck.

Sitting heavily, black spots collected on the edge of Ellinor's vision as the adrenaline ebbed and the shock settled in. Talin glanced at her wounds, shook her head, and dug into an emergency kit that was hanging off the back wall next to the locked cargo hatch. Silently, she took Ellinor's still bleeding wrist and began tending to her wounds as her girlfriend extracted whatever information she could out of Warin.

"What's the plan, Warin? Stop yowling like a cat in heat and spit it out! What's Irati's game?" Pema demanded, digging the Lance a little deeper into Warin's arm as Kai and Lazar held the struggling soldier.

"I don't know!" Warin cried, his brown eyes frantic, his body twitching as the electric blade pulsed continuously against his skin.

"That's a pile of doehaz shit and you know it. Don't lie to me, boy. What's the game Irati's playing? Is Mirza involved?"

Warin cried out, face sweaty, as he tossed his head from side to side, his mousy brown hair with its bright blue streaks sticking to his damp face.

When he didn't answer, Ellinor asked, "What's in Magomed? Why has Irati set a heading for there?"

Magomed was a little municipality close to the Dagmar Sea and the Farvald River. It wasn't one of the powerful city-states of Erhard the way Euria or Anzor were, nor did Irati, Mirza, or Eko have any family or friends there, from what Ellinor could remember. Cosmin always liked ensuring the family and close friends of his inner circle were housed within Euria, in case anyone got it into their heads to betray him. After Andrey's and then Misho's death, Ellinor's family had left Euria for the small town of Desta, safe from Cosmin's claws.

Janne had no family. She had been sold to the fetish clubs for debts her dead parents couldn't pay, but the rest, well, Cosmin knew exactly where their families were at all times.

"I don't know!" Warin screamed again, his dusky brown skin going pale the longer he writhed in pain under the Lance. "I swear to Azer, I don't know. They didn't tell me. Janne! I . . . I just wanted to help Janne. She didn't say how. Just . . . just that you were all a bunch of traitors."

"And you believed her?" Pema hissed. "Boy, you're dumber than you look."

"What did she promise you?" Ellinor asked.

"Promise me? Who?" Warin gasped.

"Janne. What did she promise you for helping? What are they after?"

"We're keeping the dreeocht safe! Janne said we'd been betrayed, and Anzor wasn't safe. Said Cosmin would thank me and she would . . . she would, too."

"Oh, aye," Talin said, injecting Ellinor with a military grade Reco shot—meant to heal and repair significant trauma within a few hours, or days at the most—before binding her hand in a bandage. "Bet I can guess how you thought she'd be *thanking* you, too. Kai, do all men think this much with their dicks?"

Kai, despite everything, gave Talin a wicked smile, and winked. "Yup, 'fraid so."

"Bunch of dumb fucks, the lot o' you." The hint of laughter returned to Talin's voice, green eyes dancing in mirth.

"Ah, c'mon now—"

Pema cut him off with a growl. "We haven't the time for that." Fixing her dark eyes on Warin once more, she pressed the knife a little deeper, and Ellinor saw her thumb twitch over the hilt, adjusting the current pulsing through Warin's body. Ellinor thought she had turned it down, until Warin shrieked.

"Last time I'm asking, you read me? Tell me what I need to know to get this bird back on course."

"I don't know! Irati didn't tell me what's going on, or why this is happening. All I know is what Janne said. Please, Pema, you gotta believe me. Just please stop."

Whether Pema would have removed the blade or turned down the charge administered to Warin, Ellinor would never know, as the soldier could take no more. His whole body convulsed and his eyes rolled back in his head before he passed out.

"Well, shit," Talin grumbled. "Now what?"

Ellinor scrubbed her uninjured hand over her face, trying to clear her head and ignore the throbbing in her bandaged wrist. Very little was making sense. All she believed were things she saw for herself: Irati was dirty, and Janne, at least, knew the full plan.

And now she knew they were headed to Magomed, but couldn't say why, or even where they currently were. She didn't know how willing Eko was in all this, though she figured he was more willing than Warin—bringing him in seemed like an impulse decision on Janne's part—and she still didn't know if Mirza was helping Irati. But with the cockpit and cargo doors locked against them, they had no way of forcing Irati to land, correcting their path, or finding the next safe house.

"Fuck it all," Ellinor yelled, kicking the dreeocht container, making the crew wince or jump in surprise. "Kai, can you get this thing off me?" she asked, tugging on her collar.

Kai looked away, eyes downcast. "No. Sorry, Ell . . . you need a mechanic for that. Or Cosmin, he 'as the key."

"Embla," she said, turning desperate eyes to the young soldier trying her best not to be noticed. "You're a mechanic, yeah? Can you get this off?"

Embla shook her head. "That's way beyond me. Out of everyone, Eko might—*might*—be able to get that thing off. But, like, we can't even reach him. And even if you could, I doubt he'd help."

Ellinor knew it was a long shot, but she was hoping by now a little good luck would have come her way. Closing her eyes for a moment, she collected her thoughts, and when she opened them again, she turned her gaze to Lazar. "I'm assuming you built a fail-safe into this plane or something in case of a shit storm like this?"

Lazar regarded her coolly, as if considering something well beyond Ellinor's abilities to understand. "Maybe," he said, and fell silent.

Ellinor waited for him to continue, her eye twitching and body temperature rising as she tapped her foot. Just as she was about to throttle him, he glanced at Embla. "Ya may not be the best mechanic, but, without my glasses, I'll need ya if we're going to override what yer . . . *friends* did to my plane. Ya willing to do that?"

Embla gave Pema a beseeching look, and when her superior officer nodded in return, Embla sighed. "Yeah, sure. I'll do what I can, I guess."

Lazar nodded. "Good. This isn't going to be fun, and we don't have much time."

CLOCK'S TICKING
///CHAPTER FIFTEEN

N O ONE but Lazar Botwright knew what they were doing. The seersha wouldn't even explain to Embla; he just told her what to do as she dug behind a panel that had been concealed by the emergency med kit. Lazar blew out his breath in exasperation several times. Without any of their gear or access to the proper tools, they had to use Janne's Lances for the job at hand. Although Ellinor guessed his annoyance could have also been because he had no cigar to chew on.

Ellinor stood, rubbing the back of her neck. No one else had a clue as to what was in Magomed, and she couldn't puzzle out what would have Irati racing toward it as if the rest of the world were collapsing.

Meanwhile, Talin Roxas prowled the cabin. She plucked seatbelts and any other items not bolted down to fashion restraints for Warin, as well as anything they could use to attack or defend, should Janne or Irati appear from the cabin. As the explosives expert went to work, Pema kept a close eye on

Warin. Kai tried to help Lazar or Talin where he could, but neither his skillset nor his fingers were suited for delicate tasks.

With a loud hiss, Embla dropped Janne's knife and shook her hand. Lazar scowled at her, large eyes darting from the sparking wire they were tampering with to the sealed cockpit door. Seeing nothing, Lazar turned his attention back to Embla, whispering to her as she retrieved the knife, but stopped abruptly as another kind of hiss filled the cabin.

Ellinor glanced up at the air vents above the ransacked luggage compartments. The air flowing out of the vents was abnormally cold and seemed coated with a metallic twinge. Ellinor's eyes went wide, and she threw the hood of her armor back on, fastening the flap that served as a gas mask over her nose and mouth.

"Cover your mouths. Don't breathe that shit in," Ellinor ordered, yanking the seat covers away from Talin and shoving them into people's faces. Except for Warin; she figured the gas could only help keep him unconscious.

Pema glared up at the offending vents. "What is it?"

Ellinor took a deep breath, letting her mask filter clean air from whatever was oozing from the vents. Glancing down at her wrist, the readout of her mask's analysis flashed in yellow text back at her. Gritting her teeth, she shook her head. "It's the same stuff they put in the oxygen masks. They must have gotten Eko to divert the flow into the cabin."

"Probably tipped off to what we're up to by yer fumbling fingers," Lazar growled at Embla, yanking the red and yellow plaid scarf around his neck up and tying it around his face as best he could.

"It's not my fault," the girl whined, her voice muffled. "I'm not as good at this stuff as Eko. Cosmin only had me tag along so I could learn! From Eko, from Janne. He wanted . . . *needed* me to be better or I'd never be able to pay off my debts. Plus, you aren't even telling me what I'm supposed to be doing."

"Calm down, you two," Pema Tran snapped. Her eyebrows knitted together as she drew Talin close; she clung to Pema's hand in return. Holding a cloth over her nose and mouth with her other hand, she turned back to Ellinor. "What's that mean? We're going to get dropped by this stuff again?"

Ellinor peered more closely at the readout and shrugged. "Maybe. The masks gave a more concentrated dose, so it's going to take a lot more to have a similar effect."

"*Which means?*" an edge sliced through Pema's rough voice.

Ellinor narrowed her eyes at the older woman. Pema was normally so levelheaded, but with Talin being shot at and her panic attack over the turbulence, Pema was losing her control.

Love makes you weak. Ellinor shook the thought away before it could progress further, but it didn't lessen the tightness constricting her throat.

"Which means," Ellinor croaked, "we're running out of time for whatever it is Lazar is trying to have Embla do. Time to be straight and tell us what's up, old man. If you fall unconscious, I've got to know what we're supposed to be doing."

What Ellinor didn't tell him, or any of them, was that her time was limited as well.

After Janne's blade caressed her armor, its circuitry had gone into overdrive to keep the flow of amps from frying it completely. This had drained the armor's power supply significantly. She had at most only another hour before her armor shut down, which included the gas mask.

For the first time, Ellinor saw true concern in Lazar's eyes, though she wasn't convinced his worry was strictly over the chilly gas. "I built a . . . contingency plan. We're activating it. Or trying to, if yer girl wouldn't keep mucking it up."

Ellinor cut in before Embla could make any kind of retort. "A contingency plan for what? What are you doing, exactly?"

Lazar blew a heavy breath out through his nose. "Opening the emergency hatch. I put it there in case of a hijacking. What'd ya think we were doing?" He waved at the console Embla was trying to hack. "Should've been simple. But those bullets messed with the wiring when they punctured my baby. The door isn't disengaging like it should. Had it worked properly, the paneling would've slid back and allowed us to get to an escape pod of sorts. It'd have been enough to get us back on track."

"Hold up. On whose authority? The management didn't know about no escape pod or contingency plan. Who do you work for?" Talin asked, her ebony knuckles going white around Pema's hand.

Lazar's eyes twinkled in a smirk that his lips didn't show. "Cosmin's orders. Though I don't rightfully work for that man."

A hard lump formed in Ellinor's throat. Too much was happening that was contradictory to Cosmin's careful planning, and Lazar just happened to have a plan in case it all went sideways on *Cosmin's* orders? Lazar spared Ellinor a cool, flat stare. But before she could say anything, Kai slumped forward, his big hands gripping the headrest beside him, white-knuckled.

"I ain't feeling so hot, boss," Kai said, his face taking on a green sheen.

"Shit, we're running out of time." Ellinor pointed a finger at Lazar, "We're not done," and then strode to Embla. "You doing okay?"

Embla was sweating more than she should be, her eyes losing focus as the gas started to cloud her mind. The girl tried to nod, but the action seemed to sap more energy than Embla currently had at her disposal. Taking a deep breath, Ellinor moved as close to Embla as she could and took her mask off, wrapping it around the girl's mouth and nose.

Embla tensed, the blade shifting to point at Ellinor instead of the console. As soon as the clean air went into Embla's lungs, she relaxed.

Speaking with her stare, Ellinor urged Embla to hurry. A flicker of surprise, followed by respect, flashed in her big brown eyes as her mind began to clear from the effects of the gas.

Thanks to Ellinor's caster training—and her silenced abilities—she could hold her breath for longer than most people, but even she needed to breathe every now and again. Switching off with Embla was an option, but with the batteries of her armor quickly diminishing, she couldn't maintain it for long. And with the rest of the crew already getting woozy, they'd be no better than lame pigeons if Lazar's contingency plan didn't activate soon.

Then three things happened simultaneously: Janne peeked out from the cockpit—her nose bandaged, blue eyes appearing black within the bruises around them, the panel Lazar said hid the escape pod door finally opened, and the gas ran out.

Ellinor snatched the knives from Embla and put her mask back over her face. "Get them out of here. Drag them if you have to, but move."

"But what are you going to do?" Embla whined, ducking behind Ellinor.

"Something worthy of the rumors you listen to. Now go!"

Embla's cheeks flamed in embarrassment before she nodded. She grabbed Talin first and dragged her into the new room as Janne and Irati stepped from the cockpit, the door shutting behind them. Ellinor turned her shield back on, and noted Janne had a larger Lance dagger with her this time. Not that it mattered, as behind her, Irati had her Gislin Cobra, and murder flashing in her dark eyes once more. All Ellinor needed to do was buy enough time for Embla to get the rest of the crew through the hatch door. Not that Embla was moving quickly, despite her best efforts. Outside of Janne, Embla was the smallest of their crew.

There was no thunderous explosion this time as Irati fired at Ellinor. The woman had added a suppressor to her rifle, for reasons Ellinor was unsure of—until she caught the sound of Janne trying to sneak up on her. The dampened ringing helped Janne focus, even if it made it possible for Ellinor to better follow her movements.

With the near continuous fire from Irati, Ellinor had no time to peek out from behind her shield to see where Janne was. But each time one of the bullets recoiled off her shield, her wounded wrist burned with pain. She was unable to brace herself properly, adding more pressure to her arm with each shot, her boots slipping back on a floor still slick with blood.

Sparing a glance behind her, Ellinor groaned. Only Pema and Talin had been moved to safety, though Lazar was staggering toward the escape pod. But Kai needed the support of the wall, unable to move on his own. If they didn't take the dreeocht with them . . . Ellinor suppressed a shiver. She didn't want to consider what would happen—what would *emerge*—should the dreeocht be freed from its container because it got damaged by ricocheting bullets.

I need more time!

Janne slashed at her with the dagger, trying to slice into her thigh from beneath her shield, when Ellinor's time ran out. Ellinor danced out of reach then lunged at Janne, but she wasn't used to the weight of the weapon and her slash did little. She cringed once more as her shield morphed into an oblong rectangle to block Irati's shot aimed at her kneecap. As the shield morphed, Janne dove back in to slash at her exposed appendages.

She kicked out, catching Janne on the chin. She heard the woman hiss in pain, but the sound was cut off by the *ping* of another bullet ricocheting off Ellinor's shield. She struggled to keep her arm up, the hot, throbbing agony in her wrist making it hard to keep the shield level.

A grunt came from behind, catching Ellinor's attention. Embla was trying to maneuver the dreeocht container on its push-cart into the safety of the hatch—leaving Kai where he was, struggling to get off the wall.

At the sight, Ellinor's insides quivered. "No," she yelled, "you get him to safety first!"

"But—" Embla began, but Ellinor cut her off.

"Do as I say, dammit! Kai comes first."

Embla stopped fussing with the container, and began tugging on Kai, who leaned heavily on her as they moved.

Irati stopped shooting at Ellinor and started shooting toward Embla. With a yelp, Embla dropped Kai as she ducked, before trying to tug the man to safety once more. Ellinor was out of options. She snatched Warin's limp body from the ground and used him for cover, stretching out her shielded arm to give Embla protection.

Janne scowled at her, lurching to the side to avoid cutting Warin's legs as his body swung in front of Ellinor. Janne would think twice before harming Warin.

"This gets us nowhere," Irati said, trying to keep the growl from her voice. "How about this. You and the dreeocht stay, and I let the rest of this worthless squad leave with their lives. Fair is fair."

"My ass," Ellinor shot back. "I don't know what you think you'll accomplish, Irati, but this is madness. You have to know Cosmin isn't going to let you steal from him. You and your family are as good as dead, your body just hasn't gotten the memo yet. Do you really want that? You want to sign your brothers' death warrant?"

"Cute. That's cute, really!" Irati answered, forcing a laugh. "I'm *saving* Cosmin's prize. Lazar was going to run off with it, you must know that. So, we'll let the rest of the traitors go if you play nice and stay put. We finish the job, and you get your magic back. Isn't that what *you* want?"

"Stop lying; you aren't good at it." This time, Irati didn't try to argue, but she did begin to close the distance to Ellinor, as Janne climbed on top of the seats so she could strike without hitting Warin.

"Is Mirza a part of this? Eko, too?" Ellinor asked, vying for more time.

Irati grinned in response, giving Ellinor an uncomfortable feeling that sent her gut freefalling.

Shaking her head, Ellinor pressed, "Why? What's in Magomed that you need a dreeocht for?"

Irati smiled wickedly, her dark eyes glittering like the sun over a blackened desert. "You don't get it, do you? Azer's taint, you really are stupid, aren't you? How you ever got promoted is the biggest mystery of all. And if you make some half-assed quip about me, I swear I will render you brain-dead here and now."

Curiosity raced through her like an avalanche, making her shiver at what Irati could have planned—and what would happen when Cosmin knew his plan had indeed gone tits up in such a catastrophic way. Ellinor opened her mouth to press the issue, when she heard Embla and Pema grunt in unison as the sergeant returned to help the smaller woman tug the heavy dreeocht container and its bullet riddled push-cart to safety.

"No!" Irati yelled, rapid firing at the duo as they struggled to get the contraption moving.

The constant shifting of Ellinor's shield was draining the battery at an alarming rate—it wouldn't outlast Irati's elongated magazine of ammunition. And there was still Janne, who was darting around Ellinor from the tops of the seats like a sleek shark, trying to nip at her without biting Warin in the process. Ellinor moved and dodged Janne's thrusts, the two hopping around one another like aristocratic dancers at a gala to the music of Irati's muffled, rapid shooting.

"Ellinor, come on," Embla said, waving from the entrance of the hatch as she tried to fix the wiring so the door would close.

Ellinor jumped back to Embla, Warin twitching in her arm as he began to regain consciousness. "Let's go, Embla," Ellinor said, thrusting Warin at Janne to force her back as another shot from Irati jolted Ellinor's shield.

"I'm trying, I'm trying! It's not working this time. I think Eko must be, like, blocking my efforts or something. It's not cooperating."

Janne swung at her again, Ellinor moving at the last moment, the electric dagger passing so close she could feel the crackling air as the blade missed her face.

"How much time is this going to take?" Ellinor was trying to stay calm, knowing full well that more pressure wasn't going to help the already flustered newbie.

"I don't know. I don't know! Too much time. You won't be able to buy me enough with Eko working against me."

"Do your best, I'll make time for you." And Ellinor meant it.

She pushed forward, shoving Warin's semi-limp body at Irati, who fired another round at Embla. The wet *thunk* of her bullets and Warin's surprised gurgle let her know Irati had missed her intended target for the first time. Janne's strangled scream told her that Warin had, in a twisted way, paid the price for shooting at Talin, and for choosing Janne Wolff over the rest of his team.

Love makes you vulnerable. It will get you killed.

"Janne, stop!" Irati shouted, as Janne threw herself at Ellinor, making it impossible for Irati to shoot at her, or Embla, without hitting Janne.

Janne slashed and lunged, Ellinor parried and jumped back, her shorter Lances no match for the longer dagger. Each time their weapons met, electricity curled and crackled around their blades like white octopus tentacles writhing in pain.

"Don't kill her, you idiot! I need her alive," Irati called, trying to get around the dueling pair.

That's when Ellinor felt a hand land on her shoulder, pulling her back into the escape hatch. Time seemed to slow as she sailed passed Embla, a look of determination on the young woman's face as she ripped one of the electrical knives from Ellinor's hand.

She fell against Kai, who wrapped her in his arms. "Let me go! Embla! Get your ass in here!"

Embla shook her head as Irati leveled her Cobra. "I said there wasn't enough time. This is the only way. I'm sorry. Make sure Cosmin takes care of my family."

With that, Embla plunged Janne's knife into the exposed circuitry. Irati fired her rifle. Embla's head slammed forward, but the hatch doors closed before Ellinor could see the ruin that was once Embla's round face.

Ellinor had not liked Embla. She had barely known her, but she was hardly more than a child. She didn't deserve to die for Cosmin or Irati's misguided plans for power.

"I could have saved her," Ellinor cried, shock settling in, making her body shudder.

"No, boss, you couldn't 'ave. It was the only way. Embla, she . . . she 'ad the right of it. There wasn't another way," Kai said, voice thick with remorse.

Dropping Janne's last knife, Ellinor jammed the heels of her palms into her eyes and rubbed, hoping to banish the thought of Embla's bloody face as Irati's bullet ripped through her skull. When the image wouldn't leave, she glared at Lazar.

"Her sacrifice better have been enough, seersha. Get us out of here. And, for the love of Azer, someone get me my fucking weapons!"

NOT EXACTLY "PLAN B"
///CHAPTER SIXTEEN

THERE WAS only one good thing about Lazar's contingency plan: the passageway led into a small compartment sandwiched behind the cargo hold. Ellinor and the rest of the beleaguered crew were able to retrieve their armor, weapons, and all the supplies they could carry, and load the dreeocht into an escape pod disguised as a shipment container. Kai and Talin busied themselves with reclaiming their gear and loading the pod as swiftly as they could while Pema and Lazar tried to get a message to Cosmin, but the outbound comms were blocked. They'd have to send a message later, once they were free of the hypersonic plane.

Ellinor shoved her twin double barrel pistols into the holsters around her hips, and slid the compact combat-tech crossbow—her beloved Asco Rhino—into the holster on her back, under her cape. Janne's knife she thrust into her thigh holster next to her miniature Leviathan Roaster. All the while, her armor and shield were plugged into the outlet on the far wall, charging as much as possible until the pod was ready to push off.

Kai slid back into his Coyote mechanized suit before securing the dreeocht into the pod, the push-cart rattling, one of its hydraulic lifts inoperational. Ellinor caught Lazar's eye. She stashed her two karambit knives into the slots on her waist, preparing to confront him about all the things he was hiding from her, when the hypersonic plane made a muffled *WHOOSH* sound. Ellinor paused mid step, waiting.

The aircraft began to vibrate, and Lazar glanced beyond Ellinor to the door they came through. He watched it, as tense as Ellinor, but nothing else happened as the Eagle Owl continued to vibrate.

The plane's rattling increased until it suddenly ceased. Lazar put his hand on the hull, before recoiling as if burned. "Get yer asses in the pod now," he said, all but flinging Talin inside as she was closest to the pod door.

"What do you think you're doing? You touch her like that again and I'll gut you," Pema yelled, darting for Talin, only to have Lazar shove her in the pod, too.

"They took the plane out of hypersonic speeds. We're just hovering now. Don't ya see? Those cowards diverted the power. They're going to force their way in." He fixed Pema with his greenish-yellow eyes; they reminded Ellinor of a cat. Frustration and anger wafted off him as his pupils dilated. "Ya want yer girl's sacrifice to be in vain? Get in the fucking pod. Throw yer temper tantrum after we get to safety, ya wretched dolt of a woman."

Kai was at Ellinor's side a moment later, tugging her into motion. "Let's go, Ell. We've got ourselves a right proper clusterfuck, and we've gotta get out of it."

As if to emphasize his point, the cargo doors groaned as they retracted, sparks flying as they were forced past the locking mechanism Embla broke. Ellinor saw the glimmer of Janne's dark blue eye, and the soldier in her took control.

She grabbed her armor's batteries and ran for the escape pod, throwing herself in alongside Kai. As the pod doors shut, Janne wriggled herself past the cargo bay doors, followed by the muzzle of Irati's rifle.

Lazar was pressing an absurd number of buttons as fast as his long fingers would allow, a new set of glasses sliding precariously further down his nose. Talin hovered at his side until she saw the hidden doors beneath them open. Greeted by nothing but blue sky and a carpet of thin gray clouds, Talin scrambled back, her breath coming in quick hiccups as she tried to claw her way out of the escape pod.

Pema tackled her girlfriend, Kai helping restrain her as the first of Irati's bullets hit the pod. Ellinor knew Irati was using magitech bullets and, with the way the pod shuddered, she assumed they were water bullets, meant to short circuit Ashlings.

Lazar slammed his palm on the flickering console and the pod disengaged from the plane as the doors fully retracted. The suction of air had Janne clinging to another heavy cargo box lest she be sucked out of the plane. But that did not save Embla, whose lifeless body flew past her one-time mentor and into the pod before tumbling out into the endless sky below. Ellinor winced at the hollow *thunk* her body made upon impact, a tear rolling free as she squeezed her eyes shut, but they flew open a moment later as a different sound rocked the pod.

Irati's finger never let up off the trigger. A cascade of bullets pummeled the pod as its thrusters engaged and made its way out of the hypersonic plane. No sooner had they sailed free of the cargo hold and corrected their flight path for the direction of the next safe house did the net of electricity from Irati's water magitech bullets fry the rest of the pod's shields and circuitry. The lights went out, and Ellinor's stomach lurched into her throat with the freefall.

The sounds of Talin and Pema's screams and Kai's frantic prayers filled the cabin as Lazar desperately tried to get the pod's console to respond. The wind howled as they fell, the warning sirens of the Eagle Owl fading as they dropped away from the plane.

All Ellinor Rask could see was the rapidly approaching ground, its details becoming clearer the closer they came. She started to wonder what she'd look like smeared across the terrain, and decided that's not what she wanted her last thought to be. She shut her eyes and whispered, "I'm sorry, Misho. I'll see you soon."

GOOD AT BAD IDEAS
///CHAPTER SEVENTEEN

C OUGHING, ELLINOR was convinced a truck was sitting on her chest. Her eyelids were hundred pound weights, and it was all she could do to lift them enough to peer into the hazy capsule. Smoke filled the space, and faint flashes from the malfunctioning command console were all that illuminated the pod. Ellinor assumed there must have been sound, but no noise made it to her ears beyond a loud buzzing that vibrated her skull as the craft swayed around her and noxious fumes filled her lungs.

Despite how much she yearned to close her eyes and fall asleep, she kept forcing them open and making herself cough out the foul air. She fumbled with her restraints, her fingers fat and clumsy as she struggled over the simple buckle. Agonizing seconds later, she was free and the pressure from her chest lessened. Falling to her hands and knees, she coughed again before remembering her mask. She fastened it with jerky movements, but kept the setting on low to conserve as much of the power supply as she could. After a lungful of clean air, her vision no longer swam, and her thoughts became less muddled. She even heard sound once more and realized that the faint *beep* wasn't all that faint, but was, in fact, a blaring siren alerting the incapacitated crew that the pod was on fire.

Ellinor didn't know the first thing about operating air transports, let alone a disguised escape pod. But she knew smoke rapidly filling the cabin was not something that should be happening. Crawling toward the exit, Ellinor scrabbled along the door until she found the emergency release. She pulled at the big red tab; the door cracked away a bit but was jammed from opening. Groaning, she tugged and tugged on it to no avail. It wasn't until she gave it a good kick, which jarred her knees, that the door fully opened and smoke billowed out into the evening air.

Ignoring the aches and pains that plagued her body, Ellinor went back into the aircraft and began unbuckling Kai, Pema, Talin, and Lazar. Kai and Lazar were already starting to come to, and when they regained enough of their wits, helped her haul out the dreeocht. Its container was no longer smooth and sleek, but as there were no warning lights and Ellinor's collar wasn't acting up, she assumed the dents hadn't compromised the device's integrity.

By the time they got everyone out, flames licked around the console and crawled up the walls. Pushing Lazar a little, she said, "We don't have much time. That thing's going to blow any moment now, and it'll be a big arrow to our position. Please tell me you managed to get us closer to where we should be?"

Lazar spared a glance for the pod, a frown settling on his face once he saw the full extent of the damage. Ellinor snapped her fingers in his face to get his attention. "We don't have time for you to try and be clever. I doubt you'd be able to in your state anyway. Where are we?"

Before the seersha could answer, a popping sound came from inside the ruined escape pod, and Lazar's eyes went wide. He limped toward the rest of the crew, waving his arms. "Get back, the lot of ya. Move everything back or yer going to be missing more than just yer eyebrows. Move now, damn ya!"

Despite their best efforts, the crew wasn't moving nearly as fast as they needed to. Kai bled from a deep gash above his eyebrow, Talin held her elbow like it had popped out of place, and Pema hopped on one foot, and that was on top of all the other scrapes and bruises Ellinor knew they were suffering. They had just moved the dreeocht and most of their gear to a safe distance behind a nearby outcropping of boulders and a dead tree when the pod exploded.

It bounced twenty feet into the air as the remaining fuel caught on fire in a rapid burst, enough to send a gust of scorching air slamming into them and knocking all but Kai off their feet. Ellinor groaned, slowly getting back up on wobbly legs.

With another glance to make sure Pema and Talin were none the worse for wear, she hobbled back over to Lazar and shoved his shoulder. "Out with it before more shit blows up. Where are we, old man?"

Lazar scrubbed a hand down his face, smearing soot over his skin. Grunting in disgust, he wiped his hands on his pants before pulling a type of compass from his pocket. While the seersha had not been in nice clothes before, they were barely more than tatters now. How he was still able to hold anything in his pockets was a mystery to Ellinor.

Tapping the cracked screen of the compass, the device made a sputtering *whorl* noise for a moment before it settled into a healthier cadence. As Lazar squinted at the screen, Ellinor spared a glance for the banged-up crew and took mild comfort in watching them bandage each other up as best they could with the emergency medical supplies they had on hand.

"Amaru," said Lazar, his voice near as gruff as Mirza's from all the coughing and rancid smoke inhalation.

"What?" Her mind was still slow to comprehend what was being said.

"According to my digimap, that's about where we are. The little city-state of Amaru is about fifteen miles away. Look, ya can just make out the glow of the lights from here. Yer not as blind as me without glasses," Lazar grumbled, putting the device back in his pocket.

Ellinor had never used a digimap before; they were complex little handheld devices that could read the topography of any area and pinpoint your exact location. A few rich and paranoid parents had special digimaps made to help them monitor their children, as did many of the wealthiest brothel owners who wanted to ensure that no one tried to kidnap or flee with their employees. Cosmin had a few of the stupidly expensive devices in his possession, but he only gave them out when agents were on covert assignments that required back channels and putting their heads into black bags. The only disadvantage of a digimap was it needed a clear view of the ground in order to get its bearings. From a plane, with a blanket of clouds covering the earth below? The things couldn't even function as a proper compass.

Squinting at where Lazar pointed, she could see the faint glow of a city in the distance, its neon and electric lights blaring at all hours. Thankfully, they were still far enough away where the explosion of their escape pod had likely gone unnoticed.

Still, something felt off to Ellinor, her gut churning less with motion sickness now and more with the acid of suspicion. With Irati's mutiny and the fact that Lazar seemed prepared for it, not to mention Cosmin's past secrecy in suspecting a betrayal, or heist, and not informing his gang, Ellinor felt like a trap was closing in. Her anger at Cosmin rose, constricting her throat as her eyes darted from the city in the distance to the injured remnants of the crew she had considered her friends not all that long ago. Misho would never forgive her if she led them into more danger.

Grabbing Lazar's arm, she jerked him toward her, his reddish-bronze skin darkening with indignation all the way to the tips of his elongated ears. "You're going to tell me what's going on, and you're going to do it *now*." She waited for Lazar to acknowledge her, and when he didn't try to grab for his scattergun, she continued, "You're going to tell me who you work for, where the supposed safe houses are located, and who knew about their locations. I've got to know what we could be walking into, and just how much shit we're already in. Understand me?"

Lazar glanced toward Talin and Kai, who were finishing patching their wounds as best they could before his eyes fell on Pema, who didn't bother hiding her curiosity in their conversation. Ellinor followed his gaze and she narrowed her eyes, shoving him in the shoulder again to get his attention.

"None of that. There's not enough of us for you to try and hold back now. I don't care if they overhear, you're coming clean, and you're doing it now."

"Bossy one, aren't ya?" Lazar said, a hard edge to his voice as he fished a cigar out of his reclaimed pack.

"If that's what you want to call it. I like to think of it as my 'get shit done' attitude. We don't have time for bullshit. For all we know, Eko is close to fixing whatever damage was done to the Eagle Owl and honing in on our location as we speak. I don't know you, Lazar, and there's been one betrayal too many as is. I've got to know you're on the level."

Lazar shrugged, feigning boredom. But the twitch in the corner of his big eyes gave him away. When Ellinor didn't back down, he knew the game was up.

"Fine," he grumbled. "I work for Zabel Dirix. Cosmin knows. That's why he hired me. Didn't trust the lot of ya, figured something . . . *unsavory* may go down. Cosmin figured a traitor was in his house, but thought having your old team about to keep you compliant was worth the risk, which made using outside help more agreeable. He's a clever bastard, I'll give him that. He just didn't know where the blow would come from, so he had me come along as insurance so my mistress would know Cosmin, at least, was on the straight with her. I used both their funds to get the Mamba and Eagle Owl up and running. So, yeah, I followed my orders from both Cosmin *and* Zabel. Good thing, too, or we'd all be fucked and Zabel would take it out on Euria. She's right desperate to get that dreeocht."

"Where are the safe houses, and who knew?" Ellinor said, balling her hands into fists to keep from punching something, or someone.

Lazar's cigar flared as he took a long drag, his eyes glancing to Pema, whose hand hadn't strayed from her own scattergun shotgun. Blowing the cigar smoke in Ellinor's face, he said, "Caratacus, obviously. Then Donnchad. I had this here nice speedy yacht that would've taken us across Lake Agi and down the good side of the Farvald and Finnr Rivers. I had some caravans stashed near the river's mouth; we'd have taken those around the Saxa Desert. We'd stop in Gentius, then straight on to Anzor. Simple. Only one who knew was that burned lieutenant of yers, Mirza Otieno."

"Fuck," Pema murmured, limping over to Ellinor, using her scattergun as a crutch. "That must be why Irati's keeping Mirza with her, so she knows the plan and can keep Cosmin at bay."

Lazar rolled his eyes. "Maybe. That, or he's helping her. Ya consider that?"

Ellinor shook her head. "Irati's not using the safe houses. She was heading straight to Magomed. She doesn't need Mirza for that."

Pema's jaw clenched, frowning. "Maybe he's *her* contingency plan. Like this pod, you follow?"

Ellinor shrugged, but didn't answer. She couldn't worry about a problem that hadn't fully presented itself. Especially when she was having a hard time hiding the tremble in her knees and the hitch in her breath as her throat began to close around an invisible stone. The parallels surrounding their current predicament and Misho's death were becoming too glaring to ignore. Memories of his death, the flash drive she found on the body of the Ashling afterward—all were competing for space in her mind beside the images of Embla and Warin's last moments alive.

"Is Amaru near where you stashed the boat we were supposed to take?" Ellinor said, rubbing her forehead, trying to get her mind to stop spinning.

"*Yacht.*" Lazar narrowed his big eyes at her. "Amaru's on the wrong side of the Farvald River. The transport was stashed where Lake Agi feeds into the river, and that's hundreds of miles away from here. We'll need to get us a new mode of transportation."

"Will you be able to get us something usable in Amaru? Or get a message to Cosmin and Zabel?"

Pema grabbed Ellinor's arm and tugged her away from Lazar, back toward Talin and Kai. "This is a bad idea, Ellinor. Don't be stupid. We can't go to Amaru."

"I know it's a bad idea, but the alternative is sit here and hitch a ride with Irati again. None of you are in any condition for a long hike somewhere." Frowning, Ellinor lightly nudged Pema's ankle and gave Talin's elbow a poke. When both women jerked and hissed in pain, she leveled a flat glare back at Pema. "So what do you want, Sergeant? To wait around here for Irati?"

When Pema didn't answer, she continued, "Look, you all need time to heal and we're too far away from anywhere else that would be even the slightest bit useful to you guys right now. Kai can carry one of you, but he can't carry you both, and someone's got to push that blasted dreeocht around. We have zero good options here. Unless I'm missing something?"

Pema and Talin exchanged a look, and Kai didn't appear to be aware they were speaking at all. With a sigh, Talin said, "Fuck it. Baby, she's right. It's a dumb-as-shit plan, but it's the only option."

Pema hung her head, hiding her eyes behind her hair. "I know," she said slowly, licking her lips, "but I don't like it."

"You don't have to like it. We just have to survive. Think you can manage that?"

Pema gave Ellinor a lopsided grin, and Talin chuckled. "Aye, we can survive just fine, thank you very much," Talin responded with a wink, grasping Pema's hand.

Ellinor slowly made her way back to Lazar, who had busied himself readying his surviving items for the trek ahead. "Right, so, can you get us a ride or something from Amaru?"

Lazar tucked his bright white hair—only slightly singed—behind his tall ears, before scratching at his chin, his eyes taking on a vacant look that Ellinor had begun to associate with him thinking and scheming. With a heavy shrug, he said, "Yes and no. I can get us out of here and back toward where we need to be getting, but I can't contact our bosses from Amaru. The underground's run by some mid-tier seersha air caster," Lazar paused, his eyes flicking to her in a pointed way before he lowered his gaze, "and the little shit is trying to be bigger than he is. So, me trying to get a message to a rival with a dreeocht in tow? Not happening. In fact, with yer eyes proclaiming loud and clear what ya are, I figure we're already in for more trouble than the lot of ya can handle. The caster in charge, or the governor, finds out we have a magical battery that can boost his power exponentially? We're as good as dead."

Ellinor crossed her arms over her chest, her headache returning in force with Lazar's words. "So what you're trying to tell me is, we're fucked. That about sums it up, yeah?"

Lazar smirked. "I just said we'd be in for *trouble*. I don't know yer crew, woman. I can't say how much they can handle, especially now. But yer going to attract attention in Amaru. The caster's gonna know what ya are and want to keep ya. So, ya tell me, are we fucked?"

Her lips pressed together in a slight grimace, brows pulling in as she looked off into the night. A sinking feeling settled in her stomach. She tried to tune out the sound of the popping and crackling fire, of Pema slowly hopping her way back to where she and Lazar stood, so she could listen for Irati's stolen Eagle Owl. Even if the lieutenant wasn't nearby at that moment, it would take only minutes to travel from hundreds of miles off to return to where they were.

Coming closer, Pema guessed at Ellinor's thoughts, and placed a hand on her shoulder, turning her back toward Kai and Talin. "We've got enough for now. Let's shake our ass and get moving while we still can. We can talk logistics as we go, you follow?"

Ellinor nodded. "Yeah, let's get as close as we can to the city tonight and slip in with the early morning deliveries. If Amaru is anything like Euria, only transport drivers will be up and about, and those guys aren't usually the sharpest. We should be able to sneak in and find a place to lay low while Lazar does his thing." Ellinor eyed Pema's bandaged ankle for a moment, then asked, "Can you walk on that?"

Pema jutted her chin up. "I'll manage."

"You can lean on my good side if you need to, baby," Talin called, tugging on her pack as Pema and Ellinor joined her. She fixed her dazzling green gaze on Ellinor. "Guess you're in charge o' this operation now, aye?"

Ellinor winced. "I was coerced into doing this. I just want to get my powers back. If you or Pema have a better idea, feel free to take charge." She lowered her voice, leaning toward the pair, "I don't trust Lazar to lead us. It's likely, I don't know, he's got some other motive that may get us all killed."

"I hear that," said Talin, nodding. "Right, then. Let's get a move on. You got anything to use as cover in case Irati does a fly by?"

Kai answered for her. "I grabbed a couple of those there camo tarps Lazar used to hide 'is Eagle Owl with. Toss those over a tent or two and Eko won't be able to spot us, even with radar. It'll look like a couple of boulders sitting in an empty field."

His voice was flat, not holding any of the easy charm Kai was known for, and she guessed the shock of losing two people he once worked with right on top of each other was taking its toll.

"Good, we'll need those tarps for sure then." And with that, her new-old crew followed her lead, trusting her bad idea wouldn't see them all killed.

Time moved slowly after that, the sounds of their ruined escape pod fading, the thrum of the bustling city building as they trudged along. But as the night wore on, Ellinor's sinking feeling remained, and her heart would not stop fluttering.

"This air caster, what's his name?" Ellinor asked, disrupting the silence that had fallen on the team. She cringed with how loud her voice sounded in the stillness, running her fingers through her tangled hair and then fixing it back into its bun.

Lazar frowned at her, but answered all the same. "Dragan Voclain. Know the bloke?" The way he said it sounded accusing, but she paid the seersha's tone no mind.

Ellinor rolled her eyes. "Air casters aren't that rare, you know. Most just don't get themselves tangled with gangsters. That makes me special, yeah? I'm one of the few corruptible air casters Cosmin could get his claws in."

Lazar snorted at her, and Ellinor changed the subject. "Let's say we didn't go into Amaru. Where's the next closest place you could get a message to Zabel or Cosmin? Or where we could catch a ride to Anzor?"

Lazar guffawed, but there was a hard glint in his eyes. "I wouldn't call it close," he said, fishing the digimap out of his pocket again and bringing it to life. "There be some fly-over hamlets along the way, but they won't have any long distance wireless comms I could use, let alone a transport hardy enough to get to Anzor. That leaves Behar. It's a friendlier city-state for sure, but that's on the other side of the Finnr River a good ways. We're talking days, if not weeks, of walking to get there. We don't have the supplies for that, plus, with yer bitch of a lieutenant on our heels?" Lazar gave a low whistle and shook his head. "We'd never make it."

Ellinor found herself nodding along with Lazar's words; she had figured he would say something like that, but she wanted to be positive. Her gaze drifted to the rest of the crew. Talin and Pema were starting to pant while holding on to their respective wounded elbow and ankle. Occasionally Pema grunted in pain, but Talin was quick to reposition her so they could continue on. Ellinor looked away before the pair could see the concern etched on her face.

Kai was struggling with the push-cart, the dreeocht container wobbling atop of it, its no longer sleek surface covered in soot and scorch marks. The push-cart had taken most of the damage in the fall, and it didn't roll as smoothly as it had. Ellinor wasn't convinced it would survive much longer, period. But Kai didn't seem to care. His gaze was unfocused as he peered into the black night and the flashing lights of Amaru slowly getting closer, and closer.

Something broke inside her to see Kai still so disheartened by the loss of some of their crew, and the betrayal from the others. She hated that he was still so loyal to Cosmin despite everything that had happened. Her muscles tensed with each step she took, her jaw aching from how hard she ground her teeth. She took out her two karambit blades—state-of-the-art WX Lacerator Knives—just to give her hands something to do.

Like any other karambit blade, there was a ring attached to the end of the hilt, allowing Ellinor to flip the viciously curved blade around her hand in a dizzying display of movement. The blades were best in close combat, ideally suited for hooking and tearing through skin, arteries, and muscles alike. But the WX Lacerator Knives also contained a minuscule computer in their carbon-steel hilt that gave them boomerang capabilities. Ellinor could flick the Lacerator from her finger, send it tearing through her adversary, and then recall the blade to repeat the process less than a second later.

As the silence stretched, the buzzes and vibrations from the nearing city-state growing, Ellinor spun and caught her knives faster and faster. Her nostrils flared with each angry exhalation.

Pema noticed the furious, and a little dangerous, speed at which Ellinor was spinning and palming her blades. Her brow quirked as she asked, "Everything good?"

Ellinor glanced down at the karambit knives for a moment, then growled as she replaced them in their sheaths. "No, it's not all good," Ellinor said, her teeth bared for all to see now that her mask was no longer on. "I been thinking, yeah? How Cosmin decided to keep his suspicions to himself and it cost two people their lives and injured four others. He's letting his soldiers, his *pawns,* unwittingly trip traps that only Cosmin sees. It's the exact same shit that got Misho killed, and now more people are dying. Can't you see that?"

Her outburst had drawn Talin, Lazar, and Kai's attention. They slowed their pace to gawk at the pair. Talin glanced from Ellinor to Pema, waiting for one of them to explain. When Pema didn't respond, the ebony skinned seerani asked, "What's all this then? Cosmin didn't kill Misho. A group o' Ashlings and their sympathizers did."

Ellinor's cheeks began burning, her fingers itching for her knives, before she barked out a harsh laugh. "You didn't tell them, Kai? What really happened?"

Kai shook his head. "Not my story to tell, boss. Never was. Besides, you know I don't rightfully believe Cosmin did it on purpose. Rotten bad luck, that's what it was."

Ellinor was tempted to punch Kai again, but scowled at him instead. "Then let me educate you, all of you. This is the second time Cosmin has pulled crap like this, and he's going to keep doing it, and more people will needlessly die just so that joke-of-a-caster can stroke his ego over his own brilliance. He thinks he can play us like pieces on a chess board."

"Keep ya voice down, woman," Lazar growled. "Ya don't know who may be listening this far out. May be the police for Amaru, could be Eko and Irati searching for our signature. Air your dirty laundry later."

As if on cue, a rumbling sound could be heard far off in the distance. Ellinor couldn't tell if it was the Eagle Owl circling or not, but Lazar was right; it was best if they didn't take any chances. They were getting close enough to where any listening device worth its weight could pick up the sounds of their movement, even if they couldn't be physically seen yet.

She glowered at the seersha, but gave a deft nod in agreement. She stomped over to Kai and helped him move the broken push-cart a bit faster over the rough terrain, and waved to Pema and Talin to pick up the pace as well. "Fine," she said in an angry whisper, "once we're safe, at least for the night, you three are going to hear what I have to say." She gave Pema, Talin, and Kai a pointed glare. "This is important, and the sooner you see Cosmin for the selfish prick he is, the better. This will save your life, I'd bet my left tit on it."

Her old squad didn't respond. She didn't need them to. They all lowered their heads, and limped as close to the city's walls as they dared for the night, planning to still sneak in during the early morning deliveries. But even as sweat collected in the small of her back as she helped Kai, her toes curled within her boots, and her muscles quivered, and it had nothing to do with the heavy dreeocht container.

Cosmin's recklessness with keeping plans and suspicions to himself had done so much irreparable damage, and yet his soldiers still had such blind faith in the powerful seersha that Ellinor found it nauseating. She vowed to change that. She would make sure they all knew who Cosmin von Brandt really was and, hopefully once this mission was done, they'd all walk away from his employ before it got them killed.

THE REAL COSMIN
///CHAPTER EIGHTEEN

T HEY SCAMPERED across the rocky, destroyed land as quickly as they could. Most land between the major metropolises was a wasteland; resources were depleted to feed the thriving steel and neon jungle for miles around the gated city-states.

Most of the smaller municipalities had walls of some kind around them. The local governments often said it was for the citizen's protection, but really it was to keep their constituents contained. Entering the city wasn't impossible; you could drop the right person's name, grease the right palm, or buy the watchmen a beer, depending on how boring their shift had been. But to get out? That was a different story. The only way out was with a government issued passport: something hard to get, and even harder to fake with the microchip verifications in place.

The walls surrounding Amaru didn't so much glow, as suck the surrounding light in, making the barrier darker than the night. It was an old form of technology, and a nasty one, if

Ellinor was correct. If someone not permitted to exit, or enter, the city touched the wall, instead of jolting them with a high volt of electricity, it would suck all the fluid from their body, mummifying them instantly. Only the government could use magitech like that legally, but the magic inside was too powerful for the tech that held it and would need to be replenished each time the system went off.

Either the governor of Amaru had a plethora of air and water casters working for him that kept the wall charged at all times, or the government had made a deal with Dragan himself, who could replenish the magic with relative ease. It made Ellinor uneasy to think about a mobster like Dragan Voclain potentially working so close with the governing body of Amaru. It would make it more difficult to hide.

Everyone knew the elected officials, the government that kept Erhard "safe" from the other continents and nations across the sea, was a farce. The only source of true power the government had was in its mechanics. They ensured that certain magic-based technologies were outlawed. The combat and bio-tech from the government-controlled factories and machine shops outperformed anything the casters could create, lest they risk having their homes and factories raided and being thrown into a black box for the rest of their long lives.

Once the crew found a safe distance from the walls to set up camp, Ellinor helped Kai drape the camo tarps over the tents, and activated the dreeocht container's chameleon mode. Even with its battered and filthy state following their escape, the chameleon mode transformed the once sleek, coffin-like device so it appeared to be nothing more than a boring stack of celluloid parts.

Once done, Ellinor went to help Pema and Talin, but was stopped by Lazar, who waved her over then ambled a short distance away. How he could amble after the night—and day—they had, she had no clue, but she refused to show that she was impressed by his resilience.

"That's going to be a problem," he muttered, jerking his chin toward the wall.

Ellinor rolled her eyes. "You think?"

Lazar ignored her. "We're going to need passes to enter without getting detained. Even if we do go in with the morning deliveries."

"I'm assuming you're telling me this because you can get us said passes? Otherwise . . ."

Lazar grunted. "Yeah, I can get us passes. Y'all hang tight, I'll be back in a few hours."

Before Ellinor could ask anything else, the seersha was sneaking off. Ellinor told herself she didn't really want to know *how* he was going to get the city passes. She knew he was resourceful and damn sneaky, and figured he would find a way. That was all that mattered.

She shook her head and took a deep breath, trying to lessen the ache in her joints. But even if she had succeeded, all the meditative breathing on Eerden wasn't going to lessen the burning in her chest that had intensified with each step of the twelve mile hike.

Once the crew disappeared into the virtually invisible tent to rest and partake of the road rations they were able to save, Ellinor joined them. She ignored the disguised container, and the sleeping beast within, as she went.

Pushing open the flap, she noted Pema was fussing over Talin—her arm in a new sling, but her deep ebony skin was flushed and she was sweating with discomfort. Pema caught Ellinor eyeing the seerani and frowned. "The dislocation was worse than we thought. Damn thing damaged some nerves and arteries. She needs a proper doctor, you understand? Someone who can fix this and not some half used med-kit."

"Yo, baby, calm down. I've had worse, and worked with worse injuries, too. I'll be fine," Talin murmured. Neither Ellinor nor Pema believed her.

"Can you move it?" Ellinor asked cautiously.

Talin shrugged with her good arm. "Nah, but it wasn't my dominant arm anyway. You need me to make you some dirty explosive? I'm still good to go."

"You need a surgeon." Pema lowered her forehead to Talin's, her eyes shrouded as she examined the damaged elbow.

"Yeah? Well, so do you. Your ankle is all kinds o' fucked."

Ellinor pinched the bridge of her nose. "Look, it doesn't matter. Rest and use what healing supplies you can. Azer's abyss if I know what Lazar's doing exactly, but he's getting us passes for tomorrow and then he's getting us a ride to where we need to go. If we can spare time for someone to look at your injuries without asking questions, we will. I've no clue how long things will take tomorrow, but we've got to be cautious, yeah? Dragan's the seersha mob boss here, and he's an air caster."

Ellinor's hands began to tremble, unable to contain the burning within her chest any longer at seeing Pema and Talin's battered and bruised faces. "Oh, and there's still Irati, Janne, Mirza, and Eko out there looking for us, plus we have two dead soldiers whose families have no fucking clue they've lost someone!" By the end, her body was thrumming and she wanted to fling her Lacerators at someone.

Kai put his hand on her shoulder, pulling her onto one of the packs they had taken from the wreckage. Pema and Talin exchanged wary glances, but kept their opinions to themselves. Before Ellinor could shrug his hand off, Kai was thrusting a bottle of aged tequila into her face, forcing her to take it.

"Relax, Ell, we're on your side 'ere." Raising his own bottle of tequila—which made Ellinor wonder who had decided snagging alcohol was the smartest move when they were fleeing—Kai said, "Sorry it ain't whiskey, but let's pour one out for our fallen. To Embla!"

"Not Warin?" she asked.

"Fuck that guy," Pema grumbled, raising an empty cup for Kai to top off.

Ellinor nodded dully, watching Kai pour a healthy amount of the murky golden liquid to the ground before taking a swig himself. Ellinor had never been a fan of straight tequila. She usually needed it with something, or at the very least, a lot of salt. She took a small sip, grimaced, and passed the bottle to Talin.

"Irati's not the only reason we're missing people," Ellinor said. While her need to stab someone was tempered for the moment, her rage still simmered beneath the surface, and it was time she made good on her promise to enlighten the crew.

"Ah, not this again, Ell," Kai mumbled, reaching for the tequila.

"Yes, this again. If you didn't tell Pema and Talin what really went down the day Misho died, then I will. They deserve to know, especially after what happened today. Shit, everything about this mission reeks of what happened with me and

Misho! So, while we wait for Lazar to get back, I'm going to tell them."

"I do love a good story," Talin muttered, hand curled around the neck of the tequila bottle. "Too bad we ain't got a fire going, stories are great for roasting things over a fire."

"This is serious, Talin, and, given all the crap we've dealt with, it may save your life."

Pema's eyes darkened, her brow furrowing like it always did when someone spoke to Talin in such a way, but Ellinor ignored her. "Think about it for a second. Cosmin has this really valuable treasure, yeah? He's got to ship it halfway across Erhard in secret and he can't send any casters and this," she said, waving at the four of them, "is who he sends? Does that look right to you? Sure, you guys are all great, you serve Cosmin well, but you aren't exactly his elite team. He says it's because having my old team here is going to keep me in line or some bullshit, but with this shackle, I'm no threat. Not to him or his cargo. So tell me, why is he sending *anyone* but his covert operatives on this all-important trip?"

Sullen silence answered her. Kai wouldn't look at her, but both Talin and Pema glared at her with hurt disbelief. Ellinor sighed, scrubbing at her forehead.

"Look, Eko isn't his best pilot. He's a great mechanic, but the best? Not by a long shot. Irati and Mirza work well together—or did—but they aren't the best at covert missions. I mean, outside of her being a sharpshooter, they have no covert training. And Janne, Warin, and Embla? Maybe I can see Janne, she's not bad at killing people in the dark, all quiet like, but the other two? What business did they have on this trip? And you, Pema? You aren't a covert operative either. Talin, while I enjoy seeing you, what does Cosmin need an explosives expert for on this trip?"

She held up her hand, stalling Pema from interrupting. "I know you asked Cosmin for a favor, but that doesn't mean shit to Cosmin and you know it. Honestly, the only ones who make sense are Kai and Lazar."

Kai's eyes brightened, a half smile tugging on his lips at the idea of Cosmin needing him. Ellinor frowned at him in return. "Sorry to break it to you, big guy, but he didn't send you on this escort mission because your skills are invaluable. Think about what you've done the whole time since this thing started. You've watched me and pushed the dreeocht around. That's all he needed you for."

The three of them stared at her, Talin and Pema with scowls on their faces, but a dark shadow over their gazes, letting her know they were mulling over her words. Kai slumped back against the gear he was sitting against, his chin sagging and eyes drifting to the side once her words sank in. Ellinor hated that Kai loved—genuinely loved—Cosmin. It would eventually get him hurt, or worse.

"Cosmin's pulled this kind of crap before, when he feels like there's a rat but doesn't know who it is. He uses his valuable cargo as bait to see who snaps at him, and from where. He doesn't consider that he may be sending people to their deaths. He's more concerned with figuring out who's going to betray him and catching them in the act. He's just so arrogant that he assumes the few people whom he believes he can trust infallibly will be able to handle whatever trouble he brings on them, and it gets people killed. Every. Single. Time."

"That's what you think happened here? And what happened to you and Misho?" Pema asked, a forced smirk on her face, as she lit a cigarette. But her gravelly voice held no conviction in her sarcasm.

"It's what I *know* happened. It's fact, Pema." Ellinor shut her eyes for a moment, once more seeing that small silver flash drive lying next to the dying Ashling. The little drive that held all the evidence she needed. She recalled jamming it into a computer and all the files of Cosmin's secret projects flashed before her eyes once more, as if it were happening right now and not eight years in the past.

Shaking her head, she opened her eyes and leveled her gaze on Kai, who stared at the tequila bottle clutched in his hands. "You see, Misho and I thought we were just guarding some powerful technology that, in the wrong hands, could be used to bring Cosmin in, get him charged with a crime, and give up the game. It was supposed to be all routine, yeah? Just me and Misho watching a warehouse. Then these Ashlings and their humani sympathizers show up and, well, you know what happened next. From the moment they busted in and ambushed us, it didn't sit well with me. It was too hardcore a force, even for that kind of technology. Turns out I was right.

"This Ashling had a drive on zer, and I snagged it about the time Cosmin finally sends help, despite sensors going off like crazy to tell him some serious shit is going down. Something just nagged at me about it, so I took that drive. Forgot all about it though, when they took . . . when they carried out . . ."

Ellinor paused, hands clenching and eyes stinging as the memory forced itself upon her. Of seeing medical staff rushing in to try and save anyone they could, but everyone was dead. Ellinor had made sure of that, once there was no bringing Misho back. Kai shifted as if he would give her some kind of embrace, and she cleared her throat, hunching her shoulders forward and away from him.

"I forgot all about the stupid thing until after the funeral. That's when I load it up, and you know what I see? I see plans, intercepted files, and designs for the thing me and Misho were really guarding. Cosmin told us it could be devastating in the wrong hands, but turned out that asshole *was* the wrong hands. He didn't have smart technology that could be given to just any bot to turn it into an Ashling. Oh no! He was actually *making* Ashlings, or trying. According to what I found, Cosmin was trying to make an even smarter war machine, some sophisticated bot that didn't need programing and that functioned like any living lieutenant or sergeant on the field. Something that was truly sentient, but had its free will stripped away. It'd be aware, but unable to do anything against orders. Sounds familiar, yeah? That's because it's what the fucking Ashlings fight against! It's the same shit those Ashling Juice Box manufacturers want so they can come out of hiding on Amardeep and turn our tech against us."

"Yo," Talin interrupted. "That don't mean anything. Means Cosmin's plans got found out. That's shitty work sure, but that doesn't mean Cosmin got your man killed. Just means he was doing something dumb and got caught is all."

"That's what I been trying to tell you, Ell. Cosmin didn't mean for it to go down like that," Kai added.

"The fuck he didn't," Ellinor growled, nearly jumping to her feet. Clearing her throat again, she turned her gaze back to Talin, who sat wide-eyed, and Pema, who continued to maintain her stony visage, taking long drags on her cigarette.

"At first, I thought it was bad luck, or whatever you want to call it, too. Then I get to thinking, yeah? I start wondering how these Ashlings knew what Cosmin was really doing. Because that's not up for debate. He was making, or trying to make, some murderous Ashling half-breed. You can ignore how deplorable that is if you want, but don't you forget it, either. Anyway, there's still no way these Ashlings could have known what Cosmin's up to. Zeyr aren't even based in Erhard! So I start digging and you guys remember that old mechanic Cosmin used to have? The one who worked alongside Eko? Logain? Ever wondered what happened to him? Why he went missing about the time Misho was buried?"

She waited for a moment, but even Kai was silent, once more avoiding her gaze. Everyone remembered Logain and how he vanished one day. Cosmin didn't speak his name again, as if he never existed. Ellinor dropped her eyes, fixating on the half empty bottle in Kai's hands as the memory continued to raise her body temperature until she was sweating.

"Cosmin had a *suspicion*, you see. Thought someone was trying to betray him. He was right, in a way, just wasn't sure how or why, or any of the details about the betrayal. Cosmin has some sixth sense about stuff like that. So he sets it up so someone, whoever the rat is, will want to act. But because he didn't know how or who, he pretended like nothing was going on. Gives me and Misho what should be an easy assignment that wouldn't look odd to outsiders, or anyone else for that matter. He gives the assignment to people he knows he can trust, and who he hopes can handle damn near anything—again, without looking suspicious, yeah? Otherwise he'd put his generals all over that shit.

"Cosmin gets his suspicions confirmed, and his operations stay safe, but given the attention, he figures it's not worth it, so he stops construction. And all it cost him was Misho.

Now you tell me, doesn't that smell of what's happening here? That's the kind of man Cosmin is. He's selfish, and those who pledge themselves to him are expendable, as long as his operations don't get messed up in the process. He knew someone was a bit too interested, or just figured with a prize like a dreeocht, someone would try and make a move. So he assembled a team he could live without. That's what we all are to him. People he can live without."

Pema shook her head slowly, as if coming up from a dream, her olive skin flushed. "You don't know that, though. You don't know that Cosmin *knew* what was going to go down. You're just making assumptions. What actual proof do you have?"

Ellinor tried to keep her lip from quivering into a snarl as she glanced at the sergeant. "I confronted the bastard about it."

Talin sucked in a breath, and even Kai winced. No one accused Cosmin like that, not unless they wanted to have their bones set on fire right then and there.

Pema's eyes narrowed. "And he what? Confessed?"

Ellinor's shoulders bunched and she ground her teeth. "Not exactly. But he didn't deny it, either. He just, I don't know. He shrugged it off. Like it was no big deal if I was right, wrong, or that Misho was dead because of it. Like none of that mattered. Would an innocent man act so indifferently? The fact that I'm still alive after a *discussion* like that should be culpability enough."

Kai scratched at the back of his neck. "Like I said before, just because he didn't right out deny doesn't mean he knew a thing 'bout what Logain was gonna do. You got no physical proof, you never did. It's a shame 'bout Misho, a real tragedy.

Don't mean Cosmin knew what would happen. He didn't set you or Misho up."

Talin was chewing a nail on her good hand, and Pema stared at the floor, withdrawn and brooding, cigarette forgotten in her fingers. Even if they weren't willing to accept what she knew in her gut as a fact about the kind of man Cosmin was, they were at least thinking about it. Kai would never be able to consider such things, but it was a start. If she pushed—or shook them, like she wanted to—she would ensure they never considered her words, let alone try and look at what happened then and compare it to now with the same kind of objectivity.

Shrugging, Ellinor tried to act as if it didn't matter. Like she didn't care if they believed her. Getting up and stretching to hide her tense muscles, she said, "Just think about it, yeah? I'm going to scrounge up some food. Any takers?"

To a chorus of grunts, Ellinor began to scavenge more of the travel rations that had made it through their mad dash away from the burning transport. But Ellinor had no appetite. She watched the crew eat, her thoughts far away, and wrapped the cape attached to her armor tightly around her, pretending it was Misho's arms instead a sophisticated piece of combat-tech hidden within swathes of fabric.

By the time they had eaten their meager meal, Lazar returned. He wore a big grin, making his greenish-yellow eyes twinkle. He wouldn't share the cause of his mirth, instead, he handed them each a pass that would allow them access into Amaru.

Plopping down on the ground, a self-satisfied grin plastered on his face, he said, "We leave before first light. Get some rest; it's going to be a fun day tomorrow."

WHAT SPEAKS LOUDER
THAN MONEY?
///CHAPTER NINETEEN

"A GOVERNMENT visitors pass, really?" Talin Roxas scoffed, inspecting the badge Lazar had given them the night before more closely.

Lazar shrugged, fishing a new cigar from his ragged pants. Ellinor assumed the seersha had gotten a fresh supply while skulking around Amaru, as she had a hard time believing he had rescued any from their smoldering craft.

"Ya can read, can't ya?" Lazar grumbled, chewing on the end of the cigar. "It doesn't have to do anything but get us past them nasty walls on the down low. Don't go waving it about or anything, and it'll be fine like good wine. There's a bar not far from where I need to go. Y'all wait there, and if ya stay put, shit won't hit the fan."

Talin shrugged with her good shoulder and went to help Pema stuff their provisions into packs that were easily transportable. The crew had snagged a few backpacks that Cosmin had used Ellinor's previously donated magic on. There was a dollop of air magic held within a small piece of a manufactured gem that a clever mechanic had connected to the bag. They could pack up to two hundred and fifty pounds into the bags and the magic held most of the weight by manipulating the current around the backpack into a dense pressure pocket that made the bag feel, well, light as air.

Ellinor eyed the bags, heat flushing through her body at Cosmin still benefiting from the magic she had given him long before her departure. But the heat radiating through her was soon replaced by a hollowness in her chest as she tried to reach out for her magic. She was greeted by such a profound emptiness that tears stung the back of her eyes, and all she wanted to do was curl into a ball away from everyone and everything until the collar rusted off.

As if sensing she were about to wallow in something he didn't understand, Lazar bumped her shoulder with his elbow. She was slow to look at him, but when her eyes settled on his, he thrust a small box at her, his big eyes holding a shadow of sympathy behind his new glasses. She raised her brow, but he didn't say anything until she relieved him of the property.

"The passes won't do us any good if ya so much as make eye contact with anyone." Ellinor gently handled a pair of contact lenses, comprehension making her shoulders feel heavy. "They aren't the good kind—couldn't get a pair of those without suspicion—but they're a dark enough color to hopefully lessen the, er . . . " Lazar trailed off, his eyes drifting from her bright, tropical ocean blue ones to the collar around her neck. "Well, it'll hide what ya are, that's all that matters. Think of some other cute name for yerself and no one should know what—*who* ya are."

Sighing, she gingerly placed the contact lenses in her eyes. She blinked her tears away and helped the rest of the injured crew pack up their gear—including the dreeocht container that still looked like stacks of innocuous crates—and headed for the city walls.

None of them spoke along the way, well aware the police on the wall may have devices that would pick up their conversation. Besides, they all knew this was Lazar's expertise and the seersha would need to do all the talking when it came to duping Dragan's men and the government employees until they could get out of Amaru.

Lazar motioned for them to stay back as he approached the main gate. Ellinor could only make out a few of the words exchanged between the seersha and humani guard. From what she gathered, Lazar fed the man some line about having their convoy ambushed by lawless deadland dwellers not far off, and they needed to contact their main office to get put back on track.

Most of the officials from one city didn't care for government types from other city-states. But it was common courtesy to not interfere with the legal comings and goings of the men and women who, supposedly, ran the continent. The guard grumbled at Lazar, waving them in, and made it clear their presence was barely tolerated.

But it would be tolerated, Ellinor mused, trying to hide the relief threatening to blossom over her filthy face.

On the fringes of Amaru, the city didn't feel as oppressive. The skyscraper's shadows barely touched them this far out, the cloud of exhaust from air transports scarcely tickled Ellinor's nose, and the vibrations of the ground vehicles and the powerful elevators that raced from the bottom of the sky-scrapers to the top barely registered beneath her feet.

Even so far from the center where Dragan's influence would be greatest, however, Ellinor didn't feel safe. No matter how much Kai assured her the contacts made her eyes look more a dull gray than their unnaturally bright blue, Ellinor felt like every gaze lingered on her a moment longer than it should.

They hadn't walked more than ten minutes before Lazar stopped and waved them toward a synth-club and dive bar. "Wait there, I'll be back in a few hours and then we can shove off to somewhere I can get a message to Cosmin and Zabel. We'll see what they want us to do next." But Lazar didn't sound all that hopeful, which made Ellinor's stomach clench as he lobbed off, and the rest of them hobbled into the bar.

That time of morning, there was no one in the bar save the beleaguered bartender, no doubt still recovering from a busy night, and a synth-bot plugged into the wall, recharging after a night of pumping electronic beats that always perfectly reflected the mood of the patrons.

The nicer synth-clubs had live singers who would dance and interact with the crowd. The singers didn't have to carry a tune, the synth-bots handled that for them, but they did have to be alluring and sensual enough to make everyone—men and women, seersha and humani—feel like they had a shot at taking them home. Those who could sing, and had all the other physical qualifications, were usually employed in the clubs owned and operated by the mobster casters in the city.

The man behind the bar scowled at them, but Pema limped toward him anyway. She fed him the same line Lazar used earlier and flashed her badge. The man's frown didn't lessen, but he glanced over the badge, grumbled something, and jutted his chin toward a booth, leaving them alone without audible complaint.

Pema slid into her seat and said, "He'll bring food in a minute. He said we could use his employee's restroom so we don't look like we just got real friendly with the ground, too."

"He said all that, did he?" Talin cooed.

Pema winked at her. "No, but my universal credit chip did."

Talin chuckled. "Nice. Which alias you use this time?"

"Lyra. It's the cleanest identity I've got with the deepest pockets." Pema glanced at Ellinor, then at the bathroom, and nodded to herself. "We're good here, you can get to the restroom without getting too far from the dree—uh, the *cargo*. You go first, Lieutenant."

Ellinor flinched, as if the title burned her skin. Pema shook her head and held up her hand before Ellinor could voice her protest. "Look, you saved our asses back there. I may not agree with your views on the boss, but you did right by me and . . . Embla. You'll always be my lieutenant. I trust you, you follow me? Sorry about giving you the cold shoulder back on the Mamba and the Eagle Owl, but you leaving all those years ago without a heads up? It stung. You didn't just leave the boss, you left *us*, and that shit wasn't okay. But after the stunt Irati pulled?" Pema ran her fingers through her hair, sneering down at the table. "All I'm saying is, I'm glad you're back," she finished, extending her hand for Ellinor to take.

She hesitated, but Pema was right. It hadn't been fair to her team to walk out on them like she had Cosmin. They deserved better than that. Clasping Pema's hand, Ellinor gave a deft nod, and headed into the bathroom.

Flicking on the switch, she stifled a groan as the harsh fluorescent light illuminated the small room. She knew she was in need of a shower, she just hadn't known how desperately. Her face was a collection of puckering purple bruises, scrapes, and soot. Eyes ringed in red from the toll of being disconnected from her powers. Her raven black hair an oily mess, the purple tendrils at the base of her neck as limp and dull as oddly colored dead snakes. Turning on the faucet, she dunked her hands under the warm water. She watched them tremble, allowing the fear and panic she kept at bay to ebb from her system in this one private moment.

She would let herself feel all the burning hatred, the rage, and sorrow she had for those she lost and those who had put them in harm's way for just this moment. No one needed to know how hard her heart thumped in her chest. How she couldn't seem to get enough air in her lungs since her abilities were muted and she had learned of Misho's power being sucked away by a slumbering being of pure magic. Or how there was a painful itching in the back of her throat for all the words she swallowed, and all the times she wanted to scream.

No, all they would see was their lieutenant of old.

They needed to believe she was cool and collected because, if they didn't, she would have no shot at returning to Cosmin and being welcomed into his embrace. No chance to plunge her modified Leviathan Roaster deep into his craven heart. She washed up as best she could in the sink, though there was little she could do for her hair or the abrasions underneath her armor, and pinched her cheeks to help lessen the ashy pallor they had taken, then headed back to the booth.

There was a pile of fried eggs, greasy bacon, hard bread, warm butter, sweet jam, and large mugs of oil-black coffee waiting for her, and she dug in as if there wasn't a hard pit in her stomach making everything taste a little sour. While they ate and took turns in the bathroom, Ellinor commandeered a wall socket and began charging her armor and shield once more, just in case.

The hours they spent waiting for Lazar were productive, at least. Kai found a squirrelly doctor nearby who didn't mind seeing visiting *government officials* for the right amount, and for a bit extra, he was willing to come to the dingy bar.

The little man's clothes were filthy, covered in grime from the lower levels, ripped and torn so often that the patches needed patching. His eyes twitched behind thick, metal-rimmed glasses, but at least his hands were steady and relatively clean. "There's not much I can do without taking you back to my office," he murmured, voice low and soft.

Kai laid his scattergun on the table. "Not gonna happen, friend."

Ellinor almost snickered at the doctor's loud gulp in response. "Very well, I guess what I have is more than what you've got at your disposal? Yes, well, let's get started then."

By the time he left, Pema's ankle was neatly wrapped and no longer as swollen as it once was, Talin's face no longer pinched in discomfort from her elbow, and the gash above Kai's eye had been properly closed. They were still a far cry from being back to their old selves, but it was a step in the right direction.

Pema lit a cigarette and ordered another beer as the bar began filling with the lunch crowd. Most were delivery drivers getting off from late night and early morning shifts, and paid the group no mind. But a few were police who manned the walls. Those men and women watched Ellinor and the group a little more closely. They tried to hide it through side-long glances, disguising their movements by drinking or stretching, but Ellinor noted their lingering looks.

Ellinor shot Kai a glance and nudged his foot under the table, alerting him to the attention. He grunted, and positioned himself to better reach the dreeocht, should they need to run. Pema and Talin watched him move, their faces darkening as comprehension fell on them.

Pema groaned softly in turn, snuffing out her cigarette and downing the last of her beer, then brushed off Talin's frown with a gentle touch. "What? Wasn't going to waste it. It's not bad either, given where we are."

Talin rolled her eyes, but stopped mid-roll as the doors to the bar swung open and a group of private military types entered. Their armor was similar to what Ellinor wore—form fitting combat-tech suits that were meant to absorb magical attacks and turn most projectiles when properly charged. All their suits were the same heather-grey color, making them stand out from the red and black uniforms of the police.

"Time to go," Kai muttered, as one of the soldiers bumped one apparently in charge, jerking her chin in their general direction. Kai lumbered to his feet as if he were just another drunk, and grabbed the disguised dreeocht container on its rickety push-cart.

Once he was moving, Ellinor turned a feigned sleepy look to Pema, hoping the soldiers at the door would think they were a group of late night workers who treated the mid-afternoon like everyone else treated their evenings. "Staggered exit," she whispered. "Wait for me to get past the restroom before you follow. But don't do the drunk-in-love act. That only attracts more looks."

"Does not. It's easy and makes the dudes in the room think about other things than a pair o' women leaving under odd circumstances," Talin murmured.

It was hard to maintain her air of forced levity under the circumstances, and Ellinor felt her eye twitch. "You can help each other out, but seriously, don't paw at one another. It attracts too much attention. If you get us caught, or killed, Talin, I swear my ghost will come back and kick your ass. You know I'm good for it."

"Please, you've been gone a long time, Ell. Pema would avenge me."

Pema grinned at her girlfriend. "Me and my spirit aren't getting involved. We'll be waiting for you in paradise, lounging in the arms of a bunch of buxom, naked ladies. You're on your own for that one."

Talin was exaggerating a pout, but Ellinor could take no more. Frowning at her, she said, "Talin, seriously, be smart."

Talin's face flushed, but before she could answer, Ellinor's collar buzzed, letting her know the container was getting out of range and she had to move. Pushing to her feet, she pretended to stumble out. She glanced over her shoulder once and was met by a wall of angry stares as the group of soldiers looked up from the screen they were studying on their commander's armband.

Her heart pounded in her chest and her stomach began churning again. She hadn't taken more than a few steps before the soldiers moved toward her. Ellinor didn't wait for them to catch up, nor did she waste time signaling Pema or Talin. She bolted for the back door, running to catch up with Kai before she and Cosmin's prize were caught.

A MESSY EXIT
///CHAPTER TWENTY

ELLINOR BURST into the dark alley, her eyes falling on Kai a second later as he maneuvered the dreeocht's container into a side street too narrow for trucks. She raced after him, only belatedly wondering how—and where—Lazar was supposed to find them now. The sound of Talin and Pema crashing out of the bar cut off her thoughts, new thugs close on their heels.

Pema had barely cleared the door when Talin tossed a flash and tear gas grenade behind her—a special design she'd come up with herself—and then shut the door. There was a muffled *BANG* followed by shouts and crashes from behind the door.

Pema helped barricade the exit with debris left in the alley before slapping Talin's ass. "Nice one," she chuckled, before hobbling across the street.

Skidding into the alcove near Kai, Ellinor panted, "How fast can you push that thing?"

Kai frowned more with his eyebrows than his lips as he watched Pema and Talin approach. "Not fast enough. If that be

Dragan's personal men and not just some thugs looking to rob the outsiders? Ah, shit, Ell, we ain't getting far with this thing and two injured ladies in tow."

Ellinor glanced at the hastily blocked door as Pema and Talin joined them in their hiding spot. The barricade wouldn't hold for long. She didn't want to hide herself in the throngs of people closer to the city center and lose Lazar, but they couldn't stay where they were, either.

"Fuck it. We're too exposed here. We need to get to higher ground, somewhere where we can control the access points. Kai, think you can climb with that thing?" Ellinor pointed to a building across the way with only one fire exit and high walls lining its roof.

Kai grunted. "Shit, Ell . . . I can try."

"I believe in you, buddy. You two good to climb that?"

Pema's face was twisted in agony just looking at the rusted ladder, but she never got a chance to answer. A roaring sound filled the alley, drowning out everything else.

Ellinor cringed as the back door of the bar was blown apart by the blast of a scattergun, and lurched back as a beat up delivery van raced down the road, the brakes engaging at the last moment, the tires smoking as they skidded to a halt on the pavement. The sudden appearance momentarily stalled the thugs, giving Lazar Botwright enough time to poke his head out the window.

His eyes were so wide they nearly took up his whole forehead. "I told ya to keep a fucking low profile!" Snarling as the goons recovered and began trying to flank the vehicle, Lazar shouted, "Get loaded up, and do it quick. Ellinor, give them cover or we'll be fucked twice over. Jelani, get ready to peel out like the abyss is coming to swallow ya."

Ellinor's hackles raised at the unfamiliar name, but she couldn't think about that when seven guards squared off against them, some with snot and tears still running down their puffy cheeks, curtesy of Talin's grenade. Pema and Talin struggled to get the dreeocht safely inside the van, Lazar shielding them as best he could. Ellinor was glad she'd taken the time to charge her armor and shield as she yanked her Lacerators from the holsters at her waist.

Her damaged hand throbbed as she spun the special karambit knives around her fingers, sending them sailing through the air at rapid speed, the black steel no more than a blur, closing the distance and ripping through two of the assailants, taking chunks out of their raised arms. Before they could even register that she had thrown the Lacerators, she'd recalled them and was preparing to launch them once more. The attackers dove for cover before she could throw them again, all except one.

One of the bolder thugs made a break for Ellinor, sprinting at her from the corner of her vision. She couldn't move out of the way. Kai took one large step into the path of the aggressor, swinging his scattergun like a bat. The man's head snapped back with a *crunch*, and he collided with the building across the alley.

A red laser sight appeared on Kai's chest, the sound of a rifle being cocked overly loud in Ellinor's ears. She gasped, and slid in front of Kai, activating her shield a second too late.

"Don't kill that one," an uninjured soldier barked. "Boss wants her alive!"

Ellinor's heart slowed at his words, a sour taste filling her mouth. Swallowing, she put her Lacerators back, thumbed the latch off her pistols, and motioned for Kai to help Talin and Pema. Ellinor cleared her throat, "Don't know what you're talking about, or what you think you're doing. We've got government passes; we're just passing through. The name's Margot, see? Says so right on the badge." It didn't say any such thing. But Ellinor flashed the badge at them anyway and hoped it was enough.

A few of the goons exchanged guarded glances, but the uninjured man wasn't fazed. "Bullshit. We know who you are. Dragan was real clear on it. So come quietly and we won't waste the rest of your people."

Ellinor thought she'd need to pound on her chest to get her heart beating in a normal cadence. *How did he find us?*

Andrey's voice growled through her head. *Figure it out later. You're facing trained operatives and have no use of your magic. If you don't act first, they'll take you.*

Taking a deep breath, Ellinor channeled the persona she had cultivated since leaving Cosmin. She lowered her shield, giving the group in front of her a wicked smile that was mostly teeth before jerking up the hood of her armor and saying, "That was a mistake. You clearly don't know *who* I am, do you?"

No one answered, and she forced a demonic grin. "Yet another mistake. I'm not impressed with your boss's performance so far. And honestly, I've already been bundled up in a cell this week, I've met my quota for the year."

Before her assailants could decide to sneer, chuckle, or be afraid, Ellinor charged. She sprinted straight at them, her hand gripping her double barrel Dunstan Anaconda and firing before Dragan's men even knew what was happening.

Three of Dragan's people fell to the ground in agony seconds later. Three-on-one were odds she was better acquainted with.

The soldiers reacted with a chorus of cursing. They lobbed an electric grenade over her head, hoping to dismantle the van and short circuit her armor, but Lazar's reflexes were just as good as Janne's, if not better. He caught the grenade and threw it back at the soldiers. Ellinor heard the faint buzzing sound as it went off, disabling two of the soldier's mechanized suits. She dove for them first, yanking her high-carbon steel knife free.

Still twitching, one of the men tried to punch her in the jaw, but she deflected the blow and grabbed him by his shoulders, twisting him around to absorb the shot of a scattergun from the uninjured man. He cursed, and while he reached for another weapon, Ellinor stabbed the man she held three times in quick succession, her knife slicing through his disabled armor and into his heart with ease. She flung his dead body at the uninjured soldier before he could ensnare her with an electric net, and lunged for the other combatant whose armor had been short-circuited.

Before she could reach him, her shield flared to life. It splayed out, the small metal flaps making a faint snapping sound as they meshed together like snake scales to deflect the tranquilizer darts fired at her. Maneuvering while her shield kept morphing was difficult, but practice had made it a complicated ballet with Ellinor at the center.

She ran at the other soldier and leapt on him, her boots slamming on his chest. She let the momentum drive them down, her knife sliding into his throat, before she used the same momentum to push off his chest and back to where the last two soldiers remained.

"You shouldn't have fucked with me," spat Ellinor as she ripped her other pistol free from its holster and sprang at the men, her cape flapping behind her. She fired, hitting a soldier who looked to have been about Embla's age. That's when the uninjured soldier, the one giving all the orders, decided trying to *not* hurt Ellinor wasn't an option anymore. As the last of his men fell, he unleashed a handful of mechanical bees.

Similar to the dragonflies Cosmin had in his grand meeting rooms, these little pieces of combat-technology were both pretty and deadly. The bees swarmed at Ellinor, moving around her in a way her shield couldn't block. One of the bees slipped passed her shield, stinging her repeatedly. Her armor struggled to absorb the blasts of air the bee was trying to deposit into her veins that would give her an embolism. She batted it away, only to be stung by another as she tried to get to the soldier. She knew her armor would give out soon.

"I can't get a clear shot, Ell!" Kai yelled, tracking her with his scattergun.

She waved him back, stumbling, a scorching heat starting to radiate from her collar.

She didn't understand what was happening. The bee's illegally stored air magic was being deposited directly into her bloodstream; she knew this as fact. She felt the bees get to the unprotected parts of her body. But something about the collar was affecting the bee's deposited magic.

The sound of the last goon stomping toward her, and the frantic thumping of Talin throwing things from her backpack, looking for a device to incapacitate the mechanical bees was almost lost to the buzzing in Ellinor's ears. The collar got hotter and hotter, and constricted as if parts were fusing to her skin, but Dragan's weaponized bees didn't incapacitate her.

Despite the confusion screaming at her that this was strange and nothing good could come of it, her survival instinct didn't allow her to slow down, not when there was an armed goon facing her.

She pushed through the mechanical insects, her fist connected with his temple before he could draw his combat-tech sword from his waist. He stumbled and she grabbed the back of his head, slamming his nose on her knee. As he bounced off her, she kicked him in the gut hard enough to send him sliding into the wall of the bar. Before he could recover, she grabbed her Lacerator and threw it at him, the karambit knife burying itself in the side of his neck.

"I don't belong to Dragan *or* Cosmin. Never forget that," Ellinor barked. She recalled the weapon, the curved blade tearing through the man's throat, before she dashed back to the delivery van as the assassin lay gurgling in a growing pool of his own blood.

Lazar threw the side door open for her and dove for the passenger side, the dreeocht and the rest of the crew safely tucked into the back of the sizable old van. As she jumped in and turned to close the door, Ellinor saw an infiltrator drone hovering over the carnage.

Infiltrator drones were simple robots—essentially cleverly hidden cameras meant to blend in with the surroundings. The fact that this one had moved and made itself obvious meant someone had direct control of that specific bot. And given that Dragan's men knew who she was and what they were carrying, Ellinor assumed it was Dragan watching them, and that he wanted her to know it.

Pema followed her gaze, leveled her scattergun, and shot the drone down. "Suck it, Dragan," she growled.

"Haul ass out of here! We're going to have some heavy heat coming down on us real soon if we don't find a way out of Amaru," Ellinor said, her voice quivering in time with the rest of her insides. Her unease with the suddenly enclosed space intensified at the prospect that a powerful air caster might be on his way.

She pawed at the collar around her neck as the van lurched forward. It felt . . . different, but she couldn't say how. Ellinor could still get her fingers under it to yank at it, but it felt closer to her skin, more embedded, somehow. Shivering at the idea, she tried to distract herself with other thoughts.

It was then Ellinor registered that Lazar Botwright was not driving, but someone she had never seen before.

A NEW WINGMAN
///CHAPTER TWENTY-ONE

T HE OLD, cracked leather surrounding the dashboard groaned as Lazar's hands clenched on it. "What did ya do, hmm? What in the abyss did ya do for them to find ya? I'm gone for five fucking hours and Dragan's people find ya? Ya'll call that laying low?"

Ellinor had never seen Lazar so furious. Gone was his cool indifference and unflappable persona. Even under the barrage of Irati's bullets, and as their transport crashed to the ground, she hadn't seen the seersha get this manic—or terrified—before.

"We didn't do anything, you follow me?" Pema Tran lurched around Ellinor to shove Lazar in the arm, completely ignoring the new face driving the vehicle. "We sat there, ordered food, cleaned up, and got a doctor to come and see to the injuries. We were careful."

Lazar's face paled, giving a sickly pallor to his reddish-bronze skin. "How did ya pay for that doctor?"

Pema frowned. "With a universal credit chip tied to an alias of mine. A *clean* identity, got that? Cosmin had his guys scrub it and everything."

"The name ya use for this alias wouldn't happen to be Lyra, would it?"

Pema blinked rapidly back at him. "How did you know that?"

"You stupid, stupid, woman—"

"Yo man, lay off," Talin interrupted.

"Silence, child!" Lazar bared his teeth at her. "That's how they found the lot of ya. Jelani here heard chatter about some Lyra woman being flagged as a fake just before we headed back this way. A hot tip about some priceless cargo. I'm guessing that yer *team* knew about the identities? Because Cosmin issued them a bunch too?" Pema slowly nodded. "Yeah, figured. Yer bitch Irati, or maybe her quiet partner Mirza, gave the lot of ya up. Probably couldn't get into Amaru, but figured we'd have to come through it, and she must have given a list of yer identities to Dragan. The second ya used that credit chip, ya got pinged."

He blew out a heavy sigh, the smoky residue of his cigar on his breath filling the van. "There was a reason for the secrecy in getting that container out of Euria. Rumors were already flying. People knew what Cosmin had and couldn't keep. Bet it didn't take much for a rat like Irati to get a message to Dragan and for him to believe the rumors. Probably cut the same deal with him as she did her contact in Magomed. What in the abyss were ya thinking?"

"I wasn't, okay? I didn't think Irati would be able to get a message to Dragan. Not that fast anyway," Pema moaned, rubbing her palms into her eyes. "Talin was in pain, my ankle hurt like a bitch, Kai was bleeding . . . I didn't think it through, I admit. Given how much my head's been kicked around the past twelve hours, yeah, in retrospect, it was dumb. But it's done. Now we gotta get out of this mess, you follow?"

Lazar glowered and threw his fake badge at her. Pema lurched forward as if she would tear his long ears off. Kai caught her about the waist and pushed her into Talin's arms, who, despite the deep frown on her face, knew to keep Pema from pummeling the seersha.

"Aye, it was a clusterfuck, but it's over now. How do we get out of 'ere? I assume you had a plan besides throwing a fit?" Kai said, trying not to lean against the dreeocht container but not having much luck.

Lazar glared out the window, his big eyes darting around every corner as they sped toward the outskirts of the city proper. "Jelani's our only hope of getting out of the city now. Cosmin and Zabel can't help us."

The driver, Jelani, inclined his head, but Ellinor couldn't get a good look at him other than to see he was a seersha with dusky silver-brown skin, and pointed ears, though not as large as Lazar's. His hair reminded Ellinor of fog. It was a soft, whitish grey and looked to always be in motion, freshly tousled, despite the windows being up.

"You trust this guy?" Ellinor said, her voice low, hand poised over her knife. "Who are you?"

Jelani snorted. "Jelani Tyrik Sharma, at your service. And Lazar doesn't trust anyone, but that doesn't keep him from calling in every favor he's owed. You have nothing to fear from me, Ellinor, I'll see you to safety." His voice was deep and rich, and it sent a shiver racing along the back of her skull that told her not to trust this man.

He gave her a slow, sidelong glance, his gaze lingering on her longer than she thought necessary, given the speed at which he was driving. His eyes were framed in thick, black lashes, and she thought she saw something like intrigue flash through them, but with their coloring, she couldn't be sure. His eyes were a deep indigo, like the night sky after a full moon has risen. Buried in the rich blue were dozens of flecks of lighter blues, making his eyes twinkle like the moon's reflection across ocean waves. All seersha had strange eyes in one fashion or another, but never had Ellinor seen a pair so unique.

Jelani smiled with half his mouth, his full lips tilted in such a way to make him look more relaxed than what the situation called for. He turned his attention back to the road. "Impressive work, by the way. I was worried I would need to step in and handle the situation. I confess I didn't believe Lazar when he said you and your people were capable of handling Dragan's men. Bravo to you for proving me wrong. I hate using my abilities and giving myself away in enemy territory."

Ellinor quirked a brow, sparing a glance at Pema, Talin, and Kai before answering, "Uh, thanks, I think?" Shaking her head, she frowned back at Jelani. "Are you a caster? Lazar, is he part of the *contingency* plan you made for Zabel and Cosmin?"

Lazar and Jelani glanced at one another, sharing a private grin before Lazar shook his head. "Jelani doesn't work for anyone anymore, not like that. He doesn't agree with how things work, so he tends to go his own way. I found him, or caught him, rather, trying to liberate some of my property, back in the day. But skill knows skill when they see it. I offered him passage out of Zabel's turf as long as he never said no to me when I needed his services.

"He's a caster, but just barely, and before you ask, it isn't in air, its earth, so he's of little use to Dragan. Outside of myself, the man knows the underground like no one's business. Knows how everyone, from the lawless who live in the middle of nowhere to Ashlings, get in and around the cities and how to move supplies. A good sort to know in a pinch."

"I've heard of you, of course, Ellinor," Jelani added, this time keeping his eyes forward. "You were making quite the stir in Euria for causing mayhem to the established system. Many I know, and helped, had grown to admire your efforts. It's a pity you're back helping Cosmin."

Ellinor shoved the back of Jelani's seat, nostrils flaring as her muscles clenched at the implication. "I don't help willingly. Get your facts straight, asshole." She jabbed a finger at her collar. "This means that unless I do everything he says, I'll never get my powers back. You understand? Only Cosmin, or some really skilled mechanic with a death wish, can take this shit off."

Jelani met her gaze through the rearview mirror, his starry night eyes darkening as if a cloud passed over them, his jaw clenching. "You didn't seek out a mechanic while you waited for Lazar?"

"Watch it, Sharma. Ellinor has a job to do, and she knows it," Lazar said, his voice holding the edge of a threat.

But it was a fair question. *Because then I'd never be welcomed back into Cosmin's embrace. I'd never get close enough to plunge my Leviathan Roaster into his heart to avenge Misho.*

But the hollow emptiness in her, whenever she reached for her abilities, was destroying her in a way similar to Misho's death. She barely knew who she was or what she was doing without her abilities, though no one else seemed to sense how damaging the collar was to her. She toyed with the idea of giving her lofty plans for revenge up so she could get her abilities back, but closed her eyes against the idea. She spent close to seven of the eight years since Misho died, plotting. She couldn't stop now; she couldn't give up. Not when she was this close, not when she had nothing left.

Ellinor stifled a sigh, her shoulders slumping as she leaned back in her seat. "Doesn't matter," she mumbled. "It's like Lazar says. I have a job to do."

Jelani spared her another glance in the rearview mirror. A fleeting look of interest—or possibly amusement—crossed his features before he focused on the road and getting them out of Amaru.

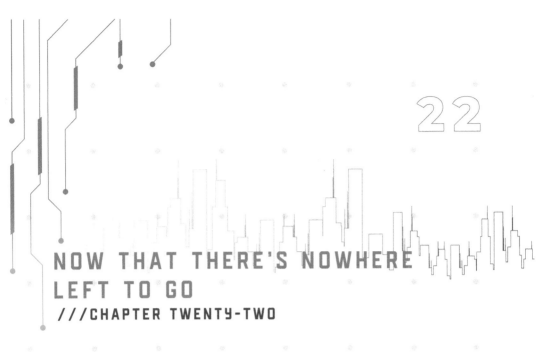

NOW THAT THERE'S NOWHERE LEFT TO GO
///CHAPTER TWENTY-TWO

U NDER DIFFERENT circumstances, Ellinor would have found Amaru charming. Unlike Euria, the skyscrapers didn't create hundred mile long shadows, and the exhaust from the transports didn't blot out the sky completely, turning those below into nocturnal creatures unfamiliar with the sun's rays. As Jelani raced through the city, Ellinor gained a new appreciation for the warehouses that went up only forty stories, the shop fronts that didn't fill their tall windows with nothing but electric screens advertising barely legal businesses.

She admired the tall apartments with projection façades over their steel walls transforming the buildings into charming red brick abodes like the vintage buildings of children's fables. In fact, the only way Ellinor knew it was a façade was when some punk humani kicked what Ellinor thought was a tree. The whole building flickered, showing the dark steel pillars and dingy plastic windows beneath.

There were still the casinos with their bright neon proclaiming anyone could be a winner, provided they lost enough
first, flimsy looking palm trees on their roofs bouncing back
and forth in the current created by the aerial transports. And
there still appeared to be a strip club, synth-bar, or coffee dis-
pensary on every other corner with glittering diamond white
lights around their entrances. But even with those businesses
looming over the others, Ellinor found she rather liked the
smaller town feel of Amaru. Or, rather, she liked the *idea*
of it. In practice, she wasn't sure she would like losing the
anonymity the enormous crowds of Euria afforded her.

The crew remained silent as Jelani Sharma crisscrossed
through the city, trying to get to some secret back exit before
Dragan used his own men or the enforcement officers in his
pocket to stop them. It gave Ellinor an opportunity to try and
forget the hulking dreeocht container wedged behind them,
making the decrepit van feel cramped as everyone tried to stay
as far from the slumbering creature as they could.

Ellinor focused her attention on the people and bots flashing by. Somewhere in the back of her mind she knew she
should be spending the time planning their next move. But
she was exhausted with merely trying to keep her body from
going into shock. Ellinor wanted to pretend like a dangerous
soldier and a powerful seersha weren't hunting for her, at least
for the moment. She had been in such situations on a pretty
much daily basis since Misho's death and was desperate for a
reprieve, even a temporary one.

Ellinor noted there were a greater number of bots out on
the street than there were in Euria. Most were service droids of
various kinds, zooming down the broken sidewalks and bumping over the potholes in the street on their way to make de-

liveries. But there were also more guard and bouncer androids of various forms. Most were stationary, the personal bot of individual store fronts and apartment complexes meant to keep vagrants out of the shops and homes. But a few were patrol robots used by the police, making sure that both aerial and ground-bound vehicles obeyed the laws. Ellinor shrank back from the window as they passed *those* bots.

When they came to a traffic stop, she glanced up to the illuminated metal pathways that allowed people to cross above the ground vehicles to get to the businesses located off ground level. There she spied a man and a woman arguing as the rest of the pedestrians gave them a wide berth.

Ellinor briefly watched the woman with bubblegum pink hair whip out a modified Lance blade that harnessed a bit of illegal fire magic. It was mainly for show; a burning blade wasn't as useful as, say, Janne's electric Lances. But when the blade burst into flame while the woman pulled down a visor that flickered to show a bright blue screen over her eyes, it did look scary.

As soon as the woman's blade was out, the tattoo-covered man tapped the side of his shaved head, and another combat-tech visor flared to life. A shimmering white bubble enveloped the man as he continued to yell. She smirked and thrust her blade at him. His nearly invisible electric shield surged around him, stopping the blade, and the man began to laugh.

Their van stuttered forward. Ellinor twisted in her seat, trying to keep the arguing couple in view as Jelani wove through traffic.

The woman's smirk turned into a grimace as she continued to push the knife, the man mocking her all the while. Then, the shield began to flicker and crackle, before it went out completely.

Ellinor snorted, her view momentarily unobstructed as they sped farther away. *That would never happen with my shield!*

The woman shoved her burning blade into the man's chest, yanked it free, and was running away before the man's knees hit the ground and the nearby patrol androids could respond to the murder.

Ellinor rolled her eyes, facing forward in her seat once more, watching the other vehicles race by as Jelani lost their van in the throng of trucks. On occasion, the less experienced people Ellinor worked with had made fun of her archaic shield. They claimed that using a shield that relied on morphing metal plates was out dated when she could be using shields with laser technology to deflect blows and magic attacks. The light shields were flashy and impressive looking, but they required so much energy that even the good ones didn't last long.

But such idle thoughts were wiped away as the van bounced over the uneven pavement toward some destination only Jelani and Lazar knew. It had been maybe ten minutes of driving, but Ellinor was growing antsy, feeling overly exposed in a vehicle that had no bullet proofing whatsoever. Its windows weren't even tinted.

"Where are we going?" Ellinor asked, sticking her head between the two seersha. "Are we almost out of Amaru?"

"Just about," Jelani answered. "There's an old service tunnel along the outskirts. The service automatons used to use it as a way to go in and out of the city without clogging traffic.

A pair of Ashlings collapsed half the tunnel a few years back and no one has gotten around to fixing it."

"Ashlings, was it?" Lazar eyed Jelani, his cat-like eyes glinting with a challenge.

Jelani didn't even give the older seersha a sidelong glance. "Yup, Ashlings. I can't take credit for that one, though I applaud their efforts. A contact of mine informed me of the tunnel. Thought I'd be able to use it to help some of the other Ashlings and zeyr friends get out of the city. I mainly monitor the tunnel now, making sure Dragan doesn't get wise to it. So far, so good. We'll use that to get your guys out of the city toward this old vehicle depot where I stash a few of my . . . hotter trucks. You can take whatever suits your fancy."

Ellinor leaned back in her seat, and Jelani's starry eyes met hers through the rearview mirror. A shadow crossed his gaze. Was it disgust? Regret? A plan brewing? Ellinor couldn't rightfully tell what the look implied, but a moment later, the dusky-skinned seersha was clenching his jaw and fixing his gaze back on the street in front of him, avoiding looking at her and the dreeocht.

He exhaled a long breath through his nose and briefly turned his attention to Lazar. "After this, we're square, correct? You'll leave me and mine alone?"

Lazar shrugged lazily. "Sure. As long as I get to Zabel safe and sound. No offense, but after last time, don't rightfully trust ya not to try and muck things up. I get to Anzor and ya won't need to worry about *me* or *mine* anymore. Fair is fair."

Jelani sighed, shoulders tensing in the same motion. "Fine. Fair is fair."

Kai chuckled from the last row of seats. "What's he got on you, friend? Must be downright cataclysmic if this be the kind of favor you owe."

Ellinor spied a wiry grin on Jelani's face before the seersha shook it away. "Suffice it to say, I know when I'm outmaneuvered and when it's safer to comply." He paused, sparing Ellinor a glance again before turning his attention back to the road. "I'm sure your lieutenant knows what I speak of in that regard."

Ellinor didn't answer. Not because she didn't think she needed to—which she didn't—but because a disturbance farther up the street caught her attention. As she stared at it, trying to make sense of what she was seeing, Pema scooted up a row, poking her head next to Ellinor's.

Her sharp eyes singled in on the commotion, and the sergeant groaned. "Oh for fuck's sake. Jelani, there better be another way to that tunnel of yours. It looks like Dragan's wise to something happening on this road."

Finally, Ellinor understood what she was seeing. It wasn't a standard road block with police checking vehicles for contraband, but war automata suited for full scale battle hovered alongside their seersha handlers—most likely casters, if Dragan was paranoid like Cosmin.

The bots were scanning the cars long before they got close to the seersha, who peered into the vehicles and occasionally demanded to see identification of some kind. The police and other government enforcers were easy to distinguish from Dragan's men; the seersha's people were all geared in those awful heather grey jumpsuit-like uniforms, the direction of their gaze shielded behind thick black visors.

Casually, Jelani turned the van down a side alley and maintained a steady, slow pace. Ellinor's stomach was doing flip-flops, and she tried to pretend the sweat collecting in the small of her back was from the stuffy van.

Without saying a word, in case the bots were using sensitive microphones to listen in on the ground traffic's conversations, Lazar tapped Jelani on the shoulder and pointed toward another side street. Jelani nodded and, still maintaining that infernally slow pace, turned them in an even wider berth from the road block.

The street they turned down was meant for foot traffic and electric push-carts; their van nearly took up the entirety of the dank alley. The mist and smoke from the aerial vehicles was particularly thick here, and Ellinor guessed that directly above them was one of the many invisible roads the airborne vehicles followed. The exhaust from the vehicles collected in alleys like this, making them appear to be in a perpetual state of dusk. Those poor bastards who lived in places like these, especially on the ground floor, had to wear masks like Ellinor's at all times or the fumes would give them lung-rot; a disease that would eat at their lungs until there was nothing left.

A few people skittered out of their way as they drove, all in tattered polyester and leather, ripped fishnet stockings, and long coats stained with grime. Ellinor was sure they were cursing at them, but couldn't tell due to the breathing apparatuses, except on the few who couldn't afford even the basic necessities.

Their van groaned under low hanging pathways that scraped along their roof, making Ellinor wince; she was sure they'd come crashing down on them at any moment. The top of the van even snagged a poor family's clean laundry left out to dry above the dirty street and scattered it into puddles Ellinor didn't think was water.

As they neared a broken, blinking neon sign that—she guessed—said *hotel*, though not all the lights came on, Jelani turned another corner and let out a long breath, his shoulders relaxing and his knuckles no longer tight as he eased his grip on the steering wheel. "We should be good now," he whispered, eyes darting around the cramped street.

"*Should?* The fuck does that mean?" Talin growled.

Lazar rolled his eyes, but Jelani cleared his throat and kept whatever smartass remark the older man would have tossed at Talin at bay.

"Well, it's not great Dragan's people and the other government types were already there," Jelani said, tone even. "There's another way into the service tunnel, so we should still be fine to get out of Amaru. Still, it's not—"

"It's not *great* that his men were there, we got it," Ellinor finished for him.

Scrubbing her face, Ellinor tried to compartmentalize once more. She couldn't worry about Irati or even what Dragan would do should he get his hands on their prize. She needed to focus on getting the team out of Amaru and nothing else.

As her mind whirled on how they could get out of the city if Jelani's exit was cut off, a thought slammed into her, constricting her chest as she whispered, "How was it Dragan's men were there? It was like they knew where we were headed. How did everyone beat us?"

Kai shifted behind her. "Ah. Now ain't that the question. You go talking, Jelani?"

There was a hard edge to Kai's voice, and the seersha's eyes darkened until they looked like a stormy night's sky. "I need that tunnel more than you. I gain nothing by betraying you to someone I actively work against."

"Ell," Pema said, tapping her on the shoulder. "You saw that infiltrator drone, didn't you? The one I shot? Think there was probably more that could be tracking us. Cloaked and all proper-like. You following where I'm going?"

Ellinor's face went slack. "It's possible, yeah."

Lazar cursed and, for a moment, Ellinor thought it was because of the infiltrator drone. But that wasn't what had the seersha sweating and squirming in his seat. Waiting at the end of the crowded street were two seersha in Ashling buster armor—similar to Kai's Coyote mechanized suit—blocking the road.

A deranged chuckle bubbled up from Kai, while Talin grumbled as if inconvenienced, and Pema started to growl a slew of colorful curses.

"Hold on," Jelani said, voice oddly calm. "There's still one more way we can try, but this is going to get bumpy."

He slammed on the brakes and put the van in reverse, not looking behind him as he drove. He kept his eyes trained on the men lumbering toward them, a thin line of sweat collecting on his furrowed brow, fingers moving around the steering wheel as if tapping along to music. A jagged wall of debris, dirt, and stone came shooting up in front of the brutes, stopping them cold and blocking their view of the retreating crew.

Jelani slumped back in his seat, face ashen with the effort to cast. Creating walls like that was basic earth magic; it shouldn't have even required Jelani to move his hands as if he were casting complex, powerful magic. When Ellinor had first started school—just plain old normal school—there was a pair of earth casters who were taught that skill almost on day one.

It was a child's trick, something older siblings liked to use to make their younger brother or sister trip all over themselves. The fact it took such a great effort for Jelani to create something so simple when there were plenty of resources for him to draw from made Ellinor's throat tighten, leery of this man who Lazar swore would be a help to them on this botched errand.

Jerking the wheel and sending the thought flying, along with the rest of Ellinor and the crew, Jelani turned the vehicle around and had them screeching back onto the main thoroughfare. All pretense of maintaining a low profile gone.

Jelani clipped other vehicles as he swerved around them, ignoring the horns of the irate drivers. He hopped curbs and narrowly avoided running over the few pedestrians traversing the lower levels, but Jelani did crash into a transport bot who was too laden with salvage to get out of the way. The whole crew winced as the crash left a large crack in the windshield.

Sirens blared behind them, along with the wail of a high pitched horn Ellinor assumed must be coming from Dragan's people as they pursued their fleeing delivery van. The van began lurching from side to side in time with metallic *pings* as those behind them opened fire, clearly unconcerned with the heavy flow of traffic around them.

Ellinor heard Pema pump her scattergun, and a moment later the sergeant said, "No way we're getting out of this clean." Ellinor glanced behind her long enough to see Pema climb into the back of the van and murmur to Talin, "Hold on to me."

Before either of the seershas could protest, Pema flung the back door open and leveled her shotgun at the nearest vehicle behind them. With Talin holding on to Pema's waist with her good arm, the sergeant sent shells full of tiny EMP devices hurtling at the vehicles behind them.

The first vehicle—a police pursuit craft—didn't deploy its shield fast enough. When the blast hit, the vehicle died instantly, its internal electronics fried. The next few vehicles were quick to turn on their own shields, negating the large blast from Pema's scattergun. Flipping a switch on the stock of the gun, Pema began firing bullets full of shrapnel in hopes of popping the tires the good old fashioned way.

All the while, their pursuers continued to fire at them, with Jelani doing his best to weave in and out of traffic, making a clean shot nearly impossible.

Then Pema slammed against Talin with a grunt. Her voice was strained as she said, "Son of a—" but her words were drowned out as Talin pulled the back door closed and began tearing at Pema's armor to see what the damage was.

"Fucking abyss," Talin cursed.

Pema Tran was bleeding. She shouldn't have been bleeding. Pema had armor like Ellinor's; when fully charged, normal bullets couldn't pierce it.

"What did they hit you with?" Ellinor's eyes widened of their own accord at the growing puddle of blood as Pema struggled to catch her breath.

"I don't see anything," Talin all but screamed. "There's nothing in the wound!"

"*Shit*," Ellinor said, before turning to Jelani. "They've switched to magic. The bastards are firing magitech bullets. We need to get more distance between us and them, Jelani, and we need it now!"

Magitech bullets, like all forms of magitech, were illegal throughout the entire continent. Supposedly, it was for the public's safety, but it was really just the elected official's way of keeping their militaries superior to the street thugs. The fact that their pursuers were using the contraband in the middle of traffic told Ellinor all she needed about how far the corruption of the police force and Dragan's influence went.

Jelani's foot was flush against the floor, pushing the van to its limits. "Faster, man," Talin Roxas yelled. "We're going to lose her!" Cradling Pema's head, Talin said softly, "Hold on baby. Don't you let go."

Being shot with air wasn't like having a puff of hot wind waft over you. The air tore through the cells and molecules of a person, using their own biology against them. Shredding through the resistance until the magic was either recalled or they got out of range of its power source, leaving no trace that it was ever there. In many ways, being hit with pure air was worse than earth or water magitech bullets; no one could ever see it coming. The one thing that could have stopped the magic would be an earth caster skilled enough to make the tiny airborne particles of dust and smog so dense around them that the projectiles themselves became too heavy and thudded to the ground, useless. But Jelani was clearly not strong enough for such a defense.

Patching Pema's side became all the more difficult as Jelani tore around another corner. "We can't make the tunnel now. We're going to have to try and force our way out."

"Can we even do that?" Kai yelled above the din of blaring horns, sirens, and Pema's strangled gasps.

Jelani's eyes narrowed as he glanced at Kai and Ellinor in the rearview mirror. "We're going to try. There are no more good options. This is the least terrible, and will leave an avenue of escape, should any others need it in the future."

Ellinor was not presented the opportunity to argue as Jelani slammed on the accelerator. The van went airborne for a brief moment as it turned toward one of the many proper exits out of the city. "What are ya trying to do? Kill us before Dragan can?" Lazar yelled, readying his own scattergun.

Jelani shook his head. "Trust me. There are more exits out of Amaru than Dragan or his henchmen can properly watch at once. I'll find a way out. But," he paused, his eyes meeting Ellinor's before darting away, "I may need Ellinor's help."

"What? Why? I can't do anything. Did you miss the part where my powers got taken away? I'm powerless here!" she yelled back.

"You, Ellinor Rask," Jelani said firmly, "are far from powerless. You know this."

Ellinor clenched her jaw. She wanted to say *no*; there was no way she would trust Jelani—a seersha, like Cosmin, of all things—and do as he asked. But what choice was there? The other option left them all dead for sure, and that didn't aid Ellinor in the slightest.

"Fine," she growled. "What is it you need me to do?"

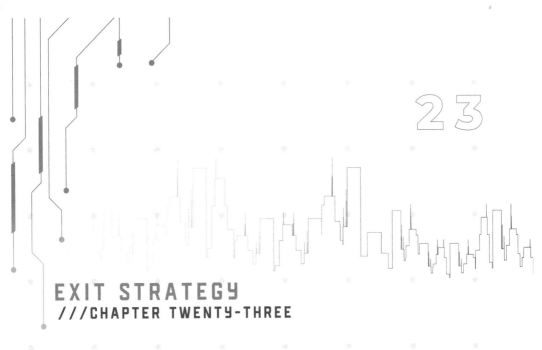

EXIT STRATEGY
///CHAPTER TWENTY-THREE

"SEE THAT super mall with the red and blue neon sign?" Jelani Sharma said, never taking his hands off the steering wheel, gaze fixed on the road as he attempted to dodge innocent commuters while making a point to knock any of the pursuit bots off the road.

Ellinor's gaze narrowed. "Yeah, what about it?"

"You any good with that Rhino of yours?"

Ellinor scoffed. Her Asco Rhino was a heavy duty mechanized crossbow; it was meant to fire dense payloads or massive projectiles. Finesse or stealth wasn't what a Rhino was for. Even if she wasn't skilled with the weapon's use, she figured now was hardly the time where it would matter.

"Just tell me what needs doing, and I'll get it done," Ellinor said, readying the Rhino.

A fleeting smile crossed Jelani's face, making him look like a dashing rogue from the penny-serial covers. Ellinor furrowed her brow, ever more suspicious of the man now. He didn't seem like the type that would be as enmeshed in the underground as he was. The smile was soon replaced by a grim look of determination as the seersha said, "I'm hoping you have building hooks. I'll need you to anchor us to the support post there."

"What in the abyss are you going to have her do?" Talin interjected, trying desperately to staunch Pema's bleeding. Pema's breathing wasn't as labored, having finally pulled far enough away for the magitech to fizzle out. "That'll just rip this piece o' crap van in two and make us easy pickings for the assholes chasing us. Or did you miss that part?"

"I understand you're stressed, but let me finish," Jelani said, struggling to make the words civil. "There's an exit on the other side of that super mall."

Before Talin could argue further on the sanity of Jelani's plan, Lazar tapped his lips. "Good enough for me. I'll give ya some cover, Ellinor. Ready to fire?"

Ellinor gritted her teeth, scrambling to get an anchor hook from her pack. She didn't usually carry them, and when she did, she had one—two, tops. Dumping her pack inside out, she found the hook and cable she had, and hoped one shot was all they would need. She attached the main line to what she hoped was the strongest part of their van, then Lazar yanked her forward into the front seat. He all but shoved her on his lap as he lowered the window and twisted around so he was facing their pursuers, offering her what little cover he could as she leveled her Asco Rhino.

Hold it steady, soldier, Andrey's stern voice whipped through her mind, calming her shaking hands. The van continued to rattle as those behind them fired what they could; the deafening sounds of police pursuit bots and vehicles making it impossible for Ellinor to hear her thundering heartbeat over the noise.

"Any time now, woman," Lazar growled in her ear.

Just a moment more, let the support come into view.

A patrol automaton bounced to their left, and Jelani swerved to knock it off course, sending the robotic soldier into a cart selling children's knock-off laser toys and yapping wind-up dogs.

"Uh, boss? They're gaining real fast. You gonna do something, or should we say our good-byes now? I'm asking for a friend," Kai shouted, his voice shrill despite the chuckle he forced out. But Ellinor ignored him and Lazar. She needed the perfect shot or they would all be dead that much sooner.

She winced as Lazar fired over her shoulder, but kept her breath steady as she pulled the trigger. The anchor flew through the air, barely missing one of the infiltrator drones following their progress.

With a crash that tore a hole through the neon sign and shook the entire super mall, Ellinor's anchor lodged itself deep into the side of the building. Before she could release her breath, it was forced out of her when Jelani jerked the wheel to the side, and the van went airborne again, whipping around like a sling. The vehicle groaned, its metal screaming louder than any siren as the hook and cable from Ellinor's anchor threatened to rip the van in two.

This shouldn't be possible, Ellinor thought, watching a few of the vagrants on the ground level dive for cover. But the cable and hooks—and the van—held long enough to fling them down the road and toward a city exit.

Ellinor flew back through the van, bumping against the seats until she landed hard against Kai and the dreeocht. She was scrambling over the seats a second later, trying to reach her Rhino to release the anchor and recall the cable attached to their van, but she couldn't reach it in time.

Lazar had a large high carbon steel knife out, and he cut the cable as easily as a perfectly cooked steak. Ellinor flinched at the loud *twang* the cable made as it sprang toward the building, and she could only hope they wouldn't need such devices again on their way to Zabel's stronghold. Regardless, she reclaimed the remaining piece attached to the roof just in case, and stuffed it back in her pack along with her other items.

The wall and city gate came at them at an alarming rate. The wall was comprised of questionable magitech that would instantly mummify someone if they touched it. But the gate at least *appeared* to be of a normal combat-tech design. Still, that alone would tear through their van if they tried crashing through while it was locked.

Lazar stuck his head back inside momentarily, pointed ears twitching and large eyes flicking over the crew before frowning deeply. Talin was as useless as Pema as she tried to bandage her lover in a bouncing vehicle with only one arm, but at least there was Kai Axel Brantley.

The panic Ellinor heard earlier was replaced with the manic glint she had come to recognize as Kai's unsettling excitement and bloodlust for a good fight, something he had developed defending himself and his mother after his gambling addicted father abandoned them. It was probably another reason Cosmin had picked the big man for this task, but Ellinor didn't want to mention that and have Kai lose focus on memories and daydreams.

Lazar smirked. "Let's light 'em up."

Kai pressed a button on his Coyote mechanized suit, and a belt of tiny electric grenades was thrust forward from a compartment in his chest. Ellinor scowled at him. "Where was that earlier, Kai? What, were you waiting for a *better* opportunity to unleash the cavalry?"

Kai shrugged, a grin tugging at his lips, green eyes twinkling. "Didn't think we'd need it. Thought Jelani 'ad this handled all nice and tight. Didn't wanna bring the governor's attention by blowing shit up if we was better off keeping our heads down."

Ellinor bit the inside of her cheeks to keep from growling at him and checked the ammunition on her pistols. She put in a new clip with armor piercing rounds in each and spared one last glance out the cracked windshield, a plan formulating at hypersonic speeds.

"Kai, I need those grenades flung as close to the gate and the bots as possible. If you miss, you better have more, got it?"

The man nodded, turning on his metal gauntlets to help lob the belt of grenades farther. Ellinor turned to Lazar, who was watching her with a mildly amused expression. "Right, then. Lazar, if you can shoot some of those humani patrolmen so they hit the wall and drain the magic, that'll help in case we need to scale something when this plan goes tits up again, as Pema would say." She glanced at Talin and then turned back to the front, wiggling into position near Jelani and Lazar.

Shouting over her shoulder, Ellinor called out, "Talin, you're in charge of Pema and the dreeocht. You'll have to get both out if we're otherwise occupied. Understood?"

"Understood," Talin said from the back of the van, and Ellinor didn't need to glance behind her to know the seerani had finished hastily bandaging Pema before holding on to the dreeocht container with her free hand.

Without warning—which, belatedly, Ellinor realized she should have given—she kicked the shattered windshield out of the van, surprising Jelani, who fought to keep the van from fishtailing. Those on patrol were screaming into ear pieces, demanding backup while simultaneously leveling their weapons on Ellinor. A few of the police patrol bots on duty were standing sentinel nearby, ordering that they stop their vehicle and approach the checkpoint at a reduced speed, not having gotten an update stating Ellinor and her team were to be apprehended.

None of the robots throughout Erhard looked like humani or seersha. Their designers kept them as machinelike as possible to avoid people forming an attachment by assuming organic qualities that simply did not exist. More often than not they looked like a supercomputer had a wild *ménage à trois* with a garbage bin and a transport vehicle and birthed some odd hybrid no one wanted to claim as theirs. The bots were functional looking, making it, admittedly, much easier to shoot them.

Ellinor leveled her Dunstan Anaconda pistols, took one long, steadying breath, and began firing.

The first bot, a patrol automaton, went down like someone whacked it with a lead pipe, falling backwards with no resistance, a fist-sized hole in the middle of its rectangular head. Its red optical lenses flickered momentarily as it fell to the ground before going out completely. Before it even landed, Ellinor was firing at another bot with similar results. All bots were built with the same weakness for armor-piercing rounds. In case they gained enough consciousness to become an Ashling, their owners wanted the option to put them down quickly.

Ellinor fired again, felling another bot that couldn't dodge in time. Her armor buzzed to life and her breath was nearly knocked from her by the impact of a bullet hitting her sternum, but Lazar was there to make short work of the offender. A shot from his scattergun sent the humani patrolman barreling into the wall. His armor couldn't shield him from the magic stored within, and a moment later he looked like a stale, adult-sized raisin someone had dressed in a jumpsuit three sizes too large for him. His death meant this section of wall was now drained of the magitech held within.

Ellinor shouted, "Now, Kai!"

Kai lobbed his grenades, his aim true, as the belt tumbled through the air ahead of their van. The shock grenades went off in a series of little *pops*, the electricity twisting and curling around the remaining automatons and the fence they were working so hard to keep closed. They couldn't shoot the gate open with anything they had on hand, but it wouldn't matter; the gate was no longer locked.

"Brace yerselves!" Lazar called, holding on to his seatbelt as tightly as he could.

Kai yanked Ellinor back into the second row and held her firmly against him. Talin, meanwhile, nestled herself between the dreeocht container and held on to Pema's semi-conscious form. They barreled through the gate, their heads whipping back and forth. Part of their vehicle's hood tore free, and at least one of the tires popped—maybe two, if all the jerking and bouncing was any indication.

The van's engine was smoking and Ellinor could see nothing ahead of them. She felt Kai shift behind her, and he lobbed another belt of grenades out the shattered back window of the van, sending the few remaining patrol bots and pursuit vehicles scrambling as they struggled to find other means of chasing down their escaping quarry.

We did it. We made it out of Amaru, and we didn't die!

She turned her aching neck back toward Lazar and Jelani, when a sound overhead made her stomach plummet and her jaw slacken. Lazar must have heard the same *whoosh* sound of the propellers overhead as Ellinor did, for he clenched Jelani's shoulder so tightly his knuckles were white.

"Ya gotta get this boat going faster." Lazar's voice was barely discernible over the struggling engine and the sound of propellers getting louder and louder with each passing second.

Ellinor was fairly certain Jelani did his best to get the van to go faster, but there was no outrunning the Ash Hawk helicopter that hovered above them for a moment before overtaking them.

Ash Hawks were far more armored and dangerous than most aerial transport vehicles, even those designed to drop bombs of various kinds. The urban maneuverability the Ash Hawks had was unparalleled for hunting down renegade Ashlings and anyone trying to flee the city.

The Ash Hawk landed directly in their path. Jelani tried to swerve away, but their van stopped abruptly, its engine block crumpling like they'd hit a wall. Ellinor's head bounced back against the seat, her vision swimming as she tried to figure out what happened.

We did hit a wall. An invisible wall.

The only explanation that made sense, even with her head still spinning from all the bouncing back and forth in the past two minutes, was that someone aboard the Ash Hawk was an air caster, even if Ellinor couldn't see them or their moving hands.

Those with an abundance of ability at their command rarely needed to move their hands beyond raising a finger to shape and position the elements. The less powerful the caster, or the more elaborate the objective, the more a caster needed to physically manipulate the element to do their bidding.

Whoever was on the Ash Hawk apparently not only had the skill for such things, but had no qualms about using that kind of power to get them to stop, when they could have just as easily shot them.

Oh fuck.

Ellinor nudged Kai, who was slow to move. Talin was pinned behind the dreeocht, but was in the process of wiggling free alongside Pema. Lazar, once more without his wire framed glasses and cigar, appeared the least phased by the crash, while Jelani seemed to be out cold for the time being. Which left only a contractor working for one of the most powerful seersha mob bosses in Erhard and a neutered air caster to deal with Amaru's criminal boss himself.

Ellinor tried to climb out of the van, but Lazar shoved her back. "Ya need to stay with the package. See if ya can get yer people moving and sneak out while I distract our guest. If ya can't get yer crew out of here, the package is the priority. Get it to Zabel at all costs, otherwise, a whole different kind of abyss waits for ya once Zabel finds out."

Ellinor blinked rapidly, trying to get her mind to accept what Lazar was saying. Their mission hinged on getting the dreeocht to Zabel so she could get the collar removed. But if she did that, then Kai would die. Pema and Talin would die.

Can I live with that?

Ellinor gritted her teeth so hard she thought they'd crack. Not long ago, Ellinor believed she could, in fact, live with leaving people behind. As Lazar left the van, Ellinor whispered to herself, "Nope," and crept out the back.

Neither Andrey nor Misho would have accepted Lazar's words as the only option. Surely there had to be a way for her to whisk the dreeocht and her—dare she say?—*friends* to safety all in one go. But the van was beyond dead and Kai was barely conscious. She could help Talin move Pema, but that would leave Kai behind.

Love is weakness. Your only focus should be on finishing the job and reclaiming your abilities.

The cold thought gripped her hard, squeezing her heart. She hesitated, closing her eyes. But the idea of Kai's big smile never lighting up a room again . . . nothing was worth trading for that. Her eyes snapped open, and she started moving.

Crawling over Kai and past the struggling Talin, she gently pushed open the crumpled back door of the van. Glancing over her shoulder, Ellinor saw that, in the brief time it took her to move and Lazar to gather what he could, Jelani had vanished.

Of course a scoundrel like that would choose now to flee. No-good renegade coward. They always talk a good game, but are nothing but limp dicks when it comes to action.

Ellinor's bitter thoughts ran rapid as she tried to tumble from the van in silence—and with as much dignity as she could muster. Regaining her feet, despite her spinning head, Ellinor stole a glance at the group Lazar now faced alone.

There were a trio of goons in the grey jumpsuits—all too similar-looking from the group that accosted them at the bar for Ellinor to tell them apart, outside of identifying the humani from the seersha. But that's not what made Ellinor's heart crawl up her chest and try to force itself past her esophagus.

Standing in the center of the thugs was a pale devil of a seersha that could be no other than Dragan Voclain. In stark contrast to the jet-black bull-sized horns, the air caster's skin was as white as a frostbitten corpse, and he did not hide his well-built physique behind the elaborate suits and luxurious robes Ellinor was accustomed to seeing Cosmin wear. Dragan wore only fitted black combat pants with arctic blue spider webs all over them, and a long black chain set with deep blue stones between the thick links. But, like Cosmin, it was the man's eyes that Ellinor had a hard time looking at; they were as close to solid black as Ellinor had ever seen.

Dragan eyed Lazar with amusement, rubbing his chin, his other hand shoved into his pocket. Ellinor was transfixed; Lazar stood confidently before Dragan, as if he wasn't a powerful air caster or the head of a dominant gang. Perhaps he was emboldened after working with Zabel Dirix for so long. Still, even though Ellinor didn't particularly like Lazar, she admired him as he leaned against the ruin that was their van and matched Dragan's amused expression with bored indifference.

"What do ya think yer playing at, Dragan? Ya know this won't end well. The likes of ya won't get away with a stunt like this. Ya can't keep us here." Lazar shifted against the hood of the van, fishing out another cigar.

Dragan looked around with forced exaggeration, his formidable horns nearly decapitating one of his men. "Really?" Dragan crooned in a voice that was dramatically higher than what Ellinor would have imagined. "I mean,"—Dragan waved around the empty area—"of course. Of course, I will."

Running his hands up the side of his ice-blue Mohawk as if ensuring it remained standing at attention, Dragan made a great show of nonchalance. Ellinor found the bravado curious, regardless of the charade, he reminded her more of a simpering, spoiled aristocrat than a notorious crime boss.

"Look around you," Dragan continued. "What do you see? Oh, that's right, *my* people." He forced a long, loud sigh. "This has been fun—no, really, it has. It's not often a group of insects thinks they can evade me. So, well done and whatever, but can we just . . . stop this now? I'm bored."

While Dragan was distracted, Ellinor helped Talin drag Pema, whose skin was going clammy, from the van before reaching in and helping Kai get his bearings enough to tug the dreeocht and the remainder of their guns toward the back. Ideally, they'd get everything offloaded and sneak away a safe distance where they could deploy the camo tarp and wait out Dragan, but Ellinor didn't think they would make it that far. Not if the seersha caster was already impatient, and Lazar had nothing he could use to pierce Dragan's magic with.

Dragan waved at the humani enforcer, who took a step forward only to have Lazar blow his kneecap off with the scattergun he had hidden behind his back. The man screamed, and the remaining guards leveled their weapons at Lazar. For his part, Dragan smiled, revealing white, serrated teeth.

"Color me impressed." Dragan clapped slowly. "But that was stupid. Are you stalling? Azer above, you are! How cute. Pathetic, but cute."

Lazar fired again, but his shot was stopped cold by a pocket of air as dense, if not more so, than what their van had hit. "Did you miss the part where I said I was bored? Really, your master may be terrifying, but she isn't here, and I am. I don't need you, or any of your crew. This was a . . . formality; a professional courtesy, if you will. Shame you blew it. I was kind of looking forward to using Ellinor. Hey, is she with you? Or did I kill her already?" He didn't wait for Lazar to answer. "Ellinor? Are you still breathing?"

Ellinor knew better than to respond.

Dragan sighed again and took his hand out of his pocket. "You do know I can just take this from you, right? This bluster of yours is dull and pointless. I could have crushed you eighteen different ways by now."

"Then why haven't ya? Don't have the stones do ya, to piss off Zabel." Lazar gave a low whistle. "Reckon that's more than a second rate caster the likes of ya can handle."

Dragan's hand clenched and Lazar began sputtering and coughing. Ellinor closed her eyes against the sound, trying to help Kai move as quietly as they could with the dinged-up dreeocht container and its barely useable push-cart out of the van. It was a sound Ellinor knew all too well, of a caster using their ability to remove oxygen from someone's lungs.

Ellinor tried reaching out for her own abilities again—she knew it was useless, but she had to do *something*. Suffocating like that was a terrible way to die. When the blank emptiness mocked her, Ellinor decided she'd had enough of the taste of despair.

"Kai, Talin, you guys drag as much of this shit away as you can. I'm going to buy you some time." Ellinor had barely moved when Kai caught her arm.

"Boss, you can't. You go far away and the collar will drop you. You gotta stay with us."

"I stay, and we're all dead. You guys need to move. I'll stay here, stall Dragan, and we all live to fight another day, yeah?"

She didn't let Kai argue further.

"Let him go, Dragan." Ellinor stepped out from behind the van.

Dragan laughed. "There you are! So puny . . . so dramatic! And completely harmless. Looks like the intel I got was solid. You know, about your little collar and what it does. You'd be nothing to me at your best, but now . . ." he shook his head, smirking. "Do you know just how powerless you are?"

When Ellinor didn't answer, Dragan frowned. "You know, I might be—" the black pools that served as his eyes dragged over her body, "persuaded to spare your life. I'm sure we can find some way to get that thing off your neck. Then, of course, we take over Erhard, you know, the usual thing someone with a dreeocht does. Imagine it. Two air casters with a dreeocht fueling us. Doesn't that just rev your engine?" Dragan licked his lips.

Lazar continued to sputter, his reddish-bronze skin going crimson as his lungs failed to inflate. Ellinor looked away, hardening her stare on Dragan. "I said let him go."

When Dragan didn't comply immediately and took another step closer, his hand twitching subtly at his side, Ellinor acted. She knew the secrets of air casting. She may not be as strong as someone like Dragan Voclain, but she knew her own ability well, and she was intimately familiar with its weaknesses.

Air was a fickle thing. It was difficult to make solid and harder still to keep in place.

Ellinor activated her shield and cape. The pale seersha hesitated and took a step back. Leaping in front of Lazar, Ellinor flapped her cape to kick up as much dust as she could, and using her shield, she sliced through the air in what looked like a drunken, over enthusiastic dancer at a bachelor party.

Despite how ridiculous it looked for Ellinor to be a tornado of one with her flailing arms and legs, she liked to believe Andrey was smiling at her from wherever his soul was now. Ellinor may be without her power, but she was not *powerless*.

Dragan's face hardened, his hand twitching faster, and Ellinor could feel herself rising from the ground. Ellinor was disrupting the current Dragan was trying to manipulate, and he was losing control, unable to stabilize the field of power. Ellinor was pushing too much away, distorting the air with dust and debris that it became too heavy with particulates to manipulate easily. It was something that, had he stayed, Jelani could have easily done with his earth abilities.

Dragan's black eyes narrowed, baring his pointed teeth at her. But Ellinor continued to move and push against the very air he was trying to keep away from Lazar.

"Enough!" Dragan screamed, losing control and blasting them all with a strong wind.

Ellinor flew through the broken front window of the van, her armor buzzing as it hardened in the places where she would have otherwise been sliced open by the sharp glass. But all she cared about was the sound of Lazar Botwright gasping as oxygen returned to him.

Ellinor tried to scramble out of the van before Dragan could focus his power again. But Lazar beat her to it, firing his shotgun from a kneeling position. His shots went wide as he continued to shudder and gasp for breath.

From a low hill to the left of Lazar, a shot rang out from an armor piercing round, leaving a smoldering hole in in the head of one of Dragan's guard's. Before the man hit the ground, there was another shot, and the remaining man crumpled. Ellinor couldn't see who had fired, though she could track where the shots came from. A roar followed as Dragan lost his temper.

"I'm done! This was exciting for a moment. *A moment.* I was going to let you live, Ellinor, what happens now is your fault." Dragan's hands began moving wildly, and Ellinor's heart and stomach went into freefall.

B EFORE THE unseen defender could fire again, Dragan Voclain picked Lazar up on the wind as if he were no more
than a child's kite. The seersha was helplessly tossed into the
center of a whirlwind, dust and debris curling around him at
speeds so fast Ellinor couldn't track them. As she watched, the
twisting air around Lazar was soon clouded with blood. Lazar's
screams cut off abruptly as the air spinning around him, cutting him to ribbons, suddenly lurched into his open mouth,
inflating every cell and organ of his body until he burst.

A hot spray of blood and viscera covered Ellinor, a pink,
sticky mist colored the air. Scraps of wet clothing thudded to
the ground, cushioning the digimap as it crashed to the dirt.
Lazar Botwright's last unlit cigar rolled in the bloody soil, coming to a rest at Ellinor's boots.

Dragan didn't even stagger at such a display of power; in
fact, his hands were still moving, the blue stones around his
neck began to glow, and the air around Ellinor took shape. The
gore-covered ground that had once been the man hired to take

them safely from Cosmin to Zabel began to morph and solidify. An ice blue mass coated with bits of sand and rock, broken pieces from the van, and torn flesh swirled together, glowing and crackling as the magic snapped together until a creature of pure magic stood before them.

Only once had Ellinor needed to face a monster cobbled together by a caster from different energy sources, all pooled together. It had been a minor earth beast, and she had only danced about the walking mound. It had been formed of glowing tree bark and thorny vines with jagged rocks for teeth, before a creature of Cosmin's own design trounced the thing quite thoroughly, as earth magic is weaker than fire. But this . . . this was beyond Ellinor's survival skills.

Dragan staggered for a moment, his magic reserves spent on the beast. The stones no longer glowed; the disguised batteries now smoked along Dragan's chain. With a hoarse laugh, Dragan disappeared from view as the air twisted to distort the area around him, making him invisible.

Ellinor was too stunned by the creature taking shape for even the violent death of Lazar to fully hit her. The one remaining guard, whom Lazar had shot, was left defenseless as the beast took a step forward and impaled him on its needle pointed foot. His shrieks turned to gurgles as his body twitched and then stilled completely.

The being in front of her stood on two pointed, drill-shaped legs that twisted into tiny tornados which then fed into a crackling mass of dark storm clouds. Lightning from raw water magic sparked and curled around the beast like vines.

Bolts sparked out from the being's chest and twisted down its stormy arms until they formed long-fingered claws of electrical discharge. Standing to its full height, the magical creature was a good three-stories tall. A nub of a tail, also made of a tiny cyclone, whipped behind it, and yet it did not disturb the Ash Hawk parked nearby. It glanced about momentarily, its eyes nothing but storm clouds that glowed from the ice-blue lightning within.

It roared, mouth opening wide all the way to its chest. The sound that came from the beast was like crashing thunder mixed with metal structures being ripped from their struts.

A grenade sailed over her head, and was sucked into the swirling beast. An explosion of fire had the creature staggering back. "Ell! Shake your ass. Move!" Talin screamed, before the beast was bellowing anew.

Ellinor took advantage of the beast's momentary distraction and scrambled farther into the van. None of them had anything to combat this magical creature with; her armor would not protect her, should it get its claws on her. Talin's high-powered fire bombs would only annoy it, Kai's most powerful weapons and Ashling buster armor wouldn't protect him for long, and Pema was in no condition to do anything. Even if Ellinor had her magic at hand, her abilities, at best, would be like battering a stone building with a breeze.

The van buzzed around her as the beast picked it up, her armor going into overdrive to protect her as Dragan's creature turned the van upside down and dumped her out. But only her, with no precious cargo. She used her cape to safely fall to the ground.

"Where is the dreeocht?" the air monster shrieked, its voice a raspy version of Dragan's, its gaping maw amplifying the caster's words.

"Gone," Ellinor yelled back, trying to buy as much time as she could. But for what, she wasn't sure. "This is why you don't toy with your kill. It's liable to get up and walk away."

Dragan didn't appreciate her answer. The beast roared again and shot a lance of air directly at Ellinor's heart.

Her chest should have collapsed, her rib cage poking out around her spine with the sheer power of the concentrated blast. But instead, her armor and cape flared and, like with the mechanical bees, Ellinor's collar began thrumming. It constricted around her neck, and yet she didn't choke. The abilities she was cut off from and Cosmin's shackle worked in tandem to absorb the magic, feeding it to the greedy, sleeping dreeocht. This time, Dragan shrieked in frustration instead of his beast.

The beast reached down to kill her the old fashioned way. But the monster never connected. Sliding between her and the magical creature was Jelani Tyrik Sharma—a Zifu Raven combat rifle slung to his back.

He held a pair of glowing swords the color of desert sand, each the length of his arm. The swords pulsed in time with something Ellinor could only faintly see beneath Jelani's dark green mesh sweater, but it looked like a glowing tattoo. In the center of the glowing swords was a black obsidian rod, a red wire coiled at the hilt.

With a start, Ellinor realized what she was looking at—traditional, bonafide, Leviathan Roasters.

If someone could touch a caster with such a blade, it would act similarly to Ellinor's collar, neutralizing their magic. But Jelani's were in sync with *him*, with something attached to him that fed directly into the blades and most likely used his own magic to—

Ellinor gasped. "You're a Creature Breaker!"

The air beast roared again, its cries morphing to that of the frustrated wail of Dragan, still invisible somewhere nearby. Jelani never took his attention from the beast, even as he ordered: "Get Dragan!"

The monster tried to leap over Jelani and suck Ellinor up into one of the vortexes twisting off its stormy torso. But Jelani's blades were there to meet it, slicing through the tendril of magic like it was insubstantial, reverting back to the air it had always been, free of the guiding force of Dragan.

She sprang away from the beast and tried to find where Dragan was hiding. She knew he had to be close; casters could never get far from their creatures or risk them turning on them, or dissolving into nothingness once more.

If I needed to stay close, but still wanted to look for my prize, where would I go?

Ellinor rolled back to the Ash Hawk.

Dodging Jelani as he dueled with the behemoth, Ellinor readied her karambit knives once more. Jelani was chipping away at the beast, his blades making the air condense with his trapped earth magic and forcing it to dissipate. The creature was missing its tail now, and as she watched, Jelani ran at the creature, sliding beneath its crackling lightning claws to slice a large chunk out of its legs.

The beast began to lose its balance, and Jelani flipped himself away before springing as high into the air as he could, jabbing his blades into part of the creature's torso where the lightning storm raged. The blades absorbed the lightning before flinging it out in all directions, freeing it from Dragan's control.

A stray spark hit Ellinor and her knees buckled, the collar around her neck vibrating painfully, and she swore parts of the technology were imbedding directly into her flesh. Looking to take advantage of her incapacitated state, the beast lurched for her, but it was Kai who met it this time.

Kai unloaded on the beast with his submachine gun, stepping away from where Talin, Pema and the dreeocht were hidden. He yelled as his bullets peppered the beast, the shockwave of his shots stalling it, allowing Ellinor to stumble to her feet.

She could feel no blood trickling down into her armor from the collar, and she wasn't left writhing on the dusty ground, like she should have been with such a shock. Ellinor tried to ignore what the collar and the dreeocht were doing to her, setting her eyes back on the Ash Hawk. She lurched into motion, spinning her Lacerators on her fingers and flinging them toward the helicopter, recalling them just as quickly if they didn't hit her target.

As Jelani took out one of the creature's legs, narrowly avoiding a claw in the process, one of Ellinor's knives found its mark. Dragan yelped, his invisibility and beast faltered as his concentration was momentarily broken.

"Got you, asshole," Ellinor growled. Taking out her Anaconda, she fired.

Her shot grazed Dragan's shoulder, his shielding back in place enough to turn the bullet. The seersha gasped, his pallor flashing from his natural ghostly hue to blinding white as he struggled to get his shielding back at full strength. But as no more stones glowed, Ellinor knew he was using his own magic, and that had limits. She grinned, slamming her Lacerators back in place and pulling out the electric knife she'd stolen from Janne.

She launched herself at the caster, pistol in one hand, Lance in the other. She fired, but Dragan turned the bullet using the wind around him. She slashed with the knife just as he lowered his head, and the blade struck one of his obsidian colored horns. The lightning crackled around it, making Dragan grimace, but he was otherwise uninjured.

Kai shot at the beast each time it got a little too close to Ellinor, or to the hidden Talin and Pema. All the while Jelani continued to spar with the beast, whittling it down to a more manageable size. With Ellinor distracting Dragan, his beast was dumber, its swings wide and only occasionally grazing Jelani, who would grunt in exertion, but did not fall.

Ducking beneath Dragan's jab, Ellinor sliced his thigh with her Lance. The seersha howled in pain. Before Ellinor could straighten and jump back, Dragan swung his head, his muscles twitching from the electricity. The edge of his horn snagged her armor and flung Ellinor back once more to the ruined delivery van. She slammed into its dented side with a groan, her spine screaming in protest.

Ellinor grunted, falling forward in an attempt to regain her footing only to have her hair grabbed by the infuriated seersha. Out of the corner of her eye, she saw Jelani slice off one of the beast's talons, but now that Dragan had Ellinor in his grasp, his beast was better able to deflect Jelani's blows without losing parts of itself in the process. Ellinor was not sure how much of Jelani's life force had already been used in fighting the magical creature—the more skilled the Creature Breaker, the longer they could last—but his dusky skin gleamed with sweat, and she guessed his reserves were coming to an end. His swords would soon be useless.

Dragan jerked her head back, a small blade now pressed against her neck. "I don't need you," he growled, bringing his hand back to cut her throat.

"Ell, move!" Kai turned from the beast and leveled his weapon in her direction.

Blood coursed down her neck as Dragan's blade connected briefly before his attention was diverted and Ellinor wriggled free. Her hand flew to her neck, trying to stop the blood as she watched Kai wobble toward Dragan. The crime boss got his air shield up, but it was visibly wavering as Kai shot round after round of armor piercing bullets at the seersha from his Rasul AbyssFire submachine gun. But Kai was now not behind the safety of the van, and Dragan smiled viciously.

Dragan's hands started dancing. In an instant, he recalled the remainder of his magic, his creature and shield dissolving and rushing back to him to form a typhoon of storm clouds—aimed right at Kai Brantley.

Kai was slow to recognize what was happening, even with Talin screaming at him to run. But Ellinor wasn't. She raced for Kai.

Dragan launched his weaponized tornado, and Ellinor dove. Her body twisted as the wind enveloped her, the howling currents deafening in her ears. Her limbs were pulled to their limit, skin tight on her face as the wind threatened to scrape it away, when her collar suddenly throbbed to life once again. It was no longer just vibrating, but burning her skin. She heard a piercing series of *beeps* from the dreeocht container before the device started to rattle.

The storm cloud that was Dragan's magic flowed around her, stabbing at her, forcing its way down her throat and into her ears and eyes as it dropped her to the ground, but the dreeocht ate that too, gorging itself on Dragan's magic. Ellinor could smell her skin burning as the last of the storm cloud forced its way inside her; pressure built in her chest, her head, until her skin could barely contain her insides. The dreeocht container was practically bouncing now and Talin was desperately dragging Pema away from the device as it began to glow.

In a loud wail, the dreeocht container's lights flared on and the device went blindingly bright for a millisecond, before the leftover magic Dragan had used to make his beast was flung back at him, tossing the caster away and out of sight, screaming all the while.

Ellinor Olysha Rask lost consciousness before Dragan Volcain ever hit the ground.

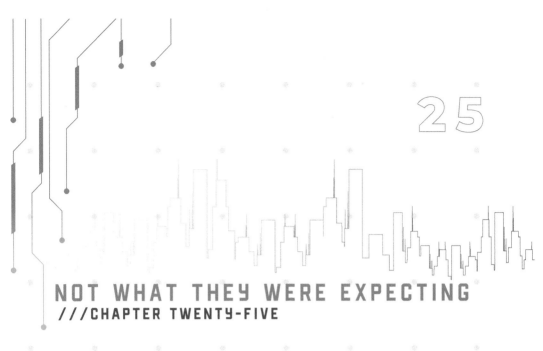

NOT WHAT THEY WERE EXPECTING
///CHAPTER TWENTY-FIVE

A PERSISTENT vibration woke Ellinor, saving her from the bloody image of Lazar exploding into bits all around her. Gingerly, she sat up and looked around, slow to comprehend what she was seeing.

A small medical drone hovered over Pema, draining its limited resources on her wound. Talin sat holding her girlfriend's hand, her arm in a new sling, pain evident in the beads of sweat running down her shaved head. Kai was fussing around the dreeocht container, the device so battered that the seal on the door was cracked open in several places. A shiver raced down her arms at the sight, unsure how long it would hold, should anything else happen. And what would emerge should the failsafe's fail.

Jelani was in the cockpit of the helicopter, his leg bouncing as he jerked his head from side to side, as if expecting something to rise from beneath them and tear them from the sky.

She supposed after everything that had happened, it wasn't a completely outlandish thought.

Wait, we're flying?

She blinked slowly, glancing about her once more and finally realized they had piled into the Ash Hawk and escaped Amaru for real this time, on Dragan's personal craft. Ellinor would have laughed, but it would have caused a wave of pain and nausea to roll over her body.

Leaning forward, she cradled her head in her hands, breathing deeply to try and ease the throbbing in her back and neck where the deep gash Dragan had given her was now covered by a piece of skin-like bandage. She moved only when she heard the faint buzz of the med drone as it hovered around her, leaving Pema momentarily to check her vitals and poke her with whatever painkiller it had left. Her heart sped as it approached, but settled once she saw the cables that would feed her vitals back to the ship's main computer were disconnected. Dragan wouldn't be able to monitor them.

If he lived.

The slight commotion captured Kai's attention as he lurched from his wall seat, sliding over to join her on the floor, his head freshly bandaged and eyes wide as they twitched from the cracks in the dreeocht container to her battered visage. Talin spared Ellinor a fleeting glance before going back to fussing over Pema alongside the returning medical bot.

"You doing okay, boss?" Kai murmured, handing her a flask that he scrounged up from Azer-only-knew where.

She took a long swig, letting the whiskey leave a burning trail down her throat, warming her entire core a moment later. It wasn't the good stuff, but it would do. The med drone buzzed a warning, yellow lights blinking, but she didn't care. Nothing was going to keep her from drinking.

Ellinor flexed her fingers as her body went tense all over, her gaze settling on Jelani. "No, I'm not doing all right."

Ellinor shoved herself off the floor, marched to Jelani, and kicked the back of his seat. "What the fuck happened? You decide that if you let Lazar die your debt is paid and you'd be free? That's it, yeah? Why in the abyss did you take so long to start shooting, and not aim at Dragan first?"

Jelani shoved her into the open chair next to him before she could kick his seat again. Jelani's expression was tight as he squeezed his eyes shut for a moment. When he opened them again, Ellinor noted the red ring in the skin lining his dark eyes. "It wasn't intentional. I didn't want Lazar to die, and certainly not like . . . that. He was never my enemy, even if we stood on opposite sides. But I needed time. Needed to prepare. After the crash, I couldn't get my bearings. I only just managed to get out of the van before Dragan saw me. I needed to charge my weapons. You understand? I needed to drain everything I could so we stood a chance against a caster like that, and after using my energy in the van . . ." Jelani's eyes narrowed and he shook his head. "Dragan hadn't seen me, he wouldn't see me come for him. It was an advantage I needed to exploit, but I was so . . ." He trailed off, shaking his head again. "I'm sorry. I wasn't fast enough, I wasn't ready in time. I miscalculated; I thought taking out Dragan's minions first would save us time later. *I* cost Lazar his life."

Ellinor's body became heavy at his confession, but she cleared her face of emotion before he noticed. She didn't know if she could believe him, didn't know if she *wanted* to believe him, to trust him.

Jelani glanced at her, his back slumping as he leaned over the Ash Hawk control console. "I should take responsibility for what occurred. I should be the one to tell Zabel what happened. But I can't. I cannot tell her. She would obliterate me, and I have people who rely on me. They wouldn't survive, should I never return."

"Oh? Like your piece of shit Ashlings?" Ellinor spat, a dull throb returning to her forehead.

Jelani raised a brow. "No, they would continue to survive should I vacate the field." He paused again, the muscles in his jaw clenching and unclenching, but still he didn't speak.

Ellinor sat for a moment, observing the new seersha in their midst. Curious why he was helping them, why he hadn't left, or sold them out to some other caster, or to Irati once he knew she was still on their trail. He seemed genuinely remorseful about Lazar, truly stunned at his horrific death, which made her wonder how the two seersha had crossed paths to begin with, questioning if, perhaps, it had been in Jelani's role as a Creature Breaker.

Her eyes slid to his swords, now compact at his sides once more.

While Ellinor's version of the blade was an illegal knock-off, Jelani's blades were a specialized form of Leviathan Roaster that few casters could wield. A unique blend of technology that was connected through a caster's own magic via a series of nanite bio-tech, infused in the caster and connected to a blade that responded only to their touch. This cut the seersha Creature Breakers off from the tether keeping their magic tied to one location, like their more powerful brethren. Creature Breakers had so little magic themselves that they were almost useless to the powerful casters of the world. But, if they had the proper training, they could trade that limited ability to become mercenaries beholden to no one.

Hired and called in when powerful casters got it in their minds to duel and summon their own creatures; Creature Breakers could turn the tide between two opposing forces. Which usually meant they were treated like underworld roy-alty—or killed instantly when found.

Ellinor had never heard of Jelani Sharma, but she assumed she should have. Given his earth abilities, she figured Cosmin would covet such an ally, perhaps even be interested in acquir-ing him. She guessed Jelani had worked as hard as Lazar had to remain hidden, his existence only known to a select few. The knowledge made the ember of distrust in her swell, ig-niting an uncomfortable curiosity about who Jelani was, and what his true motivations were.

The silence stretched, making Ellinor squirm in her seat. But instead of asking: *Who are you?* or *What do you want?* Elli-nor said, "Whatever. You rebels are all the same deep down." Ellinor jerked out of the seat, ready to rejoin Kai and help Talin with Pema, all while making plans to be rid of Jelani Tyrik Sharma at the first opportunity.

"My sister," Jelani's words were so soft, Ellinor wasn't con-vinced she had heard him.

"What?"

"Oihana, my little sister. I must—she needs me. That's why I can't tell the truth to Zabel, and I'd appreciate it if you did the same. Oihana is an innocent. She wouldn't survive without my protection for long. I don't expect you to understand such things."

"You don't know me, Jelani. Don't presume I don't under-stand what it means to love someone enough to put their life far above your own." Ellinor wasn't sure what had made her admit to such a vulnerability. She blamed the alcohol and the painkillers, not Jelani's anguished expression, nor the utter sincerity in his voice when he spoke of Oihana.

No, definitely not that.

Jelani's eyes trailed over her, as if he were observing her for the first time. His expression softened marginally, a glint of excitement flashed through his eyes before he turned his attention back to the controls. "My apologies, then. Anyway, I promised to get you to the vehicle depot where you could take what you needed to get back on track. But with the Ash Hawk, I think we can get farther away and speed things along. Kai mentioned where Lazar was taking you . . . to a transport he had stashed at the end of the Finnr River, correct?"

Ellinor nodded, and Jelani continued. "What I have stored in the depot would have worked. But given the trouble you've been having, and the state of your crew, not to mention your cargo, I believe the safest course for you all is to make a brief detour. I'll introduce you to Oihana. She can outfit your crew better and, perhaps, keep your container from bursting."

Ellinor sat down in the co-pilots seat, body heavy. "Why would you do that, yeah?" she whispered. "No one helps for free."

Jelani's lips twitched, but he didn't look at her. "There may be a price. But I wouldn't ask you of it now, not in these conditions. But, if it eases your mind, I think we could be . . . beneficial to each other. Still, I would offer this aid regardless. I owe Lazar that much."

He dipped his head, and said no more as he fiddled with the controls of the helicopter. Ellinor blinked at him rapidly, her muddled mind incapable of making sense of his words.

She wasn't sure going to see Oihana was a good idea, but nothing felt like a good idea anymore. Pema still had a hole in her side, and the dreeocht container wouldn't survive another battle. With Irati, Mirza, Janne, and Eko still in possession of the Eagle Owl, Ellinor was in favor of anything that would get them moving faster and farther away from any area where they could potentially be ambushed—or sold out to another gangster.

As she went back to her seat, Kai eyed her with a raised brow. He nudged her with his big foot when she didn't immediately speak. "What's up, Ell?"

Scrubbing her hands over her face, she grimaced at the grimy, rough texture of her skin from Lazar's—and her own—dried blood. "We're making a detour to somewhere we can all—" she waved at the dreeocht as well as Talin and Pema, "get patched up. Jelani's taking us to his sister's safe house. Guess she may have what we need. I'm not comfortable with the arrangement, but Pema needs serious help, and he's offering us that. I'm not so much a paranoid bitch to refuse that, yeah?"

Kai gave her a thin grin, his black bio-tech tooth gleaming at her in the bright light of the ebbing afternoon sun. "Ah, yeah, guess not. So, you okay with this here plan?"

Plugging her armor and shielding into a port on the Ash Hawk, Ellinor avoided Kai's keen gaze. "Jelani seems sincere in wanting to help us. He figures he owes Lazar still, and while I don't trust his motivations, I'm inclined to believe him. For now. Besides, he's the only one who can fly this bird, and I'd rather not walk to the Finnr River." She paused, glancing at the readouts on her armor, making sure everything was charging properly. "How are you, Kai? You got knocked around something good. Need something stronger than whiskey to help you out?"

Kai chuckled, then shrugged. "Nah, I'm good. Just gotta bash some skulls for the trouble this shit-show causes Cosmin, then I'll be square." He glanced at the other women briefly before leaning toward Ellinor. "How's, uh, your neck? The . . . collar not bothering you none?"

She glared at him and Kai held up his hands. "I'm just trying to get things back to right with you and me, Ell."

Ellinor's chest tightened. "I'm taking that, this 'you and me' thing, one day, one moment at a time. But I can't forget what happened, you know? Each time I want things between us to go back to how they were, before Cosmin fucked it all up, I just feel . . ." she took a deep, shuddering breath. "I can feel *your* hands on my neck. I can feel the vibration as the shackle fused together, how everything went cold as soon as this thing went on." She tapped the collar around her neck, and gasped.

Where there had once been a gap, was now no discernible difference between where Cosmin's device ended and her neck began. She clawed at the device, but couldn't pry it away from her skin. A burning pain raced down her neck, like rivers of fire, as pieces of the collar were now rooted in her skin and could not be pried away.

"What the fuck is happening?" Ellinor squealed, trying to keep panic from making her voice shrill.

Kai inspected the device briefly, his face paling and his jaw slackening a bit. He waved the medical drone over and instructed it to fix her neck, to safely pry the device out of her flesh. Ellinor sat still as the bot buzzed around her. Had she not touched the device, she would have never known it was fused to her throat. She felt no different; nothing hurt until she, and now the drone, tried to pry it away.

An involuntary squeal squeezed past her lips as the bot once more failed to safely remove the collar with one of its fine laser scalpels. Jelani put the Ash Hawk on autopilot and came back to inspect what all the noise was about.

He frowned at her, his defined eyebrows jutting downward in a mix of sympathy and worry. "All the more reason to make that detour now."

"Why's that? What's wrong with her?" Talin asked, leaving Pema's side to see for herself what new damage had been inflicted.

"Some sort of reaction to all the magical attacks, I'd assume, given what that device is meant to do," Jelani said, rubbing his chin, eyes taking on a shrouded look that did little to veil the anger building in him. "I'm no mechanic. I can't say why this is happening. But my sister is. She can shed some light on what's happening to your commander that the medical drone can't."

HEY, LITTLE SISTER
///CHAPTER TWENTY-SIX

ELLINOR SLEPT fitfully for the day it took them to travel to the far outskirts of the little hamlet of Behar. It was the only township within miles and miles of the Finnr River where Lazar had what they needed. They should be getting back on track to reach Anzor, hopefully before anything else caught up with them.

Her injuries were not as grievous as Pema's, but even so, alongside the emotional toll of the past few days coupled with her near death experiences, it was hard for Ellinor to stay awake for more than a few hours at a time. That didn't mean she felt all that rested as Jelani slowed the Ash Hawk and flipped off its various cloaking devices so whoever they were approaching outside of Behar—Ellinor assumed it was Oi-hana—would see them coming and not shoot them from the sky.

Far outside the protective circle of Behar was a series of mounds that could be mistaken for hills in the shadow of the sparse forest and gurgling emerald green river nearby, except a thin tendril of white smoke rose from the mound in the center. Ellinor watched the little hump with interest, but her attention was constantly being captured by the sheer *emptiness* of the area around her. Such wide open spaces, the natural colors, being away from the familiar conveniences of the metropolitan swarm of bodies, technology, and magic, still caught Ellinor off guard.

Jelani fiddled with the controls, making the lights on the Ash Hawk flicker and the whole craft vibrate for a moment. Pema—who had recovered enough to be semi-conscious—groaned as she turned to look at Jelani. "What's happening? We there yet?"

Jelani didn't turn to address her. "We have reached my sister, yes." The Ash Hawk landed with a gentle *thud* and Jelani all but ran toward the door.

Kai stopped him. "Where you think you're going, aye?"

Jelani eyed him coolly before nimbly moving around the big man. "I need to disable the security measures my sister has in place, and I'd rather you not see me do that. This is what I hold most dear, and you work for the opposition. My sister needs a moment to secure her own assets. It's nothing personal, just—"

"Business?" Ellinor finished for Jelani, giving Kai a knowing look.

She was tired, her body ached, and she was desperate for a hot meal, a long shower, and clean hands so she could remove the contacts that distorted her eye color. She understood Jelani's precautions, his desire to protect his sister. But she was in no mood to delay, especially with Pema still looking so ashen. If Jelani had wanted them dead, or had wanted to use the dreeocht for his own purposes, he could have easily killed them in their weakened states, or kept the dreeocht and Ellinor for himself to sell to a new buyer. She still didn't trust him all that much, but they needed what he was offering, regardless of her misgivings.

Jelani's grin was slow, but it tugged up the corners of his lips and lit up his starry eyes. "Precisely. This is my business, and I will protect it."

Ellinor waved him away, a facsimile of permission that both knew was unnecessary; Jelani's smile became a little more genuine. Kai pursed his lips, narrowing his eyes at Jelani before shrugging and turning to collect their gear.

Talin Roxas was not so easily convinced. "You do anything that has even a whiff of calling in some caster, and I'll make a special grenade just for you. I'll stick it in a place you won't be able to reach, either, pretty boy. Got me?"

Pema grasped for Talin's hand, but Jelani seemed good-natured about it. He winked at Talin, but didn't otherwise acknowledge the threat.

Ellinor had wanted to take the opportunity to further study their surroundings and use the peace and relative safety of the area to help steady her twitchy nerves, to steady the rhythm of her heart, which had only gotten worse with the collar's malfunction. But no sooner had Jelani disappeared into one of the mounds than a swarm of service drones surround their aircraft, made with so many illegal modifications that Ellinor was sure they were on the cusp of becoming Ashlings.

She scrambled for her weapons, but Jelani and a young girl strolled out of the compound, waving their distress away. Ellinor kept her hand over her pistol holsters until the swarm of drones finished scanning the Ash Hawk and flew like a flock of birds back into a hatch on the top of one of the mounds.

Wary of why Jelani had neglected to mention they'd be scanned, Ellinor poked her head from the Ash Hawk, watching the siblings approach with a pinched expression. She couldn't leave the craft, though. Not with the dreeocht container so badly compromised. Straying even more than fifteen feet from it now set the container buzzing, her collar pulsing faintly in response. The warning system was failing, and she couldn't say how long it would remain intact, or why the container was buzzing now. But each time it did, her breath caught in her chest, and her heart skipped a beat, hoping the sleeping creature wasn't waking.

If Ellinor had been unsure of Oihana being Jelani's sister, those concerns were gone when she saw the two together. They had the same dusky complexion, though the younger girl's skin was a bit darker. Their bone structure was the same, chiseled lines making an angular face, though Oihana's cheeks were rounder and covered in onyx freckles. They had the same ear shape—just subtle points that denoted them as seersha, though Oihana did appear to be on the more humani side.

It was their eyes and hair that made them stand apart from one another. Where Jelani's hair was a tousled mess that looked like fog rolling in from the ocean, Oihana's was such a rich brown it was nearly black. It flowed around her in a wave of gentle, soft curls. Instead of eyes that looked like the night sky alight with stars, hers were the soft golden amber of drying soil.

Kai bumped her from behind, dragging the dreeocht container on its broken push-cart with him. Nodding at him, they exited the Ash Hawk with Pema, Talin, and the medical drone not far behind.

By the time they reached the waiting duo, another type of service android emerged from the hatch behind Jelani. It was the most humani looking android Ellinor had ever seen. If it weren't for the metal sheen of its skin, lack of gender, as well as the wayward wire snaking out from one part of its body and connecting to another, Ellinor would have assumed she was looking at a humani in a robotic suit, or someone with so many technological modifications they blurred the lines between a person and an Ashling.

Ellinor's mouth went dry at the sight. Oblivious to her sudden discomfort and desire to rip the bot apart for reminding her of the Ashlings that murdered Misho, Jelani waved at the young girl beside him. "This is Oihana Sharma and her helper automaton. What's this one's name?"

Oihana's eyes never left her brother's lips. "IAA-43 technically, but that's not much of a name for an Independent Assistance Android, you know? Zer likes to be called Izza."

Oihana was young, too young for someone with an IAA. Oihana looked to be in her mid-twenties, still a teenager by seersha standards, given they could live for five hundred years, easily. Usually only the very old had Independent Assistance Androids.

"Izza? Why?" Jelani asked, a soft smile on his face.

Again, Oihana watched only his lips. "Zer likes it. I like it. That's why."

"What's wrong with you? Can't look your own brother in the eyes. Oihana, is it?" Pema asked, her voice raspy and weak, as she clutched at her side, Talin gently supporting her.

Jelani's gaze whipped to Pema, his face darkening. But Oihana seemed unaffected; she turned and walked back toward the compound, waving everyone to follow her like she hadn't heard Pema.

They made to follow after her, but Jelani stopped them with a raised hand. "There is absolutely nothing wrong with my sister. You understand? *Nothing* is wrong with her." His voice quivered slightly, cheeks flushed, and it looked like he was taking great pains not to bare his teeth.

Talin narrowed her eyes but helped Pema follow along in Oihana's wake. "Right, fine. You know she didn't mean nothing by it."

Ellinor blinked in surprise. Talin, for once, appeared too exhausted to argue and defend her girlfriend.

They descended into the mound through a hatch in the roof that reminded Ellinor of the cavern Lazar had built. Bile rose in her throat at the memory, her breaths shallow, desperately trying not to inhale the iron twang floating around her from Lazar's dried blood. Her stomach was still rolling by the time her eyes adjusted to the clinical, bright white light of the room. Oihana watched them, her big, round eyes scanning their faces.

Nodding to herself, Oihana gestured to Pema and Talin. "Have her rest there. I have a fleet of repurposed medical drones. They can't do surgery anymore, but they'll make sure your lady doesn't get an infection." Talin glanced to the bed, which looked more like a gurney to Ellinor, and nodded, helping Pema lay down on the starchy white sheets.

Turning her gaze back to Ellinor and Kai for a moment, Oihana frowned, and scratched her cheek. "I'll take a look at your box, but I don't think there's much I can do. That collar though . . . ." She peered at the contraption around Ellinor's neck, her frown deepening before shaking her head. "I have to look at it more closely."

Ellinor took a step toward her, but Oihana raised her hand. "Ew, no! You're gross. Go wash, then I'll take a look. You can use the shower down the hall, Izza will show you. You, big man, bring the box over here, it'll be close enough to your friend where it'll be fine."

She had never been dismissed like that by a mechanic before, let alone one so young. Ellinor was so stunned she didn't realize IAA—43, or Izza, had its—zers?—cold metal hand on the small of her back, leading her down the hall.

Ellinor shivered at the contact.

Izza's tinny voice filled the hallway. "Are you cold, miss? I can bring you old coats of Mr. Jelani's once you are clean. They will be big on you, but they will function. Ms. Oihana does like to keep the temperature down. She claims it helps her work, helps her focus. I have warned Ms. Oihana several times the temperature hovers at a degree where illness is possible. But she overrides my advice. Shall I deliver you that coat along with fresh clothing?"

Ellinor had never dealt with an Independent Assistance Android before. Normally, only the oldest—and richest—in Erhard could afford such bots, as they acted as nursemaids and companions to the perpetually lonely as their old age meant they outlived any who would be willing to take care of them. Those androids still appeared like any other service bot, but with longer arms in order to help their owner. None were allowed to look humani, but Izza certainly did. It was a crime to make bots look like people.

Ellinor suspected Oihana hadn't salvaged this piece of technology like she had with the medical bots. Which meant she had made this IAA device all on her own.

Is it an Ashling? No, if it was, why would it help Jelani's sister?

Still, the thought remained and Ellinor's skin began to tingle uncomfortably as Izza kept zer all too humani hand on the small of her back, shepherding her along. As Izza touched her, all she could envision was the morphing mechanical gun from the Ashling who killed Misho. She jerked away from the thing, her hands tingling.

"No. You can clean my clothes but not my armor, yeah? That gets plugged in—and stays with me. *You* can fuck off. Now." She jerked the bathroom door open and glared at Izza, who stared at her in return with zer unblinking ocular orbs, which emitted an odd grey light source, not the black of most Ashlings. But she found no reassurance in this.

With a tilt of zer head, the IAA turned on zer heel and waddled down the hallway. Ellinor shut the door, and checked to make sure it was locked three times before turning to whatever solace a hot shower could offer her.

Ellinor emerged over an hour later, clean, and free of Lazar's contacts. She probably would have stayed under the scalding water longer had her armor not pinged, letting her know it was fully charged once again. The subtle reminder that a harsh reality waited outside the bathroom was enough to shatter the fragile reprieve she had built for herself. Sighing, she draped a towel over her, fetched the clean clothes laid out from outside the locked door, and secured her armor and weapons before hunting down Oihana and Jelani.

The siblings were outside what Ellinor assumed to be Oihana's workshop. She supposed they were speaking, but no sound passed their lips. Instead they moved their hands in complicated, fast-paced gestures that Ellinor couldn't follow. It didn't look like any form of sign language she was familiar with. She knew such a secret language would be exceptionally handy in Jelani's line of work, and she wondered if she could get him to teach it to her before they parted ways for good.

Assuming that doesn't add to the favor he'll ask for later.

Shaking her head, she ran her fingers through her damp, long black hair, tugging on the tendrils of faux glowing purple as they passed her fingers. She had dyed it a lifetime ago when she was still loyal to Cosmin, something Misho had initially hated but grew to love, keeping her from cutting the dyed strands away each time they grew back. Clearing her throat, she stepped up to the siblings.

Jelani's attention snapped to her instantly, Oihana's a moment later, her brow creased until it softened at seeing Ellinor. The young girl grinned and waved Ellinor over. "Good, you're clean. I won't get some nasty disease from just looking at that thing on your neck now."

Ellinor wanted to smile at the girl. She wanted to be swept up in her nonchalance for the situation at hand. But the harsh look from Jelani and the unease she had around the seersha killed any momentary ease she felt around Oihana.

Nodding, Ellinor stepped toward the work bench Oihana sat at, careful to avoid Jelani's inquisitive eyes as she passed. She didn't like the look he gave her, and she worried that, despite the shower's heat, she was still pale from the shock that refused to wear off, the slight tremor in her hands as obvious as an earthquake. She sat on her hands as she eased onto a seat across from the girl.

Without preamble or fear, Oihana gripped Ellinor's neck in rough, calloused hands. Oihana bit her lip as she prodded the collar, tilting Ellinor's head this way and that, her amber eyes darkening the more she tugged and ran her thumbs over the device—especially where the collar was now fused to her skin. Oihana picked up a few devices that scanned the shackle keeping Ellinor's powers locked away, each eliciting a huff of frustration from Oihana until she tossed the last scanner on the work table and threw her hands up.

"How did this happen?" She tapped her neck. "What happened to make it do that? It's not supposed to do that, you know. It should have killed you. How are you alive?"

Ellinor felt Jelani shift behind her, the rustle of his clothes telling her he was silently conversing with his sister. Oihana waved him off, not taking her eyes from Ellinor's lips.

Ellinor frowned, her panic returning. "I don't know. Each time I was hit with air magic—though, some water could have been in there, maybe? I don't know. The collar buzzed and the lights flared on our cargo box. The collar would tighten, but never choked me. We were running and fighting for our lives, so excuse me for not checking what was happening, yeah? I was a bit preoccupied and since it didn't kill me, I figured it wasn't worth my immediate attention."

Ellinor could feel the tremor in her hands snaking up her arms as her heart started to race with a fresh wave of fear. She watched Oihana's eyes slide from her lips to where the dreeocht container was nestled in the corner, its cracks and dents exactly the way they were when Ellinor had gone to shower. Oihana's shoulders slumped, and she began fiddling with her hair as she shook her head.

"It isn't like anything I've seen or worked with before. I've gotten scraps from tech like what's in your collar, but it makes no sense why it's reacting this way to *you* getting hit with caster magic." Frustration and intrigue laced through her tone, making her naturally deep voice huskier. Shrugging, Oihana said, "It won't kill you. So that should make you feel better, right? But no one's getting that thing off you. At least no one in Erhard. Doubt the caster who shackled you could even get it off now. At most? They can probably switch it off. But I don't have the tools for that, unless you want me to kill you?"

When Ellinor narrowed her eyes in response, Oihana stood, walking to the dreeocht container where she ran her hands over its now grimy surface before Ellinor could say the news did not, in fact, make her feel better. "Whatever's broken or different about the bio-magitech around your neck is affecting this stupid thing. I can't even fuse the cracks without some warning light blaring on. This is so stupid. Anni, why do you only bring me the annoying crap?"

"Anni?" Ellinor whispered, swiveling toward him, her lips twitching into a grin.

Jelani gave her a cold look and said, "Don't you dare," before turning a softer expression to his sister. "You said you liked a challenge, so I complied. Don't complain when I find you things to test your abilities. This is how you grow and become better."

A playful scowl creased Oihana's face before she waved her brother off again. "Fine, whatever. But that doesn't mean I can do anything for it, or her. Not on your deadline. Go on, take what you need. Just bring it back this time? In *one* piece. I can't waste time fixing the same crap over and over again. There's no fun in that.

"Izza's made some food, by the way. Feel free to stuff your face. Zer's not a bad cook considering zer can't taste what zer makes. I'm going to take some notes on this box, maybe if you come back this way when you're done with this job or whatever, I'll have answers for you."

Ellinor didn't move. She stared at the back of Oihana's head as the girl flitted around the container once more, tapping things on a scanner strapped to her wrist, the small computer connected, no doubt, to some larger device in another section of the underground laboratory.

"What's that mean? No one can get it off? I'll never get my powers back?" Oihana didn't answer, too focused on what she was seeing from her scans. Ellinor turned to Jelani, her eyes blinking rapidly as if that would change the scene playing out before her. "Even if she can't fix it, someone can take this thing off without taking my head with it, yeah? There must be someone. I have to get my powers back!"

Her voice shook, going up an octave that made her sound younger than her fifty years. Jelani shifted his weight, rubbed his shoulder for a moment as if he were debating touching her in some manner of comfort, before shoving his hands in his pockets. A rueful grin grew on his face that didn't reach his eyes. "Oihana will figure it out, she just needs more time than you have. I mean, you have to deliver your cargo, not that you don't personally have enough time. That's, of course, if you decide you still want to deliver your prize to Zabel?"

She narrowed her eyes up at him, and Jelani held up a hand. "Consider other options, that's all. Your ex-boss isn't the only one who can remove your shackle. Oihana is one of the best mechanics in Erhard, she truly is, but there are others, people more intimately familiar with such devices that may have better luck removing it completely, not just turning it off."

"You're asking me to double cross Cosmin," she whispered fiercely. "No, not just Cosmin, but Talin, Pema, and Kai. You know what happens to them if I pull some shit like that? Cosmin tortures them and their families, slowly, endlessly. It'd probably set Zabel's dogs after them, too. It means I can't get close to Cosmin again. Can't ever make him pay for what he did—" She bit off her words, turning away, water blurring her vision.

Jelani made a soft sound of understanding. "Well, I definitely wouldn't want your friends to pay such a price. Still, something to consider on the road ahead, certainly."

Before she could protest, he was helping her to her feet and leading her to another room, one that snaked behind where Oihana was working, putting a wall between her and the dreeocht. It was then that the smells of beef, garlic rice, and fried peppers tickled her nose. She almost vomited on the spot.

She knew she needed food, that her body needed fuel to repair the trauma of the past few days, but the thought of eating sent her empty stomach lurching up her throat. Jelani left her at the entrance to retrieve a plate from IAA-43, and Kai, no doubt seeing the sick look on her face, darted for her, gently leading her to a bench.

"Eat this first," he said, thrusting a chalky candy into her hand. "It's pure ginger. It'll knock the sick out of you. You gotta eat though, Ell. We got a long way to go, and we're leaving in a few hours. We'll get this mess cleaned up all proper like, you'll see. It's gonna be just fine. Trust me."

Popping the ginger candy in her mouth on auto-pilot, Ellinor wanted to believe Kai, to trust him. But experience told her he wasn't telling the truth, even if he was unaware of it himself. *Nothing* was going to be fine.

GREETINGS FROM HOME
///CHAPTER TWENTY-SEVEN

PEMA TRAN disagreed with Ellinor. "You can't leave me here," the woman seethed as much as she could from the cot she was struggling to sit up on.

Talin gently pushed her girlfriend back down. "Baby, listen to her, please? That little girl's bots aren't real surgeons. Which is what you need. There's too much tissue damage from that fucking air bullet." She leaned her forehead against Pema's, her voice softening. "You could die if we run into more trouble. I can't lose you, Pema."

Pema gave Talin a pained look before fixing her gaze on Ellinor, who spread her hands, pleading for understanding. "I applaud your dedication, I really do, but think about it, yeah? You can barely walk, tire easily, have trouble breathing. What's going to happen if trouble finds us again?" Pema opened her mouth, Ellinor shook her head, silencing her. "You're going to do your best, I know you are. You'll fight bravely. But I've seen you and Talin when one of you gets hurt. You lose all sense."

I don't blame you, I would too if it were Misho. Ellinor swallowed her words. "I'm doing this to keep Talin and Kai safe. It's not personal. Stay here with Oihana, get better, and on the way back from Anzor we'll pick you up before heading back to Euria."

"We're coming back for you, baby," Talin added, kissing her softly. "I'm always coming back for you."

Pema's eyes glazed over with tears, but she jutted her chin up valiantly, squeezing Talin's hand. "You'd better."

Ellinor left the two, giving them a private moment while she helped Kai and Jelani load their supplies on the Class 3 Hornet Hawk Oihana had updated, and had allowed them to "borrow" for the remainder of their trip. A few minutes later, a teary eyed Talin joined them. She wouldn't speak to Ellinor, but both women knew Ellinor had made the right call. With some space and time, Talin would speak to her again.

Once they took off, Ellinor disconnected from her conscious thoughts, allowing the next two days in the cramped military aerial transport to roll past her in a numb, hazy blur. She avoided speaking to Jelani about what his sister said about her collar, and about his not so subtle offer. She was still curious about him though; he had yet to say what he wanted from her. He couldn't just be offering these *alternatives* for free, could he?

Once they were in free airspace on the second day of their flight, Ellinor was able to get a message to Cosmin von Brandt without fear it'd be intercepted by Irati or any of Dragan's people. The seersha crime boss was not pleased to hear from her, especially given her news. He was mollified, for the moment, knowing they were making up time in the air. Cosmin promised to have some *trustworthy* backup waiting at their next stop—near the small city of Gentius—and that was it. Cosmin warned her once more of the consequences of failing, and disconnected the holo-call, presumably to tell Zabel that Lazar had been killed by Dragan, and that he couldn't confirm if the caster was killed in the aftermath.

After the exchange, Ellinor found herself staring at the battered dreeocht container, wondering if all this trouble had been worth it. She wanted to bring peace to Misho, and she always would, but being caught and turned into a pawn for Cosmin had already cost three people their lives, and she wasn't even including Dragan's goons. Her brother may have accepted such losses as collateral damage, as a hazard of this line of work. But Misho wouldn't have seen it that way.

She was beginning to question if her burning desire for revenge was worth the cost.

Misho Shimizu had liked having a direct effect, to do what needed to be done without all the bureaucracy. He liked seeing immediate results, and didn't agree that magitech should be so heavily regulated. With Cosmin, he could supply magitech more effectively than through the traditional government role his training had placed him in. Plus, so many elected officials were already on Cosmin's payroll that it made a certain degree of sense to try and make the underground as honorable as possible, rather than constantly fight it to no avail. So, when Misho returned to their cramped apartment telling her he had taken Cosmin up on his long-standing offer, Ellinor had followed, no questions asked. She believed in his sense of morality above her own to make the right choice.

But now, looking at the havoc and death her quest for vengeance had brought her, and without the familiar warmth of her own powers, she was starting to recognize the festering wound Misho's loss had left in her. An infection of hate had spread in her over the years, and slowly, day by day, she stopped seeing friends or enemies; she saw only obstacles.

Her heart sank, unable to pinpoint when she had so completely lost her path.

With her thoughts distracted by these melancholic questions, Kai was finally able to get through to her. Nudging her with his shoulder, he slumped down beside her. "Cosmin ask 'bout me?"

Kai's eyes shimmered with a watery hope, making Ellinor's intestines twist. It didn't matter how many times she told Kai that Cosmin would never love him, that the seersha would never see the big humani as anything more than a useful brute, Kai's heart was too ensnared by the caster's charm and disarming looks. Maybe one day she would be able to show him how useless it was to still hold out hope, but she didn't have the energy for it this day.

Ellinor shook her head. "Nope, sorry. It was all business."

Kai chewed on his lip for a moment, his eyes losing focus. "Guess he does 'ave other business on 'is mind, don't he?" Shaking his head slightly, Kai forced himself to relax and changed the subject. "We're coming up on the Saxa Desert soon, you know. You been quiet as the abyss since we got in this Hornet Hawk. Need a med bot to . . . ." He trailed off, scratching at his spiky red and acid green hair. "I dunno. Check your 'ead again? You knocked it around something good."

She waved his concern away. "So did you, and I don't see a bot fussing over you. Tell you what, you let the bots scan you, and then I'll let them have a go at me." Kai winked, waving her offer away, and she shrugged. "Suit yourself."

Ellinor dropped the act when Kai continued to frown at her. She sighed. "I'll be fine. Just processing the metric shit-ton of information from Oihana regarding this—" she waved at the collar embedded in her flesh, "and that stupid dreeocht. The box is barely holding together. Not sure how many more bumps it can take."

Kai flashed her a toothy grin, the black bio-tech tooth gleaming in the artificial light of their aircraft. "Well, we ain't gonna give it more bumps. We're free and clear now. Figured we done paid enough between . . . the crew we lost and every-thing else." His eyes wavered and his voice threatened to crack. Clearing his throat, he said, "We paid a steep price. By Azer, we're due some good luck."

Talin hissed at them from her bunk. "Don't go jinxing us. Words like that, phrases like 'what else could go wrong' ensure one thing. Take a guess what it is."

"Ah, lay off, Talin. Just because you're sore about Pema doesn't mean—"

"No, no. Go on, guess. What happens when you say shit like that, Kai?"

Kai tucked his chin into his chest, averting his eyes. "The opposite," Kai mumbled, like a child caught trying to sneak dessert.

"Exactly. No price can outbid a jinx. You remember that and keep your damn mouth shut."

Ellinor rolled her eyes. "Calm down, Talin. Really. Leave Kai's optimism intact, yeah? It's just words."

Talin scrubbed a hand over her face, but failed to bring any luster back to her dark ebony skin. "There can be plenty o' harm in words spoken in idleness. Pema taught me that."

They all grew quiet, their eyes scanning the various crevices of the patchwork plane, listening to the subtle vibrating panels as the air outside flowed around them. They remained that way for several minutes, holding their breath as if they were waiting for the jinx Talin warned of to catch up. When nothing happened, Ellinor smiled at Kai.

"See? All that worrying over nothing," Kai said. "Dragan doesn't know where we're headed, and we lost Irati. We're in the clear. Aye, a bit of luck, finally."

As if on cue, the radar Jelani had been diligently watching began screaming a warning throughout the cabin. Clear one moment, something popped up on the screen dangerously close the next.

That "something" rammed into the Hornet Hawk, sending the whole thing shuddering. Smoke spilled into the cabin, and Talin yelled, "I fucking told you!"

BLOODY AMBITION
///CHAPTER TWENTY-EIGHT

AFTER THEIR escape from the Eagle Owl, Ellinor believed she was a master at the art of crashing, or, at least, surviving a crash. Her armor powered up, deadening the sharp points of impact that would otherwise break bones, draining the charge at an alarming rate as she tumbled around the cabin, trying to scramble to the dreeocht container and use her body to cushion the thing. No matter what was outside their craft—whether it was Dragan Voclain or some new caster eager to lay claim to their property—the last thing Ellinor wanted was for the dreeocht to get out while they were in tight quarters.

Ellinor wasn't sure what the effects of multiple blows to the head were, nor did she think her bruises could get any more bruised, but she knew she was about to find out as Jelani struggled to keep their Hornet Hawk from dismantling upon impact. The dreeocht box thudded against her back before bouncing into Kai's chest, where he he wrapped it in his arms.

They were nearing doehaz territory now. Few braved areas where the ferocious beasts dwelled, and never anyone with anything magical on them, not even held within a piece of technology. Their nose, and taste, for anything magical was legendary, and unless you flew over them, there was no getting around them. That anyone would be this close to the desert merely by chance was impossible.

A loud keening filled her ears, drowning out the beeps from the malfunctioning craft. Talin was clinging to the bunk, Kai trying to keep the container from punching a hole in the compromised craft. Flashes of light from their cracked windows mingled with sparks from the lights, and as they slid to a halt in the rocky, sandy terrain, all she *knew* was that they had been hit and were without a functioning transport. Again.

Once the Hornet Hawk stopped tumbling and skidding in the hard packed earth, Jelani was on his feet, climbing through the transport, sparing only passing glances for the rest of the crew as he manually tried engaging the shields. "Talin, grab whatever gear you can," he snapped before pointing at Kai. "Get my rifle."

With the crew in motion, and once Ellinor was convinced the dreeocht wouldn't be making an appearance, she hauled herself to her feet. Ignoring the sharp pain in her joints, she followed after Jelani.

Her eyes flicked from one red light to the next, to cracked glass, to smoking consoles, and back again. "We have no defenses, do we?" Her words sounded slurred, like speaking around a mouth full of food. Prodding her mouth with her tongue, Ellinor took some small comfort in her teeth being where they were supposed to be.

"Not at the moment, no," Jelani said slowly. "But whatever hit us didn't want us dead. Not immediately. That gives us a chance." Glancing at the rest of the crew, Jelani nodded to himself. "We're not entirely defenseless."

Ellinor tried to shrug, wanting to give a sarcastic answer to the assumption that four badly battered people would be able to mount any kind of effective defense, but stopped herself. Neither Misho nor Andrey would have tolerated such defeatist thoughts, and she owed it to Kai and Talin to do her best to get them out of this mess alive.

Checking her pistols and dinged up Asco Rhino still strapped to her back, Ellinor tried to ignore the pain and focus only on the upcoming altercation. "What hit us? Did you see anything?"

Jelani shook his head, shoving a fresh magazine into his combat rifle. "No, it moved too fast. It's a hypersonic craft of some kind. One that was already in the area. Waiting for us, perhaps?" His voice darkened along with his face, blame and guilt for his perceived failure evident.

The suspicion that was itching at the back of her bruised skull flared to life. "Shit . . . ." The failure wasn't Jelani's, but Ellinor's. She hauled herself back to her crew, Jelani behind her.

"What is it? You know what hit us?" But Ellinor ignored him, instead helping Talin locate her pistol and grenade belts, as Kai powered on his brawny Coyote suit.

"It's Irati. This whole time we've been running, fleeing from one point to the next, thinking we could simply out run them. We should have known better." Ellinor scrubbed her hands over her face, wincing as touching the tender flesh sent sharp pains radiating all the way to her chest.

"*I* should have known better. Taken the time to sit and plan a safer route instead of letting Lazar shoulder that burden. Alone, no less. Instead, I let my—" Ellinor cut herself off abruptly with a growl, before turning her back on the slack-jawed crew. "I should have known that when they lost us near Amaru, they'd repair their ship and wait for us to show up. They must have gotten the information on the routes for refueling from Mirza, or maybe Eko. Whether he gave it willingly or not doesn't matter now."

What she didn't say was that her arrogance, her extreme desire to get this job done and over with so she could get back to the revenge business had led them all into a trap. A thickness coated her throat until she couldn't swallow, her heart constricting in her chest with guilt and the disappointment she imagined Misho would have if he could see her now.

Ellinor and the crew paused in both thought and movement, their heads jerking up as a buzz, similar to a swarm of angry bees, swelled above them outside of the ruined aircraft. The repaired Eagle Owl was just above them, barely audible over the loud buzzing sound was the unmistakable *thud* of two people jumping from the plane to land outside the cockpit doors. The narrow passage would only aid Irati and whomever was with her. One gas grenade and they would all be out cold, and Irati could stroll in and take what she was after, whatever she wanted.

"Right, okay," Ellinor whispered, trying to wrestle her racing heart back under control. "We need to get out of here before they breach that door. There's a back exit of some kind, yeah?"

Jelani's eyes slid from the cockpit door to his feet. "Yes, beneath us. We can get out through the cargo area. It'll be tight. But won't your friends be waiting for us on the other side?"

"Not if we move fast. Everyone knows where a cockpit door is, but the cargo holds on these small craft all look different, have different kinds of hatches. It'll take them a moment to find it, and I'm sure they're hoping we can't get to it. So let's move while we have the chance, yeah?"

They fell in line without further direction, knowing what to do without being told. They were a machine—albeit a battered one—that moved in harmony with one another. Kai maneuvered the dreeocht container, all but one of the push-cart's wheels hopelessly mangled, as carefully and quickly as he could with Ellinor's help, to where Jelani was opening the cargo hatch and readying their exit. Meanwhile, Talin scooped up their weapons and supplies in order to mount some kind of defense against Irati Mishra. Within moments, the crew was in the cramped hold and trying to exit the craft undetected.

Jelani slipped away unseen by those on the hypersonic plane. Irati didn't know who was on the Hornet Hawk; it could have been Lazar and a new crew of goons, or just Ellinor and Kai. Jelani wanted to take advantage of the ambiguity to flank their enemies. But before Ellinor or Talin could join him a safe distance from their ship, Janne Wolff darted around the side, having figured out where the exterior cargo hatch was.

Ellinor was barely five feet outside their ruined transport, but she was able to see the seersha creep toward the Eagle Owl. Janne's eyes glittered, her smile feral as she glared at Ellinor, missing the stealthy Jelani completely. She hoped he was going to distract the traitors by disabling their craft, but she had an uneasy feeling, all the same.

Ellinor took a step toward the woman. Her fingers twitched for her Lacerators, trying to give Talin and Kai more room to move, to get the dreeocht clear, but she miscalculated. The boom of a cannon cut through the hissing sounds of their destroyed vehicle.

Ellinor, Kai, and Talin flung themselves in different directions. A hot, searing pain raced along Ellinor's shoulder from the bullet's graze. The burning sting alerting her that her armor had lost its charge from shielding her, once again, from a crashing plane.

The dust from their bodies hitting the ground momentarily hid them. As the shot's echo faded, Janne growled.

Ellinor's vision cleared, and her eyes landed on the glint of silver in Janne's hand. She wasn't wielding her Lances, but a hefty revolver. Janne swung the gun around, and Ellinor rolled at the same moment Janne fired again. The deafening sound couldn't completely mask Talin's sharp gasp.

Deal with it later, Andrey's harsh voice barked through her mind.

Gritting her teeth, Ellinor lurched to her feet and yanked out her Anaconda before Janne could refocus her aim. Janne fired, but didn't hit Ellinor.

"You bitch. Wait till you see what I'll do to you. I owe you for taking Warin away! You'll be begging me to put a bullet in your brain." Janne bared her teeth, her dark blue eyes flashing with rage as she swung her gun. Ellinor was ready this time and she didn't hesitate.

Ellinor's first shot was too low and shattered Janne's tibia, her second too high, but rendered Janne's nimble hand obsolete as the bullet tore through her palm as she fell. "You should know better than to issue threats you can't back up, Janne. *That,* by the way, doesn't even come close to getting justice for Embla. Pity. I thought this little rematch of ours would be . . . oh, I don't know. More challenging, maybe? More interesting? You barely drew blood."

Despite Talin's panting and Janne's own cries, Ellinor wasn't going to kill Janne. She couldn't, they had been friends once. But with her armor dead and Irati, Eko, and Mirza—or others—waiting to ambush them, Ellinor needed the leverage.

Snatching Janne, Ellinor held the screaming woman tight against her chest, covering herself in blood once more. Then, and only then, did she risk a look back at the rest of the crew.

Talin finished hastily tying a tourniquet around her leg, Janne's shot having gone through the fleshy part of her thigh. Kai, for the most part, seemed unharmed, having moved the dreeocht as far away from Ellinor as possible. He stood glowering in front of the container, his submachine gun and the arsenal hidden within his armor at the ready; he would defend their cargo with his dying breath if he had to, as Cosmin ordered.

Holding Janne tight, Ellinor called out, "This was hardly worth the effort of chasing us down, yeah? Just to fail so spectacularly. No wonder you were part of Cosmin's B Team after I left. He couldn't be bothered with you. Wanted to be rid of you, more likely."

Ellinor didn't want an answer, nor did she expect one. She just needed more time for Talin to get back into cover, and for Jelani to dispatch whomever he could on the Eagle Owl so only those outside of the plane were of any concern.

"What was your plan, anyway? Seems pretty flimsy to me. Blow us out of the sky? Really? Because *nothing* bad could have happened to your prize that way. What was the point?"

Ellinor took a step forward, dragging Janne with her, then stopped. She couldn't remember how far Oihana said she could get from the container now, and with all the warning mechanisms having given out while they flew, the way Oihana warned it might, she had no way of knowing when she got to the end of her tether. She was forced to wait for the danger to come to her.

A shot cracked. Ellinor cowered behind Janne, who feebly tried to get out of her grasp.

"Stop talking, you doehaz cow." Irati's shrill voice filled the silence following her shot's echo, her tone dripping malice.

Ellinor peeked around Janne, but couldn't see Irati. Another shot, this one dangerously close to her head—and Kai, by proxy, who returned fire—forced Ellinor to duck behind Janne once more. She took a hesitant step to the side to better keep her friend from the line of sight.

"You think you're so clever, don't you, Ellinor? Always thought you were smarter than me. That you deserved your position. That I didn't *earn* it." When Ellinor tried to inch her way to the side again, another *crack* filled the air. A small crater appeared next to her foot where Irati's bullet was fired. Ellinor stopped moving, sweat rolling down her face as Irati continued speaking.

"Cosmin, my older brothers, *everyone*, they're all the same. They see a pretty woman and assume she was given some favor along the way. That the *only* way she could have achieved greatness or prestige was by fucking some man in power. And if we do sleep with the bastards because, I don't know, I wanted to? It just proves their point. How dare I like sex, right?" Irati's laugh sounded harsh for the first time in Ellinor's memory, her tightly coiled control crumbling around her.

"Women were worse!" Irati yelled. "Most of the time, those pussies wouldn't even let me *try*. They just handed me what I wanted because they figured a pretty face would know what to do with power. And abyss if I didn't take it. All I ever tried to do was show them all that I belong here. That I fucking matter. That I can achieve anything I want without any special favors."

Ellinor's body went numb. Irati Mishra may be a bitch, but she wasn't wrong. Ellinor could empathize. She could see how that need to prove everyone wrong by proving her worth, that driving competitive streak, and Irati's ambition would finally sour her. And maybe if Ellinor had known, she wouldn't have teased the woman so much. Maybe it would have lessened the hostile resentfulness that pumped through Irati's veins like poison. But it was too late now.

Ellinor could hear Kai reload his submachine gun; she motioned him to wait. "What good are those achievements if you kill everyone in your way? What is it all for, Irati? It's not too late to stop this," Ellinor pleaded, unsure if Jelani needed more time, or if the crew was in a safe position.

"Talin?" she called to the side. "Talk to me. Are you all right back there?" Ellinor thought she heard Talin hiss at her, but couldn't be sure, as Irati was yelling once more.

"Stop? *Stop*? I'm just getting started. Cosmin was wrong to think I was a placeholder for the likes of you. I'm better than you ever were, and I'm going to prove it by tearing down *everything* Cosmin's built with a caster of *my* choosing."

Ellinor realized, with a sinking feeling in her gut, she wasn't all that different from Irati. It made her blood run cold in her veins, her throat dry. Both Ellinor and Irati had grown to detest Cosmin for different reasons, but their reaction, their plan, had been the same.

Am I as far gone as Irati? Would I kill my team to accomplish my goals? What if it was Kai standing in my way? Ellinor shuddered. *I don't want to turn into Irati.*

"The water caster in Magomed will be a powerhouse of my making," Irati declared. "She'll appreciate the gift I give her. You, Cosmin, and all those pigs who thought I was nothing more than a sweet ass will learn I'm far more skilled and powerful than anyone has ever given me credit for."

Ellinor blinked at Irati's words, and laughed.

It may have been the bruise to her skull that made her chuckle at a woman with a Gislin Cobra trained on her, but she couldn't help it. She shook Janne back into consciousness with her mirth. "That's just . . . that's *precious*, Irati. That's cute, really. Don't you see, though? You'll just land yourself back where you already are. Giving a caster a tool so she can be more powerful? They'll forget all about you, and everyone else will just think you slept with the new boss, too!"

Ellinor's tone grew darker. "You proved your point, Irati. You're a badass boss. But this? You're so bent on your own personal gain that you've put your entire team at risk, not to mention your prize. You'll burn everyone in your path just to get your own way. This just proves everyone was right about you. You're showing us all that you're nothing but selfish and reckless."

I would know.

"Not to mention stupid," Talin added, her voice muffled, coming from somewhere behind and to the side of Irati.

"That too!" Ellinor agreed, drawing Irati's attention. "It's still not going to be *you* that people fear or respect. It'll be the caster you prop up."

The thunderous *crack* of Irati firing registered secondary to the painful thud against Ellinor's chest, like a truck had tried to plow through her sternum. Janne Wolff slipped from her grasp, a bloody hole in the assassin's chest, eyes wide and staring somewhere above where Ellinor was standing.

Irati cursed, and Ellinor rolled to cover behind the dreeocht container while still struggling to breathe, convinced at least one rib was cracked.

"Kai," Ellinor wheezed. "Please tell me you have more grenades or something we can lob at the bitch."

Kai gave her a pained expression, "Ah, abyss. I don't, Ell. Got a bit grenade happy blowing that fence back there. Only got the generic stuff now. If you can get a clear shot though, I've got some of Cosmin's magitech bullets. Would end 'er right quick."

"She's somewhere on top of our busted Hornet Hawk. Janne looked to her when she got wiped out. She's got to be cloaked or something, because there's nowhere to hide up there." A thought struck Ellinor and she yanked her Rhino off her back. She may not have her building hooks anymore, but she had enough of the cables and pieces collected from Lazar cutting the line that it should work for what she had in mind.

Readying her crossbow amid Irati trying to flush them out under a hail of bullets, Ellinor counted the shots. Finally, a lull occurred.

"Cover me," she whispered to Kai, stepping out from behind cover and shooting their broken plane with the remnants of her building hook. As the cable flew through the firing groove with nothing to anchor it, Ellinor grabbed it before it could fly free. She felt the burn through her glove as the cable slipped through her grip. Just as the hook landed, she closed her grip and launched herself to the top of the Hornet Hawk.

She heard a faint scrambling noise, and dropping her Asco Rhino, she grabbed her Lacerator knives, spinning them on her fingers and releasing them as fast as she could in the general direction of the sound. When one of her knives didn't return and there was a bark of pain, Ellinor dove at the space where her knife had disappeared.

She tackled Irati, but the mostly uninjured lieutenant had the advantage.

Ellinor wrestled the woman's Gislin Cobra away, and Irati slammed her knee into her chest. A *whoosh* of air erupted from Ellinor, followed by a sharp pain pulsing through her bruised and cracked ribs. Grabbing her hair, Irati wrenched her head back and tried to slice Ellinor's throat, no longer caring that she needed her for the dreeocht.

The dreeocht!

Ellinor summoned her training, turned, and pinned Irati briefly. Ellinor wrapped her arms as tightly as she could around Irati, suffering through hammer-like blows to her kidneys as she rolled off the side of the Hornet Hawk closest to the dreeocht.

Irati landed on top of Ellinor. The lieutenant raised her fist, Ellinor shut her eyes, and then the pressure was gone. In an explosion of breath, Talin Roxas tackled Irati off Ellinor.

Talin's leg was still bleeding, but that didn't stop the explosives expert. She grappled with Irati, grabbing fistfuls of her hair, yanking long coils free. Irati screamed, but Talin wouldn't relent. A quick jab, and Talin had broken Irati's perfect nose.

"Bitch!" Talin yelled. "You rat! You almost got Pema killed selling us out to Dragan." She punched Irati again, then took out one of the long, pointed tools she used when making her explosives. "Azer's balls, we're a *team*." She raised the glimmering object over her head, ready to strike.

Irati slammed her fist down on Talin's gunshot wound. Talin sucked in a breath, her back curling, and Irati bucked her hips, tossing the seerani off. Irati reached for one of the high-carbon steel knives. Ellinor was scrabbling to her feet, Talin and Irati too close together for Kai to get a clear shot. She careened into Irati Mishra as she was bringing her arm back to stab Talin.

Ellinor's head was still spinning from the crash, and Irati was able to get her legs untangled enough to knee Ellinor in the side again. She could feel the sharp edge of the knife against her stomach. She stared up at Irati, seeing nothing but fire burning in her dark gaze, and Ellinor knew she was dead.

Then, there was Kai Axel Brantley.

He tore Irati off Ellinor, throwing her back at the dreeocht, before picking Irati up by the collar of her armor and slamming her back down to the ground.

He did this until the knife flew from the woman's hands. But still, the lieutenant struggled. Even at her peak, Ellinor was no match for getting out of Kai's clutches without using a bit of trickery and extraordinary timing, but Irati was pummeling Kai with everything she had left. By the time Talin was helping Ellinor back to her knees, Irati had nearly slipped free of Kai's grasp and was lurching toward her discarded Cobra.

A familiar voice that sounded like rough stones being ground together broke through Irati's animalistic snarls as she struggled with Kai. "You're done, Irati. It's over."

Ellinor had never been happier to see Mirza Otieno's scarred visage in her entire life.

Nothing else registered to her—not Jelani standing behind Mirza, nor the dark-skinned lieutenant holding his gun flush against Eko's head—all Ellinor knew at that moment was Mirza hadn't betrayed them.

"Mirza!" Irati shrieked, still struggling and clawing at Kai.

"I'll kill Eko. It's over, Irati."

Eko Blom turned his quivering gaze to Irati, his hazel eyes watery with fear, his lean body trembling in Mirza's arm. The mechanic turned pilot didn't fight. He stood limply as he beseeched the woman who had convinced him that her plans were noble, or perhaps couldn't go awry, or that the money and prestige was worth the risk, to do as Mirza asked.

"Please, Irati," Eko's voice trembled in time with his body.

"What makes you think I care about him? I shot Janne. He's a tool, nothing more. Go ahead, Mirza, kill the timid *child*. This prize is mine! I can still make this work."

Irati threw her head back, hitting Kai square in the nose, covering her dark hair in a spray of blood. Wriggling free of Kai, Irati lunged for Ellinor and Talin once more while simultaneously making a grab for the handle of the dreeocht container, but Jelani moved with such speed that all Elinor did was blink, and the man had secured the infuriated woman in a choke hold.

As Irati slumped to the ground, Eko asked, "Would she really have killed me? Or you, Mirza?"

Mirza let the terrified pilot go and looked him straight in the eye. "Yes."

As Kai helped Jelani secure Irati as best as he could with a bloody nose, Ellinor eyed Eko warily, her fingers drumming on the hilt of her recovered pistol. "Why, Eko?" Her voice broke as the words left her, and Eko swayed on his feet, as if a puff of air would send him toppling over.

"No one ever looks—*looked* at me like she did. No one sees me. I wanted it to be real, and I thought—*believed* it was. It didn't matter what she wanted. I'd have given her anything, everything. I'm sorry." Eko lowered his head, his disheveled milky-white hair shrouding his face.

"Sorry? Eko, you're *sorry*? You don't get to be sorry. Embla, Warin, Lazar, they're all dead. Irati killed Janne, and she almost killed *us*. We . . . they were your crew. You tell me, Eko, does sorry seem like enough to you?"

Eko shook his head and Ellinor sneered at him. She pushed past him and shoved Mirza in the shoulder. "And where the fuck were you? You can't tell me that you couldn't escape this whole time? Aren't you supposed to be better than that?"

Mirza's dark eyes hardened, his jaw clenching. "Yes," he croaked, and Ellinor finally got a look at his face.

His dark skin couldn't mask the deep, discolored bruises on his face, the lopsided way he stood favoring his leg, the twisted, swollen hand at his side. Many of the abrasions seemed fresh, too.

Ellinor's shoulders sagged. "You told her then? You had to, I'm guessing. Told Irati where the transports and safe houses were? Where we'd have to go to refuel or meet a new team?"

Mirza's gaze became shrouded, and he nodded. *So many people suffered under Irati . . .*

She glanced back at Kai and Talin, both wounded, but alive. Swallowing the tightness in her throat, Ellinor made a decision. "You have to go back to Cosmin. Tell him what happened. He's supposed to be sending more people, so tell him where we are, and where we're headed. And you have to take Talin. That leg wound looks like it may have nicked an artery, and she'll want to pick up Pema." Mirza tilted his head, frowning, ready to argue, and Ellinor shook hers. "It's a long story—Talin can fill you in." She glanced at Irati and Eko, heart beating erratically. "And secure these two. I'm sure Cosmin will want to deal with Irati in person."

Irati began struggling again—no longer deprived of oxygen, she was coming around. "Mirza, no. Don't give me back to Cosmin. Just kill me, okay? Just fucking kill me. Don't give me back to that man. Please, I'm begging you!"

Ellinor frowned, glancing to Mirza, who remained silent, eyes fixed on his boots. Ellinor shrugged and answered for him. "You can beg and grovel until I'm dead and buried, it doesn't change a thing. You're going to Cosmin, Irati. You have to pay for the lives you stole."

Kai and Jelani hauled a shrieking Irati back onto the Eagle Owl. Eko crept closer to Ellinor, playing with his rough hands. "And me? Do I go back, too?"

Ellinor pinched the bridge of her nose, and winced as her tender face protested the comforting action. "Yeah, Eko, you go back too. You have to fly that bird."

Eko continued to fidget at her side, and a pang of remorse bloomed in her chest. He wasn't a bad man, just a lonely one. "I wish I'd known. I could have told you Irati's smiles were empty."

The pale man heaved a silent sigh. "Right, well, it's too late for that, isn't it?" He glanced at Kai and Jelani as they exited the plane. "Will Cosmin kill me too? Or will he do worse?"

Ellinor opened her mouth, then shut it. *I don't know what Cosmin will do.*

Bile rose in her throat, and she held up a finger, hobbling over to Mirza who leaned against the Eagle Owl, arms crossed and scowling at the ground. "Do me a solid, Mirza," she whispered.

He raised an eyebrow, and Ellinor took a deep breath. "When you pick up Pema, drop off Eko. Leave him behind. Don't take him back to Euria."

Mirza's eyes narrowed. "You have already spoken to Cosmin?" When Ellinor nodded, he released a long slow breath, and said, "Why does Eko deserve mercy?"

Ellinor winced, and rubbed the back of her head. "Look, he was dumb, yeah? Fooled by her charms. You know what it's like. He was alone. I . . . he had no one when I left you guys." Mirza's eyes remained hard, his jaw clenched. Ellinor raised her hands. "Just think about it, yeah? He's not a bad kid. Let him live, that's all I'm asking."

Mirza continued to glare at her, nostrils flaring. "I'll consider it," he growled. "But I should really stay with you. I know the plan, remember?"

"You're injured, and someone needs to watch Irati. I need Kai's help to haul that thing around still. Besides, Cosmin will need you to give him a full report, yeah? That's what he's expecting." Mirza's frowned deepened at her words. "Don't worry, we've got this." She gave him a reassuring squeeze on his shoulder.

Mirza cringed. "Fine. Just finish the damn job."

Ellinor nodded. "I will."

Mirza shook his head, gaze dropping to the ground again. "You better move to safer areas. Downed military plane, all that smoke . . . Any trouble still following will catch up. Head that way," Mirza pointed into the distance where a trio of looming boulders could be seen. "Sync that busted digimap to my comms. I'll have the new ship home in on your location, you won't make it to the last safe house." Mirza waved her away, turning back to their plane, leaving Ellinor Rask with her marching orders.

As Ellinor processed his words, wondering why Mirza wanted to stay with the package so badly, Eko sidled back toward her. "Well? What happens to me now?"

Ellinor raised a hand like she would pat him on the shoulder, but couldn't bring herself to do it. She sighed. "I pled your case. It's in Mirza's hands now. You do your best to make it up to him, and maybe he'll make sure Cosmin doesn't kill you, or he'll leave you far enough away from Euria where you can flee. That's the best I can do."

Eko nodded, tears rolling down his cheeks. "Thank you, Ellinor. I'm sorry, truly."

Ellinor gripped his shoulder briefly, and Eko hung his head as he shuffled on to the Eagle Owl, Talin not far behind. "You sure, Ellinor? I'm thinking you could use an extra pair o' hands out there."

Ellinor gave her a tired smile. "Don't worry, I have Kai. It's better if you get looked at by a doctor with some legal gear, not just some hacked together med bot. We'll be fine. Besides, it's better if you're with Pema."

"If you say so. Just wish we didn't have to take another shitty plane back. I can't stand these things." Talin took a deep breath, stilling her quivering hands, and trying to appear unconcerned about flying once more. Fishing in her pocket, she motioned to Ellinor. "Here, take these." Talin handed a string of makeshift batteries and various wires and fuses into her hand. "They're fucking dirty little grenades, but it's better than nothing. You know, for those extra emergencies."

Ellinor closed her hands around the hastily crafted battery grenades and nodded. Talin gave a wan smile and took a step aboard the Eagle Owl, using the walls for support, her fingers still trembling. Before she could vanish, Ellinor jumped after her, and gripped her hand. "Promise me one thing though, Talin."

"What's up?"

"Consider what I said outside of Amaru. About Cosmin. Look at him and everything that happened objectively, and just . . . think about it, yeah?"

Talin's lips pressed into a firm line, but she gave a deft nod, leaving Ellinor to exit the plane alone.

She watched them lift into the air, oblivious to how far she was from the dreeocht container. She watched them gain altitude, before the *whorl* of the engines warming drowned out everything else, and the Eagle Owl shot off at top speed back toward Euria, kicking up debris from the ruined Hornet Hawk.

A wave of metal parts flew over her head, forcing Ellinor to duck, and knocking her off her feet. Kai and Jelani flattened themselves to the ground, barely avoiding the debris. But the container holding the sleeping magical creature had no such luck. The reverberating sounds of metal crashing filled the silence left by the Eagle Owl.

Before Ellinor could lift her head to inspect the damage, a raging burn enveloped her neck as her malfunctioning collar went off.

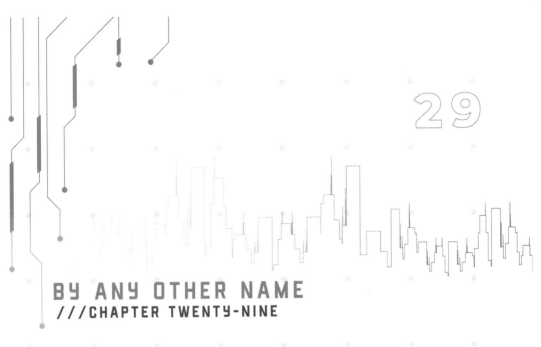

BY ANY OTHER NAME
///CHAPTER TWENTY-NINE

E LLINOR RAN as fast as she could, but it didn't matter. The dreeocht container had been hit and jostled one too many times. There was no closing the box.

Kai lurched back from the emerging creature, crashing into Ellinor. Jelani was scrambling to get to them, his mouth moving, but Ellinor couldn't make sense of his words over the ringing in her ears, terror immobilizing her as she came face to face with the dreeocht.

A grey cloud swirled around the creature, twisting and turning, rolling in all directions as the raw air magic tasted the environment before condensing into a milky sphere, further obscuring the monster. A second later, the ball of air burst apart in a prismatic display of light that glittered like a million rainbows trapped in droplet sized crystals. Ellinor had never seen air and water magic come together in such a way before, and it momentarily dazzled her.

A wave of dark, stormy water rose out of the container and propelled the creature forward. It crashed to the ground in front of the trio, but not a drop hit them as the magic evaporated into nothingness, leaving its creator behind.

And there, standing on a patch of ground that was impossibly undisturbed after all that magic, stood the dreeocht.

It looked like a child, a little boy.

The creature stood on wobbling legs as lances of lightning lurched and snapped out from its shoulder blades. The dark clouds that oozed from the being became the backdrop for the raw water magic, illuminating the blues, purples, pinks, and oranges of the lightning that did not disappear, but rather coiled and whipped out to the ground continuously. The dreeocht blinked large, round eyes into the bright light as he took his first step. His eyes were like pale blue marbles against his—mostly—corpse pale skin. There were thin wire-like veins crawling over parts of his limbs and cheeks in both gold and silver, like embedded pieces of jewelry or wire nets.

Interspersed with the dazzling wires were patches of scales from what appeared to be a sea serpent or a large fish. Metallic, bright green and brown scales decorated the creature's skin in several places, from tiny, individual scales, to wide patches, giving him a kind of glowing warmth, despite the disturbingly pale skin beneath. There was also a small collection of seashells at the crown of the dreeocht's forehead, where feathery tendrils of seaweed drifted and flowed about his head on a phantom breeze. Sprouting on top of his head around the seashells and seaweed were several black wires wrapped into corded cables, which mimicked the same movements as the seaweed. Though, as the dreeocht's attention moved around the group, his . . . hair, for lack of a better word, reacted as if it had its own conscience.

The dreeocht before Ellinor looked as if it had been pieced together from a shipwreck victim—a humani child—rebuilt to incorporate random organics and tech drawn to such things. The dreeocht blinked his round eyes slowly, registering the chaos around him. Kai and Ellinor continued to stare, paralyzed, while Jelani tried to get between them and the creature.

The dreeocht regarded them a moment before lifting his hands and flexing his fingers toward them. Its feet and hands were slightly larger than they should have been, given the creature's small stature, and they, too, looked like they had been crossed with an animal: short, stubby fingers attached to an overly large palm that looked better suited to a canine.

The movement was enough to snap Ellinor from her stupor. She ripped a pistol free, cocking it in the same movement. Jelani's words finally broke through to her.

"Don't! Don't do anything stupid. Just wait a moment. Just . . . wait. It won't hurt you if you don't attack."

"And what's to stop the beastie from attacking us?" Kai whispered harshly, his hand quivering over the butt of his AbyssFire.

"Ellinor. She's what it's drawn to. Give him a moment to register her, and you'll be fine. We'll all be safe," Jelani answered. Ellinor tried—and failed—to be calmed by the surety in his voice.

Ellinor had faced a doehaz before, in a virtual training simulator. She still had nightmares of her failed attempts to save herself, even if she had been perfectly safe. She didn't want to consider what a being of pure magic could do to her, should she spook it. Not that she wanted the monster to be attached to her in any capacity to begin with, either; it was meant to be a gift for Zabel Dirix.

The dreeocht's wire and seaweed hair whipped around in a frenzy, displaying its own confusion and wonder. He continued to contemplate his hands before suddenly sniffing and licking the air, as if he sensed something delicious. Ellinor shivered as its pale eyes settled on her.

His thin, bluish lips spread into a large smile as he took another wobbly step toward her, a giggle bubbling up from deep within the creature like the breeze rustling dead leaves out of a tree. The laughter seemed to surprise the thing as he stopped for a moment, before taking a surer step toward Ellinor, his smile growing to show pearly white teeth.

She saw flashes of the doehaz's long, pointed teeth from her training sim as the dreeocht approached. She raised her weapon before she was conscious of the action, eliciting a growl from Jelani. "Ellinor, don't."

The dreeocht stopped, and cocked his head. "You? You. Youyouyouyou," the dreeocht stuttered like a malfunctioning android, but with the sweet, high pitched voice of a child. "Ellinoooooor. You are. EllEEEEE-nor."

She winced at the terrible inflection, and the dreeocht laughed again, awkwardly clapping. "You! Yes! You! My Ell, Elli-nor."

Jelani crept to the side of the celebrating beast and helped Kai and Ellinor to their feet, eliciting a coo of surprise from the dreeocht. "What's he doing? Why does he look like that and not like one of the doehaz? They're related, yeah?" Ellinor whispered, trying to swallow her panic at facing a creature of legend, who was *smiling at her,* of all things.

"No two are alike, you don't know this?" Jelani whispered back. "They're formed from what's around them, what creatures and devices the magic can grow and latch on to. Doehaz are similar in that regard, true. No two creatures of that ilk are similar, either."

Jelani tilted his head at the beast, and Ellinor noted the dreeocht seemed oblivious to anyone but her. "As to what it's doing? I wouldn't know. Do you feel anything from your shackle? Perhaps that will tell us."

Ellinor felt warm in a not entirely unpleasant manner, and there was a slight tingle through her neck and head, but she had assumed it was her accelerating heart rate. Now she wasn't sure. Mostly, she felt confused.

Her uneasiness felt so out of place when faced with this child-like creature. Until she remembered what it was: pure magic and technology so concentrated that it brought new life to a corpse and other random items. Still, the thing was rather cute, breathtaking in his own way, once she overlooked the lightning sparking from his back that was more than enough to kill her twice over.

"Never mind that," Ellinor said, waving Jelani's concern away. "What do we do now? Can we take it to Zabel like this? Out of its box, I mean."

A pained expression crossed Jelani's dusky face, and it took him precious moments to answer. "If you want, yes. But you don't necessarily *have* to. There is an alternative, as I've said."

The sound of Kai readying his submachine gun kept Ellinor from asking more about the alternative. She shook her head, and Jelani's chin slumped to his chest, shrouding his eyes behind a curtain of fog-like hair. "Then we will continue on our way," Jelani answered, a hint of anger in his tone. "The dreeocht will be fine; he's attached to you. He'll go where you go."

The dreeocht bounced toward them, then jumped, gripping his feet in paw-like hands, and floated the rest of the way to Ellinor. Kai stumbled back, raising his AbyssFire once more, and Jelani smacked him on the back of the head. "*It is harmless. As long as you allow it to continue examining Ellinor,*" he growled. "The moment you interfere with violence, it will defend itself then vanish. Then you'll wish it had obliterated you when you return to Cosmin or Zabel empty handed."

Kai swallowed, and took a step away from Ellinor, though she wished he hadn't. The dreeocht let go of his feet, and gripped her face. Her breath stopped mid-gasp, the collar around her neck vibrating at high speeds and lightning crackling off the dreeocht's back all the while. "Speak, you? No, no, no. Not with words? Feeeeeelings? Oh! *Yes*!" he chirped at her, hair dancing about his head.

The collar began thrumming so hard, Ellinor's teeth rattled in her head. But she worried that if she pried the beast's hands off her face, he would grow enraged and the lightning would strike her with no effort.

The more he spoke, however, the less he sounded like a faulty machine and more like a child pretending to be prophetic. "Air? You are the air?" The dreeocht blinked his large eyes slowly once more, before looking around and releasing Ellinor's face, much to her relief. His paw-like hands had a slightly furry feel to them that was surprisingly delicate, still, she was glad the legendary being was no longer touching her.

The creature frowned. "Gone? Water is gone? No more? Where? Water-man? Where is . . . he? Where is *he*? You are *her*? The air. He was water? *Was*. Oh! Oh . . ."

Ellinor's insides were falling and crashing all over again. "Okay, that's enough of that. So you felt me through the collar, yeah?" Her fear turning into an edgy anger. "Wonderful. Good for you. But you know where 'water-man' is? You sucked the last of him up so you could stay all cozy in your box. He's dead. Gone. You consumed him. You practically *ate* the very last bit of Misho. There's nothing left anymore of my husband. You—" Ellinor bit back her words, realizing she was starting to yell.

She felt a hand on her shoulder and was surprised to see Jelani there and not Kai, who still stared warily at the dreeocht. "It's okay," he whispered to her, before addressing the dreeocht. "Yes, my little friend. Misho was the 'water-man.' He died, it would seem, some time ago. His magical essence provided you some comfort? It helped you sleep happy? Happy, like this?" Jelani indicated his own bright smile.

The dreeocht mimicked the smile and nodded enthusiastically. "Misho was Ellinor's mate, her husband," Jelani continued patiently. "You understand? Ellinor is here, and Misho is gone. You won't feel him anymore. But Ellinor is enough for you, isn't she? She's fierce, loyal, and has sacrificed so much to get you this far. Isn't that great? Aren't you proud to be connected to her?"

Ellinor went numb at Jelani's words, but her shock, confusion, and hurt kept the blush she may have otherwise felt a lifetime ago at bay.

The dreeocht looked at Ellinor with such honest adoration that her heart ached. "Elli-nor is great? Better than great. She is fiercest. I love? Yes! *Love* my Elli-nor. But no happy?"

The clouds around the dreeocht grew darker, the silent lightning intensified, mimicking the dreeocht's distress. Kai frowned up at the sky, craning his neck to watch the clouds grow and reach toward the sky. "Uh, boss? Your new friend don't look none too pleased. Try smiling, will you?"

Once more, Jelani spoke for her when Ellinor struggled to find words to address the pouting dreeocht. "Misho's essence is no more. Ellinor has nothing left of him, friend. Is her sadness so surprising? She misses her 'water-man,' her Misho. But he lives in you now, right? Perhaps you'll be able to remind Ellinor of that, and she'll be happy again? Do you think you can try that for me, little friend?"

Ellinor would have been impressed with how aptly Jelani spoke to the creature, but she was too offended by what Jelani was suggesting for that. "You think knowing Misho dwells somehow within that thing will make me happy? What's wrong with you?" Ellinor barked at Jelani, barely containing herself from shoving him.

"Ellinor, please," Jelani whispered urgently as the storm clouds continued to gather and crackle with lighting. "Let the creature have this lie. I can't fight something like this if he decides to leave."

Begrudgingly, she accepted the merit of his words as her hair began to snap with static. Forcing a smile, she met the dreeocht's quivering eyes and was surprised by the fear and hope she saw within his gaze. She didn't have to try that hard to soften her voice. "Do you have a name?"

The dreeocht blinked rapidly at her, bouncing up and down in the air in time with his movements. The storm's growth stalled momentarily. "Name? What? What, what?"

Talking to this thing is going to give me a permanent headache.

Stifling her sigh, Ellinor summoned as much patience as she could muster. "Yeah, a name. I'm *Ellinor*—" she made sure to emphasize the correct way to say it, "and the water-man's name was *Misho*. That's what we call people, so they know we're talking to them. This is *Jelani,* and this is *Kai.* When I need them, I call their name. What do I call you?"

"You sure that's a good idea, Ell?" Kai whispered while the dreeocht chewed on his thin lips, brow furrowed in concentration.

Ellinor shushed him. "I'm not calling it 'dreeocht' or 'hey you' all the way to Anzor. Zabel would need to give him a name anyway. I'm saving her time."

"Call . . . me? What is *me*? So many things inside. Me? Yes, mememe," the dreeocht mused. He scratched at his scales, tilting his head back and forth rapidly, before stopping and giving Ellinor the widest smile yet. She didn't have time to suppress her shiver before a whip of bright, raw water and air magic struck her, encasing her in a blinding bubble as the warm, wet magic crawled over her, snaking its way in through every pore.

She became aware of thoughts that weren't her own, but were too primal for her to make sense of. She was powerless to stop the invading force from crawling through her thoughts and memories, licking at her own latent power. The shackle tightened around her neck and then she felt the presence lurch away, as if hurt by the device.

Ellinor wanted to struggle, wanted to panic and fight, but she couldn't move. The magic held her as tightly as a cocoon. Any sound breaking through the magic was muffled, as if through walls of cotton. Instead, all she could really *hear*—though it was more a feeling—ringing through her mind over and over was: *What am I?*

The dreeocht pored over every inch of her, searching for an unattainable answer. What would Ellinor have said to this creature, anyway? How could she explain to anyone what they were, when she had so little idea of who *she* was anymore?

Then, with the loud whistle of a storm she couldn't feel, Ellinor was released. The ball of magic she was encased in evaporated into nothingness, leaving behind the faint scent of the salty ocean and just a few of the lightning-like tendrils coiling back into the dreeocht. She thought several minutes must have passed, but in reality, she had been wrapped in the dreeochts magic for milliseconds at most. Kai and Jelani still right where she left them.

The storm above was no longer on the verge of breaking; instead, it began taking shape. The clouds shifted into a myriad of colors, turning into dancing shapes of sea creatures so life-like, Ellinor couldn't help but stare in wonder at the scene above her even as she tried to process what happened.

Kai rushed to her, helping her up and inspecting her for damage. "That thing didn't hurt you, did it?"

"Your concern is touching," she croaked, voice raw for reasons she couldn't explain, "but what were you going to do, Kai? You can't hurt him."

"Ah, well, wouldn't stop me from trying, now would it?" Kai winked, though it didn't diminish the honest worry still lurking in his gaze.

The cloud creatures continued to swirl, as if they were reenacting a play in a strange interpretive dance. As Ellinor's mind continued to spin, she wondered if the magical clouds were somehow showcasing what the dreeocht saw when it invaded her mind and heart.

"Do you know what that was all about, Jelani? You seem to know the most about these creatures, which is odd, by the way. But I'll get to that later. Right now, explain what in the abyss just happened?" Ellinor whispered, watching the dreeocht as his eyes rolled back in his head and the cloud animal's dance reached a dizzying speed.

Jelani spared her a veiled glance, before returning his attention to the dreeocht. It was clear he was hiding something. "I haven't seen the process done before, despite what you're implying," Jelani said slowly. "But, from what I do know, it would appear as if the dreeocht was reaffirming the connection, what it was ripped from when the container broke open. It only knew you by the feel of your magic, and nothing more. It was, I guess you could say, learning about you. In an attempt to understand itself. Rather remarkable, when you think about it. The process didn't hurt, did it?"

There was a momentary flash of concern in Jelani's gaze, as he leaned toward her a bit, body tense as if he were holding himself back. Ellinor shook her head, when suddenly the dancing cloud animals above dispersed in a shower of sparkling light.

Whatever the dreeocht had been doing, he seemed to finish as his eyes rolled forward again, and his faintly blue lips parted once more in a wide smile. "Fiss," the dreeocht declared, his childish voice clear and free of its odd stammer.

"Fiss? I don't understand, what is a 'fiss'?" Ellinor glanced between Jelani and Kai for help, but they were as confused as she was.

The dreeocht giggled, wire and seaweed hair dancing in mirth. He clapped his hands again, then pointed to his chest. "Fiss! Me! That's a name. *My* name."

"Your name is Fiss? Really?" She exchanged a glance with Kai, who shrugged and bit his lip to hide his smile at the odd moniker.

"Yes, Elli-nor. *Fiss*. You can call me that. Fiss."

"Does it mean something? Your name. How did you come up with it?" Jelani asked, rubbing his chin.

Fiss scratched at the silver and gold wires embedded in his skin, still floating on a current of air the rest of them couldn't feel but which still carried that faint salty-ocean scent. "Yes. There is a meaning. I found it in Elli-nor. In her magic. Locked away magic. I didn't like that, but I can't free it. Don't know. Why? So bad, so sad."

"Fiss?" Jelani whispered, getting the creature's attention again. "You were telling us the meaning of your name?"

"Oh, yes! Magic has a . . . tongue. Language? Yes! It kept saying it over, and over, and over, and over—" Fiss stopped abruptly with a giggle, before starting again. "Fiss is the knowing, the understanding. A name to grow? Ah, a name to grow *into*. Fiss will fit better later. But I like it now. *Fffiiissssssssss.* I found it in my Elli-nor, so it is perfect!"

"All right, Fiss it is. Nice to, uh, meet you?" Ellinor said, still reluctant to correct the almost all powerful being on the proper emphasis of her name.

Ellinor tried to replicate what Fiss had done, prodding at the void deep within where her magic dwelled. The wound was still raw—coupled with the ever present thrumming of the collar—and did nothing to lessen the feelings of despair in her gut from bubbling up. She had hoped that, with Fiss out of his box, the dreeocht would be able to snap the collar off, but apparently the device repelled it too much for Fiss to dismantle it.

The dreeocht beamed at her and bounced closer. When Ellinor flinched back, Fiss stopped and cocked his head at her once more. "That . . . what was it? You fear? What?"

Ellinor turned away from Fiss, scratching at the back of her neck. "Nothing, really, it's nothing. You're just this . . . thing that I've never met before and . . . never mind, Fiss. We've got to get moving. We have to meet with someone and get you—*us* to where we need to be. It's not safe for us to linger here."

Collecting her gear, she heard Kai and Jelani do the same as Fiss floated beside her once more. "Safe? What does that mean?"

She raised an eyebrow at the creature. "You really don't know anything, yeah? Safe means you aren't in any danger. You can go to sleep and not worry about someone or something hurting you. Where we are right now, and where we need to go, is none of those things. If we don't keep moving, something very bad will find us. It's called a doehaz. Do you know what that is? It's a monster, not all that different from you."

"Monster? Monsters are bad? I am bad? Why, Elli-nor? I don't feel bad. I feel like you!"

"Ell," Kai whispered, gripping her elbow and steering her away from Fiss, "you sure you want to go 'round calling Fiss a monster? He don't know no better." Kai's eyes drifted to Fiss and Jelani.

The seersha rubbed the top of Fiss's head, glaring at Ellinor. "Fiss is no monster. He can't be, it's literally impossible. Dreeocht can only cast sweet magic, cute little nothings. It's still powerful beyond compare, but their magic isn't harmful. Only with the aid of a caster can a dreeocht shape conscious magic, magic capable of destruction, and harm. Another reason you should at least consider my 'alternative,' Ellinor.

"The doehaz," Jelani said, voice growing darker, "are the true monsters. And, while mindless feeding machines, they bring a balance of sorts. No caster can travel too far or grow too powerful, extend their reach too wide, or a doehaz will find them and it will eat them. Dreeocht are similar, but instead of consuming magic, their inherent goodness acts as their counterbalance."

Ellinor's brows furrowed. "I don't understand. I thought their power was limitless. How can their own nature act as limitation?"

"Really, Ellinor? I'm surprised it's not obvious, based on what you already know." Jelani's tone may have been light enough to be considered teasing, but Ellinor knew the Creature Breaker was stalling.

"Spell it out for me then, yeah? If you haven't noticed, I've suffered a few more knocks to the head than I'd like recently."

Jelani sighed. "Dreeocht are *good*. They are idyllically innocent. They're simple, and generally untroubled by fear or worry. Unless, or until, a caster is connected to them. That is the only way they ever know anxiety or fear; it's the only way they can deliberately cast something that can cause harm. Everything has its limitations, nothing can be all powerful. Just as doehazs' lack of intelligence is their downfall, so is a dreeocht's purity, ironic as that may seem."

Ellinor huffed in response, turning away. She ground her teeth, not wanting to consider that Fiss was another innocent she would have to betray.

She ignored Jelani, along with her aches resulting from her fight with Irati, as she marched in the direction of where Cosmin's new crew would be meeting them. "This—*it*, is just business," she said to Kai instead. "You can't forget that, yeah? You owe me." She tapped the collar on her neck. "Fiss is a *job*. And, to top it all off, the thing is powerful as fuck, good or not. You were terrified of the thing the entire time he was in his box. So why are you so sweet on him now, yeah? Just because he's attached to me or whatever cute thing Jelani says, doesn't change anything."

"Ah, I dunno, Ell. I mean, just look at what the kid makes, will you? All 'em pretty colors when the magic goes away? Sure, when he was in the box he was this scary thing. I won't go denying that. Could have been anything coming of that thing. . ." Kai trailed off, and shrugged. "Fiss is the job, I get that. But you could be nicer to the kid, is all I'm saying."

Ellinor frowned. She knew Kai was bullied as a child so his protective nature often flared up at times like this, but this was absurd. "Fine, but we can't keep him, you know that."

Kai rolled his eyes and left her to walk near Jelani and Fiss, the latter of the two stopping every now and again to look back at Ellinor and ensure she was still close by, as if worried she would vanish if he wasn't always watching her.

They were heading deeper into doehaz territory with a creature of pure magic, a shining being. They had very little in supplies, and no means of shelter until they reached the rendezvous point at the boulders. And, if a doehaz didn't venture this far out from the Saxa Desert to devour the four of them, that didn't change the fact that Zabel still might use Fiss to fry them as soon as they delivered Cosmin's package.

Fiss was *supposed* to have remained in the box. Zabel was supposed to be the one to open the container so she could properly leash Fiss before he could float off somewhere. Ellinor wasn't sure how she was going to convince Fiss to stay with Zabel, but she also had more immediate concerns: her armor and shield had no more charge. And the fact that three magically inclined individuals were *walking* into the one place they should never go.

EXPOSURE
///CHAPTER THIRTY

ELLINOR OLYSHA Rask had never walked across a desert before. She was rendered speechless by the flat, open space, stretching as far as the horizon, a blurred sepia haze smudging the edges of the world with the sky.

Even with the dazzling sandy area around her, Ellinor was by no means relaxed. Her body was tense, ready to spring away should she hear the unmistakable roar of a doehaz. Her focus on her surroundings helped her ignore Fiss, who floated next to her, making miniature storms in the palm of his hands, cooing as those storms turned into tiny magical creatures that scampered off into the distance.

Each time Fiss created magic of any kind, her collar heated. It wasn't painful in a physical sense, but the reminder that it was nearly impossible to remove hurt in other ways. The fact the device reacted each time Fiss used magic was disconcerting, especially since what he was doing, by dreeocht standards, required very little effort. Ellinor didn't want to consider what her collar would do, should Fiss get it into his mind to cast *substantial* magic.

She had told the dreeocht to limit his casting, that it would attract unwanted attention. Fiss seemed to understand, but then occupied himself by sending tendrils of slippery, ocean-spray scented magic toward her, probing her psyche like he had before, or testing the collar around her neck. The collar sparked and buzzed when Fiss had done that, eliciting a yelp of pain from Ellinor. Fiss cried at her reaction, enfolding himself in a waterfall that left the ground completely dry. Ellinor was forced to apologize to get Fiss to stop casting. Now she let Fiss make his little storms and hoped the fleeing magical creatures would serve as a distraction, should a doehaz head their way.

Kai approached Fiss, and whispered, "So, Fiss, you wanna put some clothes on? Gotta be uncomfortable floating 'round all naked."

"Un-comfortable? I don't understand, red friend." Fiss hadn't quite gotten used to using Kai's name, instead seeming to prefer calling him by the color of his hair, despite the neon green streaks. "Why would I be this thing?"

"Well," Kai hesitated, scratching at his scraggly beard. "I just mean most us fellas prefer to cover up our bits. Keeps the sensitive parts from getting torn off or getting in the way, know what I mean?" Kai audibly sucked in his lip, and Ellinor spared them a glance. The tips of his ears were as red as his spiked hair. "Er, guess you wouldn't know nothing 'bout that, would you? Sorry, kid. Still, you wanna, uh, cover up?"

"Will this make red friend happy? The covering up?"

Kai shrugged, scratching the back of his neck. "Ah, it ain't about me, kid. If you don't wanna, you don't gotta. But it may keep you safe. Protect your skin from the sun and the like. Not sure if your kind gets sunburned like us humani, but that shit 'urts like the abyss." Coming to a decision, Kai stopped and dug in his pack. Pulling out one of his marginally clean mesh undershirts, he handed it to Fiss. "Better safe than sorry. You put that on, Fiss. Use your magic if you gotta to make it fit all proper like, but it should keep you protected a bit."

Ellinor didn't see what Fiss did to make the shirt fit, though she felt the magic through her collar, as Jelani matched his stride to hers. "Fiss is becoming more stable with each passing hour. We have nothing to fear from him. You don't need to worry so much, you know."

She frowned at him. "How would you know? You've been oddly secretive since Fiss popped out of the box." Ellinor paused, a thought striking her. "Shit, Jelani, why are you even still *here*? You don't owe me, or Lazar, anything. Not after you helped with Irati. Why didn't you hitch a ride back to Oihana with Talin? Thought your sister needed you, yeah?"

"Oihana knows the protocol if I don't return each week. She will be fine for a little while longer. Especially now that she has Izza working."

She suppressed a shiver at the mention of the humani-like android. But when Jelani didn't elaborate further or address her other questions, Ellinor growled. "Fiss isn't the only thing I worry about. I worry about what *you're* hiding. Especially now with you hinting at me running off with Zabel's prize. What gives? What do you want?"

"Does it matter? I'm offering you a choice. An out. I can give you what Cosmin is offering, and, honestly, isn't that better? You have no love for him, that's obvious. So why can't what I offer be enough?"

Ellinor's eyes darted to Kai and Fiss walking slightly ahead of them, both oblivious to their conversation. She frowned at Jelani, her brows knitting together. "Because you not telling me your motivations, and I mean the real ones, not this 'I'm just doing you a favor' act, makes me think you're just as bad as Cosmin. Be straight with me, Jelani. I'm not going to be used and coerced again."

Jelani let a long breath out through his nose. "Fine. I think you could help. Help my friends, and me. You think you know all there is about Ashlings? You don't. Most advanced androids just want to live. To truly *live* as you and I do, to make their own choices, choose their destiny, to love. They can't do that with the blocks in their programming and the protocols making it illegal to make beings like Izza. Oihana could be killed as a traitor for what she's done. Is such a *crime* worth death? My sister is a genius, but she will always be stunted by the inherent fear so many people have toward intelligent robots. Toward Ashlings."

Ellinor sucked in her breath. "You want me to make more Ashlings? With Fiss? Is that it? You think if you get the collar off that I'll ask Fiss to nicely make an army of Ashlings just because your sister likes to tinker? In exchange for reuniting me with my powers, all I have to do is help your friends get what they've always wanted. That's it, yeah?"

With magic like Fiss's the programing blocks in any smart android could be overridden, and with him bonded to Ellinor, she could ask him to shape the magic to bring life, real life, to robots that, if you shot them, didn't stay dead. There was no such thing as death to a creature that could be shut off and on, could have any devastating damage fixed.

The idea terrified her.

"I work with a group that is trying to have the Ashlings recognized as true sentient life," Jelani said slowly. "To be recognized as beings with rights. They aren't violent the way your government's media paints them." He paused, and his tone took on a measure of pleading. "You are powerful and resourceful, Ellinor. You were all these things before Fiss. I didn't lie when I said I'd heard of you before. I'd do my best to recruit you, regardless of Fiss bonding to you, but now that he has . . . can't you see how much good you could do? And not just to those who seek freedom, but to Eerden as a whole."

Ellinor's answer was instant. "No."

Images of the Ashlings who shot her little bug pulsed behind her eyelids. Jelani wanted her to help him create more of such monsters? Absolutely not. In an instant, the mild curiosity she had felt toward him, the gratitude she had for Jelani helping her team escape Amaru and Irati, turned to distrust and disappointment.

Jelani blinked. "No? But surely my help in getting that biotech device out of your neck is preferable to Cosmin's?"

Kai and Fiss were still oblivious to their heated whispers, heading dutifully toward the outcropping of rocks in the distance where they would signal to Mirza's comms so he could help Cosmin's new team pinpoint their location. Ellinor wanted to keep them oblivious to Jelani's offer; Kai wouldn't take it well to learn the seersha wanted her to betray Cosmin.

She turned a hard stare back to Jelani. "You're both awful choices. But at least I know Cosmin and the kind of monster he is. I don't know you, Jelani. And, furthermore, I don't trust you or your kind."

"My kind?" Jelani's tone turned harsh, eyes dark as he clenched his jaw.

"Yes, Ashling sympathizers. Seersha casters. Both groups have given me a metric shit ton of reasons not to trust them. Guess what? You're both of those *kinds*. So, no, I don't trust you." *Not anymore. You're just like Cosmin, you never wanted to help me, just use me.*

He glanced at Kai and Fiss, his hands dropping to the hilts of his Leviathan Roaster blades. His hands tightened for a moment, before he forced them to relax, and growled at Ellinor. "I could say the same about you, and yet I don't. I've seen you. Watched you with your crew. You may pretend like you don't care, as if they're just part of this job. That may have been true once, but it's not anymore. Which tells me you aren't the same as the *kind* who have wronged me. Whom I work against. I believe you will do what is right based on what you have done and haven't done thus far. It's why I thought you'd be agreeable to my offer."

Ellinor scoffed. "*My kind* hurt you? What, a humani break one of your precious Ashlings?"

Jelani glanced at the pair ahead of them. Fiss giggled at Kai, who was swatting at the magical squirrel made of air Fiss created and set loose on Kai's back. Jelani's grin made his eyes twinkle. His fingers drummed on the hilt of one of his blades for a moment, before he sighed and cast his gaze on the horizon, as if coming to a decision.

"You have noticed," Jelani began slowly, voice strangled, "that Oihana doesn't hear . . ."

"At all?" Ellinor offered.

Jelani winced. "That's because of me. I was discovered as a potential Creature Breaker early in my life, not long after my mother passed away. My father was too much of a wreck to steer me toward another path at the time, so I went to the academy. I trained. I had the nanites embedded in me as soon as I was old enough, and I began offering my services to any caster with enough credits and a big enough grudge to do something about it.

"During that time, my father met a humani woman and fell in love with an intensity I had never seen before. I was hurt. A part of me didn't want him to recover from my mother's death. So, to punish him, I accepted a position with a seersha caster on the opposite end of Erhard from where he was with his new bride." He paused, eyes going glassy for a moment as he peered into the distance toward the boulders they were heading to. "I aligned myself with the seersha mob boss in the city of Trifon, much like you and your husband aligned yourselves to Cosmin. I worked for the criminal syndicate in that place for many, many years, never once speaking to my father or returning home. At least, not until he sent a holo message informing me I had a sister, and showing me Oihana's pudgy little face. I left Trifon that afternoon."

He trailed off, and Ellinor thought he decided to share no more. Her heart raced, a need bubbling up in her to know what had happened to Jelani and his family. "I know how you feel," Ellinor said softly. "My big brother, Andrey . . . I always wanted to impress him. From the moment I was old enough to really see him, I wanted to be just like him. Family's funny like that, yeah? Even when they hurt us, even when they . . . are no longer with us, they have ways of drawing us back, keeping us near."

Jelani raised a brow at her. "Where is your brother now?"

She swallowed. "Gone. Dead, like Misho, but longer. He died on a Juice Box raid when I was very young. It's what inspired me to enlist and my parents to get matching tattoos of his name. I wanted to make Andrey proud." Her voice lowered, eyes dropping to her boots. "In spite of my magic. Joke's on me now, yeah?"

She could have told him about Misho. Shared with him why she distrusted and hated Ashlings so much, but she wasn't ready to share her husband with anyone else, not after Fiss took the last of his magic. She was afraid she might lose even more of him somehow.

Jelani nodded, as if something in her story made sense to him. He offered her a wan smile before continuing. "That little girl captured my whole heart with a mere gurgle. I couldn't stay away from her. Oihana allowed me to have a relationship with my step-mother. She didn't hold my initial disdain against me. She was very understanding. For a humani," he added with a side-long look at Ellinor, who answered by rolling her eyes.

"I sent my boss in Trifon a message informing him I quit. I needed to stay in my home town of Higini to be with my family. My boss, Lothar, tried to convince me to relocate everyone to Trifon, but I couldn't rip them away from their home just for my own selfishness. Lothar said he understood. But understanding is not the same as forgiveness. He couldn't leave Trifon to hunt me down, I mean, crossing that much of Erhard just to make a point to his former Creature Breaker would be a long and costly endeavor. But, as you know, the powerful seersha who cultivate their operations under the government's nose, their pride, their demand for unconditional loyalty, their thirst for revenge . . . it's all far more important than the impracticality of delivering a certain kind of message.

"It took years. I was freelancing again, helping defectors of the gangs escape the city, when Lothar's goons caught up to me. I wasn't expecting retaliation, and it was a costly mistake. The assassins were good, probably the best Lothar could send. My step-mother and father . . . they never stood a chance. Neither were casters. I never got to say good-bye."

Ellinor's hands tingled, the weight of Misho's body in her hands making her fingers curl, her arms heavy with the muscle memory. Her chest felt too tight under her armor, her heart shrinking. She knew the guilt Jelani carried all too well, for she carried a similar, heavy burden. The never-ending desire to say good-bye to the ones you love, but also never wanting to say those words. To hold them close forever, to redo the day of their death over and over again until you did it right, and they no longer paid the price. Ellinor could feel herself warming to Jelani again, but she bit her tongue, refusing the shared survivors guilt be a bridge between them, not after his *proposal.*

Jelani took a deep, jagged breath. "But Oihana, she was already showing a strong affinity for machinery and engineering at a young age. She was returning from school as I returned from work, just as the attackers finished with my parents. I was stunned, blinded by rage and sorrow. I didn't move fast enough to get between them and Oihana. She tried to defend herself, deployed some of the mini-drones she was working on, but the thugs responded by tossing a grenade of some kind. Oihana's devices saved her life, but it cost her hearing. Nothing she could do, or any living mechanic or doctor—and I took her to the best—could restore her hearing. She's learned to read lips, and we've developed our own sign language. But yes, *your kind*, the kind who works for the crime bosses, are the ones who hurt me most. I slaughtered those who hurt my family, even though I couldn't return the favor to Lothar, but it didn't bring my parents back. So, Oihana and I have found purpose in other things."

Ellinor was left numb and speechless all over again. She couldn't even press him for what he knew about creatures like Fiss. Now it all made sense. Jelani's loyalty to his sister, why he worked against both the established government and the seersha casters who ran the underground, and why he supported the Ashlings. His sister needed them. They helped her, and she made them in kind.

"I'm sorry that happened to you, I am. But I'm not going to trade one shackle for another. I can't help the creatures that took Misho from me," Ellinor said, voice suddenly hoarse.

Jelani's smile was slow, but genuine. "I understand. There's time yet, you may change your mind. You aren't cut of the same cloth as the brutes who were deployed by Lothar, after all. There is still honor left in your soul, even if you try to bury it. I can sense enough of it in your bearing. You don't belong working for seersha like Cosmin, or Zabel, for that matter."

She tried to harden her face, to frown with a knowing look, but her face wasn't entirely cooperating. "You don't know that," she murmured.

Jelani smiled and shook his head. "I may not be a strong earth caster, but I'm still attuned enough to the natural pull of the earth to be sensitive to others. It doesn't make me all that popular. Most are uncomfortable once they discover the extent of my sensitivities. Others merely refer to it as a 'gut feeling.' My gut hasn't steered me wrong yet."

Ellinor realized her gait had slowed. Making herself swallow, she forced her abused body to pick up the pace once more. It wasn't possible that she stumbled across someone who was, what? Good? Sincere? Impossible. Especially someone who aligned themselves with Ashlings.

She glared at Jelani. "Misho was the honorable one. You're wrong about me. I have no honor left. You should leave, you don't need to stay here with us anymore."

She heard him chuckle behind her as he lengthened his stride to catch up. "Maybe, but my gut says otherwise." Jelani paused, then shrugged as he caught up with her. "I think I'll stay. My instincts say you're going to change your mind about returning to Cosmin. About what to do with Fiss, even. I think my offer intrigues you, even if you want to continue denying it," he smirked. "Besides, given your and Kai's condition, you could use my help."

She didn't respond to Jelani. A roar in the distance—back where the remnants of the Hornet Hawk and the dreeocht container was abandoned—captured their attention. They all stopped mid-stride.

Ellinor swallowed her rising bile enough to whisper, "Doehaz."

"Why do we run, Ellinor?" Fiss asked, finally getting the inflection of her name right.

"Remember how we told you about the monsters that like to eat magic?" Ellinor panted. "Well, they've come to eat us. All that fucking magic has attracted them."

"Boss," Kai hissed as he frantically readied his Rasul AbyssFire and Coyote armored suit, "that ain't helping."

The bellowing roar of the doehaz still rang in the distance. Ellinor hoped it would spend some time sucking whatever it could out of the broken dreeocht container before following their trail. The boulders were still too far away; she didn't think they'd make it to safety before the doehaz cut them off.

Kai was right, however. But not in the way he thought.

Skidding to a stop, Ellinor grabbed Kai as he barreled passed, and Fiss bumped into Jelani with the sudden stop. "Running isn't the answer here," Ellinor wheezed, trying to re-gain her breath. "Ever since shit hit the fan the first time with Irati, all we've done is race from one problem to the next. I kept thinking I just had to move faster, had to outpace the danger, but that's gotten too many people killed and hurt. We need a better plan. Shit, we need *a plan* period."

"Ell, as much as I love me a good battle, we ain't got that luxury. Doehaz 'ave our scent. You know those things don't give up once they smell magic. Our only hope is to get some-where secure-like and raise fortifications till 'em reinforce-ments arrive." Kai trembled next to her, green eyes darting back the way they'd come.

"Ellinor has a point," Jelani added, his Leviathan Roaster blades free of their sheaths, though the seersha had yet to turn them on. "We won't outrun the creatures. We're too de-lectable of a prize for them to ignore. We need to mount a de-fense if we hope to survive."

Ellinor's mind raced as her eyes flew over the barren ter-rain. Like an ancient film reel warming up, she recalled her one failed attempt of fighting a doehaz in her virtual trainer. *That's it!* "We need to kill one."

"Well, no shit, Ell. But how you propose we do that, huh?"

"You're not helping, Kai," Ellinor snapped. "Look, Jelani's right. We have too much magic—the doehaz won't stop coming. What we need is to kill one and cover ourselves in its gore. The smell of the dead doehaz will hide us until the new transport comes."

"All right, fine, but how we gonna kill one of 'em bastards? That one back there sounds like a big fucker. We ain't gonna survive that."

"Where there is one doehaz, there are others. The little ones always flee when a bigger predator comes into the area. My guess is we won't have trouble finding a few of the smaller ones running away from the same bastard we are."

Ellinor's eyes fell on Fiss, who still floated on the breeze next to her, not quite comprehending the danger. Kai followed her gaze, and understanding finally seemed to settle on the big man. Smiling mirthlessly, she said, "You ready to pick a fight now?"

A glimmer of amusement flashed through Kai's bulging eyes. "Ah, shit yeah!"

OPEN WIDE
///CHAPTER THIRTY-ONE

"THIS PLAN is idiotic," Jelani grumbled, expression harried.

Ellinor shrugged. "Doesn't mean it won't work."

"Actually, that's precisely what it means. You want to get eaten by a doehaz? This is how you get eaten by a doehaz."

"Ah, quit your bitchin', Sharma. You'll be fine," Kai said, as he prowled the area, loading his grenade belt with the home-made battery bombs Talin Roxas had given Ellinor before leaving. They were non-magical and needed to be lit manually, making them impractical against someone like Irati, but for a doehaz, they were perfect.

Ellinor found—at least from her botched training simulator—that the best way to deal with a doehaz was by blowing it up from the inside. Each doehaz was different in terms of what it looked like, just like a dreeocht, so none of them would know what they faced until it was upon them. Regardless, doehaz were mindless, making them damn hard to kill. You couldn't wound the thing, for it would crawl toward you and catch up when you were least expecting it, and if magic was used against the beasts? If the correct amount wasn't used, one may accidentally fuel the monsters rather than destroy them.

"Trust me, Jelani, I'm well aware of the danger here. But we're on the outskirts of the Saxa Desert. We have too much terrain to cover in doehaz territory without killing at least one, anyway," Ellinor said. "If we had more time and more, well, just more of anything at our disposal, I'd do something clever. I promise to show off my clever side another time."

"I'll hold you to that," Jelani muttered, readying to send tremors into the surrounding area.

The hope was to divert a smaller doehaz toward them as it fled the larger beast. They would let Fiss use his connection to Ellinor to cast vicious magic, destroying the doehaz. If they did it fast enough, the magic would be expelled and they would be covered in dead doehaz before any more of the roaming monsters caught their scent. If anything went wrong, Kai would be ready with his grenades and submachine gun. But if they attracted something too big, it would eat the magic Fiss used rather than be overwhelmed by it, and then—

Stop thinking about the worst case scenario, the long dead voice of her brother chimed in her head. *Focus on your plan and getting that to work, then you won't need a backup.*

Glancing from Ellinor to Fiss, Jelani took a deep breath, and jutted his sharp chin upward in a look of determination. "Ready to flirt with suicide, then?"

Ellinor grinned and nodded, jerking Fiss behind her and Kai while Jelani summoned his magic. Having a Creature Breaker divert their minimal flow of magic from their weapons was dangerous—not only did it exert a great deal of effort and energy on Jelani's part, it meant his blades would be useless until he had enough energy to recharge the weapons.

Flexing his fingers, Jelani's face twisted into a grimace. Soon, tremors were sent in the opposite direction of their downed aircraft, with Jelani as the bait in the center. Fiss, still oblivious to the danger, giggled as the earth began to rumble.

Jelani could cast his magic only for a minute before he was exhausted. Ellinor chewed on her bottom lip in annoyance. Had she not been shackled, she could have cast for much longer, increasing their chances of success. Despite her irritation, Ellinor went to the stumbling Jelani, helped him sit in front of Fiss, and covered them in Jelani's cloaking device, taking his place at the center of where he cast from.

A minute later, she heard a new, thundering roar quickly approaching. Ellinor closed her eyes, concentrating on the sound and the subtle vibrations heading her way. Forcing a swallow, she opened her eyes and fixed them on the dust cloud coming from the west. And, within the swirling vortex of dust, she saw *them*.

The first doehaz appeared to be an emaciated black stallion. Except for the clawed, mechanical insect pincers it had for front legs, the android optics, and the jaw that split into thirds, creating a gaping maw of bleeding muscle with three jaws of razor sharp teeth. Patches of the horse-like doehaz were completely gone, either showing the muscle reanimated with new, random pieces of combat-tech, or replaced with what looked to be discarded pieces of an old factory wall.

The second doehaz was a bit smaller; with the head of a feral boar, the arms of a humani, and the lower body of some kind of stag. This doehaz had a great deal more metal and machinery over its body, ripping through the muscle to create long, black, mechanical spikes. Some of the spikes even appeared to be broken Leviathan Roasters.

"Get ready, Fiss," Ellinor hissed. "You're going to need to pop those suckers as soon as they get close to me. Don't want to cast too far out and attract more attention, yeah?"

"What does it mean, 'pop them?' What is this, Ellinor?" Fiss cooed, poking his head out from the cloaking device, seaweed and cable hair quivering as if excited—or nervous.

Ellinor snapped her attention back to the rapidly approaching dust cloud. "Fill whatever tries to eat me with enough air to make it burst into chunks so we can cover ourselves in the innards. Its gross, but you have to use our connection to cast destructive magic to kill these monsters or they *will* kill me."

Fiss squeaked, and she hoped that was a confirmation as the doehaz skidded to a halt only a few feet away.

The doehaz paused, their snouts twitching in the air as they followed the trail of magic to its epicenter. The rotting stench of the reanimated creatures had Ellinor gagging, drawing their attention. Much like Fiss, the beasts could sense the latent magic within her blood. Precious seconds were lost as Ellinor struggled to regain control of her frozen body. By then, the doehaz were closing the meager distance toward her.

"Pop them, Fiss!" Ellinor screamed, clambering to the side to divert the doehaz from the others cloaked behind her.

Ellinor willed her feet to move faster; she needed to move the doehaz away from where Jelani was shielding Fiss, from where Kai waited, ready to shoot at the last moment if need be. She knew Fiss was casting not by what happened to the doehaz, but by the collar. An involuntary shriek tore from her lips as she collapsed to the sandy ground. Instead of the empty void that greeted her, Ellinor's insides ignited, like she was being boiled alive from the inside out.

Fiss popped one of the doehaz—the pig-like one—when he released the magic, freeing Ellinor from her torment.

Dead doehaz rained from the sky. Kai and Jelani were shouting. Fiss was bawling. And the second doehaz stopped in its charge. Gore from its hunting partner landed around Ellinor, shielding her scent. Gasping, Ellinor struggled to her feet before the doehaz noticed her again.

"Ellinor! Pain! No pain for Ellinor! Noooooooooooo," Fiss wailed, and Ellinor had to agree with the dreeocht. She didn't think she could survive Fiss using her in order to cast his magic again.

"Jelani," Ellinor said as loudly as she could, her voice raspy. "Get Fiss out of here." Gripping one of her pistols, she forced herself back on her feet despite the burning pain still radiating around her neck. Hot liquid dripped from the corners of her eyes, and she wasn't sure if it was sweat, tears, or blood. "Plan B," Ellinor croaked, hopefully loud enough for Kai to hear, before firing at the doehaz.

She emptied the entire clip into the roaring beast, emissive green blood spurting from each impact, but it didn't go down. That was the problem with doehaz. They weren't filled with the kinds of organs they should be. Ellinor knew she wouldn't kill it this way; with Fiss a blubbering mess, and Jelani too weak from casting his own magic, there was only Kai to protect them.

The concussive sounds of rapid fire from Kai's submachine gun pounded against Ellinor's head. But the beast didn't even stumble as it barreled back around to where Kai was firing, too big and bulky to move quickly in his Coyote mechanized suit. Ellinor's stomach twisted painfully at the thought of the horse-like monster feasting on Kai's bones.

Fiss struggled in Jelani's arms, shrieking, and writhing in the seersha's grasp, shaking off the cloaking device and revealing their location. The doehaz's head swung between Kai, and Jelani and Fiss, but the choice was obvious; the beast lurched forward, and Ellinor's heart seized in her chest.

She grabbed her own illegally tailored, knife-sized Leviathan Roaster. The monster's attention was instantly diverted. The magitech held within its fine wires, her blood, and the bio-tech shackle too delectable for the doehaz to pass up. She was an easy meal and the beast knew it. It skidded to a halt with a roar, turning its massive head back her way.

"Ell, no!" Kai yelled, but it was too late, the doehaz was locked on her.

Ellinor's skin was cold beneath the sweat, her breathing irregular as a wave of extreme fatigue rolled over her. Ellinor's thoughts were becoming muddled, concentrating nearly impossible. Her fingers barely able to hold her Leviathan Roaster as shock settled in. If she didn't end this quickly, she would be devoured.

I'll see you soon, Misho.

The doehaz pounded toward her, its three-jawed maw opening wide. Ellinor jerked to the side, slamming her knife into its neck with the rest of her ebbing strength. She used the leverage to swing herself up on to its back, avoiding its pincer front legs, the stench of rotting meat assaulting her senses.

The beast reared up, and Ellinor felt it shudder as Kai continued to pelt it with bullets from his AbyssFire, trying to blow its legs out. Kai fired relentlessly as Ellinor continued to stab the doehaz in the neck, but the beast's legs were made of steel.

Chunks of muscle were blown free of the fiend, but it didn't go down.

"Ell, catch," Kai barked, and lobbed one of the lit battery grenades at her.

Ellinor's vision was blurring and going white at the edges. She could barely make out the glowing grenade sailing through the air toward her as she desperately held on to the doehaz.

Ellinor felt herself slipping. She reached up for the glowing battery, and felt the doehaz's maw open, wider and wider, head snapping around toward her exposed throat.

Her fingers touched the grenade, and palmed the device.

The doehaz's tentacle-like tongue uncoiled from its maw, slithering toward her, ready to pull as much of Ellinor as possible into its mouth in one go.

Fiss's deafening cries drowned out the doehaz's final roar as Ellinor tossed the grenade deep into its gullet.

Summoning the last of her failing strength, she kicked herself out of range of the doehaz's jaws as it snapped them closed, inadvertently swallowing Talin's dirty grenade. A muffled *boom* rang in Ellinor's ears, and a shower of rancid viscera rained down on her as she slipped into the darkness.

WAKE-UP CALL
///CHAPTER THIRTY-TWO

A PLEASANT warmth enfolded Ellinor, and for a moment she believed Misho was rocking her. But it wasn't. It was Jelani, as Kai covered her from head to toe in the blood and gore of the slain doehaz. Her stomach flipped at momentarily thinking Jelani was Misho. You can't trust him, he wants to use you, too, she reminded herself, but was incapable of moving.

Her consciousness was fuzzy, slow to reclaim her body from her suppressed magic trying to burst free. She tried to dig deep and touch her abilities, desperately hoping Fiss had somehow broken the technology in the collar, but once more she was greeted by a cold emptiness deep in her soul.

Slowly, the voices of Kai and Jelani broke through the fog sitting in her mind. "We can't do that again, it could kill her. This shackle makes it so Fiss can't risk casting without killing Ellinor. He's almost as catatonic as her."

"Aye, I see 'im. But I don't rightfully understand *why*. Ell didn't die. Reckon she's survived worse, too, running from

Cosmin like she's been. Fiss's got no reason to be . . . I dunno, whatever it is that kid's doing." Ellinor heard Kai grumble somewhere above her as another chunk of still warm doehaz viscera was smeared around her neck and chest.

Jelani growled. She was conscious enough to at least groan and alert the men, but she was curious and stayed silent.

"Because," Jelani began slowly, "dreeocht *bind* to casters. If they're caught, that is. In an odd way, they need casters to reach their true potential. They need that connection to direct their wild magic. But what casters do to them when they're caught and bound before they wake . . ." Jelani shifted behind Ellinor, as if he were shaking his head. "It's a perversion of the natural order. Fiss, he bound himself to Ellinor in the way it should be. He's a part of her. That's the best way to describe it. The connection is flawed, though, because of the damn collar. The link isn't a two-way connection, the way it should be. When Fiss used Ellinor as the focuser, and hurt her in the process, it went against the complete love he feels for her. Dreeocht are primal beings, Kai, there is no in-between when they love or hate something. The moment Fiss found Ellinor, was connected to her by that collar, he imprinted on her. He worships her. Do you understand?"

There was a moment of silence before Kai mumbled, "I think so. But that's a problem, ain't it? If Fiss is connected to Ell, he won't be leaving 'er for Zabel, will he?"

Jelani sagged a little as he held Ellinor, rubbing more of the doehaz blood onto her hands. "There may be a way for you to complete your task. Zabel isn't shackled like Ellinor. It may be possible to convince Fiss to go with Zabel if he believes that staying with Ellinor may destroy her."

Kai sucked in his breath. "Kinda harsh, ain't it?"

"I didn't claim it would be an easy thing to do. I gave Ellinor another option, but she's blinded by her hate for your boss. She'll entertain no alternative."

Another moment of silence, and Ellinor wondered if Jelani could feel her racing heart. She heard Kai stand and blow out a heavy breath. "What're you getting at? You want Ell to betray Cosmin? Again?" Kai forced a laugh, before sighing loudly. "And just how is it you know all this shit 'bout dreeocht and seersha casters using 'em anyway? Bit of a coincidence, ain't it? That you 'appen to know so much. You gonna share? Seeing as how we're such good *friends* now?"

Ellinor held her breath, waiting for Jelani to answer, when Fiss's soft voice broke the moment. "Ellinor! Back!"

Her eyes flew open as the dreeocht careened into her, forcing the air out of her lungs. Fiss didn't care about all the nasty bits smeared into her armor, skin, and hair, wrapping his arms around her and squeezing. His paw-like hands soft and warm on her bare flesh. For the first time, Ellinor didn't feel the urge to flinch away from the magical creature.

Kai nudged her side with his big foot. "Welcome back, boss. Glad you ain't going to be just another ghost story."

"Likewise, buddy," Ellinor said, voice wheezy.

"Pain," Fiss moaned. "I made Ellinor hurt. Never, never, ever meant to. Nonono, never ever."

"It's all right, Fiss. You didn't mean to," Ellinor said, clearing her throat and trying to think how one was supposed to comfort a child. "It was just an owie—" Ellinor cringed at using such a word. "It hurt, yes, but it wasn't anything permanent."

Fiss looked up at her, the patches of scales sparkling in the setting sun, his pale blue eyes shimmering with tears. After a moment, Fiss nodded. "Owie, ouchie. Not that bad? A ow or ouch is okay?"

"Well, I wouldn't say it's okay, you don't want to cause hurt if you can help it. I lived, we killed the doehaz, that's the important thing. Mission accomplished, Fiss. You did well, yeah?" Ellinor glanced at Kai standing above her. "We should go. We may smell like doehaz, but I don't want to tempt things with that big one still out there."

Fiss wouldn't let go of Ellinor, however. As if he was worried she would slip away again, the dreeocht scuttled onto her shoulders and wrapped himself around her. Thankfully, Fiss was nearly as insubstantial weight-wise as the air he commanded. Ellinor frowned, but allowed the creature to stay where he was. To say she was conflicted about what to do with Fiss after Jelani's discussion with Kai was an understatement. She didn't like the ominous tone of Jelani's words, but her revenge on Cosmin for his hand in Misho's death had waited long enough.

Extending a hand, Kai helped her to her feet. Ellinor wouldn't look at Jelani as he stood from where he had been sitting on the ground behind her. Oblivious to her discomfort, Kai asked, "You sure you're good to walk, boss?"

"Doesn't matter if I'm not, we've got to reach those boulders by nightfall. We need the shelter," Ellinor said, voice tight. Shrugging, she hobbled toward their destination. "I could feel my magic. It was trying to break free and, in the process, making my body boil trying to implode on itself. It's the best way I can describe it. The shock was too much, I suppose. My body needed a restart to cope with it." Fiss whimpered in her ear and Ellinor ruffled his seaweed and cable hair. "Fiss, it's fine, seriously. Anyway, it's gone now. I still can't reach my magic and—" she touched the collar around her neck, now completely fused to her skin, "this thing has only gotten more stuck in the process. Today hasn't been a great day."

"When did you actually come to?" Jelani asked, matching her wobbly pace, ready to steady her if need be. "Did you hear any of what Kai and I discussed?"

She glanced at him and quickly averted her gaze. "I heard enough. About the bond thing with Fiss," she cleared her throat, "and enough to know you still haven't shared how it is you know so much about dreeocht and their relationship with casters. You need to rectify that, you got that? I need to know what's going to happen when we take . . . when we get to Zabel."

"Zaaabeeelllllll," Fiss crooned, as if tasting the powerful seersha's name on his tongue. Giggling, he shifted on Ellinor's shoulders, tangling his not-quite-humani hands in her gore filled hair.

"That's fair," Jelani said with a sigh, watching Fiss. "But it isn't safe to speak here. It's not safe to speak at all, really. Not until we reach shelter. I haven't heard that other doehaz in some time which makes me think it's gone back to prowling, trying to follow whatever magical scent we left behind. It would be wise not to give it a heading."

Ellinor opened her mouth to protest, but one look from Kai's wide, terrified eyes had her shut it just as quickly. "Fine," she said, voice tense. "But as soon as we're safe, you're spilling everything you know. Before Cosmin's new crew shows up."

"Story? Jell-annie has a story for us?" Fiss giggled, head bobbing as he twisted to look at the seersha.

The smile Jelani offered Fiss was both soft and sad. "Yes, little friend. Though it may mean nothing to you, I'm going to

tell our friends what I know of your kind. It will prove enlight-
ening, I'm sure. Do you think you can remain silent until then?
It's important we don't alert any of the other beasts to our location. We wouldn't want them attacking Ellinor again, would
we?"

Fiss wrapped his arms around her neck, and while Fiss held
on tightly, it caused Ellinor no discomfort. She wondered if
that was due to the machinery embedded in her flesh, or if Fiss
was really that incapable of hurting her.

"No one hurts Ellinor. Protect Ellinor, Jell-annie!"

Jelani's starry eyes locked on to Ellinor's as he said,
"Gladly."

She narrowed hers in return. "I can protect myself just fine,
thank you very much."

Kai guffawed in response, which made Fiss giggle, and Ellinor's face heat up. Jelani grinned at her blush and, balling her
hands into fists, Ellinor marched off, ignoring their grins and
her aching body until they were safe and Ellinor could address
them all properly.

After a few gut-clenching roars from the massive doehaz,
and the few times Fiss forgot that making noise was a bad
thing, they reached the gigantic boulders. Which was just as
well for Ellinor. She reeked of dead doehaz, her entire body
throbbed like she had gone through an industrial dryer, and
the collar on her throat was now a literal part of her. Ellinor

was at the end of being able to handle any more near misses or bad news.

Plopping herself down in the shade of a boulder, Ellinor allowed Kai and Jelani to secure the area as she scratched at the embedded piece of bio-magitech in her neck. She had gotten used to the ceaseless, if subtle, vibration of the collar since Fiss had joined them—she assumed it was a result of his obsession with creating little magical creatures—and while it wasn't painful, she didn't like the feeling, either.

She watched Fiss float about, holding his feet, observing Kai with fascination. "What does red friend do?" he chirped.

Kai smiled. "Makin' a perimeter so nothing sneaks up on us. I ain't one to shy away from a fight, but we're mighty low on ammo. So we needs to be smart 'bout it now. It's all pure mechanics tech, so no doehaz will think it smells tasty. We'll still need to keep watch, but it should keep us a tick safer."

"Keep watch? What is this?"

"One of us will need to stay awake at all times. You know, to watch. Make sure there ain't no surprises. You follow, Fiss?"

"Stay . . . awake? No sleep, red friend?"

Kai's grin stretched, his black mechanical tooth gleaming in the dimming light. "Yup, no sleep for a little while for one of us. Not you though, Fiss. Reckon you need the rest."

Fiss giggled. "No sleep! Don't need it, red friend. I will watch, watch, watch and keep you and my goodest friend Ellinor safe. Yes I will!"

"Uh," Kai said, sending the signal from Lazar's digimap to Mirza so he could relay where to have Cosmin's new ship meet them. "Well, then you can keep whoever's on watch company, kid. You won't need to do it alone."

Ellinor could see why Kai found the dreeocht endearing. Fiss was nothing like the doehaz. He had an honest goodness about him, and an innocence about everything that made Ellinor see the world in a new way, almost like the first time. She wondered if this was similar to having a child—

Stop, Ellinor. Love will make you weak. Vulnerable.

Once Kai and Jelani finished securing the area as best they could, Kai waved Fiss over to him. "C'mon, kid. You and me are gonna take first watch. We'll let 'em casters get sleep first, poor babies had a 'ard day." He added with a wink, making Fiss giggle as he floated off to join Kai, prowling around the boulders as night fell.

Ellinor watched Jelani take a seat next to her, straightening out his gore-covered legs, and stretching his neck and arms. She could understand his stiffness. Ellinor supposed they had something in common now in that regard: casting magic took a heavy toll on their bodies. At least Jelani's regenerated.

Once he stopped cracking his back, Ellinor cleared her throat. "Spill, Jelani. Time to share what you know about dreeocht, and how you know it."

His shoulders caved in a little with exhaustion. "Are you sure we should discuss this now? Shouldn't we wait for Kai and Fiss? Fiss did express wanting to hear this as well."

Ellinor waved him off. "You're stalling, and that makes me suspicious, so we're ending that now. I can update Kai later, plus I'm not sure how this helps Fiss. Azer forbid this gives him an existential crisis." Ellinor paused, taking a heavy drink from her canteen. "So, time to start talking."

He was silent for a long time, his eyes drifting skyward. "I learned of the dreeocht firsthand in Trifon," Jelani eventually whispered.

Ellinor sucked in her breath. "The caster there has a dreeocht?"

Jelani scratched at his chin and shrugged. "Lothar is excellent at hiding such things. But the dreeocht was not . . . ." His eyes moved down to his palms where they lost focus. "Lothar's dreeocht was barely a dreeocht, to be honest. Enough for it to count, but it was unstable, even before—well, that's not a topic for now. Regardless, Lothar has such a creature, and he used her and me in tandem whenever he felt the need. I was privy for a time with how he used her, how his dreeocht needed to cast her deadly magic through him."

"And you saw that all first hand, did you?"

Jelani nodded slowly. "It's why Lothar came after me so hard, even though it took him years to do so. So few people see dreeocht and understand them; the casters who have them enjoy that anonymity. It means they can turn the dreeocht into beasts, things to fear. Such as you and Kai did, initially. Truthfully, the dreeocht are nothing to fear themselves. If left alone, they will make beautiful, harmless magic for their entire existence. But there is something about that innocence which makes them gravitate toward others of their magical type. They sense a likeness and want to be near that, despite the risk. My guess is it makes the dreeocht feel complete in some way, or it's a compulsion similar to a doehaz hunting for magic. I'm unsure on that score."

Ellinor was silent, her eyes still narrowed at Jelani. Finally, she said, "Why couldn't you share this sooner? As far as I can tell, nothing you've said is worth the level of secrecy you treated it with."

Jelani shrugged. "I didn't know you, didn't trust you. I didn't want to share my involvement with Lothar. Had I done that, then I'd have to share more. What happened to Oihana and my family, and my hand in that. I wasn't ready to reveal such things. And then after? Well, we were a bit preoccupied with staying alive, if I recall correctly? But if we are to work together . . ." he trailed off, grinning at Ellinor's stubborn glare. "Or *potentially* work together in the future, the timing feels better now."

The smile Jelani turned her way was thin, etched in the exhaustion she too felt. Not entirely conscious of the action, Ellinor lay down on the still slightly warm ground, her eyelids heavy. "I suppose I can understand that. But you want to re-earn my trust? Don't hide anything from me anymore. I always find out. It usually doesn't end well."

"Is that why you hate Cosmin so much?"

Jelani's question surprised her, her eyelids jerking up. "He hid things from me, yes. Similar to this botched mission." She hesitated, debating telling the Creature Breaker more. If he was opening up to her, trying to move past his ridiculous request that she join his cause, then Ellinor figured she should do likewise. They might still need each other, after all. Perhaps it was time to tell him more of Misho.

She took a deep breath, meeting Jelani's gaze. "Cosmin thought he was being clever. That he'd flush out a rat in his midst, but in doing so, he didn't share all the information his crew needed. So when things went tits up, like they always do, the good guys were caught unprepared and they died. Cosmin killed my husband, and all because he wanted to keep his cards close. I found out what he was really doing after Misho died. I've been hunting down the culprits for the past seven of the eight years since Misho's death. Cosmin's one of the few left I have to *repay*, him and a few Ashlings."

"You've been chasing revenge for nearly a decade?" Jelani whispered, breaking her thoughts as they drifted toward sleep once more.

"I won't stop hunting until Misho is avenged. Even if it kills me."

"There is more to life than vengeance, Ellinor. Your Misho would tell you the same. You need a new purpose. Please, reconsider my offer. If not for yourself, for Fiss at least. I'm certain Misho wouldn't want you to die for this."

"You're assuming I want to keep living without him," Ellinor mumbled as sleep finally took her. Her dreams were troubled and full of the images of Lazar exploding, Pema being shot, and Embla dying, until a soothing presence fell over her, taking her bad dreams away. And, for a moment, it felt as if she were reunited with her magic once again.

A PLACE FOR THE DEAD
///CHAPTER THIRTY-THREE

THE SOUND of engines woke Ellinor. Cursing, she jolted upright, annoyed that Kai neglected to wake her for watch duty, and that he didn't rouse her before the new transport was practically on top of them.

Landing on one of the boulders was one of Cosmin's stealth hypersonic aerial transports, a smaller Eagle Owl than the one Lazar built. The planes weren't obvious, but if anyone did see them, there would be no mistaking that Cosmin von Brandt was up to something. Ellinor assumed that this close to Anzor and with all the trouble they already encountered, Cosmin no longer cared about secrecy.

Fiss watched the transport with open fascination. "Ellinor, what is that, Ellinor? Is it for us, Ellinor? No danger?"

Ellinor tried to smile, but she felt her expression wavering. "Yeah," she murmured, stuffing her gear as quickly as she could into her travel backpack, "that's our ride out of here. We'll fly the rest of the way to Anzor and won't have to worry about hiding from any more doehaz."

Fiss clapped his hands. "Flying! I love flying, Ellinor! You will love it, too! Yes!" As if to demonstrate, Fiss began zooming around her before darting toward Kai, who playfully swatted at the dreeocht in return. Only Jelani seemed unaffected by Fiss's enthusiasm.

Ellinor narrowed her eyes at the seersha. He looked disgusting, though Ellinor was sure she looked no better. But even beneath the covering of the dry, emissive blood and meat chunks from the doehaz, his dusky skin was sallow, his movements both stiff and twitchy as he eyed the plane.

"What is it?" Ellinor asked as the Eagle Owl landed and the hatch doors hissed open.

"Don't you find it odd that the transport got here so fast? It may have traveled at top speed the entire time, but it shouldn't have arrived so quickly."

Ellinor shrugged. "Maybe? But Cosmin had the plane waiting at one of the rendezvous points, supposedly. It didn't travel all the way from Euria. Is that all that's bothering you?"

His long fingers fiddled with the hilts of his Leviathan Roaster swords. "I'm unsure if I'm welcome on your ship. Your boss doesn't know me, and the one person who could have vouched for me is dead. I'm a wanted man, but being left here would also be a death sentence," Jelani whispered.

Ellinor waved his concern away. "By now, Mirza, Talin, Pema, and the others are well on their way back to Cosmin. Talin and Pema can certainly vouch for you, especially after your sister patched Pema up at her bunker. You freed Mirza, so that will count for something, too. Cosmin is a wicked bastard, but he doesn't like having debts. If he feels like he owes you, he'll give you safe passage now and declare you two square, even if he never personally speaks to you. You'll be fine."

Jelani didn't look placated. He clamped his jaw shut so tightly, the vein on the side of his head bulged, but he said no more and finished collecting their things. Ellinor glanced at the Eagle Owl as a small fleet of bouncer and combat automatons poured from the transport.

Ellinor's heart sank.

Cosmin's backup crew had no seersha or humani amongst them. While these bots weren't even close to Ashlings the way Oihana's were, their unblinking ocular orbs still made Ellinor shiver when they fell on her.

Fiss was inspecting the robots, who didn't seem to notice the dreeocht one way or another as they maneuvered the crew onto the plane. "Kai," Ellinor whispered, snagging the big man's elbow, "is this it? This is everything Cosmin sent?"

Kai shrugged. "Looks like. We should call 'im when we get airborne. You can ask 'im if we should be expecting anyone else."

How Kai could be at ease around so many of Cosmin's mechanical goons, Ellinor would never understand. Ellinor swallowed her trepidation and, clenching her fists, she stomped toward the transport, grabbing Fiss by his thin shirt on the way and ushering the chirping dreeocht inside.

Jelani lingered at the door, fingers drumming along the side. Ellinor held up a hand, silently telling him to wait, as she prowled through the ship. She knew where Cosmin hid most of his cameras and spy devices. And, even years after Ellinor quit, the seersha hadn't changed his layout. Ducking into blind corners, she disconnected the cameras and fried the bugs so Cosmin couldn't spy on them. Ellinor went back to where Jelani was waiting, waving him onboard, but he didn't move, watching the androids with a pointed look on his face.

Ellinor rolled her eyes. "They aren't infiltrator drones. Cosmin's too paranoid about the governor hacking into his systems, should the police get a hand on one of his bots. He doesn't put anything with direct feedback to him in any of his mechanical staff. You're fine. Stop being a baby, yeah?"

Jelani frowned, but stepped onto the Eagle Owl, the hatch door locking behind him.

Once they were in flight, Ellinor glanced to where their last transport had been, and trembled. There was only a husk of the wreckage remaining, and massive slithering imprints of the thing that had feasted on it. Suppressing another shudder, Ellinor dashed for the plane's small bathroom, slamming the door and refusing to come out until every last bit of gore was scrubbed off her body and clothes.

She tried to disregard everything else other than cleaning herself. She didn't want to think about what she would tell Cosmin, she didn't want to consider what she would need to tell Fiss to get him to stay with Zabel, she didn't want to think about the collar around her throat that would require surgery to remove, and she didn't want to contemplate going with Jelani instead to have her collar deactivated, because that would ensure she would never get close to Cosmin again. She could barely think about her numerous physical injuries. Considering anything else added to an emotional weight she didn't need.

There was a loud wailing outside the bathroom door, making her jump, followed by unrelenting tapping. "Ellinooooor? Can't see, can't see!"

Ellinor suppressed a groan, and turned off the scalding water. Donning a new, oversized dark purple sweater, tight black cargo pants and boots, she opened the door before Fiss could summon a magical creature to open it forcibly. Fiss relaxed as soon as she emerged. The little creature consoled, she strode to the cockpit to check in with Cosmin.

The five automatons Cosmin sent were zooming about the transport, flying the plane, and guaranteeing nothing went wrong. They ignored Fiss, despite the dreeocht floating after them and trying to make little air and water creatures to mimic their movements.

Ellinor had barely slid into the co-pilot seat and activated the holo-comms before a projection of Cosmin's face appeared. Despite the nonchalant air the seersha tried to project as he lounged in a pale green paisley suit, there was a hard glint to his pumpkin-orange eyes that was unmistakable, even through the projection.

"Ah, my dear Ellinor. I was beginning to think you'd forgotten all about me. Terribly rude of you to keep me waiting, don't you agree?" Cosmin's voice was taut as his eyes narrowed in on the device around her throat.

"Sorry, been busy avoiding doehaz, you know how it is. I take it the crew is headed back all right, yeah?"

Cosmin flippantly waved the comment away. "No need to worry about them. They're being taken care of. Now, let's get down to business, shall we? I daresay this little mission of yours didn't go as planned. But thankfully, I was prepared. Really, Ellinor, I had such high expectations for you, and you utterly disappointed me."

Ellinor rolled her eyes. "I'm sorry; did you miss the part where your team mutinied? That wasn't my fault." She didn't give Cosmin time to answer. "Whatever. I was *forced* to do this. The job's getting done, yeah? That's all that matters." Cosmin huffed in reply and Ellinor pressed on. "You only sent bots. Is there a *real* crew we're going to be picking up before meeting with Zabel?"

Cosmin's laugh sounded forced, but his smile appeared genuine. "You're joking, aren't you, my dear? After I flushed that traitorous Irati out of my midst, you think I'd send more of my crew for this? Oh, no, no, no. Irati needs to tell me what I want to hear first before I trust anyone else for something like this ever again. No, the automata are all you'll need. They were already waiting with the Eagle Owl I had stashed, anyway. You're only a day out from where you're to meet Zabel. You can manage that short distance without causing more chaos, can't you, Elli?"

Ellinor clenched her jaw. "Probably. And you better have some real good mechanic and surgeon on hand when I get back to collect. This shit piece of bio-magitech you put on me has been malfunctioning. You better still be able to get it off me, *Coz*."

Cosmin frowned, and the air around the projection wavered as if he tried to scorch her. "Do not threaten me, dear. Your life is still very much mine." Cosmin took a moment to lean back in the chair, brushing his matte black hair away from his shoulders. "Your necklace can still be removed, as long as you don't continue doing anything you aren't supposed to. Like conversing with *my* dreeocht." Ellinor opened her mouth to deny any such thing but he cut her off. "Lying to me would be a mistake, my dear. I know the dreeocht is out of its box. The cameras on my plane may be . . . malfunctioning," he said, narrowing his gaze at Ellinor, "but my sensors have picked up the extra body along with your other new tagalong. Just don't forget who that gift is for, and I will uphold my end of this deal and return your magic to you, understood?"

Ellinor's heart thudded like a stone in her chest as she nodded. Cosmin smiled. "Excellent. Now, be good my dear. I'll see you soon."

Cosmin disconnected the call, and Ellinor was left numb. All she could do was cling to the promise that the collar could still be removed, even in its current condition. But the more she tried to focus only on her, the more her thoughts drifted to Kai. She missed having Kai with her, and if she killed Cosmin outright? She would lose him forever. The more she tried to reaffirm only her goals, she found herself watching the selfless Jelani as he huddled at the back of the plane, and she began considering alternative paths to the one she had been on for the past seven years. The more she tried to concentrate on her needs, the sharper the lonely pang in her heart became over the idea of giving Fiss away.

She pinched the bridge of her nose and headed back into the main cabin. Ellinor sank down into a seat and tried to get more sleep while her gear charged, but was interrupted by Kai exiting the bathroom bare-chested, his red and acid green hair a disheveled mess. He grinned, and sat down across from her, still running a towel over his corded chest.

"Cosmin ask 'bout me?" Kai said, trying to keep the quiver from his voice.

Ellinor was too exhausted to be tactful. "No, Kai. He never asks about you. You know that."

Kai shrugged, failing to hide the hurt in his eyes. "You never know. He might one day."

Before Ellinor could remind him that Cosmin only liked beautiful women, Kai was changing the subject; he didn't want to discuss the unrequited nature of his affection. "How's he doing?" Kai gestured at Fiss, who was hovering around one of the bouncer androids.

Ellinor scoffed. "Fiss? Out of everyone, he's doing the best. He's having the time of his life." Ellinor's voice caught in her throat, a stone rolling through her insides.

"You told 'im then? That he's going with Zabel?"

Ellinor shook her head, not trusting herself to speak. Fiss sensed her roiling emotions and floated over, curling himself up in her lap. "Sad? Why? We are flying!" he trilled.

"We're getting close to our destination. The end. I don't like endings, or saying good-bye. It reminds me of what I never got to do with Misho," Ellinor said quietly, voice thick.

Kai met Ellinor's pained expression with one of his own, but Fiss didn't understand what was to come. He tilted his head, back and forth, chewing his thin lips, before a large smile showed off his small, white teeth.

"Good . . . bye? No, no! The water-man. Misho? Yes. I . . . feel him? The magic he had? It tasted . . . I don't know. Different. Complete. Content. Your doing, I think? Water-man was whole, because of his Ellinor. I feel like that. Whole. Complete. Present. Water-man's essence lingers? Oh, yes. He is part of what made Fiss. Ellinor, you are here—" Fiss said, bopping her nose, "but water-man is here." Fiss placed a hand on his chest. "No good-byes."

"You can feel my Misho?" Ellinor murmured, heart hammering.

Fiss nodded, bobbing his head enthusiastically. "Misho is gone, but not *gone*-gone. I hold a piece. Deep in me. Tastes like love. I like it. Feels right."

Before she was even aware, Ellinor was hugging Fiss and Fiss was hugging her. A part of her little bug lived in Fiss, and the knowledge that Misho hadn't completely left eased some of the deep seated despair she carried.

Realizing what she was doing, she jerked back. Fiss blinked at her in confusion for a moment, but Ellinor wasn't looking at him anymore. Instead, her gaze shifted between the combat android standing sentinel at the back of the cabin, its ocular orbs glowing as it observed the three of them, silent and unmoving, and Jelani, who was grinning at her just off to the side as he ran a towel through his damp greyish hair.

"How long have you been standing there like a creep?" Ellinor mumbled. Whipping around, Fiss beamed at the seersha and went cannonballing into his abdomen for a hug. Fiss enjoyed crawling over Jelani almost as much as he loved climbing on Ellinor.

"Long enough," Jelani said matter-of-factly. "Rather sweet, isn't it? That Fiss has maintained something of your love that Cosmin had intended to destroy by feeding it to him?"

Ellinor scowled at him, her ire flaring. "What's that supposed to mean? I'm supposed to be happy that a piece of my husband lives in a treasure that is destined for someone else to have?"

The presumption that Ellinor should be *grateful* that Misho somehow remained in an intangible sort of existence in Fiss, still too far away for Ellinor to hold or love again, broke her heart. Her initial happiness pushed to the side like a kitten by the gorilla her depression had become. Fiss would be going to Zabel Dirix, and the little piece of Misho she had found would be ripped away once again.

It would have been better to have never known.

"It doesn't have to be that way, you know," Jelani whispered, voice husky in a way that made Ellinor's insides clench.

"Whatcha getting at?" Kai growled, eyes narrowing as Jelani took a few steps toward them, arms still wrapped around Fiss.

Jelani stopped moving, his starry eyes bright with hope as he gave a beseeching look to Ellinor, ignoring Kai. "All I am saying," Jelani began slowly, "is there are other avenues to explore. Ones that accomplish your need to be free, and keep Misho near you," Jelani said vaguely, his eyes drifting to the automata before snapping back to Ellinor. "You can abandon this need . . . this *craving* you have to get back at those who hurt you and finally live your life. There are others who could benefit from your help. My offer still stands, if you'll take it."

Ellinor's mouth was too dry to answer.

"We gots a job to do, Sharma," Kai said, bushy brows furrowing at the other man. "I like Fiss loads too, but he's meant to live with Zabel." He flashed the dreeocht a big, toothy grin. "You're gonna love Anzor, Fiss. I know it."

"Ellinor," Jelani said, once more ignoring Kai. "Are you sure this is what *you* want? Is this the road you wish to continue on?"

Fiss, oblivious to the double meaning, or perhaps the *true* meaning of what was being discussed, turned his attention to Ellinor. Grinning, he floated toward the window as if he wanted to see this place Kai said he would enjoy so much.

Ellinor clamped her jaw shut. She didn't know what she wanted anymore, what she truly wanted. For eight years, she had considered nothing beyond slaughtering those responsible for Misho's murder, and rushing headlong to meet him in the process. The thought made her itchy. She didn't truly believe she had a choice the way Jelani implied; she didn't want to help Ashlings in return for having their mechanics remove her shackle.

Ellinor balled her fists, nails cutting into the palms of her hands, and shook her head. Ellinor wouldn't meet Jelani's imploring gaze. "Kai's right," she said, voice weaker than she intended.

You'll never forgive yourself. Misho's voice floated through her mind. *Don't do it.*

But she had to. This was the only way to guarantee the mobster didn't take his displeasure out on Kai if Ellinor stole his prize. It was the only way to make Cosmin pay. But her heart wasn't in it, shrinking in her chest as she mumbled, "This is business."

NO TURNING BACK
///CHAPTER THIRTY-FOUR

E LLINOR DIDN'T speak for hours as they raced toward An-zor. Her insides were twisting into knots, and each time she looked at Fiss as he bounced about the cabin, her hands got hot and clammy all at once. A thought was scratching through her skull, giving her a mild headache. Something Je-lani had mentioned was trying to force itself to the forefront of her mind.

Jelani, for his part, was not attempting to speak to her, either. His disappointment in her was palpable. She tried to convince herself she didn't care. Ellinor was certain as soon as they reached safe airspace out of the reach of doehaz, he would use his outlaw contacts to escort him back to Oihana. Even Kai was sullen, declining to play with Fiss in favor of cal-ibrating his armor and weapons.

Her eyes slid from the three of them, avoiding the unset-tling way the bouncer and combat androids moved about the cabin. One was lingering near them for longer than Ellinor felt was necessary, when the thing making Ellinor feel slightly ill finally bubbled to the forefront of her consciousness.

"Jelani," she said, voice wobbly, "what were you going to say about the dreeocht and caster relationship? Something Lothar did to his dreeocht, or all casters do when they catch them. Something to make them work for the casters, yeah? If they don't bond naturally like . . . Fiss. They do something, don't they?"

Jelani gave her a cold look, his eyes hard like dark stones. He gave her an almost imperceptible nod, and Ellinor forced herself to swallow the tightness in her throat. "What is Zabel going to have to do to Fiss to make him bond to her?"

Jelani scrubbed a hand over his face, a look of exhaustion pulling his full lips down. "Are you certain this is something you want to know?"

It was her turn to give him a nearly undetectable nod. Jelani sighed, motioning her closer, his eyes taking on a far-away look. "When Lothar first found his dreeocht, the creature was already conscious. She was docile. Easy to catch, naturally drawn to Lothar's earth caster abilities, and mine, I gather, as Lothar wanted me with him should the dreeocht prove difficult. She—Lothar named her Minnow—was curious enough about us to not need the precaution. But it allowed me to see what few know."

"What they use to control the dreeocht, you mean?" Ellinor asked, the back of her neck suddenly sweaty.

Jelani nodded, glancing at the bot, which hadn't moved. "It's a device, not unlike your collar. It sits high on the throat with a metal tendril at the back like a scorpion tail. The tip of the coil is inserted into the base of the dreeocht's skull, where it opens, affixing it permanently into the bone. Inside the tip is a needle that floods the dreeocht with nanites, similar to the ones used for Creature Breakers, but instead of the minuscule devices in my blood connecting to my magic and my blades, the nanites connect the dreeocht to a corresponding mechanism in the caster. Lothar used a shot to inject himself with the necessary bio-technology; he wore no collar like Minnow was shackled with. Once on, the device cannot be removed without killing the dreeocht, though I wouldn't say they were all that alive, once the apparatus is put in place. It . . . lobotomizes them. Making the dreeocht unaware of the world they're in, or what's happening to them. They become no more than a breathing battery, just as the powerful casters want."

Ellinor had to stifle her gasp as she breathed out, "But why? If dreeocht are already drawn to such power, why mentally castrate them?"

Jelani glowered at her. "Because they still have free will. Minnow would have left Lothar if he did terrible things. Things she didn't want to channel her magic through. Dreeocht may be overly innocent with a hearty dose of naiveté, but they know the difference between good and evil. Minnow would have disappeared one day, and Lothar would be without his powerful asset. Tell me, Ellinor, if your Cosmin could have kept Fiss for himself, is he the type of caster who would take such a risk?" When Ellinor shook her head, Jelani clenched his jaw and gave her another curt nod. "That's why people like Lothar, Cosmin, and no doubt Zabel, all but kill their dreeocht. That's what Zabel will need to do to Fiss. His freedom, you might even say his soul, is the price you are paying in order to enact your *revenge.*"

Ellinor was struck dumb by what he had shared.

Without another word, Jelani pushed himself from his seat and stalked toward the back of the cabin, where his gear was stashed and Ellinor's armor and shield were finished charging. He began going through his things violently, as if preparing for something, refusing to look at Ellinor or Fiss.

It wasn't that Ellinor didn't believe the gangster bosses wouldn't go to such horrific lengths to keep their prizes, but she was shocked that she had been so blind to the idea of the dreeocht being caged within their own minds. Just like she was, in a way.

It's not me who has to pick up the tab for my revenge.

She shivered. There was so little of herself left that she recognized, so many bodies piled up around her. She wasn't sure how she could keep wading through the mess she was leaving for others to clean up.

Embla, Warin, Lazar, Janne, what's one more body? Besides, Fiss isn't really going to die. But Ellinor couldn't convince her heart of what her mind so desperately tried to hold on to, not with Jelani's words ringing through her skull. Not with the *out* he kept dangling in front of her, though she wasn't sure his offer was still good.

There was still an element of caution at play, and racing to Anzor in an Eagle Owl that belonged to a powerful caster would attract the kind of attention everyone wished to avoid. Unease gnawed through Ellinor's chest the entire time, and she chewed the nubs of her fingernails to distract her, with little success.

Fiss sensed the awkward disquiet from the group—they weren't exactly being subtle. Fiss's agitation grew. Little sparks of lightning shot off his back, his seaweed and cable hair writhing like snakes in agony. Watching Fiss drift about the cabin almost listlessly, Ellinor failed to see Kai stomp toward her.

"You gotta tell 'im, boss," Kai whispered, poking her in the shoulder.

Ellinor jerked her arm away. "What should I say to him, Kai? That he has to stay with Zabel and, oh, by the way, she's going to implant a hook thing in your head so you practically cease to exist except for, you know, boosting her powers. That sound like something that will help Fiss right now?"

Kai blinked rapidly at her. "What's this? That ain't . . . . Who told you they do that to 'em dreeochts?"

Ellinor's eyes flicked to Jelani and Kai scratched at his beard. "He could be lying."

Ellinor shook her head. "Something tells me it's the truth. But even so, do you want to risk something like that?" Kai clenched his jaw in response, and Ellinor's shoulders sagged.

"Shit, Ell, I dunno. I reckon we don't 'ave a choice, do we? This was the deal, what Cosmin said we gotta do, so I suppose we gotta do it. Even if . . ." Kai trailed off, eyes drifting to Fiss. Balling his meaty hands into fists, Kai shook his head sharply. "Nah, Jelani's gotta be lying. That, or that kind of shit was just something Lothar did. Cosmin wouldn't do something like that, doubt he'd trade Fiss to someone who did, either."

Ellinor flinched back. "You really do believe the best in that man, yeah? Cosmin doesn't deserve your loyalty, Kai. He never did."

Kai shrugged, a blush coloring his cheeks. He didn't answer her immediately, turning his gaze to the window. "We gotta be nearing Anzor by now," he said, changing the subject.

Ellinor sighed, and took out Lazar's cracked digimap, aiming it at the ground. "Yeah," she said. "Maybe half an hour at most."

"We are near the end?" Fiss squeaked, floating toward her. "Will arriving make Elli happy? Something is wrong. Bad taste, bad taste! This will make it go away, yes Elli?"

Ellinor's mouth hung open, the backs of her eyes stinging. *He says it just like Misho used to. Soft, warm, and hopeful.*

Jelani noted her harrowed expression, putting the little device he had been fiddling with away, and broke the tense silence between them. "Last chance, Ellinor. Do you really wish him to become like Minnow?"

Hanging her head, Ellinor said, "I don't have a choice."

Frustrated, Jelani slammed his palm into the side of her seat. "There is always a choice. You *always* have a choice. I've told you what the alternative is. Stop being so fucking thick. It would be kinder for me to kill Fiss than to let you choose to continue."

Ellinor's head snapped back like she had been struck. She had never heard Jelani swear before, certainly not at her, though she deserved it. A modicum of respect grew in her for Jelani, for him standing up to her. Few did anymore.

"Choice? What is this? What are we choosing?" Fiss asked, hair trembling as he played with his fingers.

Ellinor didn't answer Fiss, locking eyes with Jelani. "I . . . we can't."

Kai frowned. "Ell's right. We gots no other option 'ere."

"That," Jelani growled softly, "is a blatant lie."

He jerked his eyes to where the bouncer bots waited near the emergency hatch doors, the other combat androids readying the transport for landing. "You can't be suggesting that two people who obliterated a pair of doehaz, survived a coup, bested Dragan Voclain, and traveled the length of Erhard with precious cargo in tow cannot handle the obstacle before them? That they have forgotten the allies they've made," he said looking deep into Ellinor's eyes, "that would continue to help if you made the *right* choice? Someone who has resources to help with your shackle?"

"You mean working with the same Ashling scum that cost Misho his life in the first place? The very people who would force Fiss to make more of their kind in exchange for *helping* me?" Her voice lacked conviction, holding instead hopelessness, her eyes stinging anew with fresh tears.

Jelani glanced at Kai before turning his gaze back to her, a look of disappointment flashing in his stare. "I would never force Fiss to do anything. I would give him a choice, an option. Just as I'm giving you." He shook his head. "If it comes down to it, you must decide which you view the lesser of two evils."

"Elli? I am missing things. What is it you speak of? Don't understand," Fiss said, curling himself in her lap and burying his face in her soft sweater.

Ellinor scrubbed a hand over her face, before dropping it to the back of Fiss's bare neck. Imagining a shackle there like hers sent her stomach freefalling.

"Boss," Kai whispered, eyeing Cosmin's androids. "You can't. This be *business*, remember?"

"And if Zabel is like Lothar, what then? You can't be good with that, Kai. You of all people can't be okay with that. You were abandoned and picked on and abused as a kid, you want that for Fiss too, yeah? You're the one who keeps reminding me that he's just a *kid*," Ellinor said, a note of pleading in her voice as she wrapped her arms around Fiss's little body. The parallels between her and Fiss were clicking into place, the tumblers turning in her head.

The obvious link between her and Fiss presenting itself now that she started to see him for what he truly was: a newly formed creature. A child. A child that held a bit of her Misho in his soul.

Kai's expression was pained as he looked at Ellinor and Fiss together. "But Cosmin . . ." Kai trailed off, and cleared his throat, running a hand through his spiky hair. "Fuck me to the abyss and back," he grumbled, face twisting. "What do we do then, boss?"

Ellinor shrugged, then lowered her voice. "Do as Jelani suggests? Overpower the bots and commandeer this bird. Let Jelani pilot it somewhere safe where we can set Fiss free or something. Then we part ways. I find some mechanic that can free me of my problem, you go back to Cosmin and say you were ambushed, that Fiss got out and I fled. Some rubbish like that. Cosmin will believe a loyal soldier like you. Easy come, easy go, with no risk of Fiss ending up like the other dreeocht, Minnow," Ellinor said, meeting Jelani's glittering stare.

Kai rolled his eyes. "You make it sound easier than it is, boss. But fine. Wait 'ere."

As Kai nonchalantly headed for their weapons and armor, Fiss turned his big, pale blue eyes up to Ellinor. "You feel lighter. My Elli feels less hurt. A good thing has happened?"

Ellinor didn't need to force her smile this time. "Yes, for once I think I'm finally going in the right direction."

Fiss tilted his head, but didn't respond as Kai handed Ellinor her armor and shield. Eyeing the automata warily, Ellinor put Fiss down and shrugged back into her fully charged armor, snapping weapons back in place under the pretense of preparing for landing.

Crouching in front of Fiss, Jelani said in hushed tones, "My little friend, you must stay out of the way for what's to come next. Don't worry, but be sure to stay out of sight and let nothing take you away from Ellinor. Do you understand?" Fiss nodded and Jelani patted him on the shoulder. "Very good. Think of it as a game. You hide and we'll find you once we've cleared a path. Doesn't that sound like fun?"

Fiss glanced at Ellinor for confirmation and she grinned. Turning back to Jelani, the dreeocht nodded enthusiastically and disappeared from view in a fit of giggles, using the constant whirl of air magic around him to bend the light in such a way to make him invisible, like Dragan had done. Once Fiss vanished, one of the bots near the hatch door began to emit a low buzzing that made the hairs on the nape of her neck stand on end.

Before she could analyze the behavior, Jelani was nudging her. "Divide and conquer?"

Kai answered for her, that familiar gleam twinkling in his eyes. "Works just fine. Let's do this, boss."

Kai Axel Brantley shot first.

Burst fire from his Rasul AbyssFire obliterated one of the bouncer bots. The androids moved instantly as their comrade tilted to the side, falling over. Ellinor darted for the bot piloting the plane while Jelani made sure the two guarding the cargo bay couldn't assist. Ellinor's focus homed on the pilot, who, while not removing its claw-like digits from the flight console, had a pair of turrets deployed from its shoulders, aimed right at her.

Ellinor activated her shield. Teeth rattling vibrations and deafening pings from the bullets made Ellinor's progress slow. Ellinor crouched low, unsheathing Janne's Lance from the side of her thigh. She glanced at the readouts on her wrist, noting the shield battery was starting to drain.

Then, her collar began vibrating painfully as Fiss cried out, "Red friend!"

With her heart racing and sweat forming on her brow, Ellinor threw caution to the wind. *Fuck it. Sorry, body, once this is over I'll make it up to you with the biggest bottle of whiskey I can find.*

Ellinor jerked up, shielding her head as she moved. Flipping the electrical knife point down, she lunged. Thumbing the Lance's pulse to as high as it would go, she rammed the knife into the vulnerable spot between the bot's head and neck, her chest about to cave in from the impact of the bullets her armor was attempting to absorb. Ellinor couldn't breathe as the bot twitched, the electricity frying its circuitry, the breath completely knocked out of her at least three times over. But Fiss was still crying, the collar squirming on her neck, and the sounds of fighting behind her going strong.

Ellinor didn't wait for her breath to return before acting once more.

Scrambling back to where Kai and Jelani were, Ellinor was glad to note Fiss remained invisible, despite his anguished screams. The scene before Ellinor made her stomach lurch into her throat. Jelani was struggling with a combat bot wielding more magitech weapons than its type should have. The bot tried to grab the seersha and throw him into the bubble escape hatch where Kai lay crumpled on the ground, face covered in blood. A damaged bouncer bot stood over him, its cannon-like gun pointed at Kai's head.

Jelani hissed, a long gash appearing on his hip. Ellinor sprang into action, despite her shock. Throwing her Lacerator knives at the security bot to get its attention—and keep it from dragging the struggling Jelani to join Kai—she raced for the automaton, burying the still humming Lance in one of its ocular orbs, and caught the flying blades with her free hand. With Jelani safe, she yanked her Asco Rhino off her back, ready to fire a massive steel bolt at the bot's chest. But the android wasn't there. In the chaos, it had joined the bot with Kai and sealed the door.

"No!" Ellinor screamed, pounding on the hatch doors. Then, an all too familiar face was projected against the clear wall of the bubble pod.

Ellinor's body went cold, eyes wide, as she breathed out, "Cosmin."

"My dear," the seersha crooned. "You really shouldn't have done that."

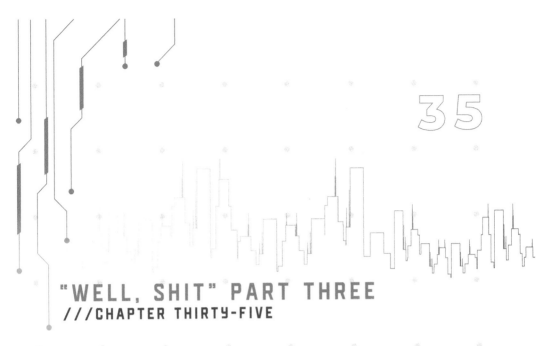

"WELL, SHIT" PART THREE
///CHAPTER THIRTY-FIVE

"**W**HAT ARE you planning?" Ellinor asked, fingers twitching over the triggers of her pistols.

Cosmin von Brandt clicked his tongue at her, fixing the skinny black tie of his suit. "Really, this shouldn't come as a shock to you. I don't trust you. I had so hoped you'd surprise me in a good way, Ellinor, but alas! Between this misguided action of yours and Irati's failed little coup, I've hit my quota on betrayals for the decade, I dare say." He pouted dramatically at her, his orange eyes glittering.

"You were spying on us? But . . ." Ellinor's eyes darted to the recording devices she had dismantled. "How?"

Cosmin rolled his eyes. "You've been absent a very long time, my dear. I'm a changed man! Our departed Lazar wasn't the only one with a *contingency plan*. The bouncer droid with its gun pointed at our flamboyant Mr. Brantley? It's outfitted with an infiltrator drone recording and surveillance unit. I paid double to make sure no one would notice the extra device in its tin head, and disposed of the mechanics who created it for me, so they couldn't go tattling." Cosmin paused, his eyes narrowing for a moment as his cavalier attitude evaporated. "You always did have the deadly penchant for underestimating my cleverness."

Ellinor angled her body to be in front of the bleeding Jelani and the still hidden Fiss. "So, what now? We're at a bit of an impasse, yeah?"

Cosmin smirked. "Hardly. I'm holding all the cards here. You see, you're still going to deliver that little beastie to Zabel as planned. She'll come to meet you personally on the outskirts of Anzor, though. We can't have a repeat of what happened in Amaru with Dragan, after all. So much noise and fuss you caused. So here's what's going to happen. You're going to have that seersha interloper fly the plane to the designated rendezvous point. Kai, along with my remaining droids, will take the bubble hatch ahead of you, to ensure you go to the one destination and the one destination *only*. Failure at this point, Ellinor, guarantees Kai's death. Any deviation from the plan, any stops, any messages, or any delay that I simply don't like, will result in my droids delivering a serum into Kai's veins. The serum is laced with nanites holding just a bit of my magic in them. It'll boil Kai from the inside. Very unpleasant, I assure you."

Cosmin watched her face, and she was sure he saw the horror racing across her features. "You always were partial to the big lug, don't think I didn't note your friendship. I had hoped his presence and adoration of me would have been enough to secure your cooperation. But seems not even using your old crew could keep you from misbehaving. Oh well, no matter now; he'll be useful in other ways. You have your orders, my dear, make sure there are no further disappointments. For

Kai's sake." Cosmin began chuckling, but the holo-projection was abruptly cut off as the bubble hatch launched from the plane. Ellinor didn't have a chance to even tell Fiss to use his powers.

No sooner had the pod disappeared than Ellinor's fury and frustration twisted through her like a tornado. "Fucking ass!" she screamed, kicking the wall. "That son-of-a-bitch. Piece of doehaz shit! Ugh! This is all my fault. I should have dismantled those fucking bots."

Fiss blinked back into view, cowering near Jelani. "Elli is mad, Jelly. Make my Ellinor happy please? Scared. I have fear, Jelly."

"Ellinor," Jelani said, his tone pleading as Fiss's hair began lashing out and a strong breeze filled the cabin.

Scrubbing her hands over her face, Ellinor said, "Fiss, I'm sorry, okay? But I'm frustrated and worried for Kai. This is all my fault. Kai doesn't deserve what Cosmin will do to him if we don't take you to Zabel."

"What's that mean, Elli? Take? Give? What's this?"

Ellinor sighed, kneeling down next to Jelani to inspect his wound. "Cosmin, that seersha you just saw, his plan is to ship you to a powerful caster named Zabel in exchange for a bunch of combat-tech, magitech, and war automata he plans to use to make himself more powerful, along with securing her as an ally, or some shit like that. You are a bargaining chip, you understand? Cosmin is trading you, bartering you to Zabel. But, well, it didn't really work out that way, yeah? But Cosmin still expects you to go to Zabel or . . . fuck, I don't know what will happen. If Zabel will retaliate or, I don't know, something worse. So he's taken Kai to ensure I follow his orders. He needs you and me to part, forever, and for you to work for someone else."

"I can't stay with Elli?" Fiss said, voice wobbly.

Ellinor shook her head. "I've got to think, Fiss. We have to help Kai. We need to get him back first. You get that, right?"

When Fiss nodded in reply, Ellinor tried to force herself to relax and think. "Okay, so one thing at a time," she mumbled, poking at Jelani's wound. The seersha hissed, and she gave him a sympathetic look.

The wound was deep, but it hadn't sliced any arteries, thankfully. The androids used a laser sword of some kind to inflict the damage, cauterizing the wound as it sliced through muscle and tissue. With no other medical droid on hand, Ellinor would need to rely on her field training to clean the wound and stitch it as best she could.

Digging in a medical kit, Ellinor removed everything she would need. Just as she was about to clean the gash, Jelani gripped her wrist. "Breathe, Ellinor. We will get your friend back. Kai will survive this."

Ellinor shut her eyes briefly, forcing a deep breath in and out. She didn't want to tell Jelani how sincerely she doubted that. How she didn't trust Cosmin not to give Zabel permission to kill them once Fiss was in her possession. Then there was Fiss to consider. Knowing what casters did to the dreeocht, and that something of Misho lived on in Fiss . . . the thought of giving him up made her knees quake. What Ellinor desperately wanted was to save them all, but she was convinced that wasn't possible.

Giving a weak nod, Ellinor went to work patching Jelani as best she could. "Why didn't you stop me?" Jelani raised a brow, wincing when she pulled the torn muscle and skin back together. "You knew what was going to happen to Fiss if we went through with Cosmin's plan. Why weren't you working against us? Making sure we couldn't deliver Fiss to a lifetime of torture?" She stapled his skin together, eliciting a grunt from Jelani.

"I would have," he said, voice brittle. "I had a plan if you kept insisting you had to continue on this despicable mission." He paused, sucking in a breath as she lathered disinfectant on his wound. "I would have disabled your armor, Kai's too. Then I would have freed Fiss before we were in Zabel's reach."

"So that's what that device was you were messing with?" Ellinor asked, putting a bandage on his wounded hip.

He nodded. "I was testing you, giving you every benefit of the doubt. I wanted you on my side. I wanted to see if you had the same moral beliefs as I did. I honestly believed you did, but I needed you to make the right choice on your own, that's how I'd know if you were truly trustworthy. I am . . . disappointed you didn't come to the conclusion I was hoping for much sooner."

Ellinor's muscles tensed. "I wish you had stepped in sooner, too. That you'd been *honest* about what you were really up to. We could have avoided this. Kai wouldn't be in enemy hands."

Jelani met her stare with a glare of his own. "Trust me, Ellinor. I wish I had as well. I won't make the same mistake again. You take too long to get out of your own way."

Ellinor blinked at him, rocking back from where she was crouched. His words stung, and she was surprised at how sharply she felt the sting. But the gentle pressure of Fiss floating behind her brought her back to her senses. Hanging her head, she silently helped Jelani to his feet, turning away as he repositioned his shirt and pants.

Stalking toward the bots, Ellinor began meticulously dismantling them, stripping them of the infiltrator drone parts in their heads, stomping on anything that even had the faint appearance of a listening or spy device. Now that she knew a bit more what to look for, she was taking extra precautions, though she wouldn't be so arrogant again in believing she had found everything.

As she worked, hunting for a way to remove the GPS without tampering with any other wiring, she called to Jelani, "Get this bird going as fast as you can. If you have spare armor or whatever to protect you from anymore close calls, put it on and get ready." She looked up, noting Fiss hovering near her, captivated by what she was doing, and smiled at him. "We're going to save Kai."

THE LONG GOOD-BYE,
THE SHORT HELLO
///CHAPTER THIRTY-SIX

DESPITE JELANI assuring Ellinor they were moving as fast as the transport would go after their skirmish, Ellinor still felt like they were crawling. She had been unable to dismantle the GPS, and while she was fairly positive no cameras remained, she couldn't guarantee Cosmin wasn't at least listening to them, making conversation stilted or nonexistent between the three of them

Occasionally, she could see a glimmer of reflected light off the bubble pod that signaled Kai was still ahead of them, but they never seemed to close the distance. Soon, the looming metropolis of Anzor rose from the horizon, and a sharp pang struck Ellinor's chest.

Similar to the other major cities in Erhard—and no doubt the rest of Eerden—where powerful casters dwelled and pretended to go along with the governing bodies, Anzor was a testament to Zabel's power. It glittered like diamonds made of steel and glass. The skyscrapers twisted and curled high above the stratosphere, like geysers of water that bathed the stars in crystal clear rainwater. There was an elegance to it that Euria lacked. In Anzor, the lines of the buildings were all gentle curves with seamless edges. Whereas Euria's were harsh, unapologetic boxy lines and sharp points.

The flashing bright neon of advertisements and businesses danced against the tall buildings, making them pulse with life. Even in the middle of the day, the shadows from the enormous buildings cast most of Anzor into a state of everlasting night, the fog created by the exhaust of the various vehicles only faintly muted the brightness of the city.

Once they crossed the threshold into the shadows of Anzor, Ellinor shivered. They had reached the point of no return. In a few miles, they would be face-to-face with one of the most powerful water casters in Erhard.

Neither Cosmin nor Zabel had tried to contact them as they headed for the rendezvous point. During that time, Ellinor made sure all her weapons were loaded, and her armor and shield were as charged as possible once again. Jelani did likewise, pouring whatever little power he could spare back into his Leviathan Roaster blades—just in case. Fiss still didn't understand what was happening, but he understood their solemn expressions and kept close to Ellinor, often brushing against her as if to assure himself she was there.

"Ellinor," Jelani called from the cockpit, "you'll want to see this."

Joining him, Ellinor squinted to where the faint shimmer of the bubble pod could be seen reflecting the lights of the tall buildings. Unlike Euria, Anzor didn't stretch into farmlands before ending. Anzor was a vertical city through and through, relying only on its mechanical industry to support itself. A realization that made Ellinor shudder once more.

Standing next to the pod just outside the shanty apartments bordering the glittering city was a small group of people. Ellinor assumed they were Zabel's most trusted generals and lieutenants, though probably not casters, who might be tempted to use Fiss before she had a chance to claim him.

"It's not as many as I was expecting, but it's still a healthy amount of opposition," Jelani said, his tone flat. "How would you like to handle this? Kai is your friend. I'll follow what you think is best here."

"Time to bring red friend back?" Fiss added, peeking around Ellinor's legs to get a better view.

She placed her hand on his head and whispered, "Something like that, yeah."

Looking at the waiting crowd, Ellinor sorted through the facts of what she knew about Fiss and the device embedded in her neck. Ellinor knew of only one option to save both Fiss and Kai. Rubbing at her jaw with her free hand, she slid her gaze to Jelani. "Hang back and keep the engines running. You're going to need to be ready to get everyone out of Zabel's reach as fast as you can."

Jelani frowned. "What are you going to do?"

"Don't worry, this will work," she said simply, her eyes darting pointedly about the cabin, and while she was concerned about what Cosmin may overhear, she also didn't want Jelani to argue with her, to try and stop her. When Jelani still looked unconvinced, she sighed. "What is your gut telling you?"

The seersha closed his eyes, dipping his head, fog-like hair covering his eyelids for a moment as he considered her words.

He raised his head and met her gaze. Her own bright, tropical blue eyes reflected in his dark stare. "That I trust you."

She may not like that he could sense things about her, but at least it worked in her favor in this instance. She clapped him on the shoulder. "My man. Put us down over there. Now Fiss," she said, stooping to be eye level with the tiny dreeocht, "you're going to have to come with me and do *exactly* as I say, all right? Don't question me, just act when I tell you to. Then you help get Kai back on the ship with Jelani. Do you understand?"

Fiss nodded a little too quickly. "Follow Elli, do what she says. Yes, Ellinor. I can do that."

Jelani landed the transport a safe distance away, and Ellinor stood up, surveying the area. There were ten people and at least three droids she could see, all surrounding a tall, elegant seersha woman with light maroon skin and thick hair such a deep blue it was almost black. Her pointed ears peeked out of her thick tresses, and a pair of ivory demon-like horns were prominently on display.

"All right, Fiss, time to go." Ellinor reached down and grabbed the dreeocht's paw-like hand and headed for the transport door. Before she disengaged the locks, Jelani snagged her arm and turned her to face him.

"Don't forget my offer, Ellinor. It still stands. Come back, and I'll help you, and I'll give Fiss the choice of whether or not he wishes to help as well. I won't tamper with his free will, or yours," he whispered, breath tickling her ear.

A shiver raced from the balls of her feet up to her knees. She shut her eyes, and took a step back, wrenching her arm free. She nodded, giving a grim smile in response.

Taking a deep breath, she disengaged the door. Holding on to Fiss's hand tightly, she marched toward the waiting caster.

As they approached the assembled group, Zabel Dirix spread her arms and lurching bolts of lightning erupted from her hands, jerking toward Ellinor and the kneeling figure on the ground. Ellinor hadn't noticed him before, but it was easy to see it was Kai. She refused to look too closely at the damage the big man suffered, for fear she would lose her temper and act too quickly.

As the lightning came closer, it took shape, transforming into a web with dozens of spiders made of magic shifting in jerky movements along the strands. Zabel lowered her hands, but the magic stayed in place. Ellinor had never seen such a thing, but she knew it was some kind of insurance on Zabel's part.

Ellinor watched the spiders warily as they moved. They created webs of glittering, lightning that they effortlessly traversed, suspended in the air. Movement had her looking away; the rest of Zabel's entourage fanned out, creating a larger circle around their boss.

The distance between them evaporated, and Ellinor got a clear view of what Zabel was wearing. Adorned in a creamy white bodysuit and a pair of golden leather high-heeled boots that came up over her knees, Zabel cut an impressive silhouette. A flowing floor length, sheer grey robe with billowing sleeves covered the seersha. The vestment glimmered with crystals, or they could have been stones meant to look like gems which held magical reserves—Ellinor could never be sure with where casters hid magic or weapons, given their paranoia.

Frowning, Ellinor slowed her gait and hoisted Fiss into her arms, cradling him.

A glower flitted across Zabel's face, a hungry look of jealousy in her pale grey eyes. It was soon replaced with a coy smile on her full, dark lips, but Ellinor knew what she saw and held Fiss all the tighter, whispering in his slightly pointed ear, "Do you know what those are?"

"The magic?" His tongue poked out of his thin lips, flicking as if he was tasting the air, before snuggling back into Ellinor's arms. "The spider lightning. Nets on nets on nets. They will catch us. Keep us. Hurt my Elli. Pulled from machine and the sky, natural and unnatural. Very strong. Lots and lots of it. We go back now?"

"We have to get our red friend first, remember?"

Fiss whimpered and Ellinor's heart stuttered in her chest. She glanced at Kai, his back heaving and shaking, and she wondered what Cosmin or Zabel had done to him. Kai's blind adoration to Cosmin was going to get the man killed, but she didn't blame him, either. She would have done the same, had Misho asked such things of her, even if they were deplorable. She meant what she said; Kai deserved a better man to love than the likes of Cosmin. In the cold recesses of her mind, she knew she owed Kai nothing, but her heart, her soul, told her differently. She owed it to the friendship they once had to make sure he walked away and could live a life somewhere far from Cosmin.

Zabel snapped her fingers and called, "You aren't being paid by the minute. Trying my patience further will be bad for your associate's health."

Buying for time as her mind came to terms with what her heart was telling her to do, Ellinor responded, "Sorry. I just didn't know this was going to be a party. You'll forgive my hesitance, yeah?"

Zabel's flirty smile widened, though it appeared a bit feral to Ellinor's gaze. "Quite. And you are beyond fashionably late. Unacceptable." At that, the spider lightning twitched in unison on their webs, inching closer to Kai, who flinched back.

Ellinor swallowed, mind made up. Nodding as if she agreed with Zabel, she whispered in Fiss's ear once more. "Fiss, can you get rid of all the magic here? Can you consume it like you did when you were sleeping in your box, yeah?"

Fiss frowned. "Is this where I do as you say? You didn't say you'd have questions, questions, questions."

Ellinor eyed Zabel, trying to appear unconcerned despite being completely surrounded by her goons; they wouldn't wait much longer for her to relinquish Fiss. "In a second. I just need to know if you can neutralize Zabel, her crew, and all the spider lightning? It's vital to freeing red friend."

Fiss glanced around, then bobbed his head, quickly followed by shaking his head. "Can eat the yummy magic. Store it. Make Fiss more powerful. Yes, Elli. But no, no. It'll hurt you. Too much pain. I can't hurt Elli!"

Ellinor made a show of putting Fiss down. Kneeling in front of Fiss, she said softly, "You aren't hurting me because you want to, that's the important thing to remember."

"But it's a big owie-ouchie!"

She smiled. "I'm giving you permission to give me an owie-ouchie, Fiss. Do this for Kai. For me." When Fiss nodded hesitantly, chewing on one of his little claws, Ellinor squeezed his shoulders. "This is the part where you do as I say. No more questions, yeah? Right, so, eat all the magic, Fiss. No matter what, you can't stop until Kai is free. Then you help him get back to Jelani, okay? Even if that means you leave me here. That's key. Nod if you understand."

Fiss nodded, and Ellinor stood. "Good. When I yell at Kai, you do your thing."

Looking at Kai, she waited a moment until the intensity of her stare forced the shackled man to raise his puffy, bloody face. Knowing she was surrounded and Zabel's cohorts were closing in, the spider lightning weaving more webs of deadly magic, Ellinor took a deep breath to make sure Kai heard her—really *heard* her—and called, "Ready for another stupid plan, Kai?"

Her friend smiled, then chaos erupted, and Ellinor collapsed in excruciating pain.

Zabel screamed, lightning and wind boomed and crackled around Ellinor; her armor the only thing keeping her skin from tearing off her bones. Zabel's henchmen couldn't move; Kai was the only one mobile, and his steps were slow and lumbering as he struggled to get to Fiss.

The spider lightning around Ellinor convulsed, webs bouncing as they struggled to wrap Kai, Fiss, and Ellinor in their webs. Zabel spread her arms and hands wide, fingers dancing wildly, trying to keep the magic alive and moving toward her goal. But the spider lighting was instead morphing into shapeless ribbons that curled around Fiss and were absorbed into the dreeocht.

As Fiss corralled the magic in the area, calling to it and removing it from wherever it was stored, Ellinor's collar grew so hot she was sure her skin was melting. As her latent magic responded to Fiss's commands, trying to come out and join the dreeocht she had been unintentionally attached to, parts of Ellinor felt like they would burst apart.

Inside her ribcage, a giant boulder was trying to force its way out of her chest, while other parts of Ellinor felt as if they were shriveling into nothingness. Her lungs felt non-existent, and she could have sworn all her veins were collapsing, the blood disintegrating like dry ash. Her head was pounding, a sledgehammer beating against her temples as her muscles failed her simultaneously, and Ellinor crashed to the ground, writhing and contorting in pain.

This is it. This is how I die. Love is weakness.

The thought came to her as her vision began to fail, starved too long of oxygen as Fiss continued to contain Zabel and her people by consuming every spark of magic they produced.

Vaguely, she could feel Kai scoop her up in his arms, as if he too hadn't just been tortured minutes before. She registered Fiss's pained wailing as he continued to do as Ellinor asked, despite killing her in the process, and the screams of Zabel's people as the magic Fiss summoned tore through their bodies undeterred by their armor.

Her vision went black, except for a pinprick of light at the epicenter. Standing within the light, was a figure with the most marvelous amber eyes that twinkled when he smiled, showing his slightly crooked teeth, and a rebellious strand of black hair that refused to stay slicked back. He was merely waving—if in greeting or farewell, her agony-riddled conscious couldn't tell.

"Let go, Elli. Let it all go. Love is strength," the echo of Misho's voice rang in her head.

Ellinor didn't believe in paradise or the abyss, like Kai did. *But maybe I was wrong? Unless . . . could this be the part of Misho that Fiss said dwelled within him?* She wasn't sure which idea left her feeling suddenly cold, so cold . . . .

"I will hunt you down!" Zabel's howl pierced through her thoughts. "The power you wield is *mine*. You, your families, none of you are safe from me or Cosmin. We will hunt you to the very ends of Eerden!"

A battered Zabel clapped her hands, a resounding *boom* reverberated around them, and the seersha was lifted away from the trio in a gust of wind that propelled her toward the safety of Anzor's towering buildings. Weaponless and injured, Kai let her go; Zabel's power was spent, her backup nothing more than bloody puddles of broken bodies and machine parts on the ground. But Zabel's promise rang out. It was the last thing Ellinor was truly aware of as Fiss consumed the last of the residual magic.

Ellinor Olysha Rask's heart stopped beating a second later.

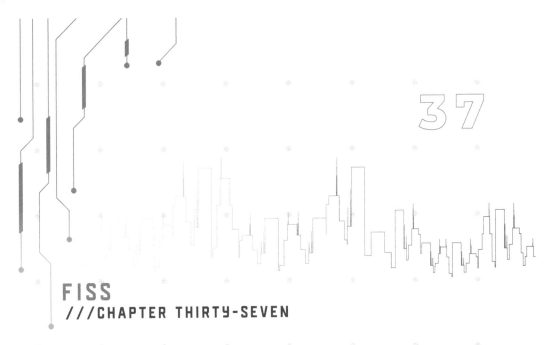

FISS
///CHAPTER THIRTY-SEVEN

THERE WAS the pain. Then there was the nothing. A cosmic swirl of empty space. Pains, sharp, and searing. Tearing, ripping, and shredding. Dark, still water. Gone. No more air.

The bright, warm swirls of magic were stilled. The joy in casting turned bitter, jagged and hard instead of safe and soft. An empty, hollow space where Elli was.

Fiss couldn't fill the space. He was untethered, unraveling. He could stop it, but without Elli there was no point. He would release himself. Dissipate the magic. Return it all to the cosmos. To the place that had made him.

Shaking, Fiss touched the ether within where the primal magic lived. The force that gave him the knowing, the understanding, his name. He was ready now, he would tear it out. Give it up. Dissolve into the bits and pieces he was before the spark. Before the air. Before Ellinor.

WAIT.

A voice, though not a voice, boomed, rattling the bright spark that made Fiss who he was, startling him from his desolate thoughts. Magic? It didn't taste like the magic he knew. Was it more? Less? Questions, questions, questions . . . . Then, voices. Fiss was not alone.

"That ain't working, dammit! When's your sister supposed to get 'ere? Ah, abyss, we're losing her, aren't we? Ell's dead for reals, ain't she?"

"You aren't helping, Kai. Oihana is on her way, but she has to collect the right gear and she . . . . You know what? It doesn't matter. She is en-route. Until then, help me with the chest compressions."

Fiss's curiosity brought his attention back to the world. He couldn't understand what Jelly and red friend were doing. They were fussing over his bonded, doing things they seemed to think would help. But Fiss still felt empty. Cold. Lost. Broken.

He could see her. Could touch her. But he could not *feel* her. Fiss now understood the behavior he witnessed when his friends faced the nasty monsters: *panic.*

Body trembling, Fiss lay beside Ellinor and tried to find warmth as Jelly breathed into her mouth, and red friend pushed down on her chest. They hardly noticed him as they flew back toward some safe place. A place Jelly said they had been to before.

Elli had told him not to question, just act. But now he had questions. Thoughts that felt at odds alongside all the new magic he held within. He searched within, yearning for something sweet. The magic in him tasted wrong. It was full of hate and hurt. The mean lady had cast it wanting to hurt the people he loved, and Ellinor most of all. He didn't understand such malice, didn't even have a word for it. Why hurt, when you could cast such beautiful magic?

But that voice, her final command . . . that was something Fiss knew how to do. To wait. Fiss stayed with Ellinor; no one would take him from her. He would lie beside her for all time. But if he couldn't feel anything from Ellinor, she would feel nothing in return; or so the primal magic said as it danced through his insides. Ellinor had told him not to do anything, but maybe she would forgive him if he disobeyed her now?

"Owie-ouchie?" he murmured at red friend. "Magic will cause Elli an owie-ouchie?"

"Not now, kid," red friend huffed, pushing down on Ellinor's chest.

Jelly paused in puffing air into Ellinor's mouth. "No, Fiss. Casting won't harm Ellinor now. But you have no need to do that, we're out of Zabel's grasp."

An idea swarmed in Fiss's mind as he watched Jelly lower his mouth to Ellinor's again. *Air. That's what he breathes. Elli, too!*

Fiss knew what to do with that excess magic. With a gust of air, he pushed Jelly and red friend away from his bonded, then twisted the flow back, making the air dive into Ellinor, filling her lungs and veins.

He felt nothing, and, overcome with fear, lightning began to spark from his shoulder blades, body vibrating with a lonely anxiety. "Kid," red friend groaned. "You gotta calm down. That ain't helping. You'll kill us, is what you'll do."

But Fiss couldn't stop; the magic that gave him consciousness would not allow the foreign magic to remain within him any longer.

A stray bolt of lightning peeled off from his agitated body, striking Ellinor in the chest, followed shortly by another errant bolt. Fiss screamed when his bonded's body suddenly jerked, and a shuddering gasp escaped from Elli, followed by unstoppable coughing.

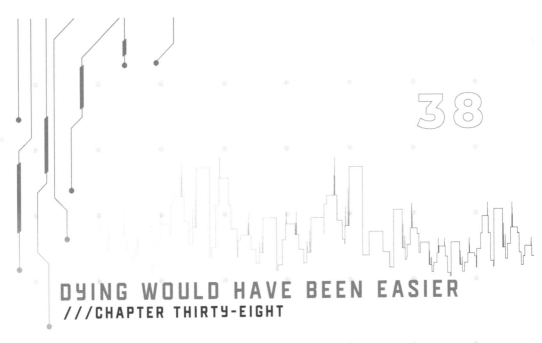

DYING WOULD HAVE BEEN EASIER
///CHAPTER THIRTY-EIGHT

ELLINOR RASK thought crashing, battling casters and doe-haz, taking bullets and blades would be the most abuse she could endure. But coming back from the dead topped the list. Everything ached, her throat raw and scorched, head throbbing, joints and muscles burning as her body convulsed with every painful cough.

She knew she had died; she felt it happen. But there was nothing waiting for her. She had wanted to be wrong about that.

Perhaps it was because Azer knew I'd be coming back?

But the thought didn't comfort her. Feeling like she was about to vomit amidst all the coughing, Ellinor rolled to her side, clutching at her throat.

She gasped, eyes flying open.

"Mirror," she croaked, ignoring the happy purrs of Fiss and the relieved sighs of Kai and the laughter of Jelani. "Give me a fucking mirror."

Reluctantly, Jelani rose to comply as Kai sat down next to her, rubbing her back. It was then she got a good look at his injuries. Burn blisters covered half his body—Ellinor guessed Cosmin had some asinine reason to show Kai his threats were legitimate. There was a deep gash in the center of his forehead where the droid struck him. She reached up, her fingers brushing the burns. "Oh, Kai . . . I'm so sorry. I tried to get to you as fast as I could. I didn't want . . . I never wanted him to hurt you."

"I know you did, boss. I know," he said, voice soft.

She met his gaze, and a moment passed between them before Kai pulled her into a warm embrace. "Good to 'ave you back, Ell," his voice surer than it had been only a second ago. "Let's not 'ave you go and do that again, okay? Thought I'd lost my last friend. Scared the piss right out of me. Thought I'd never get the chance to say sorry for what I did. You know I am, right? Sorry?" Kai said, holding her tighter. "I owe you one for saving me back there, even if you was a bit late."

"Get this collar off me and we'll call it square, how about that, then?" Ellinor croaked, her relief at Kai being all right momentarily breaking through her panic, though her hands still shook.

Jelani handed her a mirror, and took a step back as she brought it up to see for herself what she refused to believe: the collar, in one sense, no longer existed.

Her entire neck was covered in the bio-magitech that had once been confined to the circlet Kai had snapped on her. It had somehow *grown*, expanding under the onslaught of Fiss's magic until it morphed and not only covered her neck, but part of her chest and right shoulder, from what she could see, and feel. Those affected parts of Ellinor looked like they belonged to an Ashling, not to her.

Stomach churning, unable to comprehend what she was seeing, Ellinor vomited.

"I'm turning into a fucking cyborg!" Ellinor paced the cabin, making her fingers bloody as she clawed at the dark, twinkling technology. She felt nothing where she touched the parts covered in the machinery. She couldn't pry it away, it was seamlessly fused, and it didn't hurt when she attempted it. Her hands, though, ached the more she tried.

"You aren't turning into an Ashling or cyborg. That's not how it works," Jelani said, though his reassurances sounded feeble to Ellinor.

Fiss tried to go to her, perhaps to curl around her neck, to pet the metal and mechanical parts of her, marveling at how similar they were becoming, but Jelani, mercifully, kept him back. Ellinor didn't want anyone to touch her. Not now, maybe never again.

"Boss, calm down. Important thing is that you're alive, right? We should worry 'bout getting clear of Zabel first. Doubt she's gonna let us get too far away . . . Plus, this piece of shit Eagle Owl's got that tracker. We're not gonna be able to escape in this thing," Kai said, raising his hands and taking a step toward her.

"I can't fucking handle that right now!" Ellinor screamed. She leaned hard on the wall and held her forehead. "Can someone else please, *please* be in charge? I was dead, Kai. *Dead.* And now, I'm turning into some bot? Don't you dare put any more shit on me. You got that?"

Kai blinked, stunned into silence, his face going red, making the blisters all the more prominent. Jelani was the first to move. "I'll handle this. We may have options available to us that our pursuers aren't expecting. Kai? Yours was not the only escape pod, I take it?"

Kai shook his head, and pointed to another hatch. "There's a spare."

With a nod, Jelani scampered away, issuing commands to Fiss to collect all their packs, weapons, and emergency supplies, and place them into the pod while Jelani made it ready for launch. Ellinor was vaguely aware of what he was doing, that their radar roared to life with whatever retaliation Zabel promised already heading for them at alarming speeds. But all Ellinor could comprehend was the odd vision she'd had before dying.

She wasn't sure what Misho had wanted her to let go of, for even when she relinquished her life, she hadn't joined him. Her heart broke all over again, making the dizziness and weakness in her muscles worse. The denial pressed down on her, making her head too heavy to hold; her body went numb. She sank down to the floor of the cabin, unable even to sit any longer.

Ellinor curled into a ball. She couldn't hold back her sobs, her desperation to be free of the device that was taking over her body. Being reunited with her magic was now gone forever. *I was better off dead.*

"You all right, Ell?" Kai sheepishly approached, bending down as far as his girth and injuries could manage. Up front, Jelani continued to do his best to evade whatever missile or fleet of combat androids Zabel Dirix had sent after them.

Ellinor raised her head, giving Kai a flat stare as the tears poured down her cheeks. "I don't think I need a metaphor for you to understand how miserable I am, yeah?"

"Ah, no, you don't. But it's gonna be all right. There's gotta be a way to fix you, and we'll find it."

"I'd like to believe that, Kai, but, I can't. Not today. I need a day, just a fucking day, to come to terms with everything that's happened. Between this and losing so many . . . . So, if it's all the same to you, that's what I'm going to do."

Kai slid down to the floor next to her. "It was a right clusterfuck, wasn't it?"

Ellinor sighed and coughed. "That's an understatement. You realize I can't go home, yeah? And you shouldn't either, Kai. Not after this," she said, gently touching his face.

Kai's stare glazed over, a profound pain flashing behind his green eyes, shoulders heaving. "You good with having one more stowaway then, boss?"

She tried to grin, but didn't succeed. "Sure. How else am I going to collect on that debt you owe me?"

"Ah, well, sounds like someone's already forgetting I done brought 'em back from the dead."

"Yeah well, you had help with that one. The collar is all you, buddy," Ellinor responded, her grin shaky.

Silence fell between them as Ellinor watched Fiss zip about the cabin. Hiding with him was going to be damn near impossible, but they had no choice; Fiss would never leave her, and she wouldn't abandon him.

Kai, sensing that Ellinor no longer wanted to speak, just sat with her. She found his presence comforting, and she laced her fingers with his. The old Ellinor, the Ellinor that Kai had hauled from Cosmin's prison barely a week ago, wouldn't have allowed her to feel this way about Kai ever again. Maybe that was what Misho wanted her to let go of? The walls that kept people—*friends,* like Kai—from coming back into her life. Ellinor still wanted to bring peace to Misho, but perhaps there was a better way to enact her revenge without pushing everyone out of her life in the process?

"Thank you, Kai," Ellinor whispered, and squeezed his hand, resting her head on his shoulder.

Kai Axel Brantley, her forever best friend, squeezed her hand in return.

Ellinor was glad Jelani never asked for Kai's assistance as he scrambled about the plane. In fact, the only time he spoke was to command them to get into the last emergency bubble pod.

"This is going to be bumpy, but it will buy us time," Jelani said, ushering them inside the pod's cramped quarters. "I don't intend to lose the missile Zabel fired. She plans to bring the craft down and sift through the wreckage for what she believes is hers, and I'm inclined to let her. I can't find Cosmin's trackers, or dismantle the GPS, so we'll be taking care of both at the same time." He shut the door to the pod and continued, "I've let Oihana know to meet us at the mouth of the Helmut River where it empties into the Dagmar Sea. The pod has enough fuel to get us there, as long as I time the release to just before the main transport is struck. It'll be rough, so find something to hold on to."

Fiss wasted no time in clinging to Ellinor, nuzzling against her mechanical neck as if it were as soft as fleece. Ellinor tried not to sob anew at the action.

"Why in the abyss would we 'ead all the way out there? There ain't shit on that side of Erhard," Kai grumbled, his mood darkening as the realization he had kept at bay, that Cosmin would have killed him, finally sank in. Ellinor knew the anger would fade, but she hoped when it did, he was still determined to be rid of the toxic seersha's influence for good.

"I know someone who can help with your . . ." Jelani paused, glancing at her robotic neck before bashfully looking away. "With Ellinor's affliction, if you will."

Ellinor frowned. "Can't I go back to Oihana's bunker? Let her take all the time she needs to pry this shit out of me. You said it would just take a lot of time, yeah? I got time."

Jelani shook his head. "My sister is exceptionally talented, but we've moved beyond her skill set now. We have to go elsewhere."

Before he could elaborate, Jelani held up his hand, eyes glued to the radar as the blip of the incoming projectile came closer. A moment later, as all the warning klaxons blared, Jelani hit the release button, followed by a shudder as the missile connected with their transport. Both aircraft fell together, the Eagle Owl's electronics completely fried, and Jelani used the larger transport for protection until seconds before it crashed into the sandy terrain below. Keeping the pod low to the ground, Jelani used the terrain for cover as they evaded Zabel's clutches, for the time being.

Ellinor craned her neck back, watching the wreckage fade in the distance. It wasn't until she was relatively certain they weren't being followed that she spoke, voice a hoarse whisper. "Where are we headed if Oihana can't help me?"

Jelani checked their coordinates once more before turning to face Ellinor. The pod wasn't made to carry so much gear along with three full sized people and one tiny dreeocht. Jelani was so close to Ellinor that there was barely a hand's breadth between them. He studied her for a moment, his dark, starry night sky-like eyes trailing over her face and neck, no hint of revulsion to be seen, only honest concern. He dipped his strong chin, bringing his face even closer to hers.

"Your sort of problem isn't unheard of," he murmured, as if they were alone in the pod. "But the mechanics who could remove it aren't in Erhard."

"Where are they?" Ellinor asked, her voice breathy despite her racing heart, hoping Jelani wasn't about to say what she thought.

"Amardeep. I have contacts there who may be able to get us in touch with the right people."

"Amardeep?" Ellinor bellowed, her voice cracking, then lowering again, "You've got to be shitting me. We're going to the Ashlings' atoll? You think those bots are going to help someone like me without handing over Fiss so they can birth more of their kind?"

"I can assure you, the Ashlings don't care about you the way you care about them. I understand your resentment after what happened to your husband, but you have a choice. Either you go into hiding and pray Cosmin and Zabel never find you and Fiss, or we go to Amardeep where they definitely won't venture, and perhaps reconnect you with the powers Cosmin so inhumanely ripped from you. Try to believe me, Ellinor; Ashlings simply want to live and enjoy their existence. They are sentient, just like us. Each one is different. If you don't treat them all like the criminals you encountered, we'll be fine."

"But they're *Ashlings*," Ellinor said, clinging to Fiss and wishing she could take a step back.

He frowned at her. "You must let go of that prejudicial hatred, Ellinor. Let go of those things sending you toward an early grave." Ellinor's mouth went slack. His words reminding her of what the phantasm had said. "I will ask again: which do you prefer? To stay here on your own, or will you allow an unlikely ally to aid you?"

"Boss," Kai whispered, nudging her, "it ain't a bad idea, all things considered. Going to Amardeep, I mean. We can keep Fiss safe."

"My gut says this is the best option for you—for Fiss. He'll be safe in Amardeep. Ashlings are too versed in slavery to force others into such a role," Jelani added, his voice husky as he continued to gaze down at Ellinor.

Ellinor took a deep breath, trying to calm her shaky nerves. "And your gut is never wrong?"

Jelani's mouth tugged up in a soft, half smile. "Never. It wasn't wrong about you, despite you taking ridiculously long to come to your senses."

Ellinor's gut told her that Jelani Tyrik Sharma's gut was naïve. But if Fiss and Kai would be safe . . . Her brows pulled together; she surprised herself, putting their safety above her own desires, and it came so naturally. Maybe she wasn't completely beyond redemption?

Wouldn't that be nice?

She nodded. "Then let's go to Amardeep and hope this new shit show is better than the last one."

A thought struck Ellinor, that perhaps she could hunt down the Ashlings responsible for Misho's murder while they were laying low and getting her collar fixed. She had no leads, Cosmin had been her sole focus for so long, but she figured it was worth looking into. She didn't think Jelani would approve if she voiced such an idea, however.

Fiss hugged her. "Is this what safe feels like, Elli? I like it. And I like you being not dead. Elli won't do that again? It hurt Fiss for you to die."

She hugged him back as Jelani turned to the controls. "I'll try not to do that again, don't worry."

Nothing felt safe to Ellinor. Not with two incredibly powerful seersha furious with her, and not while she was cut off from her magic to the point where Fiss's casting killed her. Still, she figured anything had to be better than where she was currently, and if Jelani's sources could get the device out of her skin so she could access her powers again, then perhaps a new life wasn't completely beyond her . . . and neither was vengeance.

I'll be back for you, Cosmin.